PRAISE FOR THE
Bestselling Authors

Barbara Delinsky

"When you care to read the very best,
the name of Barbara Delinsky should
come immediately to mind."
—*Rave Reviews*

Elizabeth Lowell

"For smoldering sensuality and exceptional
storytelling, Elizabeth Lowell is incomparable."
—*Romantic Times*

Anne Stuart

"Ms. Stuart's talent shines like the
brightest of stars."
—*Affaire de Coeur*

Barbara Delinsky was born and raised in suburban Boston. She worked as a researcher, photographer and reporter before turning to writing full-time in 1980. With more than fifty novels to her credit, she is truly one of the shining stars of contemporary romance fiction! This talented author has received numerous awards and honors, and her books have appeared on many bestseller lists. Today there are over twelve million copies in print worldwide.

Elizabeth Lowell is a *New York Times* bestseller with over four million copies of her books in print. One of romance's most versatile and successful authors, she has won countless awards. She has written several romance bestsellers as Elizabeth Lowell, and with her husband, Evan Maxwell, she has written mysteries as A.E. Maxwell and romantic suspense as Ann Maxwell.

Anne Stuart has become synonymous with sizzling romance. She published her first book in 1974 and, in the over fifty novels and countless short stories she's written since then, has demonstrated an uncanny ability to touch readers with witty repartee and her trademark taut sexual tension. Anne Stuart has won every major writing award, including three prestigious RITA awards from the Romance Writers of America, and, in 1996, a Lifetime Achievement Award. She lives in Vermont with her husband, daughter and son.

Barbara Delinsky
Elizabeth Lowell
Anne Stuart

Summer Lovers

Harlequin Books

TORONTO • NEW YORK • LONDON
AMSTERDAM • PARIS • SYDNEY • HAMBURG
STOCKHOLM • ATHENS • TOKYO • MILAN
MADRID • WARSAW • BUDAPEST • AUCKLAND

HARLEQUIN BOOKS

by Request—SUMMER LOVERS

Copyright © 1998 by Harlequin Books S.A.

ISBN 0-373-20149-4

The publisher acknowledges the copyright holders of the individual works as follows:

FIRST, BEST AND ONLY
Copyright © 1986 by Barbara Delinsky

GRANITE MAN
Copyright © 1991 by Two of a Kind, Inc.

CHAIN OF LOVE
Copyright © 1983 by Anne Kristine Stuart Ohlrogge

This edition published by arrangement with Harlequin Books S.A.

Printed in U.S.A.

CONTENTS

FIRST, BEST AND ONLY

by Barbara Delinsky

1

INSTINCT TOLD MARNI LANGE that it was wrong, but she'd long ago learned not to blindly trust her instincts. For that very reason she'd surrounded herself with the best, the brightest, the most capable vice-presidents, directors and miscellaneous other personnel to manage those ventures in which she'd invested. Now her staff was telling her something, and though she disagreed, she had to listen.

"It's a spectacular idea, Marni," Edgar Welles was saying, sitting forward with his arms on the leather conference table and his fingers interlaced. His bald head gleamed under the Tiffany lamps. "There's no doubt about it. The exposure will be marvelous."

"As vice-president of public relations, you'd be expected to say that," Marni returned dryly.

"But I agree," chimed in Anne Underwood, "and I'm the editor in chief of this new baby. I think you'd be perfect for the premier cover of *Class*. You've got the looks and the status. If we're aiming at the successful woman over thirty, you epitomize her."

"I'm barely thirty-one, and I'm not a model," Marni argued.

Cynthia Cummings, Anne's art director, joined the fray. "You may not be a model, but you do have the looks."

"I'm too short. I'm only five-five."

"And this will be a waist-up shot, so your height is irrelevant," Cynthia went on, undaunted. "You've got classic features, a flawless complexion, thick auburn hair. You're a natural for something like this. We wouldn't be suggesting you do it if that weren't true."

Anne shifted in her seat to more fully face Marni, who had opted to sit among her staff rather than in the high-backed chair at the head of the long table. "Cynthia's right. We have pretty high stakes in this, too. You may be putting up the money, but those of us at the magazine have our reputations on the line. We've already poured thousands of hours into the conception and realization of *Class*. Do you think we'd risk everything with a cover we didn't think was absolutely outstanding?"

"I'm sure you wouldn't," Marni answered quietly, then looked at Edgar. "But won't it be awfully...presumptuous...my appearing in vivid color on every newsstand in the country?"

Edgar smiled affectionately. He'd been working with Marni since she'd taken over the presidency of the Lange Corporation three years before. Personally, he'd been glad when her father had stepped down, retaining the more titular position of chairman of the board. Marni was easier to work with any day. "You've always worked hard and avoided the limelight. It's about time you sampled it."

"I don't like the limelight, Edgar. You know that."

"I know you prefer being in the background, yes. But this is something else, something new. Lange may not be a novice at publishing, but we've never dealt with fashion before. *Class* is an adventure for the publications division. It's an adventure for *all* of us. You want it to be a success, don't you?" It was a rhetorical question, needing no answer. "It's not as though you're going to give speech after speech in front of crowds of stockholders or face the harsh floodlights of the media."

"I'd almost prefer that. This seems somehow arrogant."

"You have a right to arrogance," broke in Steve O'Brien. Steve headed the publications division of the corporation, and he'd been a staunch supporter both of Marni and of *Class* from the start. "In three years you've nearly doubled our annual profit margin. *Three years.* It's remarkable."

Marni shrugged. She couldn't dispute the figures, yet she was modest about flaunting them. "It's really been more than three years, Steve. I've been working under Dad since I graduated from business school. That adds another four years to the total. He gave me a pretty free hand to do what I wanted."

"Doesn't matter," Steve said with a dismissive wave of his hand. "Three, five, seven years—you've done wonders. You've got every right to have your picture on the cover of *Class*."

"One session in a photographer's studio," Edgar coaxed before Marni could argue further. "That's all we ask. One session. Simple and painless."

She grimaced. "Painless? I *hate* being photographed."

"But you're photogenic," came the argument from Dan Sobel, *Class*'s creative director. He was a good-looking man, no doubt photogenic himself, Marni mused, though she felt no more physical attraction for him than she did for either Edgar or Steve. "You've got so much more going for you than some of the people who've been on magazine covers. Hell, look what Scavullo did with Martha Mitchell!''

Marni rolled her eyes. "Thanks."

"You know what I mean. And don't tell me *she* had any more right to be on a cover than you do."

Marni couldn't answer that one. "Okay," she said, waving her hand. "Aside from my other arguments, we're not talking Scavullo or Avedon here. We're talking Webster." She eyed Anne. "You're still convinced he's the right one?"

"Absolutely," Anne answered with a determined nod. "I've shown you his covers. We've pored over them ourselves—" her gaze swept momentarily toward Cynthia and Dan "—and compared them to other cover work. As far as I'm concerned, even if Scavullo or Avedon had been available I'd have picked Webster. He brings a freshness, a vitality to his covers. This is a man who loves women, loves working with them, loves making them look great. He has a definite way with models, and with his camera."

Marni's "Hmmph" went unnoticed as Dan spoke up in support of Anne's claim.

"We're lucky to get him, Marni. He hasn't been willing to work on a regular basis for one magazine before."

"Then why is he now?"

"Because he likes the concept of the magazine, for one thing. He's forty himself. He can identify with it."

"Just because a man reaches the age of forty doesn't mean that he tires of nubile young girls," Marni pointed out. "We all have friends whose husbands grab for their *Vogue*s and *Bazaar*s as soon as they arrive."

Dan agreed. "Yes, and I'm not saying that Webster's

given up on nineteen-year-old models. But I think he understands the need for a publication like ours. From what he said, he often deals with celebrities who are totally insecure about the issue of age. They want him to make them look twenty-one. He wants to make them look damned good at whatever age they are. He claims that some of the most beautiful women he's photographed in the last few years have been in their mid-forties."

"Wonderful man," Anne said, beaming brightly.

Marni sent an amused smile in her direction. Anne was in her mid-forties and extremely attractive.

Dan continued. "I think there's more, though, at least as to why Webster is willing to work with us. When a man reaches the age of forty, he tends to take stock of his life and think about where's he's going. Brian Webster has been phenomenally successful in the past ten years, but he's done it the hard way. He didn't have a mentor, so to speak, or a sponsor. He didn't have an 'in' at any one magazine or another. He's built his reputation purely on merit, by showing his stuff and relying on its quality to draw in work. And it has. He calls his own shots, and even aside from his fashion work gets more than enough commissions for portraits of celebrities to keep him busy. But he may just be ready to consolidate his interests. Theoretically, through *Class*, his name could become as much a household word as Scavullo or Avedon. If we're successful, and *he*'s successful, he could work less and do better financially than before. Besides, his first book of photographs is due out next summer. The work for it is done and that particular pressure's off. I think we lucked out and hit him at exactly the right time."

"And he's agreed to stick with us for a while?"

Marni asked, then glanced from one face to another. "It was the general consensus that we have a consistent look from one issue to the next."

"We're preparing a contract," Steve put in. "Twelve issues, with options to expand on that. He says he'll sign."

Marni pressed her lips together and nodded. Her argument wasn't really with the choice of Webster as a photographer; it was with the choice of that first cover face. "Okay. So Webster's our man." Her eyes narrowed as she looked around the group again. "And since I have faith in you all and trust that you're a little more objective on the matter of this cover than I am, it looks like I'll be your guinea pig. What's the schedule?" She gave a crooked grin. "Do I have time for plastic surgery first? I could take off five pounds while I'm recuperating."

"Don't you dare!" Anne chided. "On either score." She sat back. "Once Webster's signed the contract, we'll set up an appointment. It should be within the next two weeks."

Marni took in a loud breath and studied the ceiling. "Take your time. Please."

IT WAS ACTUALLY CLOSER to three weeks before the photographer's contract had been signed and delivered and Marni was due to be photographed. She wasn't looking forward to it. That same tiny voice in the back of her mind kept screaming in protest, but the wheels were in motion. And she did trust that Edgar, Anne and company knew what they were doing.

That didn't keep her from breaking two fingernails within days of the session, or feeling that her almost shoulder-length hair had been cut a fraction of an inch too short, or watching in dire frustration while a tiny pimple worked its way to the surface of her "flawless" skin at one temple.

Mercifully, she didn't have to worry about what to wear. Marjorie Semple, the fashion director for *Class*, was taking care of that. All Marni had to do was to show up bright and early on the prescribed morning and put herself into the hands of the hairstylist, the makeup artist, the dresser, numerous other assistants and, of course, Brian Webster. Unfortunately, Edgar, Steve, Anne, Dan, Cynthia, Marjorie and a handful of others from the magazine were also planning to attend the session.

"Do you *all* have to be there?" Marni asked nervously when she spoke with Anne the day before the scheduled shoot.

"Most of us do. At least the first time. Webster knows what kind of feeling we want in this picture, but I think our presence will be a reminder to him of the investment we have in this."

"He's a professional. He knows what he's being paid for. I thought you had faith in him."

"I do," Anne responded with confidence. "Maybe what I'm trying to say is that it's good PR for us to be there."

"It may be good PR, but it's not doing anything for my peace of mind. It'll be bad enough with all of Webster's people there. With all of *you* there, I'll feel like I'm a public spectacle. My God," she muttered under her breath, "I don't know how I let myself be talked into this."

"You let yourself be talked into it because you know it's going to be a smashing success. The session itself will be a piece of cake after all the agonizing you've done about it. You've been photographed before, Marni. I've seen those shots. They were marvelous."

"A standard black-and-white publicity photo is one thing. This is different."

"It's easier. All you have to do is *be* there. Everything else will be taken care of."

They'd been through this all before, and Marni had too many other things that needed her attention to re-hash old arguments. "Okay, Anne. But please. Keep the *Class* staff presence at a minimum. Edgar was go-ing to take me to the studio, but I think I'll tell him to stay here. Steve can take me—*Class* is his special pro-ject. The last thing I need is a corporative audience."

As it happened, Steve couldn't take her, since he was flying in from meetings in Atlanta and would have to join the session when it was already underway. So Ed-gar swung by in the company limousine and picked her up at her Fifth Avenue co-op that Tuesday morn-ing. She was wearing a silk blouse of a pale lavender that coordinated with the deeper lavender shade of her pencil-slim wool skirt and its matching long, oversized jacket. Over the lot she wore a chic wool topcoat that reached mid-calf and was suitably protective against the cold February air.

In a moment's impulsiveness, she'd considered showing up at the session in jeans, a sweatshirt and sneakers, with her hair unwashed and her face per-fectly naked. After all, she'd never been "made over" before. But she hadn't been able to do it. For one thing, she had every intention of going to the office directly from the shoot, hence her choice of clothes. For an-other, she believed she had an image to uphold. Wear-ing jeans and a sweatshirt, as she so often did at home alone on weekends, she looked young and vulnerable.

But she was thirty-one and the president of her family's corporation. Confidence had to radiate from her, as well as sophistication and maturity. True, Webster's hairstylist would probably rewash her hair and then do his own thing with it. The makeup artist would remove even those faint traces of makeup she'd applied that morning. But at least she'd walk into the studio and meet those artists for the first time looking like the successful, over-thirty businesswoman she was supposed to be.

The crosstown traffic was heavy, and the drive to the studio took longer than she'd expected. Edgar, God bless him, had his briefcase open and was reviewing spread sheets aloud. Not that it was necessary. She'd already been over the figures in question, and even if she hadn't, she was a staunch believer in the delegation of authority, as Edgar well knew. But she sensed he was trying to get her mind off the upcoming session, and though his ploy did little to salve her unease, she was grateful for the effort.

The limousine pulled to the curb outside a large, seemingly abandoned warehouse by the river on the west side of Manhattan. Dubious, Marni studied the building through the darkened window of the car.

"This is it," Edgar said. He tucked his papers inside his briefcase, then snapped it shut. "It doesn't look like much, but Brian Webster's been producing great things inside it for years." He climbed from the limousine, then put out a hand to help her.

Moments later they were walking past piles of packing crates toward a large freight elevator, which carried them up. Marni didn't waste time wondering what was on the second, third and fourth floors. She was too busy trying to imagine the scene on the fifth, which, according to the button Edgar had pressed, was where they were headed.

The door slid open. A brightly lit reception area spread before them, its white walls decorated with a modest, if well-chosen, sampling of the photographer's work. The receptionist, an exquisite young woman with raven-black hair, amber eyes and a surprisingly shy smile, immediately came forward from behind her desk and extended her hand.

"Ms. Lange? I'm Angie. I hope you found us all right."

Marni shook her hand, but simply nodded, slightly awed by the young woman's raw beauty. Because of it, she was that little bit more unsettled than she might have been if Webster's receptionist had been middle-aged and frumpy. Not only was Angie tall, but she wore a black wool minidress with a high-collared, long-sleeved fuchsia blouse layered underneath, fuchsia tights and a matching belt double-looped around her slender waist. She was a model, or a would-be model, Marni realized, and it seemed far more fitting that she should be there than Marni herself.

Angie didn't seem at all disturbed by the silence. "I think just about everyone else is here. If you'll come this way..."

Marni and Edgar followed her to a door, then through it into what was very obviously the studio. It was a huge room, as brightly lit as the reception area had been. Its central focus was a seamless expanse of white wall, curving from the ceiling to the floor without a break. Numerous lights, reflecting panels and other paraphernalia were scattered around the area, and at the center was a tripod and camera.

Marni absorbed all of this in a moment, for that was

all the time she was given. Anne was quickly at her
side, introducing her to Webster's chief assistant and to
the others who'd be aiding in one way or another.
Marni was beginning to feel very much like a fish in a
bowl when Anne said, "Brian will be back in a minute.
Angie's gone to call him down."

"Down?"

"He lives upstairs. When he saw that everything
was set up here, he went back to make a few phone
calls." Her gaze skipped past Marni, and she smiled.
"There he is now. Come. I'll introduce you."

Marni turned obediently, but at the sight of the tall,
dark-haired man approaching, her pulse tripped. A
face from the past...yet vaguely different; she had to be
imagining. But she was frozen to the spot, staring in
disbelief as he drew nearer. Webster was a common
name...it wouldn't be him, not *him*. But he was looking
at her, too, and his eyes said she wasn't mistaken.
Those blue eyes...she could never mistake those eyes!

Her breath was caught in her throat, and her heart
began to hammer at her chest as though it were caught,
trapped, locked in a place it didn't want to be. Which
was exactly the way she felt herself. "Oh, no," she
whispered in dismay.

Anne felt both her momentary paralysis and the ensuing trembling. "It's okay," she murmured soothingly by Marni's ear. "He may be gorgeous, but he's a
nice guy to boot."

Marni barely heard her. She stared, stunned and
shaken, as Brian Webster approached. His eyes were
on her, as they'd been from the moment she'd turned
and caught sight of him, but they held none of the
shock Marni's did. He'd known, she realized. Of
course. He'd known. There was only one Lange Cor-

poration, and only one Marni Lange to go with it. But Webster? It was a common name, as was Brian. Not that it would have made a difference. Around her house he'd been referred to as "that wild kid" or simply "him." As for Marni, she'd never even known his first name. He'd been "Web" to her.

"Brian," Anne was saying brightly, "this is Marni."

He'd stopped two feet away, taking in the look in Marni's eyes, the ashen hue of her skin, her frozen stance. "I know," he said softly, his voice barely carrying over the animated chatter of the others in the room. "We've met before."

"You've met...but I don't understand." Anne turned confused eyes on Marni. "You didn't say..." Her words trailed off. She'd never seen a human being turn into a shadow before, but that was exactly what seemed to be happening. "Marni?" she asked worriedly. "Are you all right?"

It was Web who answered, his eyes still glued to Marni's. "I think she needs a minute alone." He took her arm gently, adding to Anne, "We'll be back soon. Coffee and doughnuts are on the way, so that should keep everyone satisfied until we're ready." His fingers tightened fractionally, and he led Marni back across the floor. She wasn't sure if he was afraid she'd make a scene and resist, or if he simply sensed she needed the support. As it was, she could do nothing but go along with him. Her mind was in too great a turmoil to allow for any other action.

The din of the studio died the minute Web closed the door behind them. They were in a bright hall off which no less than half a dozen doors led, but it was to the open spiral staircase that he guided her, then up through another door and into the large living room that was obviously his own. Natural light poured through skylights to give the simply but elegantly furnished room an aura of cheer, but none of that cheer seeped into Marni, who was encased in a crowding prison of memory.

He led her to a chrome-framed, cushioned chair, eased her down, then turned and headed for the bar.

Marni watched him go. He moved with the same fluidity, the same stealthy grace he'd possessed years before when she'd known him. He seemed taller, though perhaps he'd just filled out in maturity. His legs were lean and long as they'd been then, though they were sheathed in clean, stylishly stitched, button-fly jeans rather than the faded, worn denim he had once sported. The muscle-hugging T-shirt had been replaced with a more reputable chambray shirt, rolled to the elbows and open at the neck. His shoulders seemed broader, his hair definitely shorter and darker.

He'd aged well.

"I know it's a little early in the day to imbibe," he said, giving a brittle smile as he returned to her, "but I think you ought to drink this." He placed a wineglass in her shaky fingers, then watched while she took a healthy swallow of the pale amber liquid. Her eyes didn't leave his, not while she drank, nor when he crossed to the nearby sofa and sat down.

He propped his elbows on his outspread thighs and dangled his hands between his knees. "You didn't know," he stated in a very quiet voice.

Marni took another swallow of wine, then slowly shook her head.

He was grateful to see that she'd stopped shaking, and could only hope that a little more wine would restore the color to her cheeks. He sympathized with her, could understand what she was feeling. He'd been living with the same feelings for the past three months, ever since he'd first been approached by *Class*. And those feelings had only intensified when he'd learned that the editorial staff had decided to use the chief executive officer on its first cover.

He'd had the advantage that Marni hadn't, and still he was stunned seeing her, being with her after all that had happened fourteen years before.

"I'm sorry," he said, meaning it. "I thought for sure that you'd have been involved on some level when the decision was made to hire me."

"I was," Marni heard herself say. Her voice was distant, weak, and it didn't sound at all like her own. She took a deep, unsteady breath and went on, trying to sound more like the executive she was. "I've been involved with every major decision involving *Class*, including the one to hire you. But I never knew your name was Brian, and even if I had I probably would never have guessed *the* Brian Webster to be you."

His half smile was chilly. "I've come a ways since we knew each other."

"That's two of us," she murmured somberly. She looked down at her glass, looked back at Web, then finally took another swallow. Afterward she clutched the stem of the wineglass with both hands and frowned at her whitened knuckles. "I had bad vibes about this from the start. Right from the start."

"About hiring me?"

"About posing for the cover. I argued with my people for a good long time, but I've always been one to delegate authority. In the end I told myself that they were specialists and had to know what they were doing. I couldn't possibly have known who you were, but

I was *still* reluctant to do it. I shouldn't have agreed." She punctuated her words with one harsh nod, then another. "I should have stuck to my guns."

There was a lengthy silence in the room. As long as Marni was thinking of business, as long as she wasn't looking at Web, she felt better. Maybe the wine had helped. Tipping her head back, she drained the glass.

"I think they're right," Web said softly.

Her head shot up and, in that instant, the fact of his identity hit her squarely in the face again. The bright blotches that had risen on her cheeks faded quickly. "You can't be serious," she whispered tremulously.

"I am." He leaned back and threw one long arm across the back of the sofa. His forearm was tanned, corded, lightly furred with hair. "You're right for the cover, Marni. I've spent a lot of time going over the concept of the magazine with your staff, and you're right for the cover. You've got the looks. You've always had the looks, only they're better now. More mature. And God knows you've got the position to back them up."

His voice took on a harder edge at the end. Marni thought she heard sarcasm in it, and she bolted to her feet.

It was a mistake. She swayed, whether from the wine or the lingering shock of seeing Web after all these years, she didn't know. But that was irrelevant; before she could utter a protest, she found herself back in the chair with her head pressed between her knees.

Web was on his haunches before her. "Deep breaths. Just relax." His large hand chafed her neck, urging the flow of blood back to her head. But the flood that came to Marni was of memories—memories of a gentler touch, of ecstasy, then of grief, utter and total. Seared by pain she hadn't known in years, she threw his hand off and pressed herself back in the chair, clutching its arms with strained fingers.

"Don't touch me," she seethed, eyes wide and wild.

Web felt as though she'd struck him, yet she looked as though she'd been struck herself. As he watched, she seemed to crumble. Her chest caved in, her shoulders hunched, and she curled her arms protectively around her stomach. She was shaking again, and it looked like she might cry. She blinked once, twice, took a slow breath, then forcibly straightened her body. Only then did she look at him again.

"You knew. I didn't, but you did. Why did you agree to this?"

"To work for *Class*? Because I think it's an idea whose time has come."

"But you had to have learned pretty quickly who the publisher was. Why did you go ahead?"

"If your father had still been at the helm, I might not have. I wouldn't have worked for him. I knew he'd been kicked upstairs, and I'd been told you ran everything, but I wasn't sure how involved he still was. For a while there I waited to get that thank-you-but-no-thank-you call, and if it had been from him I would have said the words before he did."

"He only comes in for quarterly meetings," she said, defending her father against the bitterness in Web's tone. "He isn't interested in the details of the business anymore. And even if he'd heard your name, I doubt he'd have said anything."

Web gave a harsh laugh. "Don't tell me he's forgiven and forgotten."

"Not by a long shot," she muttered, then added pointedly, "None of us has. But he wouldn't have associated that...that Web we once knew with Brian Webster the photographer any more than I did." Her renewed disbelief mixed with confusion. "But *you* knew, and still you went ahead. Why?"

He shrugged, but it was a studied act. "I told you, the idea was good. I felt it might be the right move for my career."

"I don't recall your being ambitious."

A muscle in his jaw flexed. "I've changed."

He'd spoken in a deep voice that held cynicism, yes, but a certain sadness, even regret as well. All of it worked its painful way through Marni's system. When she spoke, her voice was little more than a whisper. "But when you found out you'd be photographing me, didn't you have second thoughts?"

"Oh, yes."

"And still you agreed to it. *Why?*"

It took him longer to answer, because he wanted to give her the truth. He felt he owed her that much. "Curiosity," he said at last.

She shook her head, unable to believe him. If he'd said "revenge" or "arrogance" or "sadism," she might have bought it, but he wouldn't have said any of those. He'd always been a charmer.

She couldn't take her eyes from his, and the longer she looked the more mired in memory she became. "This isn't going to work," she finally said in a low, shaky voice.

Web stood, feeling nearly as stiff as she looked. One part of him agreed with her, that part swamped with pain and guilt. The other part was the one that had grown over the years, that had come to accept things that couldn't be changed. He was a professional now. He had a name, a reputation and a contract. "You can't back out, Marni," he forced himself to say. "There's an entire crew out there waiting to go to work."

She eyed him defensively. "I don't care about the crew. I'll pay for the services they would have given today, and for yours. We can find another model for this cover."

"On such short notice? Not likely. And you've got a production deadline to meet."

"We're way ahead, and if necessary we'll change the schedule. I can't do this."

His eyes hardened. He wasn't sure why—yes, he'd had personal reservations when the idea had first been presented to him—but he was determined to photograph her. Oh, he'd been curious all right, curious as to what she'd be like, what she'd look like fourteen years later. He hadn't expected to feel something for her, and those feelings were so confused that he couldn't quickly sort them out. But they were there. And he *was* going to photograph her.

He wondered if it was the challenge of it, or sheer pride on his part, or even the desire for a small measure of vengeance. Marni Lange's family had treated him like scum once upon a time. He was damned if one of them, least of all Marni, would ever do it again.

"Why can't you do it?" he asked coolly.

She stared at him, amazed that he'd even have to ask. "I didn't know you'd be the photographer."

"That shouldn't bother you. You smiled plenty for me once upon a time."

She flinched, then caught herself. "That was a world away, Web."

"Brian. I'm called Brian now…or Mr. Webster."

"I look at you and I see Web. That's why I can't go through with this."

"Funny," he said, scratching the back of his head, another studied act, "I thought you'd be above emotionalism at this point in your life." His hand dropped to his side. "You're a powerful woman, Marni. A powerful businesswoman. You must be used to pressure, to acting under it. I'd have thought you'd be able to rise to the occasion."

He was goading her, and she knew it. "I'm a human being."

He mouthed an exaggerated "ahhhhh."

"What do you want from me?" she cried, and something in her voice tore at him quite against his will.

His gaze dropped from her drained face to her neck, her breasts, her waist, her hips. He remembered. Oh, yes, he remembered. Sweet memories made bitter by a senseless accident and the vicious indictment of a family in mourning.

But that was in the past. The present was a studio, a production crew and equipment waiting, and a magazine cover to be shot.

"I want to take your picture," he said very quietly. "I want you to pull yourself together, walk out into that studio and act like the publisher of this magazine we're trying to get off the ground. I want you to put yourself into the hands of my staff, then sit in front of my camera and work with me." His voice had grown harder again, though he barely noticed. Despite his mental preparation for this day, he was as raw, emotionally, as Marni was.

He dragged in a breath, and his jaw was tight. "I want to see if this time you'll have the guts to stand on your own two feet and see something through."

Marni's head snapped back, and her eyes widened, then grew moist. As she'd done before, though, she blinked once, then again, and the tears were gone. "You are a bastard," she whispered as she pushed herself to her feet.

"From birth," he said without pride. "But I never told you that, did I?"

"You never told me much. I don't think I realized it until now. What we had was...was..." Unable to find the right words when her thoughts were whirling, she simply closed her mouth, turned and left the room. She walked very slowly down the winding staircase, taking one step at a time, gathering her composure. He'd issued a challenge, and she was determined to meet it. He wanted a picture; he'd get a picture. She *was* the publisher of this magazine, and, yes, she was a powerful businesswoman. Web had decimated her once before. She was not going to let it happen again.

By the time she reentered the studio, she was concentrating on business, her sole source of salvation. Anne rushed to her side and studied her closely. "Are you okay?"

"I'm fine," she said.

"God, I'm sorry, Marni. I didn't realize that you knew him."

"Neither did I."

"Are you over the shock?"

"The shock, yes."

"But he's not your favorite person. You don't know how *awful* I feel. Here we've been shoving him at you—"

"But you were right, Anne. He's a superb photographer, and he's the right man for *Class*. My personal feelings are irrelevant. This is pure business." Her chin was tipped up, but Anne couldn't miss the pinched look around her mouth.

"But you didn't want to be on the cover to begin with, and now you've got to cope with Brian."

"Brian won't bother me." It was Web who would...if she let him. She simply wouldn't allow it. That was that! "I think we'd better get going. I've got piles of things waiting for me at the office."

Anne gave her a last skeptical once-over before turning and gesturing to Webster's assistant.

In the hour that followed, Marni was shuttled from side room to side room. She submitted to having her hair completely done, all the while concentrating on the meeting she would set up the next day with the management of her computer division. She watched her face as it was cleaned, then skillfully made up, but her thoughts were on a newly risen distribution problem in the medical supplies section. She let herself be stripped, then dressed, but her mind was on the possibility of luring one particularly brilliant competitor to head Lange's market research department. As a result, she was as oblivious to the vividly patterned silk skirt and blouse, to the onyx necklace, bracelet and earrings put on her as she was to the fact that the finished product was positively breathtaking.

The audience in the main room was oblivious to no such thing. The minute she stepped from the dressing room she was met by a series of "ooohs" and "ahhhs," immediately followed by a cacophony of chatter.

But she was insulated. In the time it had taken for Webster's people to make her camera-ready, she'd built a wall around herself. She was barely aware of being led to a high, backless stool set in the center of the seamless expanse of curving white wall. She was barely aware of the man who continued to poke at her hair, or the one who lightly brushed powder on her neck, throat and the narrow V between her breasts, or the woman who smoothed her skirt into gentle folds around her legs and adjusted the neckline of her blouse.

She was aware of Web, though, the minute he came to stand before her with his legs planted apart and his eyes scrutinizing what she'd become. She felt her heart beat faster, so she conjured the image of that particularly brilliant competitor she wanted to head the market research division. She'd met the man several times, yet now his image kept fading. She blinked, swallowed and tried again, this time thinking of the upcoming stockholders' meeting and the issues to be dealt with. But the issues slipped from mind. Something about rewriting bylaws…hostile takeover attempts…

Web turned to issue orders to his assistants, and she let out the breath she hadn't realized she'd been holding. A quartz floodlight was set here, another there. Reflectors were placed appropriately. A smaller spotlight was put farther to one side, another to the back, several more brought down from overhead. Web moved around her, studying her from every angle, consulting his light meter at each one.

She felt like a yo-yo, spinning to the end of its rope when he looked at her, recoiling in relief when he looked away. She didn't want to think ahead to when he'd be behind his camera focusing solely on her, for it filled her with dread. So she closed her eyes and thought yoga thoughts, blank mind, deep steady breaths, relaxation.

She'd never been all that good at yoga.

She put herself into a field of wildflowers glowing in the springtime sun. But the sun was too hot, and the wildflowers began doing something to her sinuses, not to mention her stomach. And there was a noise that should have been appropriate but somehow was grating. The chirping of birds, the trickle of a nearby stream... No, the sounds of a gentle piano...a lilting love song...

Her eyes riveted to Web, who approached her barehanded. "That music," she breathed. "Is it necessary?"

He spoke as softly as she had. "I thought it might relax you, put you in the mood."

"You've got to be kidding."

"Actually, I wasn't. If it bothers you—"

"It does. I don't like it."

"Would you like something else?"

"Silence would be fine."

"I need to be put in the mood, too."

"Then put on something else," she whispered plaintively, and breathed a sigh of relief when he walked to the side to talk with one of his assistants, who promptly headed off in the other direction. Marni barely had time to register the spectators gathered in haphazard clusters beyond camera range, sipping coffee, munching doughnuts and talking among themselves as they observed the proceedings, when Web returned. He stood very close and regarded her gently. She felt the muscles around her heart constrict.

He put his hands on her shoulders and tightened his fingers when she would have leaned back out of his grasp. "I want you to relax," he ordered very softly, his face inches above hers. He began to slowly knead the tension from her shoulders. "If we're going to get anything out of this, you've got to relax."

The background music stopped abruptly. "I can't relax when you're touching me," she whispered.

"You'll have to get used to that. I'll have to touch you, to turn you here or there where I want you."

"You can tell me what to do. You don't have to do it for me."

His hands kept up their kneading, though her muscles refused to respond. "I enjoy touching you. You're a very beautiful woman."

She closed her eyes. "Please, no. Don't play your games with me."

"I'm not playing games. I'm very serious."

"I can't take it." Just then the music began again, this time to a more popular, faster beat. Her eyes flew open. "Oh, God, you're not going to have me *move*, are you?"

He had to smile at the sheer terror in her eyes. "Would it be so awful?"

Her expression was mutinous. "I won't do that, Web. I'm not a model, or a dancer, or an exhibitionist, and I *refuse* to make an utter fool out of myself in front of all these people."

He was still smiling. At the age of thirty-one, she was more beautiful than he'd ever imagined she'd be. Though he had no right to, he felt a certain pride in her. "Take it easy, Marni. I won't make you dance. Or move. We'll just both flow with the music. How does that sound?"

It sounded awful, and his smile was upsetting her all the more. "I'm not really up for flowing."

"What are you up for?"

Her eyes widened on his face in search of smugness, but there was none. Nor had there been suggestiveness in his tone, which maintained the same soft and gentle lilt. He was trying to be understanding of her and of the situation they'd found themselves in, she realized. She also realized that there were tiny crow's-feet at either corner of his eyes and smile lines by his mouth, and that his skin had the rougher texture maturity gave a man. A thicker beard, though recently shaven, left a virile shadow around his mouth and along his jaw.

His hands on her shoulders had stopped moving. She averted her gaze to the floor. "I'm not up for much right about now, but I guess we'd better get on with this."

"A bit of pain...a blaze of glory?"

She jerked her eyes back to his, and quite helplessly they flooded. "How *could* you?" she whispered brokenly.

He leaned forward and pressed his lips to her damp brow, then murmured against her skin, for her ears alone, "I want you to remember, Marni. I want you to think about what we had. That first time on the shore, the other times in the woods and on my narrow little cot."

Too weak to pull away from him, and further hamstrung by the people watching, she simply closed her eyes and struggled to regain her self-control. Web drew back and brushed a tear from the corner of her eye.

"Remember it, Marni," he whispered gently. "Remember how good it was, how soft and warm and exciting. Pretend we're back there now, that we're lovers stealing away from the real world, keeping secrets only the two of us share. Pretend that there's danger, that what we're doing is slightly illicit, but that we're very, very sure of ourselves."

"But the rest—"

"Remember the good part, babe. Remember it when you look at me now. I want confidence from you. I want defiance and promise and success, and that special kind of feminine spirit that captivated me from the start. You've got it in you. Let me see it."

He stepped back then and, without another word, went to his camera.

Stunned and more confused than ever, Marni stared after him. Brushes dabbed at her cheeks and glossed her lips; fingers plucked at her hair. She wanted to push them away, because they intruded on her thoughts. But she had no more power to lift a hand than she had to get up and walk from the room as that tiny voice of instinct told her to do.

It began then. With his legs braced apart and his eyes alternating between the camera lens and her, Web gave soft commands to the lighting crew. Then, "Let's get a few straightforward shots first. Look here, Marni."

She'd been looking at him all along, watching as he peered through the lens, then stepped to the side holding the remote cord to the shutter. She felt wooden. "I don't know what to do. Am I supposed to…smile?"

"Just relax. Do whatever you want. Tip your head up…a little to the left…atta girl." Click.

Marni made no attempt to smile. She didn't want to smile. What she wanted to do was cry, but she couldn't do that.

"Run your tongue over your lips." Click. "Good. Again."

Click. Click. "Shake your head…that's the way… like the ocean breeze…warm summer's night…"

Marni stared at the camera in agony, wanting to remember as he was urging but simultaneously fighting the pain.

He left the camera and came to her, shifting her on

the stool, repositioning her legs, her arms, her shoulders, her head, all the time murmuring soft words of encouragement that backfired in her mind. He returned to the camera, tripped the lens twice, then lifted the tripod and moved the entire apparatus forward.

"Okay, Marni," he said, his voice modulated so that it just reached her, "now I want you to turn your face away from me. That's it. Just your head. Now close your eyes and remember what I told you. Think sand and stars and a beautiful full moon. Let the music help you." The words of a trendy pop ballad were shimmering through the room. "That's it. Now, very slowly, turn back toward me...open your eyes...a smug little smile..."

Marni struggled. She turned her head as he'd said. She thought of sand—she and Web lying on it—and stars and a beautiful full moon—she and Web lying beneath them—and she very slowly turned back toward him. But when she opened her eyes, they were filled with tears, and she couldn't muster even the smallest smile.

Web didn't take a shot. Patiently, he straightened, then put out a hand when Anne started toward Marni. She retreated, and Web moved forward. "Not exactly what I was looking for," he said on a wistfully teasing note.

"I'm sorry." She blinked once, twice, then she was in control again. The music had picked up, and she caught sight of feet tapping, knees bending, bodies rocking rhythmically on the sidelines. "I feel awkward."

"It's okay. We'll try again." He gestured for his aides to touch her up, then returned to stand by his camera with the remote cord in his hand. "Okay, Marni. Let your head fall back. That's it. Now concentrate on relaxing your shoulders. Riiiiight. Now bring your head back up real quick and look the camera in the eye. Good. That's my girl! Better." He advanced the film once, then again, and a third time. What he was capturing was better than what had come before, he knew, but it was nowhere near the look, the feeling he wanted.

He could have her hair fixed, or her clothes, or her makeup. He could shift her this way or that, could put her in any number of poses. But he couldn't take the pain from her eyes.

He'd told her to remember the good and the beautiful, because that was what he wanted to do himself. But she couldn't separate the good from all that had come after and, with sorrow on her face and pain in her eyes, he couldn't either.

So he took a different tack, a more businesslike one he felt would be more palatable to her. He talked to her, still softly, but of the magazine now, of the image they all wanted for it, of the success it was going to be. He posed her, coaxed her, took several shots, then frowned. He took the stool away, replaced one lens with another his assistant handed him and exposed nearly a roll of film with her standing—straight, then with her weight balanced on one hip, with her hands folded before her, one hand on her hip, one hand on each, the two clasped behind her head. When her legs began to visibly tremble, he set her back on the stool.

He changed lights, bathing the background in green, then yellow, then pale blue. He switched to a hand-held camera so that he could more freely move around, changing lenses and the angle of his shots, building a momentum in the hopes of distracting Marni from the thoughts that brought tears to her eyes every time he was on the verge of getting something good.

For Marni it was trial by fire, and she knew she was failing miserably. When Web, infuriatingly solicitous, approached her between a series of shots, she put the blame on the self-consciousness she felt, then on the heat of the lights, then on the crick in her neck. One hour became two, then three. When she began to wilt, she was whisked off for a change of clothes and a glass of orange juice, but the remedial treatment was akin to a finger in the dike. She ached from the inside out, and it was all she could do to keep from crumbling.

The coffee grew cold, the doughnuts stale. The by-standers watched with growing restlessness, no longer tapping their feet to the music but looking more somber with each passing minute. There were conferences—between Edgar, Anne, Marni and Web, be- tween Dan, Edgar and Web, between Cynthia, Anne and Marni.

Nothing helped.

As a final resort, when they were well into the fourth hour of the shot, Web turned on a small fan to stir Marni's hair from behind. He showed her how to stand, showed her how to slowly sway her body and gently swing her arms, told her to lower her chin and look directly at him.

She followed his instructions to the letter, in truth so exhausted that she was dipping into a reserve of sheer grit. She couldn't take much more, she knew. She *wouldn't* take much more. Wasn't she the one in command here? Wasn't she the employer of every last person in the room?

While she ran the gamut of indignant thought, Web stood back and studied her, and for the first time in hours he felt he might have something special. Moving that way, with her hair billowing softly, she was the girl he remembered from that summer in Maine. She was direct and honest, serious but free, and she exuded the aura of power that came from success.

He caught his breath, then quickly raised his camera and prepared to shoot. "That's it. Oh, sunshine, that's it...."

Her movement stopped abruptly. *Sunshine.* It was what he'd always called her at the height of passion, when she would whisper that she loved him and would have to settle for an endearment in place of a returned vow.

It was the final straw. No longer able to stem the tears she'd fought so valiantly, she covered her face with her hands and, heedless of all around her, began to weep softly.

2

MARNI LANGE WAS on top of the world. Seventeen and eager to live life to its fullest, she'd just graduated from high school and would be entering Wellesley College in the fall. As they did every June, her parents, brother and sister and herself had come to their summer home in Camden, Maine, to sun and sail, barbecue and party to their hearts' content.

Ethan, her older brother by eight years, had looked forward to this particular summer as the first he'd be spending as a working man on vacation. Having graduated from business school, he'd spent the past eight months as a vice-president of the Lange Corporation, which had been formed by their father, Jonathan, some thirty years before. Privileged by being the son of the founder, president and chairman of the board of the corporation, Ethan was, like his father, conducting what work he had to do during the summer months from Camden.

Tanya, Marni's older sister by two years, had looked forward to the summer as a well-earned vacation from college, which she was attending only because her parents had insisted on it. If she'd had her way she'd be traveling the world, dallying with every good-looking man in sight. College men bored her nearly as much as her classes did, she'd discovered quickly. She needed an older man, she bluntly claimed, a man with experience and savvy and style.

Marni felt light-years away from her sister, and always had. They were as different as night and day in looks, personality and aspirations. While Tanya was intent on having a good time until the day she reeled in the oil baron who would free her from her parents and assure her of the good life forever, Marni was quieter, serious about commitment yet fun-loving. She wanted to get an education, then perhaps go out to work for a while, and the major requirement she had for a husband was that he adore her.

A husband was the last thing on her mind that summer, though. She was young. She'd dated aplenty, partying gaily within society's elite circles, but she'd never formed a relationship she would have called deep. Too many of the young men she'd known seemed shallow, unable to discuss world news or the stock market or the latest nonfiction best-seller. She wanted to grow, to meet interesting people, to broaden her existence before she thought of settling down.

The summer began as it always did, with reunion parties among the families whose sumptuous homes, closed all winter, were now buzzing with life. Marni enjoyed seeing friends she hadn't seen since the summer before, and she felt that much more buoyant with both her high school degree and her college acceptance letter lying on the desk in her room back at the Langes' Long Island estate.

After the reunions came the real fun—days of yachting along the Maine coast, hours sunning on the beach or hanging out on the town green or cruising the narrow roads in late-model cars whose almost obscene luxury was fully taken for granted by the young people in question.

Marni had her own group of friends, as did Tanya, but for very obvious reasons both groups tagged along with Ethan and his friends whenever possible. Ethan never put up much of a fight...for equally obvious reasons. Though his own tastes ran toward shapely brunettes a year or two older than Tanya, he knew that several of his group preferred the even younger blood of Marni's friends.

It was because of the latter, or perhaps because Ethan was feeling restless about something he couldn't understand, that this particular summer he made a new friend. His last name was Webster, but the world knew him simply as Web—at least, the world that came into contact with the Camden Inn and Resort where he was employed alternately as lifeguard, bellboy and handyman.

Ethan had been using the pool when he struck up that first conversation with Web, whom he discovered to be far more interesting than any of the friends he was with. Web was twenty-six, footloose and fancy-free, something which, for all his social and material status, Ethan had never been. While Ethan had jetted from high-class hotel to high-class hotel abroad, Web had traveled the world on freighters, passenger liners or any other vehicle on which he could find employment. While Ethan, under his father's vigilant eye, had met and hobnobbed with the luminaries of the world, Web had read about them in the quiet of whatever small room he was renting at the time.

Web was as educated as he and perhaps even brighter, Ethan decided early on in their friendship, and the luxury of Web's life was that he was beholden to no one. Ethan envied and admired it to the extent that he found himself spending more and more time with Web.

It was inevitable that Marni should meet him, nearly as inevitable that she should be taken with him from the first. He was mature. He was good-looking. He was carefree and adventurous, yet soft-spoken and thoughtful. Given the diverse and oftentimes risky things he'd experienced in life, there was an excitement about him that Marni had never found in another human being. He was free. He was his own man.

He was also a roamer. She knew that well before she fell in love with him, but that didn't stop it from happening. Puppy love, Ethan had called it, infatuation. But Marni knew differently.

After her introduction to Web, she was forever on Ethan's tail. At first she tried to be subtle. She'd just come for a swim, she told Web minutes before she dived into the resort pool, leaving the two men behind to talk. But she wore her best bikini and made sure that the lounge chair she stretched out on in the sun was well within Web's range of vision.

She tagged along with Ethan when he and Web went out boating, claiming that she had nothing to do at home and was bored. She sandwiched herself into the back of Ethan's two-seater sports car when he and Web drove to Bar Harbor on Web's day off, professing that she needed a day off too from the monotony of Camden. She sat intently, with her chin in her palm, while the two played chess in Web's small room at the rear of the Inn, insisting that she'd never learn the game unless she could observe two masters at it.

Ethan and Web did other things, wilder things—racing the wind on the beach at two in the morning on the back of Web's motorcycle, playing pool and drinking themselves silly at a local tavern, diving by moonlight to steal lobsters from traps not far from shore, then boiling them in a pot over a fire on the sand. Marni wasn't allowed to join them at such times, but she knew where they went and what they did, and it added to her fascination for Web...as did the fact that Jonathan and Adele Lange thoroughly disapproved of him.

Marni had never been perverse or rebellious where her parents were concerned. She'd enjoyed her share of mischief when she'd been younger, and still took delight in the occasional scheme that drew arched brows and pursed lips from her parents. But Web drew far more than that.

"Who *is* he?" her mother would ask when Ethan announced that he was meeting with Web yet again. "Where does he come from?"

"Lots of places," Ethan would answer, indulging in his own adult prerogative for independence.

Jonathan Lange agreed wholeheartedly with his wife. "But you don't know anything about the man, Ethan. For all you know, he's been on the wrong side of the law at some point in his, uh, illustrious career."

"Maybe," Ethan would say with a grin. "But he happens to know a hell of a lot about a hell of a lot. He's an extension of my education...like night school. Look at it that way."

The elder Langes never did, and Web's existence continued to be viewed as something distasteful. He was never invited to the Lange home, and he became the scapegoat for any and all differences of opinion the Langes had with their son. Starry-eyed, Marni didn't believe a word her parents said in their attempts to discredit Web. If anything, their dislike of him added an element of danger, of challenge, to her own attempts to catch his eye.

She liked looking at him—at his deeply tanned face, which sported the bluest of eyes; his brown hair, which had been kissed golden by the sun; his knowing and experienced hands. His body was solid and muscular, and his fluid, lean-hipped walk spoke of self-assurance. She knew he liked looking at her, too, for she'd find him staring at her from time to time, those blue eyes alight with desire. At least she thought it was desire. She never really knew, because he didn't follow up on it. Oh, he touched her—held her hand to help her from the car, bodily lifted her from the boat to the dock, stopped in his rounds of the pool to add a smidgen of suntan lotion to a spot she'd missed on her back—but he never let his touch wander, as increasingly she wished he would.

Frustration became a mainstay in her existence. She dressed her prettiest when she knew she'd see Web, made sure her long auburn hair was clean and shiny, painted her toenails and fingernails in hopes of looking older. But, for whatever his reasons, Web kept his distance, and short of physically attacking the man, Marni didn't know what more she could do.

Then came a day when Ethan was ill. Web was off duty, and the two had planned to go mountain climbing, but Ethan had been sick to his stomach all night and could barely lift his head come morning. Marni, who'd spent the previous two days pestering Ethan to take her along, was sitting on his bed at seven o'clock.

"I'll go in your place," she announced, leaning conspiratorially close. Her parents were still in bed at the other end of the house.

"You will not," Ethan managed to say through dry lips. He closed his eyes and moaned. "God, do I feel awful."

"I'm going, Ethan. Web has been looking forward to this—I heard him talking. There's no reason in the world why he has to either cancel or go alone."

"For Pete's sake, Marni, don't be absurd."

"There's nothing absurd about my going mountain climbing."

"With Web there is. You'll slow him down."

"I won't. I've got more energy than you do even when you're well. I've got youth on my side."

"Exactly. And you think Web's going to *want* you along? You're seventeen and absolutely drooling for him. Come on, sweetheart. Be realistic. We both know why you want to go, and it's got nothing to do with the clean, fresh air." He rolled to his side, tucked his knees up and moaned again.

Marni knew he was indulgent when it came to her attraction for Web. He humored her, never quite taking her seriously. So, she mused, fair was fair... "Okay, then. I'll go over to his place and explain that you can't go."

"Call him."

She was already on her feet. "I'll go over. *He* can be the one to make the decision." And she left.

Web was more than surprised to find Marni on his doorstep at the very moment Ethan should have been. He was also slightly wary. "You're trying to trick me into something, Marni Lange," he accused, with only a half smile to take the edge off his voice.

"I'm not, Web. I like the outdoors, and I've climbed mountains before."

"When?" he shot back.

"When I was at camp."

"How long ago?"

"Four...five years."

"Ahhh. Those must have been quite some mountains you twelve-year-old girls climbed."

"They were mountains, no less than the one you and Ethan were planning to climb."

"Hmmph.... Do your parents know you're here?"

"What's that got to do with anything?"

"Do they know?"

"They know I won't be home till late." She paused, then at Web's arched brow added more sheepishly, "I told them I was driving with a couple of friends down to Old Orchard. They won't worry. I'm a big girl."

"That's right," he said, very slowly dropping his gaze along the lines of her body. It was the first time he'd looked at her that way, and Marni felt a ripple of excitement surge through her because there was a special spark that was never in his eyes when Ethan was around. It was the spark that kept her spirits up when he went on to drawl, "You're a big girl, all right. Seventeen years old."

When she would have argued—like the seventeen-year-old she was—she controlled herself. "My age doesn't have anything to do with my coming today or not," she said with what she hoped was quiet reserve. "I'd really like to go mountain climbing, and since you'd planned to do it anyway, I didn't see any harm in asking to join you. Ethan would have been here if he hadn't been sick." She turned and took a step away from his door. "Then again, maybe you'd rather wait till he's better."

She was halfway down the hall when he called her back, and she was careful to look properly subdued when he grabbed his things from just inside the door, shut it behind him, then collared her with his hand and propelled them both off.

It was the most beautiful day Marni had ever spent. Web drove her car—he smilingly claimed that he didn't trust her experience, or lack of it, at the wheel—and they reached the appointed mountain by ten. It wasn't a huge mountain, though it was indeed higher and steeper than any Marni had ever climbed. She held her own, though, taking Web's offered hand over tough spots for the sake of the delicious contact more than physical necessity.

The day had started out chilly but warmed as they went, and they slowly peeled off layers of clothing and stuffed them in their backpacks. By the time they stopped for lunch, Marni was grateful for the rest. She'd brought along the food Cook had packed for Ethan and had made one addition of her own—a bottle of wine pilfered quite remorselessly from the huge stock in the Langes' cellar.

"Nice touch," Web mused, skillfully uncorking the wine and pouring them each a paper cup full. "Maybe not too wise, though. A little of this and we're apt to have a tough time of it on the way back down."

"There's beer if you prefer," Marni pointed out gently. "Ethan had it already chilled, so evidently he wasn't worried about its effects."

"No, no. Wine's fine." He sipped it, then cocked his head. "It suits you. I can't imagine your drinking beer."

"Why not?"

He propped himself on an elbow and crossed his legs at the ankle. Then he looked at her, studying her intently. Finally, he reached for a thick ham sandwich.

"You're more delicate than beer," he said, his eyes focusing nowhere in particular.

"If that's a compliment, I thank you," she said, making great efforts—and succeeding overall—to hide her glee. She helped herself to a sandwich and leaned back against a tree. "This is nice. Very quiet. Peaceful."

"You like peaceful places?"

"Not all the time," she mused softly, staring off into the woods. "I like activity, things happening, but this is the best kind of break." And the best kind of company, she might have added if she'd dared. She didn't dare.

"Are you looking forward to going to Wellesley?"

Her bright eyes found his. "Oh, yes. It was my first choice. I was deferred for early admission—I guess my board scores weren't as high as they might have been—and if I hadn't gotten in I suppose I would have gone somewhere else and been perfectly happy. But I'm glad it never came down to that."

Web asked her what she wanted to study, and she told him. He asked what schools her friends were going to, and she told him. He asked what she wanted to do with her future, and she told him—up to a point. She didn't say that she wanted a husband and kids and a house in Connecticut because she'd simply taken that all for granted, and it somehow seemed inappropriate to say to Web. He wasn't the house-in-Connecticut type. At this precise moment, being with him as she'd dreamed of being so often, she wasn't either.

They talked more as they ate. Web was curious about her life, and she eagerly answered his questions. She asked some of her own about the jobs he'd had and their accompanying adventures, and with minor coaxing he regaled her with tales, some tall, some not. They worked steadily through the bottle of wine, and by the time it was done and every bit of their lunch had been demolished, they were both feeling rather lazy.

"See? What did I tell you?" Web teased. He lay on his back with his head pillowed on his arms. Marni was in a similar position not far from him. He tipped his head and warmed her with his blue eyes. "We might never get down from this place."

Her heart was fluttering. "We haven't reached the top yet."

"We will. It's just a little way more, and the trip down is faster and easier. Only thing is—" he paused to bend one knee up "—I'm not sure I want to move."

"There's no rush," she said softly.

"No," he mused thoughtfully. His eyes held hers for a long time before he spoke in a deep, very quiet, subtly warning voice. "Don't look at me that way, Marni."

"What way?" she breathed.

"That way. I'm only human."

She didn't know if he was pleased or angry. "I'm sorry. I didn't mean—"

"Of course you didn't mean. You're seventeen. How are you supposed to know what happens when you look at a man that way?"

"What way?"

"With your heart on your sleeve."

"Oh." She looked away. She hadn't realized she'd been so transparent, and she was sure she'd made Web uncomfortable. "I'm sorry," she murmured.

Neither of them said anything for a minute, and Marni stared blindly at a nearby bush.

"Ah, hell," Web growled suddenly, and grabbed her arm. "Come over here. I want you smiling, not all misty-eyed."

"I wasn't misty-eyed," she argued, but she made no

argument when he pulled her head to the crook of his shoulder. "It's just that...maybe Ethan was right. I am a pest. You didn't want me along today. I'm only seventeen."

"You were the one who pointed out that your age was irrelevant to your going mountain climbing."

"It is. But..." Her cheeks grew red, and she couldn't finish. It seemed she was only making things worse.

He brushed a lock of hair from her hot cheek and tucked it behind her ear. The action brought his forearm close to her face. Marni closed her eyes, breathed in the warm male scent of his skin, knew she was halfway to heaven and was about to be tossed back down.

"I think it's about time we talk about this, Marni," he said, continuing to gently stroke her hair. "You're seventeen and I'm twenty-six. We have a definite problem here."

"I'm the one with the problem," she began, but Web was suddenly on his elbow leaning over her.

"Is that what you think...that you're the only one?"

Her gaze was unsteady, faintly hopeful. "Am I wrong?"

"Very."

She held her breath.

"You're a beautiful woman," he murmured as his eyes moved from one of her features to the next.

"I'm a girl," she whispered.

"That's what I keep trying to tell myself, but my body doesn't seem to want to believe it. I've tried, Marni. For the past month I've tried to keep my hands off. It was dangerous to come here today."

Marni reached heaven by leaps and bounds. Her body began to relax against his, and she grew aware of his firm lines, his strength. "You didn't do it single-handedly."

"But I'm older. I should know better."

"Are there rules that come with age?"

"There's common sense. And my common sense tells me that I shouldn't be lying here with you curled against me this way."

"You were the one who pulled me over," she pointed out.

"And you're not protesting."

She couldn't possibly protest when she was floating on a cloud of bliss. "Would you like me to?"

"Damn right I would. One of us should show some measure of sanity."

"There's nothing insane about this," she murmured, distracted because she'd let her hand glide over his chest. She could feel every muscle, every crinkling hair beneath his T-shirt, even the small dot of his nipple beneath her palm.

"No?" he asked. Abruptly he flipped over and was on top of her. His blue eyes grilled hers heatedly, and his voice was hoarse. "Y'know, Marni, I'm not one of your little high school friends, or even one of the college guys I'm sure you've dated." He took both of her hands and anchored them by her shoulders. Though his forearms took some of his weight, the boldness of his body imprinted itself on hers. "I've had women. Lots of them. If one of them were here instead of you, we wouldn't be playing around. We'd be stark naked and we'd be making love already."

Marni didn't know where she found the strength to speak. His words—the experience and maturity and adventure they embodied—set her on fire. Her blood was boiling, and her bones were melting. "Is that what we're doing...playing?"

He shifted his lower body in apt answer to her question, then arched a brow at the flare of color in her cheeks. "You don't want to play, do you? You want it all."

She was breathing faster. "I just want you to kiss me," she managed to whisper. The blatancy of his masculinity was reducing her to mush.

"Just a kiss?" he murmured throatily. "Okay, Marni Lange, let's see how you kiss."

She held her breath as he lowered his head, then felt the touch of his mouth on hers for the first time. His lips were hot, and she drew back, scalded, only to find that his heat was tempting, incendiary where the rest of her body was concerned. So she didn't pull back when he touched her a second time, and her lips quickly parted beneath the urging of his.

He tasted and caressed, then drank with unslaked thirst. Marni responded on instinct, kissing him back, feeding on his hunger, willingly offering the inside of her mouth and her tongue when he sought them out.

His breathing was as unsteady as hers when he drew back and looked at her again. "You don't kiss like a seventeen-year-old."

She gave a timid smile. She'd never before received or responded to a kiss like that, but she didn't want Web to know how inexperienced she really was. "I run in fast circles."

"Is that so?" His mouth devoured her smile in a second mind-bending kiss, and he released one of her hands and framed her throat, slowly drawing his palm down until the fullness of her breast throbbed beneath it. "God, Marni, you're lovely," he rasped. "Lovely and strong and fresh…"

Her hands were in his hair, sifting through its thickness as she held him close. "Kiss me again," she pleaded.

"I may be damned for this," he murmured under his breath, "but I want it, too." So he kissed her many, many more times, and he touched her breasts and her belly and her thighs. When his hand closed over the spot where he wanted most to be, she arched convulsively.

"Tell me, Marni," he panted next to her ear, "I need to know. Have you done this before?"

She knew he'd stop if she told him the truth, and one part of her ached so badly she was tempted to lie. But she wasn't irresponsible. Nor could she play the role of the conniving female. He'd know, one way or the other. "No," she finally whispered, but with obvious regret.

Web held himself still, suspended above her for a moment, then gave a loud groan and rolled away.

She was up on her elbow in an instant. "Web? It doesn't matter. I want to. Most of my friends—"

"I don't give a damn about most of your friends," he growled, throwing an arm over his eyes. "You're seventeen, the kid sister of a man who's become my good friend. I can't do it."

"Don't you want to?"

He lifted his arm and stared at her, then grabbed her hand and drew it down to cover the faded fly of his jeans. The fabric was strained. He pressed her hand against his fullness, then groaned again and rolled abruptly to his side away from her.

Her question had been answered quite eloquently.

Marni felt the knot of frustration in her belly, but she'd also felt his. "Can I...can I do something?" she whispered, wanting to satisfy him almost as much as she wanted to be satisfied herself.

"Oh, you can do something," was his muffled reply, "but it'd only shock you and I don't think you're ready for that."

She leaned over him. "I'm ready, Web. I want to do it."

Glaring, he rolled back to face her, but his glare faded when he saw the sincerity of her expression. His eyes grew soft, his features compassionate. He raised a hand to gently stroke the side of her face. "If you really want to do something," he murmured, "you can help me clean up here, then race me to the top of this hill and down. By the time we're back at the bottom, we should both be in control. Either that," he added with a wry smile, "or too tired to do anything about it."

It was his smile and the ensuing swelling of her heart that first told Marni she was in love. Over the next week she pined, because Web made sure that they weren't alone again. He looked at her though, and she could see that he wasn't immune to her. He went out of his way not to touch her and, much as she craved those knowing hands on her again, she didn't push him for fear she'd come across as being exactly what she was— a seventeen-year-old girl with hots that were nearly out of control. She knew that in time she could get through to Web. He felt something for her, something strong. But time was her enemy. The summer was half over, and though she wanted it to last forever, it wouldn't.

She was right on the button when it came to Web and his feelings for her. He wasn't immune, not by a long shot. He told himself it was crazy, that he'd never before craved untried flesh, but there was something more that attracted him to her, something that the women he'd had, the women he continued to have, didn't possess.

So when a group of Ethan's friends and their dates gathered for a party at someone's boat house, Web quite helplessly dragged Marni to a hidden spot and kissed her willing lips until they were swollen.

"What was that for?" she asked. Her arms were around his neck, and she was on tiptoe, her back pressed to the weathered board of the house.

"Are you protesting?" he teased, knowing she'd returned the kiss with a fever.

"No way. Just curious. You've gone out of your way to avoid me." She didn't quite pout, but her accusation was clear.

He insinuated his body more snugly against hers. "I've tried. Again…still. It's not working." He framed her face with his hands, burying his fingers in her hair. "I want you, Marni. I lie in bed at night remembering that day on the mountain and how good you felt under me, and I tell myself that it's nonsense, but the chemistry's there, damn it."

"I know," she agreed in an awed whisper.

"So what are we going to do about it?"

She shrugged, then drew her hands from his shoulders to lightly caress the strong cords of his neck. "You can make love to me if you want."

"Is it what you want?" His soberness compelled her to meet his gaze.

She blinked, her only show of timidity. "I've wanted it for days now. I feel so…empty when I think of you. I get this ache…way down low…"

"Your parents would kill you. And me."

"There are different kinds of killing. Right now I'm dying because I want you, and I'm afraid you still think of me as a little kid who's playing with fire. I may only be seventeen, but I've been with enough men to know when I find one who's different."

He could have substituted his own age for hers and repeated the statement. He didn't understand it, but it was the truth, and it went beyond raw chemistry. Marni had a kind of depth he'd never found in a woman before. He'd watched her participate in conversations with Ethan and his friends, holding her own both intellectually and emotionally. She was sophisticated beyond her years, perhaps not physically, but he felt that urgency in her now.

"I'm serious about your parents," he finally said. "They dislike me as it is. If I up and seduce their little girl—"

"You're not seducing me. It's a mutual thing." Made bold by the emotions she felt when she was in this man's arms, she slid her hand between their bodies and gently caressed the hard evidence of his sex. "I've never done this to another man, never touched another man this way," she whispered. "And I'm not afraid, because when I do this to you—" she rotated her palm and felt him shudder and arch into it "—I feel it inside me, too. Please, Web. Make love to me."

Her nearness, the untutored but instinctively perfect motion of her hand, was making it hard for him to breathe. "Can you get out later?" he managed in a choked whisper.

"Tonight? I think so."

He set her back, leaving his fingers digging into her shoulders. "Think about it until then, and if you still feel the same way, come to me. I'll be on the beach behind the Wayward Pines at two o'clock. You know the one."

She nodded, unable to say a word as the weight of what she was about to agree to settled on her shoulders. He left her then to return to the group. She went straight home and sat in the darkness of her room, giving herself every reason why she should undress and go to sleep for the night but knowing that she'd never sleep, that her body tingled all over, that her craving was becoming obsessive, and that she loved Web.

It didn't seem to matter that he was a roamer, that he'd be gone at the end of the summer, that he couldn't offer her any kind of future. The fact was that she loved him and that she wanted him to be the first man to know, to teach her the secrets of her body.

Wearing nothing but a T-shirt, cutoffs and sandals, she stole out of the house at one-forty-five and ran all the way to the beach. It was an isolated strip just beyond an aging house whose owner visited rarely. As its name suggested, tall pines loomed uncharacteristically close to the shore, giving it a sheltered feeling, a precious one.

Web was propped against the tallest of the pines, and her heart began to thud when he straightened. Out of breath, and now breathless for other reasons, she stopped, then advanced more slowly.

"I wasn't sure you'd come," he said softly, his eyes never leaving hers as he held out his hand.

"I had to," was all she said, ignoring his hand and throwing her arms around his neck. His own circled her, lifting her clear off her feet, and he held her tightly as he buried his face in her hair.

Then he set her down and loosened his grip. "Are you sure? Are you sure this is what you want?"

In answer, she reached for the hem of her T-shirt and drew it over her head. She hadn't worn a bra. Her pert breasts gleamed in the pale moonlight. Less confidently, she reached for one of his hands and put it on her swelling flesh. "Please, Web. Touch me. Teach me."

He didn't need any further encouragement. He dipped his head and took her lips while his hands explored the curves of her breasts, palms kneading in circles, fingers moving inexorably toward the tight nubs that puckered for him.

She cried out at the sweet torment he created, and reached for him, needing to touch him, to know him as he was coming to know her. He held her off only long enough for him to whip his own T-shirt over his head, then he hauled her against him and embraced her with arms that trembled.

"Oh, Web!" she gasped when their flesh came together.

"Feels nice, doesn't it?" His voice held no smugness, only the same awe hers had held. She was running her hands over his back, pressing small kisses to his throat. "Easy, Marni," he whispered hoarsely. "Let's just take it slow this first time."

"I don't think I can," she cried. "I feel…I feel…"

He smiled. His own hands had already covered her back and were dipping into the meager space at the back of her shorts. "I know." He dragged in a shuddering breath, then said more thickly, "Let's get these off." He was on his knees then, unsnapping and unzipping her shorts, tugging them down. She hadn't worn panties. He sucked in his breath. "Marni!"

Her legs were visibly shaking, and she was clutching his sinewed shoulders for support. "Please don't think I'm awful, Web. I just want you so badly!"

He pressed his face to her naked stomach, then spread kisses even lower. "Not any more so than I want you," he whispered. Then he was on his feet, tugging at the snaps of his jeans, pushing the denim and his briefs down and off.

Seconds later they were tumbling onto the sand, their greedy bodies straining to feel more of the other's, hands equally as rapacious. Marni was inflamed by his size, his strength, the manly scent that mixed with that of the pines and the salty sea air to make her drunk. She felt more open than she'd ever been in her life, but more protected.

And more loved. Web didn't say the words, but his hands gave her a message as they touched her. They were hungry and restless, but ever gentle as they stimulated her, leaving no inch of her body untouched. Her breasts, her back, her belly, thighs and bottom—nothing escaped him, nor did she want it to. If she'd ever thought she'd feel shy at exposing herself this way to a man, the desire, the love she felt ruled that out. There was a rightness to Web's liberty, a rightness to the feel of his lips on her body, to the feel of his weight settling between her thighs.

Her fingers dug into the lean flesh of his hips, urging him down, crying wordlessly for him to make her his. She felt his fingers between her legs, and she arched against him as he stroked her.

"Marni...Marni," he whispered as one finger ventured even deeper. "Oh, sunshine, you're so ready for me...how did I ever deserve this..."

"Please...now...I need you..." When he pulled back, she whimpered, "Web?"

"It's okay." He was reaching behind him. "I need to protect you." He took a small foil packet from the pocket of his jeans and within minutes was back, looming over her, finding that hot, enfolding place between her splayed thighs.

He poised himself, then stroked her cheeks with his thumbs. "Kiss me, sunshine," he commanded deeply.

She did, and she felt him begin to enter her. It was the most wonderful, most frustrating experience yet. She thrust her hips upward, not quite realizing that it was her own inner body that resisted him.

He was breathing heavily, his lips against hers. "Sweet...so sweet. A bit of pain...a blaze of glory..." Then he surged forward, forcefully rupturing the membrane that gave proof of her virginity but was no more.

She cried out at the sharp pain, but it eased almost immediately.

"Okay?" he asked, panting as she was, holding himself still inside her while her torn flesh accommodated itself to him. It was all he could do not to climax there and then. She was so tight, so sleek, so hot and new and all his.

"Okay," she whispered tightly.

"Just relax," he crooned. He ducked his head and teased the tip of her nipple with his tongue. "I'm inside you now," he breathed, warm against that knotted bud. "Let's go for the glory."

She couldn't say a word then, for he withdrew partway, gently returned, withdrew a little more, returned with growing ardor, withdrew nearly completely, returned with a slam, and the feel of him inside her, stroking that dark, hidden part was so astonishing, so electric that she could only clutch his shoulders and hang on.

Nothing else mattered at that moment but Web. Marni wasn't thinking of her parents and how furious they'd be, of her brother and how shocked he'd be, of her friends and how envious they'd be. She wasn't thinking of the past or the future, simply the present.

"I love you," she cried over and over again. His presence had become part and parcel of her being. Without fear, she raised her hips to his rhythm, and rather than discomfort she felt an excitement that grew and grew until she was sure she'd simply explode.

"Ahhh, sunshine...so good...that's it...oh, God!"

His body was slick above hers, their flesh slapping together in time with the waves on the shore. Then that sound too fell aside, and all awareness was suspended as first Marni, then Web, strained and cried out, one body, then the next, breaking into fierce orgasmic shudders.

It was a long time before either of them spoke, a long time before the spasms slowed and their gasps quieted to a more controlled breathing. Web slid to her side and drew her tightly into his arms. "You are something, Marni Lange," he whispered against her damp forehead.

"Web...Web...unbelievable!"

He gave a deep, satisfied, purely male laugh. "I think I'd have to agree with you."

She nestled her head more snugly against his breast. "Then I...I did okay?"

"You did more than okay. You did *super*."

She smiled. "Thank you." She raised her head so that she could see those blue, blue eyes she adored. At night, in the moonlight, they were a beacon. "Thank you, Web," she said more softly. "I wanted you to be the first. It was very special...very, very special." She wanted to say again that she loved him, but he hadn't returned the words, and she didn't want to put him on the spot. She was grateful for what she felt, for what he'd made her feel, for what he'd given her. For the time being it was more than enough.

They rested in each other's arms for a while, listening to the sounds of the sea until those became too tempting to resist. So they raced into the water, laughing, playing, finally making love again there in the waves, wrapped up enough in each other not to care whether the rest of the world saw or heard or knew.

In the two weeks that followed, they were slightly more cautious. Unable to stay away from each other, they timed their rendezvous with care, meeting at odd hours and in odd places where they could forget the rest of the world existed and could live those brief times solely for each other and themselves. Marni was wildly happy and passionately in love; that justified her actions. She found Web to be intelligent and worldly, exquisitely sensitive and tender when she was in his arms. Web only knew that there was something special about her, something bright and luminous. She was a free spirit, forthright and fresh. She was a ray of sunshine in his life.

Marni's parents suspected that something was going on, but Marni always had a ready excuse to give them when they asked where she was going or where she'd been, and she was careful never to mention Web's name. Ethan knew what was happening and, though he worried, he adored Marni and was fond enough of Web to trust that he was in control of things. Tanya was jealous, plainly and simply. She'd been stringing along another of Ethan's friends for most of the summer, but when—inevitably, through one of Marni's friends—she got wind of Marni's involvement with Web, she suddenly realized what she'd overlooked and sought to remedy the situation. Web wasn't interested, which only irked her all the more, and at the time Marni made no attempt to reason with her sister.

It was shortsighted on her part, but then none of them ever dreamed that the summer would end prematurely and tragically.

With a week left before Labor Day, Web and Ethan set out in search of an evening's adventure in the university town of Orono. Marni had wanted to come along, but Ethan had been adamant. He claimed that their parents had been questioning him about her relationship with Web, and that the best way to mollify them would be for him to take off with Web while she spent the evening home for a change. She'd still protested, whereupon Ethan had conned Web into taking the motorcycle. It only sat two; there was no room for her.

For months and months after that, Marni would go over the what ifs again and again. What if she hadn't pestered and the two had taken Ethan's car as they'd originally planned? What if she'd made noise enough to make them cancel the trip? What if her parents hadn't been suspicious of her relationship with Web? What if there hadn't been anything to be suspicious of? But all the what ifs in the world—and there were even more she grappled with—couldn't change the facts.

It had begun to rain shortly after eleven. The road

had been dark. Two cars had collided at a blind inter-
section. The motorcycle had skidded wildly in their
wake. Ethan had been thrown, had hit a tree and had
been killed instantly.

3

"OKAY," WEB SIGHED, straightening. "That's it for today."

Anne rushed to him, her eyes on Marni's hunched form. "But you haven't got what you want," she argued in quiet concern.

"I know that and you know that, but Marni's in no shape to give us anything else right now." He handed his camera to an assistant, then raked a hand through his hair. "I'm not sure I am either," he said. In truth he was disgusted with himself. Sunshine. How could he have slipped that way? He hadn't planned to do it; the endearment had just come out. But then, it appeared he'd handled Marni wrong from the start.

Dismayed murmurs filtered through the room, but Web ignored them to approach the stool where Marni sat. He put an arm around her shoulder and bent his head close, using his body as a shield between her and any onlookers. "I'm sorry, Marni. That was my fault. It wasn't intentional, believe me."

She was crying silently, whitened fingers pressed to her downcast face.

"Why don't you go on in and change. We'll make a stab at this another day."

She shook her head, but said nothing. Web crooked his finger at Anne, then, when she neared, tossed his head in the direction of the dressing room and left the two women alone.

"Come on, Marni," Anne said softly. It was her arm around Marni's shoulders now, and she was gently urging her to her feet.

"I've spoiled everything," Marni whispered, "and made a fool of myself in the process."

"You certainly have not," Anne insisted as they started slowly toward the dressing room. "We all knew you weren't wild about doing this. So you've shown us that you're human, and that there are some kinds of pressure you just can't take."

"We'll have to get someone else for the cover."

"Let's talk about that when you've calmed down."

Anne stayed with her while she changed into her own clothes. She was blotting at the moistness below her eyes when a knock came at the door. Anne answered it, then stepped outside, and Web came in, closing the door behind him.

"Are you okay?" he asked, leaning against the door. Though he barred her escape, he made no move to come closer.

She nodded.

"Maybe you were right," he said. "Maybe there are too many people around. You felt awkward. I should have insisted they leave."

She stared at him for a minute. "That was only part of the problem."

He returned her stare with one of his own. "I know."

"I told you I couldn't do this."

"We'll give it another try."

"No. I'm not going through it again."

He blinked. "It'll be easier next time. Fewer people. And I'll know what not to do."

Marni shook her head. "I'm not going through it again."

"Because it brought back memories?"

"Exactly."

"Memories you don't want."

"Memories that bring pain."

"But if you don't face them, they'll haunt you forever."

"They haven't haunted me before today."

He didn't believe her. She probably didn't dwell on those memories any more than he did, but he knew there were moments, fleeting moments when memory clawed at his gut. He couldn't believe she was callous enough not to have similar experiences. "Maybe you've repressed them."

"Maybe so. But I can't change the past."

"Neither can I. But there are still things that gnaw at me from time to time."

Marni held up a hand. "I don't want to get into this. I can't. Not now. Besides, I have to get into the office. I've already wasted enough time on this fiasco."

Web took a step closer. His voice was calm, too calm, his expression hard. "This is what I do for a living, Marni. I'm successful at it, and I'm respected. Don't you ever, ever call it a fiasco."

Too late she realized that she'd hit a sore spot. Her voice softened. "I'm sorry. I didn't mean it that way. I respect what you are and what you do, too, or else we'd never be paying you the kind of money we are. The fiasco was in using me for a model, particularly given what you and I had...what we had once." She looked away to find her purse, then, head bent, moved toward the door.

"I'm taking you to dinner tonight," Web announced quietly.

Her head shot up. "Oh, no. That would be rubbing salt in the wound."

"Maybe it would be cleansing it, getting the infection out. It's been festering, Marni. For fourteen years it's been festering. Maybe neither of us was aware of it. Maybe we never would have been if we hadn't run into each other today. But it's there, and I don't know about you, but I won't be able to put it out of my mind until we've talked. If we're going to work together—"

"We're not! That's what I keep trying to tell you! We tried today and failed, so it's done. Over. We'll get another model for the cover, and I can go back to what I do best."

"Burying your head in the sand?"

"I do *not* bury my head in the sand." Her eyes were flashing, but his were no less so, and the set of his jaw spoke of freshly stirred emotion.

"No? Fourteen years ago you said you loved me. Then I lay there after the accident, and you didn't visit me once, not once, Marni!" His teeth were gritted. "Two months I was in that hospital. *Two months*, and not a call, not a card, nothing."

Marni felt her eyes well anew with tears. "I can't talk about this," she whispered. "I can't handle it now."

"Tonight then."

She passed him and reached for the door, but he pressed a firm hand against it. "Please," she begged. "I have to go."

"Eight-thirty tonight. I'll pick you up at your place."

"No."

"I'll be there, Marni." He let his hand drop, and she opened the door. "Eight-thirty."

She shook her head, but said nothing more as she made good her escape. Unfortunately, Edgar and Steve, Anne, Cynthia, Dan and Marjorie were waiting for her. When they all started talking at once, she held up a hand.

"I'm going to the office." She looked at the crew from *Class*. "Go through your files, put your heads together and come up with several other suggestions for a cover face. Not necessarily a model, maybe someone in the business world. We'll meet about it tomorrow morning." She turned her attention to Edgar and Steve, but she was already moving away. "I'm taking the limousine. Are you coming?"

Without argument, they both hurried after her.

Web watched them go, a small smile on his lips. She could command when she wanted to, he mused, and she was quite a sight to behold. Five feet five inches of auburn-haired beauty, all fired up and decisive. She'd change her mind, of course, at least about doing the cover shot. He'd *make* her change her mind...if for no other reason than to prove to himself that, at last, he had what it took.

EIGHT-THIRTY THAT NIGHT found Marni sitting stiffly in her living room, her hands clenched in her lap. She jumped when the phone rang, wondering if Web had changed his mind. But it was the security guard calling from downstairs to announce that Brian Webster had indeed arrived.

She'd debated how to handle him and had known somehow that the proper way would *not* be to refuse to see him. She had more dignity than that, and more respect for Web professionally. Besides, he'd thrown an accusation at her earlier that day, and she simply had to answer it.

With a deep breath, she instructed the guard to send him up.

By the time the doorbell rang, her palms were damp. She rubbed them together, then blotted them on her skirt. It was the same skirt she'd worn that morning, the same jacket, the same blouse. She wanted Web to know that this was nothing more than an extension of her business day. Perhaps she wanted to remind herself of it. The prospect of having dinner with him was a little less painful that way.

What she hadn't expected was to open the door and find him wearing a stylish navy topcoat, between whose open lapels his dark suit, crisp white shirt and tie were clearly visible. He looked every bit as businesslike as she wanted to feel, but he threw her off-balance.

"May I come in?" he asked when she'd been unable to find her tongue.

"Uh, yes." She stood back dumbly. "Please do." She closed the door behind him.

"You seem surprised." Amused, he glanced down at himself. "Am I that shocking?"

"I, uh, I just didn't expect...I've never seen you in..."

"You didn't expect me to show up in a T-shirt and jeans, did you?"

"No, I...it's just..."

"Fourteen years, Marni. We all grow up at one point or another."

She didn't want to *touch* that one. "Can I...can I take your coat? Would you like a drink?" She hadn't planned to offer him any such thing, but then she didn't know quite *what* she'd planned. She couldn't just launch into an argument, not with him looking so...so urbane.

He shrugged out of the topcoat and set it on a nearby chair. "That would be nice. Bourbon and water, if you've got it," he said quietly, then watched her approach the bar at the far end of the room. She was still a little shaky, but he'd expected that. Hell, he was shaky, too, though he tried his best to hide it. "This is a beautiful place you've got." He admired the white French provincial decor, the original artwork on the walls. Everything was spotless and bright. "Have you been here long?"

"Three years," she said without turning. She was trying to pour the bourbon without splashing it all over the place. Her hands weren't terribly steady.

"Where were you before that?" he asked conversationally.

"I had another place. It was smaller. When I took over from...took over the presidency of the corporation, I realized I'd need a larger place for entertaining."

"Do you do much?"

She returned with his drink, her full concentration on keeping the glass steady. "Much?"

"Entertaining." He accepted the drink and sat back.

"Enough."

"Do you enjoy it?"

She took a seat across from him, half wishing she'd fixed a hefty something for herself but loath to trust her legs a second time. "Sometimes."

He eyed her over the rim of his glass. "You must be very skilled at it...upbringing and all." He took a drink.

"I suppose you could say that. My family's always done its share of entertaining."

He nodded, threw his arm over the back of the sofa and looked around the room again. It was a diversionary measure. He wasn't quite sure what to say. Marni was uncomfortable. He wanted her to relax, but he wasn't sure how to achieve that. In the end, he realized that his best shot was with the truth.

"I wasn't sure you'd be here tonight. I was half worried that you'd find something else to do—a late meeting or a business dinner or a date."

She looked at her hands, tautly entwined in her lap, and spoke softly, honestly. "I haven't been good for much today, business or otherwise."

"But you went back to the office after you left the studio."

"For all the good it did me." She hadn't accomplished a thing, at least nothing that wouldn't have to be reexamined tomorrow. She'd been thoroughly distracted. She'd read contracts, talked on the phone, sat through a meeting, but for the life of her she couldn't remember what any of it had been about. She raised her eyes quickly, unable to hide the urgency she felt. "I want you to know something, Web. That time you were in the hospital...it wasn't that I wasn't thinking about you. I just...couldn't get away. I called the hospital to find out how you were, but I...I couldn't get there." Her eyes were growing misty again. It was the last thing Web wanted.

"I didn't come here to talk about that, Marni. I'm sorry I exploded that way this morning—"

"But you meant it. You're still angry—"

"Not this minute. And I really *didn't* come here to talk about it."

"You said we had to talk things out."

"We will. In time."

In time? In *future time?* "But we haven't got any time." She looked away, and her voice dropped. "We never really did. It seemed to run out barely before it had begun."

"We've got time. I spoke with Anne this afternoon. She agrees with me that you're still the best one for this cover. You said yourself that we're well ahead of the production schedule."

A spurt of anger brought Marni's gaze back to his. "I told you, it's done. I will not pose for that cover. You and Anne can conspire all you want, but I'm still the publisher of this magazine, and as such I have the final say. I'm not a child anymore, Web. I'm thirty-one now, not seventeen."

He sat forward and spoke gently. "I know that, Marni."

"I won't be told what's good for me and what isn't."

"Seems to me you could *never* be told that. In your own quiet way, you were headstrong even back then."

She caught her breath and bowed her head. "Not really."

"I don't believe you," was his quiet rejoinder. When she simply shrugged, he realized that she wasn't ready to go into that. In many respects, he wasn't either. He took another drink, then turned the glass slowly in his hands. "Look, Marni. I don't think either of us wants to rehash the past just yet. What I'd like—the real reason I'm here now—is for us to get to know each other. We've both changed in fourteen years. In addition to other things, we were friends once upon a time. I don't know about you, but I'm curious to know what my friend's been doing, what her life is like now."

"To what end?" There was a thread of desperation in her voice.

"To make it easier for us to shoot this picture, for one thing." When she opened her mouth to protest, he held up a hand and spoke more quickly. "I know. You're not doing it. But the reason you're not is that working with me stirs up a storm of memories. If we can get to know each other as adults—"

"You were an adult fourteen years ago. I was a child—"

"I was a man and you were a woman," he corrected, "but we were both pretty immature about some things."

She couldn't believe what he was saying. "You weren't immature," she argued. "You were experienced and worldly. You'd lived far more than I ever had."

"There's living, and there's living. But that's not the point. The point is that we've both changed. We've grown up. If we spend a little time together now, we can replace those memories with new ones...." He stopped talking when he saw that she'd shrunk back into her seat. Was that dread in her eyes? He didn't want it to be. God, he didn't want that! He sat forward pleadingly. "Don't you see, Marni? You were shocked seeing me today because the last thing we shared involved pain for both of us. Sure, fourteen years have passed, but we haven't seen or spoken with each other in all that time. It's only natural that seeing each other would bring back all those other things. But it doesn't have to be like that. Not if we put something between those memories and us."

"I'm not sure I know what you're suggesting," she said in a tone that suggested she did.

"All I want," he went on with a sigh, "is to put the past aside for the time being. Hell, maybe it's a matter of pride for me. Maybe I want to show you what I've become. Is that so bad? Fourteen years ago, I was nothing. I wandered, I played. I never had more than a hundred bucks to my name at a given time. You had so much, at least in my eyes, and I'm not talking money now. You had a fine home, a family and social status."

Marni listened to his words, but it was his tone and his expression that reached her. He was sincere, almost beseechful. There was pain in his eyes, and an intense need. He'd never been quite that way with her fourteen years before, but she suddenly couldn't seem to separate the feelings she'd had for him then from the ache in her heart now. It occurred to her that the ache had begun when she'd first set eyes on him that morning. She'd attributed it to the pain of memory, and it was probably ninety-nine percent that, but there was something more, and she couldn't ignore it. Fourteen years ago she'd loved him. She didn't love him now, but there was still that...feeling. And those blue, blue eyes shimmering into her, captivating her, magnetizing her.

"I want to show you my world, Marni. I'm proud of it, and I want you to be proud, too. You may have thought differently, but my life was deeply affected by that summer in Camden." For a minute the blue eyes grew moist, but they cleared so quickly that Marni wondered if she'd imagined it. "Give me a chance, Marni. We'll start with dinner tonight. I won't pressure you for anything. I never did, did I?"

She didn't have to ponder that one. If anyone had done the pressuring—at least on the sexual level—it had been her. "No," she answered softly.

"And I won't do it now. You have my word on it. You also have my word that if anything gets too tough for you, I'll bring you back here and leave you alone. You *also* have my word that if, in the end, you decide you really can't do that cover, I'll abide by your decision. Fair?"

Fair? He was being so reasonable that she couldn't possibly argue. What wasn't fair was that he wore his suit so well, that his hair looked so thick and vibrant, that his features had matured with such dignity. But that wasn't his fault. Beauty was in the eye of the beholder.

She gave a rueful half smile and slowly nodded. "Fair."

He held her gaze a moment longer, as though he almost couldn't believe that she'd agreed, but his inner relief was such that he suddenly felt a hundred pounds lighter. He pushed back his cuff and glanced at the thin gold watch on his wrist.

"We've got reservations for five minutes ago. If I can use your phone, I'll let the maître d' know we're on our way."

She nodded and glanced toward the kitchen. When he rose and headed that way, she moved toward the small half bath off the living room. She suddenly wished she'd showered, done over her hair and makeup and changed into something fresher. Web was so obviously newly showered and shaved. She should have done more. But it was too late for that now, so the best she could do was to powder the faint shine from her nose and forehead, add a smidgen more blusher to her cheeks and touch up her lipstick.

Web was waiting when she emerged. He'd already put on his topcoat and was holding the coat she'd left ready and waiting nearby. It, too, was the same she'd worn that morning, but that decision she didn't regret. To wear silver fox with Web, even in spite of his own debonair appearance, seemed a little heavy-handed.

He helped her on with the coat, waited while she got her purse, then lightly took her elbow and escorted her to the door. They rode the elevator in a silence that was broken at last by Marni's self-conscious laugh. "You're very tall. I never wore high heels in Camden, but they don't seem to make a difference." She darted him a shy glance, but quickly returned her gaze to the patterned carpet.

He felt vaguely self-conscious, too. "I never wore shoes with laces in Camden. They add a little."

She nodded and said nothing more. The elevator door purred open. Web guided her through the plush lobby, then the enclosed foyer and finally to the street. He discreetly pressed a bill into the doorman's hand in exchange for the keys to his car, then showed Marni to the small black BMW parked at the curb. Before she could reach for it, he opened the door. "Buckle up," was all he said before he locked her in and circled the car to the driver's side.

The restaurant he'd chosen was a quiet but elegant one. The maître d' seemed not in the least piqued by their tardiness, greeting Web with a warm handshake and offering a similarly warm welcome to Marni when Web introduced them, before showing them to their table.

Web deftly ordered a wine. Then, when Marni had decided what she wanted to eat, he gave both her choice and his own to the waiter. Watching him handle himself, she decided he was as smooth in this urban setting as he'd been by the sea. He had always exuded a kind of confidence, and she assumed it would extend to whatever activity he was involved in. But seeing him here, comfortable in a milieu that should have been hers more than his, took some getting used to. It forced her to see him in a different light. She struggled to do that.

"Have you been here before?" he asked softly.

"For a business dinner once or twice. The food's excellent, don't you think?"

"I'm counting on it," he said with a grin. "So...tell me about Marni Lange and the Lange Corporation."

She shook her head. Somewhere along the line, she realized he was right. They'd been...friends once, and she *was* curious as to what he'd done in the past years. "You first. Tell me about Brian Webster the photographer."

"What would you like to know?"

"How you got started. I never knew you had an interest in photography."

"I didn't. At least, not when I knew you. But the year after that was a difficult one for me." His brow furrowed. "I took a good look at myself and didn't like what I saw."

She found herself defending him instinctively. "But you were an adventurer. You did lots of different things, and did them well."

"I was young, without roots or a future," he contradicted her gently. "For the first time I stopped to think about what I'd be like, what I'd be doing five, ten, fifteen years down the road, and I came up with a big fat zip."

"So you decided to be a photographer, just like that?" She was skeptical, though if that had been the case it would be a remarkable success story.

"Actually, I decided to write about what I'd been doing. There's always a market for adventure books. I envisioned myself traveling the world, doing all kinds of interesting things—reenacting ancient voyages across oceans, scaling previously unscaled mountain peaks, crossing the Sahara with two camels and canteens of water..."

"Did you do any of those things?"

"Nope."

"Then...you wrote about things you'd already done?"

"Nope." When she frowned, he explained. "I couldn't write for beans. I tried, Lord how I tried. I sat for hours and hours with blank paper in front of me, finally scribbling something down, then crossing it out and crumbling the sheet into a ball." He arched a brow in self-mockery. "I got pretty good at hitting the wastebasket on the first try."

A small smile touched her lips. "Oh."

"But—" he held up a finger "—it wasn't a total waste. Y'see, I'd pictured my articles in something like *National Geographic*, and of course there were going to be gorgeous photographs accompanying the text, and who better to take them than me, since I was there—actually I was in New Mexico at the time, on an archaeological dig."

"Had you ever used a camera before?"

"No, but that didn't stop me. It was an adventure in and of itself. I bought a used camera, got a few books, read up on what I had to do, and...click. Literally and figuratively."

He stopped talking and sat back. Marni felt as though she'd been left dangling. "And...?"

"And what?"

"What happened? Did you sell those first pictures?"

"Not to *National Geographic*."

"But you did sell them?"

"Uh-huh."

Again she waited. He was smiling, but he made no attempt to go on. She remembered that he'd been that way fourteen years ago, too. When she'd asked him about the things he'd done, there'd been a quiet smugness to him. He'd held things back until she'd specifically asked, and when his stories came out they were like a well-earned prize. In his way he'd manipulated her, forcing her to show her cards. Perhaps he was manipulating her now. But she didn't care. Hadn't he been the one to say that they should get to know each other?

"Okay," she said. "You photographed a dig in New Mexico and sold the pictures to a magazine. But photographing a dig is a far cry from photographing some of the world's most famous personalities. How did it happen? How did you switch from photographing arrowheads, or whatever, to photographing *head* heads?"

He chuckled. "Poetically put, if I don't say so myself. You should be the writer, Marni. You could write. I could photograph."

"I've already got a full-time job, thank you. Come on, Web. When did you get your first break?"

Just then the wine steward arrived with an ice bucket. He uncorked the wine, poured a taste for Web, then at Web's nod filled both of their glasses.

Web's thoughts weren't on the wine, but on the fact that he was thoroughly enjoying himself. The Marni sitting across from him now was so like the Marni he'd known fourteen years before that he couldn't help but smile in wonder. She was curious. She'd always been curious. She couldn't help herself, and he'd been counting on that. Personalities didn't change. Time and circumstances modified them, perhaps, but they never fully changed.

"Web…?" she prodded. "How did it happen?"

"Actually it was on that same trip. The dig I was working at was being used as the backdrop for a movie. Given the way I always had with people—" he winked, and she should have been angry but instead felt a delicious curling in her stomach "—I got myself into the middle of the movie set and started snapping away."

"Don't tell me that those first shots sold?"

"I won't. They were awful. I mean, they had potential. I liked the expressions I caught, the emotions, and I found photographing people much more exciting than photographing arrowheads or whatever. Technically I had a lot to learn, though, so I signed on with a photographer in L.A. After six months, I went out on my own."

"Six months? That's all? It takes years for most photographers to develop sufficient skill to do what you do and do it right."

"I didn't have years. I felt I'd already wasted too many, and I needed to earn money. There's that small matter of having a roof over your head and food enough to keep your body going, not to mention the larger matter of equipment and a studio. I started modestly, shooting outside mostly, working my buns off, turning every cent I could back into better equipment. I used what I'd learned apprenticing as a base, and picked up more as I went along. I read. I talked with other photographers. I studied the work of the masters and pored through magazine after magazine to see what the market wanted and needed. I did portfolios for models and actors and actresses, and things seemed to mushroom from there."

"Did you have a long-range goal?"

"New York. Cover work. Independence, within limits."

"Then you've made it," she declared, unaware of the pride that lit her eyes. Web wasn't unaware of it though, and it gave him unbelievable pleasure.

"I suppose you could say that," he returned softly. "There's always more I want to do, and the field keeps pace with changes in fashion. The real challenge is in making my work different from the others. I want my pictures to have a unique look and feel. I guess I need that more than anything—knowing I'll have left an indelible mark behind."

"Are you going somewhere?" she teased.

There was sadness in his smile. "We're all mortal. I think about that a lot. At the rate I'm going, my work will be just about all I do leave behind."

"You never married." It was a statement, offered softly, with a hint of timidness.

"I've been too busy.... What about you?"

"The same."

The waiter chose that moment to appear with their food, and they lapsed into silence for a time as they ate.

"Funny," Web said at last, "I'd really pictured you with a husband and kids and a big, beautiful home in the country."

She gave a sad laugh. "So had I."

"Dreams gone awry, or simply deferred?"

She pondered that for a minute. "I really don't

know. I've been so caught up with running the business that it seems there isn't time for much else."

"You must do things for fun."

"I do...now and again." She stopped pushing the Parisienne potatoes around her plate and put down her fork. "What about you? Are you still working as hard as you did at first?"

"I'm working as hard, but the focus is different. I can concentrate on the creative end and leave the rest to assistants. I have specialists for my finish work, and even though I'm more often than not at their shoulders, approving everything before it leaves the studio, I do have more free time. I try to take weekends completely off."

"What do you do then?"

He shrugged. "Mostly I go to Vermont. I have a small place there. In the winter I ski. In the summer I swim."

"Sounds heavenly," she said, meaning it.

"Don't you still go to Camden?"

She straightened, and the look of pleasure faded from her face. "My parents still do. It's an institution with them. Me, well, I don't enjoy it the way I used to. Sometimes staying here in New York for the summer is a vacation in itself." She gave a dry laugh. "Everyone else is gone. It's quieter."

"You always did like peace and quiet," he said, remembering that day so long ago when they'd gone mountain climbing.

Marni remembered, too. Her gaze grew momentarily lost in his, lost in the memory of that happy, carefree time. It was with great effort that she finally looked away. She took a deep breath. "Anyway, I try to take an extra day or two when I'm off somewhere on business—you know, relax in a different place to shake off the tension."

"Alone?"

"Usually."

"Then there's no special man?"

"No."

"You must date?"

"Not unless I'm inspired, and I'm rarely inspired." Just then her eye was caught by a couple very clearly approaching their table. Following her gaze, Web turned around. He pushed his chair back, stood and extended his hand to the man.

"How are you, Frank?"

The newcomer added a gentle shoulder slap to the handshake. "Not bad."

Web enclosed the woman's hand in his, then leaned forward and kissed her cheek. "Maggie, you're looking wonderful. Frank, Maggie, I'd like you to meet Marni Lange. Marni, these are the Kozols."

Marni barely had time to shake hands with each before Frank was studying her, tapping his lip. "Marni Lange...of the Lange Corporation?"

She cast a skittish glance at Web, then nodded.

"I knew your father once upon a time," Frank went on. "Gee, I haven't seen him in years."

"He's retired now," she offered gracefully, though mention of her father in Web's presence made her uneasy.

"Is he well? And your mother?"

"They're both fine, thank you."

Maggie had come around the table to more easily chat with her. "Frank was with Eastern Engineering then, though he went out on his own ten years ago." She looked over to find her husband engrossed in an animated discussion with Web, and she smiled indulgently. "You'll have to excuse him. I know it's rude for us to barge in on your dinner this way, but he's so fond of Brian that he simply had to stop in and say hello."

Marni smiled. "It's perfectly all right. Have you known...Brian long?"

"Several years. Our daughter is—was—a model. When she first went to Brian to be photographed, she was pretty confused. He was wonderful. I really think that if it hadn't been for him, she would have ended up in a sorry state. She's married now and just had her first child." Maggie beamed. "The baby's a jewel."

"Boy...girl?" Out of the corner of her eye, Marni saw Web standing with one hand in his trousers pocket. He looked thoroughly in command, totally at ease and very handsome. She realized that she was proud to be with him.

"A boy. Christopher James. He's absolutely precious."

Marni retrained her focus on Maggie. "And you're enjoying him. Do they live close by?"

"In Washington. We've been down several times—"

"Come on, sweetheart," Frank cut in. "The car's waiting, and these folks don't need us taking any more of their time."

Maggie turned briefly back to Marni. "It was lovely meeting you." Then she gave Web a kiss and let her husband guide her off.

"Sorry about that," Web murmured, sitting down again. He pulled his chair closer to the table.

"Don't apologize." It was the first time she'd ever met any friends of Web's. "They seemed lovely. Maggie was mentioning her daughter. They're both in your debt, I take it."

He shrugged. "She was a sweet kid who was lost in the rat race of modeling. Maggie and Frank say that she was 'confused,' and she was, but she was also on drugs and she was practically anorexic."

"Isn't that true of lots of models?"

"Mmm, but it was particularly sad with Sara. She had a good home. Her folks are loaded. I'm not sure she even wanted to model in the first place, but she had the looks and the style, and she somehow got snagged. If she hadn't gotten out when she did, she'd probably be dead by now."

Marni winced. "What did you do for her?"

He grew more thoughtful. "Talked, mostly. I took the pictures and made sure they were stupendous. Then I tried to convince her that she'd hit the top and ought to retire."

"And just like that she did?"

"Not...exactly. I showed her my morgue book."

"Morgue book?"

"Mmm. I keep files on everyone I've photographed, with a follow-up on each. I have a special folder—pictures of people who made it big, then plummeted. When I'm feeling sorry for myself about one thing or another, I take it out, and it makes me grateful for what I've got. I don't show it to many people, but it gave Sara something to think about. She came back to see me often after that, and I finally convinced her to see a psychiatrist. Maggie and Frank are terrific, but Sara was their daughter, and the thought that she'd actually need a psychiatrist disturbed them."

"But it worked."

"It helped. Mostly what helped was meeting her husband. He's a rock, a lawyer with the Justice Department, and he's crazy about her. He supported her completely when she decided to go back to school to get the degree she missed out on when she began modeling." He cleared his throat meaningfully. "I think the baby has interrupted that now, but Sara knows she can go back whenever she's ready."

"That's a lovely story," Marni said with a smile. "I'll bet you have lots of others about people you've photographed." She propped her elbow on the table and set her chin in her palm. "Tell me some."

For the next hour, he did just that. There was a modesty to him, and she had to coax him on from time to time, but when he got going his tales fascinated her every bit as much as those he'd told fourteen years before had done. The years evaporated. She listened, enthralled, thinking how exciting his life was and how he was fully in control of it.

By the time they'd finished their second cup of coffee, they'd fallen silent and were simply looking at each other. Their communication continued, but on a different level, one in which Marni was too engrossed to analyze.

"Just like old times," Web said quietly.

She nodded and smiled almost shyly. "I could sit listening to you for hours. You were always so different from other people. You had such a wealth of experience to draw on. You still do."

"You've got experience of your own—"

"But not as exciting. Or maybe I just take it for granted. Do you ever do that?"

"I wish I could. If I start taking things for granted, I'll stop growing, and if that happens I'll never make it the way I want to."

"That means a lot to you...making it." So different from how he'd been, she mused. Then again, perhaps he'd only defined success differently fourteen years ago.

"Everyone wants success. Don't you? Isn't that why you pour so much of yourself into the business?"

She didn't answer him immediately. Her feelings were torn. Yes, she wanted to be successful as president of the Lange Corporation, but for reasons she didn't want to think about, much less discuss. "I guess," she said finally.

"You don't sound sure."

She forced herself to perk up. "I'm sure."

"But there was something else you were thinking about just now. What was it, Marni?"

She smiled and shook her head. "Nothing. It was really nothing. I think I'm just tired. It's been a long day."

"And a trying one."

"Yes," she whispered.

Not wanting to push her too far, Web didn't argue. He'd done most of the talking during dinner, and though there were still many things he wanted to know about Marni, many things he wanted to discuss with her, he felt relatively satisfied with what he'd accomplished. He'd wanted to tell her about his work, and he had. He'd wanted to give her a glimpse of the man he was now, and he had. He'd wanted to give her something to think about besides the past, and he had. He was determined to make her trust him again. Tonight had simply been the first down payment on that particular mortgage. There would be time enough in the future to make more headway, he mused as he dug into his pocket to settle the bill. There would be time. He'd make time. He wasn't sure what he wanted in the long run from Marni, but he did know that their relationship had been left suspended fourteen years ago, and that it needed to be settled one way or another.

They hit the cold night air the instant they left the restaurant. Marni bundled her coat around her more snugly, and when Web drew her back into the shelter of the doorway and threw his arm around her shoulder while they waited for the car, she didn't resist. He was large, warm and strong. He'd always been large, warm and strong.

For an instant she closed her eyes and pretended that that summer hadn't ended as it had. It was a sweet, sweet dream, and her senses filled to brimming with the taste, the touch, the smell of him. She loved Web. Her body tingled from his closeness. They were on their way to a secret rendezvous where he'd make the rest of the world disappear and lift her onto a plane of sheer bliss.

"Here we go," he murmured softly.

She began to tremble.

"Marni?"

Web was squeezing her shoulder. She snapped her eyes open and stared.

"The car. It's here."

Stunned, she let herself be guided into the front seat. By the time she realized what had happened, the neon lights of the city were flickering through the windshield as they passed, camouflaging her embarrassment.

Web said nothing. He drove skillfully and at a comfortable pace. When they arrived at her building, he left his keys with the doorman and rode the elevator with her to her door. There he took her own keys, released the lock, then stood back while she deactivated the burglar alarm.

With the door partially open, she raised her eyes to his. "Thank you, Web. I've...this was nice."

"I thought so." He smiled so gently that her heart turned over. "You're really something to be with."

"I'm not. You carried most of the evening."

He winked. "I was inspired."

Her limbs turned to jelly and did nothing by way of solidifying when he put a light hand on her shoulder. His expression grew more serious, almost troubled.

"Marni, about that cover—"

"Shhhh." She put an impulsive finger on his lips to stem the words, then wished she hadn't because the texture of his mouth, its warmth, was like fire. She snatched her hand away and dropped her gaze to his tie. It was textured, too, but of silk, and its smooth-flowing stripes of navy, gray and mauve were serene, soothing. "Please," she whispered. "Let's not argue about that again."

"I still want to do it. Don't you think it would be easier for you now?"

"I...I don't know."

"Will you think about it at least? We couldn't try it again until early next week anyway. Maybe by then you'll be feeling more comfortable."

She dipped her head lower. "I don't know."

"Marni?"

She squeezed her eyes shut, knowing she should slip through her door and lock it tight, but was unable to move. When he curved one long forefinger under her chin and tipped it up, she resisted. He simply applied more pressure until at last she met his gaze.

"It's still there," he whispered. "You know that, don't you?"

Eyes large and frightened, she nodded.

"Do we have to fight it?"

"I'm not ready." She was whispering, too, not out of choice, but because she couldn't seem to produce anything louder. Her heart was pounding, its beat reverberating through her limbs. "I don't know if I'm...ready for this. I suffered so...last time..."

He was stroking her cheek with the back of his hand, a hand that had once known every inch of her in the most intimate detail. His blue eyes were clouded. "I suffered, too. You don't know. I suffered, too, Marni. Do you think I want to go through that again?"

She swallowed hard, then shook her head.

"I wouldn't suggest something I felt would hurt either of us."

"What *are* you suggesting?"

"Friday night. See me Friday night. There's a party I have to go to, make a quick appearance at. I'd like you to come with me, then we can take off and do something—dinner, a movie, a ride through the park, I don't care what, but I have to see you again."

"Something's screwed up here. I was always the one to do the chasing."

"Because I was arrogant and cocksure, and so caught up in playing the role of the carefree bachelor that I didn't know any better." His thumb skated lightly over her lips. "I'm tired of playing, Marni. I'm too old for that now. I want to see you again. I *have* to see you again.... How about it? Friday night?"

"I can't promise you anything about the picture."

"Friday night. No business, just fun. Please?"

If fourteen years ago anyone had told Marni that Web would be pleading with her to see him, she would never have believed it. If thirteen years ago, ten years ago, five or even one year ago anyone had told Marni that she'd *be* seeing him again, she would never have believed it.

"Yes," she said softly, knowing that there was no other choice she could possibly make. Web did something to her. He'd *always* done something to her. He made her feel things she'd never felt with another man. Shock, pain, shimmering physical awareness...she was alive. That, in itself, was a precious gift.

4

THE PARTY WAS unbelievably raucous. Pop music throbbed through the air at ear-splitting decibels, aided and abetted by the glare of brightly colored floodlights and the sea of bodies contorting every which way in a tempest of unleashed energy.

The host was a rock video producer whom Web had met several months before through a mutual subject of their respective lenses. The guest list ran the gamut from actors to singers to musicians to technicians.

Marni could barely distinguish one garishly lit face, one outrageously garbed body from another, and she would have felt lost had it not been for the umbilical cord of Web's arm. He introduced her to those he knew and joined her in greeting others he was meeting for the first time. Marni couldn't say that it was the most intellectually stimulating group she'd ever encountered, but then her own mind could barely function amid the pulsating hubbub of activity.

In hindsight, though, it was an educational hour that she spent with Web at the party. She learned that he was well-known, well-liked and held slightly in awe. She learned that he didn't play kissy-and-huggy-and-isn't-this-a-*super*-party, but maintained his dignity while appearing fully congenial and at ease. She learned that he disliked indiscriminate drinking and avoided the coke corner like the plague, that he hated

Twisted Sister, abided Prince, admired Springsteen, and that he was not much more of a dancer than she was.

"I think I'm getting a migraine," he finally yelled at her over the din. "Come on. Let's get out of here." He tugged her by the hand, leading her first for their coats, then out the door. Once in the lobby, where the music was little more than a dull vibration, he leaned back against the wall. Their coats were slung over his shoulder. He hadn't released her hand once. "Sorry about that," he said, tipping his head sideways against the stucco wall to look at her. "I hadn't realized it'd be so wild. Well, maybe I had, but I promised Malcolm I'd come. Are you still with me?"

She, too, was braced against the wall, savoring their escape. She gave his hand a squeeze and smiled. "A little wilted, but I'm still here."

"I want you to know that these aren't really my friends. I mean, Malcolm is, and I know enough of the others, but I don't usually hang around with them in my free time. Even if I did it'd be one at a time and in a quieter setting, but I really do have other, more reputable friends.... What are you laughing at?"

"You. You were so confident back there, but all of a sudden you're like a little boy, all nervous and apologetic." She punctuated her words with a chiding headshake, but she was grinning. "I'm not your mother, Web. And I'm not here to stand in judgment on your friends and acquaintances."

"I know, but...why is it I suspect that your friends are a little more...dignified?"

She grimaced. "Maybe because I'm the staid president of a staid corporation."

"Hey, I'm not knocking it…. What *are* your friends like?"

"Oh…diverse. Quieter, I guess." She paused pensively. "It's strange. When I think back to being a teenager, to the group I was with then, I remember irreverent parties and a general law-unto-ourselves attitude."

"You were never really that way."

"No, but I was on the fringe of it. When I think of what those same people, even the most rebellious ones, are doing now, I have to laugh. They're conventional, establishment all the way. Oh, they like a good time, and by and large they've got plenty of money to spend on one, but they seem to have outgrown that wildness they so prided themselves on."

"You say 'they.' You don't identify with them?"

She plucked at the folds of the chic overblouse she'd worn with her stirrup pants. "It wasn't that I outgrew it. I was shocked into leaving it behind. Somehow I lost a taste for it after…after…"

"After Ethan died," he finished for her in a sober voice. When she didn't reply, he took her coat from his shoulder. "Come on," he said gently. "Let's take a walk."

Without raising her head, she slipped her arms into the sleeves of the coat and buttoned it up, then let Web take her hand and lead her into the February night. The party had been in SoHo at the lower end of Manhattan. They'd taxied there, but a slow walk back uptown was what they both needed.

"You still miss him, don't you?" Web asked.

The air was cold, numbing her just enough to enable her to talk of Ethan. "I adored him. There were eight years between us, and it wasn't as though we were close in the sense of baring our souls to each other. But we shared a special something. Yes, I miss him."

Web wrapped his arm around her shoulders and drew her close as they walked. "He would have been president of Lange, wouldn't he?"

"Yes."

"You took over in his place."

"My parents needed someone."

"What about your sister...Tanya?"

Marni's laugh was brittle. "Tanya is hopeless. She ran in the opposite direction when she thought she might have to do something with the business. Not that Dad would have asked her. Maybe it was because he *didn't* ask her that she was so negative about it. She never did get her degree. She flunked out of two different colleges and finally gave up on the whole thing."

"What is she doing now?"

"Oh, she's here in New York. She's been through two husbands and is looking around for a third. She's got alimony enough to keep her living in style, so she spends her days shopping and her nights partying."

"Not *your* cup of tea."

"Not...quite."

"Were you ever close, you and Tanya?"

"Not really. We fought all the time as kids, you know, bickered like all siblings do. When I read things about sibling placement, about how the middle child is supposed to be the mediator, I have to laugh. Tanya was the *instigator*. It's like she felt lost between Ethan and me, and had to go out of her way to exert herself. I was some kind of threat to her—don't ask me why. She's prettier, more outgoing. And she can dance." They both chuckled. "But she always seemed to think that I had something she didn't, or that I was going to get something better than what she did."

"She was two years older than you?"

"Mmmm."

"Maybe she resented your arrival. If Ethan was seven when she was born, and she was the first girl, she was probably pampered for those first two years of her life. Your birth upset the applecart."

Marni sighed. "Whatever, it didn't—doesn't—make for a comfortable relationship. We see each other at family events, and run into each other accidentally from time to time, but we rarely talk on the phone and we never go out of our way to spend time together. It's sad, when you think of it." She looked up at Web. "You must think it's pathetic…being an only child and all."

"I wasn't an only child."

Her eyes widened. "No? But I thought…you never mentioned any family, and I always assumed you didn't have any!"

His lips twitched. "Just hatched from a shell and took off, eh?"

"You know what I mean. What *do* you have, Web? Tell me."

"I have a brother. Actually a half brother. He's four years younger than me."

"Do you ever see him?"

"We work together. He's my business manager, or agent, or financial advisor, or whatever you want to call it. Lee Fitzgerald. He was there Tuesday morning…but you don't remember much of that, do you?"

She eyed him shamefacedly. "I wasn't exactly at my best Tuesday morning."

"You wouldn't have had any way of knowing he

was my brother. We don't look at all alike. But he's a nice guy, and very capable."

Marni was remembering what Web had said that Tuesday morning, in a moment of anger, about his being a bastard. "The name Webster?"

"Was my mother's maiden name."

"Did you ever know your father?"

"Nope. It was a one-night stand. He was married."

"Do you ever...wonder about him?"

He caressed her shoulder through the thickness of her coat as though he needed that small reassurance of her presence. Though his tone was light, devoid of bitterness, almost factual, Marni suspected that he regretted the circumstances of his conception.

"I wouldn't be human if I didn't. I used to do it a lot when I was a kid—wonder who he was, what he looked like, where he lived, whether he'd like me. I can almost empathize with Tanya. I spent all those years wandering, traveling, never staying in one place long. Maybe I didn't want to learn that he wasn't looking for me. As long as I kept moving, I had that illusion that he might be looking but, of course, couldn't find me. Pretty dumb, huh? He doesn't even know I exist."

Marni's heart ached for him. "Your mother never told him?"

"My mother never *saw* him, not after that one night. She knew his name, but he was a salesman from somewhere or other. She didn't know where. And she knew he was married, so she didn't bother. She married my stepfather when I was two. He wasn't a bad sort as stepfathers go."

They turned onto Fifth Avenue, walking comfortably in step with each other. "Is your mother still living?"

"She died several years ago."

"I'm sorry, Web," Marni said, feeling all the more guilty about the times she'd resented her own parents. At least they were alive. If she had a problem, she had somewhere to run. "Do you still wonder about your father?"

"Nah. I reached a point when settling down meant more than running away from the fact that he didn't know about me. I decided I wanted to do something, be something. I'm proud of what I've become."

"You should be," she said softly, holding his gaze for a minute, until the intensity of its soul-reach made her look away.

They walked silently for a few blocks, their way lit frequently by storefront lights or the headlights of cars whipping through the city night. The sound of motors, revving, slowing, filled the air, along with the occasional honk of a horn or the squeal of brakes or the whir of tires.

"What about you, Marni? I know what you've become, but what would you have done if...things had been different. I knew you wanted a college degree, but you hadn't said much more than that. Had you always wanted to join the corporation?"

"I hadn't thought that far. Business, a career—they were the last things on my mind—" her voice lowered "—until Ethan died. I grew up pretty fast then."

"Why? I mean, you were only seventeen."

"Ethan had already started working, and I knew he was being groomed to take over Dad's place one day. It wasn't like I wanted the presidency per se, but my father needed someone, and it seemed right that I should give it a try."

"Did you go to Wellesley after all?"

"Mmmm. I did pretty lousy my first term. I was still pretty upset. But after that I was able to settle down. I got my M.B.A. at Columbia, and joined the corporation from there."

"Are you sorry? Do you ever wish you were doing something else?"

"I wish Ethan were here to be president, but given that he's not, I really can't complain. I do have an aptitude for business. I think I'm good at what I do. There's challenge to the work, and a sense of power because the corporation is profitable and I'm free to venture into new things."

"Like *Class.*"

"Like *Class.*"

They turned from Fifth Avenue onto a side street that was darker and more deserted. Marni couldn't remember the last time she'd walked through the city like this at night. She'd always been too intent on getting from one place to another, via cab or car or limousine, to think of walking. Yet, now it was calming, therapeutic, really quite nice. Of course, it helped that Web was with her. Talking with him was easy. He made her think about things—like Ethan—and doing so brought less pain than she'd have expected. Ethan was gone; she couldn't bring him back. But Web was here.

He'd never take the place of her brother; for that matter, she couldn't even *think* of Web as a brother. It wasn't a brother she wanted anyway. She wasn't sure just what she did want from Web—she hadn't thought that far. But his presence had an odd kind of continuity to it. Tonight, even Tuesday night when he'd taken her to dinner, she'd felt an inner excitement she hadn't experienced since she'd been seventeen years old. She felt good being with him—proud of what he was, how he looked, how he looked at *her*—and she felt infinitely safe, protected with his arm around her and his sturdy body so close.

Just then, a muffled cry came from the dark alleyway they'd just passed. They stopped and looked at each other, and their eyes grew wider when the sound came again. Suddenly Web was moving, pressing Marni into the alcove of a storefront. "Play dead," he whispered, then turned and ran back toward the alley. He'd barely reached its mouth when a body barreled into him, sending him sprawling, but only for an instant. Acting reflexively, he was on his feet and after the man, who was surprisingly smaller and slower than he.

But smaller and slower was one thing. When he dragged the nameless fugitive to the ground nearly halfway down the block, he found that he was no match for the shiny switchblade that connected with his left hand. Shards of pain splintered through him, and he recoiled, clutching his hand. He had no aspirations to be a hero or a martyr. Letting the man go, he ran back to where he'd left Marni. She was gone.

"Maaaarni!" he yelled, terrified for the first time.

"In here, Web! The alley!"

He swore, then dashed into the alley, skidding to a halt and coming down on his haunches beside her. She was supporting a young woman who was gasping for air.

"It's all right," Marni was saying softly but tightly. "It's all right. He's gone."

"Did he rape her?" Web asked Marni. He could see that the woman's clothes were torn.

She shook her head. "Our passing must have scared him off. He took her wallet. That's about it."

Web put a hand on the woman's quivering arm. "I'm going to get the police. Stay with Marni until I get back."

Her answering nod was nearly imperceptible amid her trembling, but Marni doubted she could have moved if she'd wanted to.

Web dashed back to the street, wondering where the traffic was when he wanted it. He ran to the corner of Fifth Avenue, intent on hailing some help. Cars whizzed by without pausing. The cabs were all occupied, so they didn't bother to stop. And there wasn't a policeman or a cruiser in sight. Spotting a pay phone, he dug into his pocket for a quarter, quickly called in the alarm, then raced back to the alley.

Marni was where he'd left her, still cradling the woman. Frightened, she looked up at him. "He must have hurt her. She has blood on her sleeve, but I don't know where it's coming from."

"It's mine," Web said, crouching down again. He was feeling a little dizzy. Both of his hands were covered with blood, one from holding the other. Tugging the scarf from around his neck, he wound it tightly around his left hand.

"My God, Web!" Marni whispered. Her heart, racing already, began to slam against her ribs. "What *happened*?"

"He had a knife. Lucky he used it on me, not her."

"But your hand—"

"It'll be all right."

The woman in Marni's arms began to cry. "I'm sorry…it's my fault. I shouldn't have…been walking alone…."

Marni smoothed matted strands of hair from the young woman's cheeks. She couldn't have been more than twenty-two or twenty-three, was thin and not terribly attractive. Yes, she should have known better, but that was water over the dam. "Shhhh. It's all right. The police will be here soon." She raised questioning eyes to Web, who nodded. Then she worriedly eyed his hand.

"It's okay," he assured her softly. He turned to the woman who'd been assaulted. "What's your name, honey?"

"Denise...Denise LaVecque."

"You're going to be just fine, Denise. The police will be along shortly." As though on cue, a distant siren grew louder. "They're going to want to know everything you can remember about the man who attacked you."

"I...I can't remember much. It was dark. He just...jumped out..."

"Anything you can remember will be a help to them."

The siren neared. It hit Marni that Denise wasn't the only one in for a long night. "They'll want to know everything you remember, too," she told Web.

He closed his eyes for a minute, frowning. His hand was beginning to throb. He wasn't sure if his wool scarf had been the best thing to wrap around it, but he'd needed to hide its condition from Marni—and from himself, if the truth were told. "I know."

Marni's hand on his cheek brought his eyes back open. "Are you really okay?" she whispered tremulously.

He gave a wan smile and nodded.

The siren rounded the corner and died at the same time a glaring flash of blue and white intruded on the darkness of the alley. It was a welcome intrusion.

The next few minutes passed by in a whir for Marni. A second police car joined the first, with four of New York's finest offering their slightly belated aid, asking question after question, searching the alley for anything Denise's assailant may have dropped, finally bundling Denise off in one car, Web and Marni in another. Marni wasn't sure what their plans were for Denise, but she was vocal in her insistence that Web be taken to a hospital before he answered any further questions.

The drive there was a largely silent one. Marni held Web's good hand tightly, worriedly glancing at him from time to time.

"It's just a cut," he murmured when he intercepted one such glance, but his head was lying back against the seat and the night could hide neither his pallor nor the blood seeping through the thickness of his scarf.

"My hero," was her retort, but it was more gentle than chiding, more admiring than censorious. She suspected that he'd acted on sheer instinct in chasing after the man who'd attacked Denise, and in a city notorious for its avoidance of involvement in such situations she deeply respected what Web had done. Of course, tangling with a switchblade hadn't been too swift....

The nurse at the emergency room desk immediately took Web to a cubicle, but when she suggested that Marni might want to wait outside, Marni firmly shook her head. She continued to hold Web's hand tightly, releasing it only to help him out of his coat and to roll up his sleeve. He sat on the examining table with his legs hanging down one side; she sat with her legs hanging down the other, her elbow hooked with his, her eyes over her shoulder focusing past him to his left hand, which a doctor was carefully unwrapping.

She didn't move from where she sat. Her arm tightened periodically around Web's as the doctor cleaned the knife wound, then examined it to see the extent of the damage. When Web winced, so did she. When he grunted at a particularly painful probe, she moaned.

"You okay?" he asked her at one point. The doctor had just announced that the tendon in his baby finger had been severed and that it would take a while to heal, what with stitches and all.

"I'm okay," she told Web. "You're the one who's sweating."

He grinned peakedly. "It hurts like hell."

Feeling utterly helpless, she turned on the doctor. "He's in pain. Can't you help—"

"Marni," Web interrupted, "it's only my hand."

"But the pain's probably shooting up your arm, and don't you tell me it isn't!" She felt it herself, through her hand, her arm, her entire body. Again she accosted the doctor. "Aren't you going to anesthetize him or something?"

The doctor gave her an understanding smile. "Just his hand. Right now." He took the needle that the nurse assisting him had suddenly produced, and Marni did look away then, but only until Web rubbed his cheek against her hair.

"You can open your eyes now," he said softly, a hint of amusement in his tone. "It's all done."

What was done was the anesthetizing. The gash, which cut through his baby finger and continued across his palm, was as angry-looking as ever.

"You may think this is funny, Brian Webster," she scolded in a hoarse whisper, "but I don't. Who knows what filthy germs were on that knife, or how you're going to handle a camera with one hand immobilized."

"Do you think I'm not worried about those same things?" he asked gently.

"No need to worry, Mr. Webster," the doctor interjected. "I'll give you a shot to counter whatever may have been on the knife, and as for your work, it's just your pinkie that will be in a splint. Between your thumb and the first two fingers of that left hand, you should be able to manage your camera. Maybe a little awkwardly at first, but you'll adapt."

"See?" Web said to Marni. "I'll adapt."

Marni didn't reply. She felt guilty for having badgered him, but she was worried and upset, and she'd had to let off the tension somehow. Turning her gaze back to his wound, which the doctor was beginning to stitch, she slid her free arm over Web's shoulder. He reached up, grasped her hand and wove his fingers through hers.

"Does it hurt?" she whispered.

He, too, was closely following the doctor's work, but he managed to shake his head. "Don't feel a thing."

"I'm glad one of us doesn't," she quipped dryly, and he chuckled.

Millimeter by millimeter the doctor closed the gash. Once, riding a wave of momentary fatigue, Marni pressed her face to the crook of Web's neck. He tipped his head to hold her there, finding intense comfort in the closeness.

When the repair work was done, the doctor splinted the finger and bandaged the hand. He gave Web the shot he'd promised, plus a small envelope with painkillers that he claimed Web might need as soon as the local anesthetic wore off. Marni would have liked nothing more than to take him home at that point, but the police were waiting just beyond the cubicle to take them to the station.

"Can't this be done tomorrow?" Marni asked softly. "I think he should be resting."

Web squeezed her hand. "It's okay. If we go now, we'll get it over with. The sooner the better, before the numbness wears off. Besides, I'm not sure I want to spend my Saturday poring through mug shots."

She would have argued further, but she realized he had a point. "You'll tell me if you start feeling lousy?"

"I think you'll know," he returned, arching one dark brow. She hadn't let go of him for a minute, and he loved it. Barely five minutes had gone by when she hadn't looked at his face for signs of discomfort or asked how he felt, and he loved it. He'd never been the object of such concern in his life. And he loved it.

He didn't love wading through page after page of mug shots in search of the man he'd seen and chased, but the police were insistent, and he knew it was necessary. He particularly didn't love it when the wee hours of the morning approached and they were still at it, he and Marni. His hand was beginning to ache again, and as the minutes passed, his head was, too. He knew that Marni had to be totally exhausted, and while he wanted to send her home, he also needed her by his side.

"Nothing," he said wearily when the last of the books were closed. "I'm sorry, but I don't think the man I saw tonight is here."

The officer who had been working with them rose from his perch on the corner of the desk and took the book from Web. "Hit and run. They're the damnedest ones to catch. May have been wearing a wig, or have shaved off a mustache. May not have any previous record, if you can believe that."

Marni, for one, was ready to believe anything the man said, if only to secure her and Web's release. Not only was she tired, but the events of the night had begun to take an emotional toll. She was feeling distinctly shaky.

"Is there anything else we have to do now?" she asked fearfully.

"Nope. I've got your statements, and I know where to reach you if we come up with anything."

Web was slipping his coat on. He didn't bother to put his left arm into the sleeve. It wasn't worth the effort. "Do you think you will?"

"Nope."

Web sighed. "Well, if you need us…"

The officer nodded, then stood aside, and Web and Marni wound their way through the maze of desks, doorways and stairs to the clear, cold air outside. They headed straight for a waiting taxi.

"I'd better get you home," he murmured, opening the door for Marni. As she slid in, she leaned forward and gave the cabbie Web's address. Web didn't realize what she'd done until they pulled up outside his riverfront building, at which point he was dismayed. "I can't send you home alone in a cab," he protested. "Not after what happened tonight."

Some of her spunk had returned. "I have no intention of going home alone, *especially* after what happened tonight. Come on, big guy." She was shoving him out the door. "We could both use a drink."

He was paying the cabbie when she climbed out herself. She was the one to put her arm around his waist and urge him into the building. "This is not…

what...I'd planned," he growled, disgusted when he looked back on an evening that was supposed to have been so pleasant. "I never should have taken you to that party. If we hadn't gone, we wouldn't have been walking down that street—"

"And that poor girl would have been raped." Marni pressed the elevator button. The door slid open instantly, and she tugged him inside. "What ifs aren't any good—I learned that a long time ago. The facts are that we did go to the party, that we were walking down that street, that we managed to deter a vicious crime, that your hand is all cut up and that we're both bleary-eyed right about now." The elevator began its ascent. "I'm exhausted, but I'm afraid to close my eyes because I'll see either that dark alleyway, that girl, or your poor hand.... How is it?"

"It's there."

"You wouldn't take one of the painkillers while we were at the police station. Will you take one now?"

"A couple of aspirin'll do the trick."

He ferreted his keys from his pocket and had them waiting when the elevator opened. Moments later they'd passed through the studio, climbed the spiral staircase and were in his living room. He went straight to the bar, tipped a bottle into each of two glasses without thought to either ice or water, took a long drink from his glass, then handed the other to Marni.

"Come. Sit with me." He moved to the sofa, kicked off his loafers and sank down, stretching out his legs and leaning his head back.

"Where's the aspirin?" Marni asked softly.

"Medicine chest. Down the hall, through the bedroom to the bathroom."

She found her way easily, so intent on getting something into Web that she saw nothing of the rest of his apartment but the inside of the medicine chest above the sink. When she returned, he downed the aspirin with another drink from his glass. She sat facing him on the sofa, her elbow braced on the sofa back.

"You look awful," she whispered.

He didn't open his eyes. "I've felt better."

"Maybe you should lie down."

"I am." He was sprawled backward, his lean body molded to the cushions.

"In bed. Wouldn't you be more comfortable there?"

"Soon."

Very gently, she lifted his injured hand and put it in her lap. She wanted to soothe him, to do something to help, but she wasn't sure what would be best. She began to lightly stroke his forearm, and when he didn't complain she continued.

He smirked. "Some night."

"It certainly was an adventure. You were always into them. This is the first one I've taken part in."

"I think I'm getting too old for this. I'm getting too old for lots of things. I should be up in Vermont. It's quieter there."

"Why aren't you? I thought you went up every weekend."

He opened one eye and looked at her. "I wanted to be with you. I didn't think you'd go up there with me." When she said nothing, he closed his eye and returned his head to its original position. "Anyway, I often wait till Saturday morning to drive up. If there's something doing here on a Friday night."

"You can't drive tomorrow! Well, you can, I suppose, but your hand will be sore—"

"Forget my hand." He made a guttural sound. "The

way I feel now, I don't think I'm going to be able to drag myself out of bed before noon, and by then it'd be pretty late to get going."

"You'll go next weekend. It'll still be there."

"Mmmm." He lay still for several minutes, then drained his drink in a single swallow.

Marni set her own glass firmly on the coffee table. She took his empty one, put it beside hers, then gently slid her hand under his neck. "Come on, Web," she urged softly. "Let me get you to bed."

Very slowly and with some effort he pushed himself up, then stood. His hand was hurting, his whole arm was hurting. For that matter, his entire body felt sore. The aftermath of tension, he told himself. He *was* getting old.

Marni led him directly to the bed. The king-sized mattress sat on a platform of dark wood that matched a modern highboy and a second, lower chest of drawers. A plush navy carpet covered the floor. Two chairs of the same contemporary style as those in the living room sat kitty-cornered on one side of the room, between them a low table covered with magazines. Large silk-screen prints hung on the walls, contemporary, almost abstract in style, carrying through the navy, brown and white scheme of the room.

Clear-cut and masculine, like Web, Marni mused as she unbuttoned his shirt and eased it from his shoulders. As soon as it was gone, he turned and whipped the quilt back with his good arm, then stretched out full-length on the bed and threw that same arm across his eyes.

Marni stood where she was with his shirt clutched in her hands and her eyes glued to his bare chest. He was every bit as beautiful as he'd been fourteen years ago, though different in a way that made her heart beat faster than it ever had then. His shoulders were fuller, his skin more weathered. The hair that covered his chest was thicker, more pervasive, even more virile, if that were possible.

Anything was possible, she thought, including the fact that she was as physically attracted to him now as she'd been fourteen years before. Biological magnetism was an amazing thing. Web had been her first, but there'd been others. None of them had turned her on in quite the same way, with quite the intensity Web did.

None of them had stirred feelings of tenderness and caring that Web did either, and he was hurting now, she reminded herself with a jolt. Pushing all other thought aside, she dropped his shirt onto the foot of the bed and came to sit beside him. She unsnapped his jeans and was about to lower the zipper when his arm left his eyes and his hand stilled hers.

"I was...just trying to make you more comfortable," she explained, feeling the sudden flare of those blue eyes on her. "Wouldn't it be better without the jeans?"

"No. I'm fine as I am." Most importantly, he didn't want her to see his leg. She'd had as rough a night as he had, and he didn't feel she was ready to view those particular scars. They were old and well-faded, true, but the memories they'd evoke would be harsh.

Trusting that she wouldn't undress him further, he returned his arm to his eyes and gave a rueful laugh. "Y'know, since I saw you last Tuesday morning, I've been dreaming of having you again. Making love to you...here in my bed. Now here you are and I feel so awful that I don't think I could do a thing even if you were willing."

His words hung in the air, unresolved. Marni

couldn't get herself to give the answer she knew Web wanted to hear. There was no doubt in her mind that on the physical level she was willing. Emotionally, well, that was another story. Much as she'd opened up to him since their reunion, much as she'd been able to talk of Ethan more easily than she had in the past, there were still thoughts that she couldn't ignore, raw feelings going back to that summer. Illogical perhaps, but logical ones as well. She knew from experience that one time with Web wouldn't be enough. He'd been an addiction that summer in Maine. She wasn't sure that if she gave in to him, to herself, it would be any different now. And the question would be where they went from there.

"I don't think the time's right for either of us," she said in a near-whisper. "You're right. You're feeling awful. And I feel a little like I've been flattened by a steamroller." She reached for the second pillow and carefully worked it under his bandaged hand. Then she rose from the bed. "I'll just sit over here—"

He raised his arm and looked at her. "You won't leave, will you?"

"No, I won't leave."

"Then why don't you lie down, too. The bed's big enough for both of us."

She wasn't sure she trusted herself that far. "In a little bit," she said, but paused before she sank into the chair. "Can I get you anything?"

Eyes closed, he shook his head. "I think I'll just rest…"

When his voice trailed off, she settled into the chair, studying him for a long time until a reflexive twitch of his good hand told her he was asleep. Soon after, her own eyelids drooped, then shut.

Ninety minutes later she came to feeling disoriented and stiff. The first problem was solved when she blinked, looked around the room, then saw Web lying exactly as he had been. The second was solved when she switched off the light, stretched out on the empty half of the bed, drew the quilt over them both and promptly fell asleep.

She awoke several times during the night when Web shifted and groaned. Once she felt his head and found it cool, and when he didn't wake up she lay down again. Her deepest sleep came just before dawn. When next she opened her eyes, the skylit room was bright. The same disorientation possessed her for a minute, but it vanished the minute she turned her head and saw Web.

He was still sleeping. His hair was mussed, and his beard was a dark shadow on his face. But it was his brow, corrugated even in sleep, that drew her gaze. He'd had an uncomfortable night. Silently, she slipped from beneath the sheet and padded to the bathroom for aspirin and water.

He was stirring when she returned, so she sat close by his side, raised him enough to push the aspirin into his mouth and give him a drink, then very gently set his head back down.

"Thanks," he murmured, coming to full awareness. He hadn't been disoriented, since this was his home. Finding Marni sitting beside him, well, that was something else.

"You're welcome. How does it feel…or shouldn't I ask?"

"You shouldn't ask," he drawled, then stretched, twisting his torso. When he settled back, his eyes were on her. "Actually, it's not bad. The discomfort's localized now. It was worse when I was sleeping, because I couldn't pinpoint it and it seemed to be all over." He raised the hand in question and glared at the white gauze. "Helluva big bandage. I'll have to get rid of some of this stuff."

"Don't you dare! If it was put on, it was put on for a reason."

"How am I gonna shower?"

"Hold your hand up in the air out of the spray...or forget the shower and take a bath."

"I never take baths."

She shrugged. "Then take a shower with your hand in the air, and be grateful it's your left hand. If it had been your right, you'd be in *big* trouble."

He ran his palm over the stubble on his jaw. "You've got a point there." His gaze skittered hesitantly to hers. "I must look like something the cat dragged in."

She couldn't have disagreed with him more. He looked a little rough, but all man, every sinewy, stubbly, hairy inch. "You look fine, no, wonderful, given the circumstances." Her voice softened even more. "I've never seen you in the morning this way. We...we never spent a full night together."

He smiled in regret, his voice as soft as hers. "So now we've done it, and we haven't even *done* it." He raised his good hand and skimmed a finger over her lips, back and forth, whisper-light. "Do you know, I haven't even kissed you? Lord, I've wanted to, but I didn't know if you wanted it, and it seemed more important to talk."

Marni felt her insides melting. "Fourteen years ago it was the other way around."

"We're older now. Maybe we've got our priorities straight.... But I still want to kiss you." He was stroking her cheek ever so gently, and she'd begun to tremble. "Will you let me?"

"You always had the bluest eyes," she whispered, mesmerized by them, drowning in them. "I could never deny you when you looked at me that way."

"What way?"

"Like you wanted me. Like you knew that maybe it wasn't the smartest thing, but you wanted me anyway. Like there was something about *me* that you wanted, just me."

"There is." He slid his fingers into her hair and urged her head down. "There is, Marni. You're ... very ... special...." The last was whispered against her lips, the sound vanishing into her mouth, which had opened, and waited, but was waiting no more.

It started gently, a tender reacquaintance, kisses whispered from one mouth to the other in a slow, renewing exchange. For Marni it was a homecoming; there was something about the taste of Web, the texture of his lips, the instinctive way he pleased her that erased the years that had passed. For Web the homecoming was no less true; there was something about the softness of Marni's lips, the way they clung to his, the way her honeyed freshness poured warmly into him that made him forget everything that had come between this and their last kiss.

Familiarly their lips touched and sipped and danced. As it had always done, though, desire soon began to clamor, and whispered kisses were no longer enough. Web's mouth grew more forceful, Marni's demanded in return, and it was fire, hot, sweet fire surging through their veins, singeing all threads of caution.

Eyes closed under the force of sensation, Marni took everything he offered and gave as much in return. His mouth slanted openly against hers, hungrily devouring it. Her mouth fought fiercely for his, possessing it in turn. He ran his tongue along the line of her teeth and beyond; she caressed it with her own, then drew it in deeper. And while his hand wound restlessly through her hair, her own spread feverishly across his chest.

"C'mere," he growled, and swiftly rolled her over him until she was on her back and he was above her. Her neck rested in the crook of his elbow, and it was that elbow that propped him up so he could touch her as she'd done him.

Even had their mouths not come together again, she wouldn't have said a word in protest, because the fire was too hot, the sweetness too sweet to deprive herself of this little bit of heaven. Web had always been this for her, a flame licking at her nerve ends, spreading a molten desire within her that water couldn't begin to quench.

He cupped her breast through the knit of her overblouse, molding it to his palm, kneading and circling until at last his fingers homed in on the tight nub at its crest. Her flesh swelled, and she arched up, seeking even closer contact with the instrument of such bliss. She'd been starving for years; now she couldn't get enough. It was sheer relief when he impatiently tugged the overblouse from her hips.

"Lift up, sweet...there...I need...to touch you, Marni!"

She helped him, because she needed the very same thing, and she was tossing the blouse aside even as Web unhooked her bra and tore it away. Then he was lying half over her again, his large hand greedily rediscovering her blossoming flesh, and she was moaning in delight, straining for more, bunching the damp skin of his back in hands that clenched and unclenched, shifted, then clenched again.

She was in a frenzy. The tight knot in her belly was growing, inflamed not only by his thorough exploration of her nakedness but by the hardness of his sex pressing boldly against her thigh. When he slid down, she dug her fingers into his hair, holding on for dear life as his mouth opened over her breast, his tongue bathed it, his teeth closed around one distended nipple and tugged a path to her womb.

"Web!" she cried. "Oh, God, I need…I need…"

He slid back up, and her hand lowered instinctively to him, cupping him, caressing him until even that wasn't enough. His hand tangled with hers then, clutching at the tab of his zipper, tugging it down. He took her fingers and led them inside his briefs. He was trembling as badly as she was, and his voice shook with urgency.

"Touch me…touch me, sunshine…"

This time the pet name was so perfectly placed, so very right that it was stimulation in and of itself. She touched him, stroked him, pleasured him until he gave a hoarse cry of even greater need. Then he was tugging at her pants, freeing her hips for his invasion.

What happened then was something neither Marni nor Web had expected. She felt his tumescence press against the nest of curls at the apex of her thighs, and it was so intense, so electric that she recoiled and, in a burst of emotion, began to cry.

"Web…oh…" she sobbed, tears streaking down her cheeks and into the hairs of his chest. "Web…I…I…"

She couldn't say anything else. Her crying prevented it. He held her head tightly to his chest with his left arm and ran his good hand over and around her naked back, knowing that he could easily be inside her but ignoring that fact because, at the moment, her emotional state was far more important.

"It's okay. Shhhhh. Shhhhh."

"I want," she gulped, "want you...so badly, but...but..."

"Shhhhh. It's okay."

She wiped the tears from her eyes, but they kept flowing. She felt frustrated and embarrassed and confused. So she simply gave herself up to the outpouring of whatever it was and waited until at last the tears slowed before trying to speak again.

"I'm sorry...I didn't mean to do that...I don't know what happened..."

"Something's bothering you," he said softly, patiently. "Something snapped."

"But it's awful...what I did. A woman has no right to do that to...to a man."

"I know you want me, so you're suffering, too."

She raised wide, tear-filled eyes to his. "Let me help you." Her hand started back down. "Let me do it, Web—"

He flattened her body against his, trapping her hand. "No. I don't want that."

"But you'll be uncomfortable—"

"The discomfort is more in my mind than my body." Her tears had instantly cooled his ardor. He allowed a small space between them. "Feel. You'll see. Go on."

She did as he told her and discovered that he was no longer hard. Her eyes widened all the more, and she suddenly grappled with her pants, tugging them up. "You *don't* want me..."

He gave a short laugh and rolled his eyes to the ceiling. "I'm damned if I do and damned if I don't." His gaze fell to catch hers. "Of course I want you, sunshine. You are my sunshine, y'know. You're bright and warm, the source of an incredible energy, but only when you're sure of yourself, when you're happy. Something happened just now. I don't know exactly what it was, but it's pushed that physical drive into the background for the time being."

Marni wasn't sure what to think. She nervously matted the hair on his chest with the flat of her finger. "It used to be that nothing could push that physical drive into the background."

"We're older. Life is more complex than it used to be. When I was twenty-six, sex was a sheer necessity. It was a physical outlet, sure, but it was also a means of communicating things that either I didn't understand or didn't see or didn't want to say." His arm was beginning to throb. Shifting himself back against the pillow, he drew Marni against him, cradling her with his right arm, letting his left rest limply on the sheet.

"If I was still twenty-six, I'd have made love to you regardless of your tears just now. I wouldn't have had the strength to stop, the control. But I'm not twenty-six. I'm forty. I have the control now, and the strength." He paused for a minute, but there was more he wanted to say. "I haven't been a monk all these years, Marni. For a while I was with any and every woman who turned me on. Then I realized that the turn-on was purely physical, and it wasn't enough. Maybe I've mellowed. I've become picky. I think...I think that when we do make love, you and I, it'll be an incredibly new and wonderful experience."

To her horror, Marni began to cry again. "Why do

you...do you *say* things like that, Web? Why are...are you so incredibly understanding?"

He hugged her tighter. "It hurts me when you cry, sunshine. Please, tell me what's bothering you. Tell me what happened back there."

"Oh, God," she cried, then sniffled, "I wish I knew. I was so high, so unbelievably high, and then it was like...like this door opened somewhere in the back of my mind, and in a lightning-quick instant I felt burned to a crisp, and frightened and nervous and guilty..."

He held her face back. "Guilty?"

She looked at him blankly, her lashes spiked with tears when she blinked. "Did I say that?" she whispered, puzzled.

"Very clearly. What did you mean?"

"I don't know. Maybe...maybe it's that we haven't been together long..."

"Maybe," he returned, but skeptically. "You've been with other men since that summer, haven't you?"

She nodded. "But it's been a long time for me and...maybe it was too easy and that bothered me."

"You've always been honest with me, Marni," he chided softly. "Tell me. These are modern times, and you're a fully grown, experienced woman. If you met a guy and felt something really unique with him, and if he felt the same, and the two of you wanted desperately to make love, would you hold out on principle?" When she didn't answer, he coaxed gently, "Would you?"

"No," she whispered.

"But you do feel guilty now. Why, sunshine? Why guilty?"

"Maybe it was too fast. And your hand..."

"My hand wasn't hurting just then. Loving you blot-

ted everything out. I wasn't complaining, or moaning.
Come on, Marni. Why guilty?"

Her gaze darted blindly about the room. She
frowned, swallowed hard, then began to breathe raggedly. "I guess...I guess that...maybe I felt that...well,
we'd made love so much during that summer, and it
was so good and right, and then...and then..." Her
eyes were wide when she raised them to his. Fresh
tears pooled on her lower lids but refused to overflow.
"And then the accident happened and Ethan was
killed and you were in the hospital and my parents...forbade me to...see you..."

Web closed his eyes. An intense inner pain brought a
soft moan to his lips, and he slipped both arms around
her. "Lord, what they've done...what they've done..."

He held her for a long time without saying a word,
because only then did he realize the enormity of the
hurdle he faced.

WEB HAD MUCH to consider. He understood now that there was a link in Marni's mind between their love-making of fourteen years ago and Ethan's death. He understood that, though she may not have been aware of it at the time, some small part of her had felt guilty about their affair, and Ethan's death must have seemed to her a form of punishment. And he understood that her parents had done nothing to convince her it wasn't so.

Much to consider...so much to consider. He held Marni tightly, wanting desperately to protect her, to take away the pain. She was such a strong woman, yet still fragile. He tried to decide what to do, what to say. In the end he wasn't any more ready to discuss this newly revealed legacy of that summer in Maine than she was.

"Marni?" he murmured against her hair. He ran his hand soothingly over her naked back, then kissed her forehead. "Sweetheart?"

Marni, too, had been stunned by what she'd said. But rather than think of it, she'd closed her eyes and let the solid warmth of Web's body calm her. She took a last, faintly erratic breath. "Hmmm?"

"Are you any good at brewing coffee?"

She knew what he was doing and was grateful. A

faint smile formed against his chest, and she opened
her eyes. "Not bad."

"Think you could do it while I use the bathroom?
I'm feeling a little muzzy right about now."

His voice did sound muzzy, so she took pity on him.
Reaching for her discarded blouse, she dragged it over
her breasts as she sat up. "I think I could handle that."

He was looking at the blouse, then at the hands that
clutched it to her. "Hey, what's this?" he asked very
softly, gently. When he met her gaze, his blue eyes
were infinitely tender. "You never used to cover up
with me."

Embarrassed, she looked away. "That was fourteen
years ago," she whispered.

"And you don't think that what we have now is as
close?"

"It isn't that..."

He lightly curled his fingers over her slender shoulders. "What is it, sunshine? Please, tell me."

Her eyes remained downcast. "I...I'm older...I look
different now."

"But I saw you a few minutes ago. I touched you and
tasted you, and you were beautiful."

"That was in the heat of passion."

"And you're afraid I'll look at you now and see a
thirty-one-year-old body and not be turned on?"

She shrugged. "Time does things."

"To me, too. Don't you think I'm aware that my
body is older? I'm forty, not twenty-six. Do you think
I'm not that little bit nervous that you'll see all the
changes?"

Her gaze shot to him. "But I saw you last night, and
not in passion, and you're body's better than ever!"

"So is yours, Marni," he whispered. Very slowly he

eased the knit fabric from her hands and drew it away. His eyes took on a special light as they gently caressed her bare curves. "Your skin is beautiful. Your breasts are perfect."

"They're not as high as they used to be."

"They're fuller, more womanly." He didn't touch her, but his heart was thumping as he captured her gaze. "If I wanted a seventeen-year-old now, I'd have one. But I don't want that, Marni. I want a mature woman. I want you." Very gently he pulled her forward and pressed a warm kiss to each of her breasts in turn. She sucked in a sharp breath, and her nipples puckered instantly. "And if you don't get out of here this minute, mature woman," he growled only half in jest, "I'm going to have you." He shot a disparaging glance at the front of his jeans, then a more sheepish one back at her.

"Oh, Web," Marni breathed. She threw herself forward and gave him a final hug. "You always know the right thing to say."

He wanted to say that he didn't, but the words wouldn't come out because he'd closed his eyes and was caught up enjoying the silken feel of her against him. Only when the pressure in his loins increased uncomfortably did he force a hoarse warning. "Marni...that coffee?"

"Right away," she whispered, jumping up and running for the door, then returning, cheeks ablaze, for her bra and blouse before dashing for the kitchen.

Not only did she brew a pot of rich coffee, but by the time Web joined her she'd scrambled eggs, toasted English muffins and sliced fresh oranges for their breakfast.

"So you can cook," he teased. He remembered her

telling him, during those days in Camden, that Cook had allowed no interference in the kitchen.

Marni put milk in his coffee, just as he'd had it that night when they'd been at the restaurant, and set the mug beside him. Then she joined him at the island counter. "I may not be a threat to Julia Child, but I've learned something. Post-graduate work, if you will."

He sipped the strong brew and smiled in appreciation. "An A for coffee." He took a forkful of the eggs, chewed appreciatively, then smacked his lips together. "An A for scrambled eggs. Very moist and light."

She laughed. "Don't grade the muffins or the orange. I really can't take much credit for either."

"Still, you didn't burn the muffins."

"You have a good toaster."

"And the orange is sliced with precision."

"You have a sharp knife, and I have a tidy personality." Amused, she was watching him eat. "You'll choke if you don't slow down."

"I'm suddenly starved. You should be, too. We didn't get around to having dinner last night."

Marni ate half of her eggs, then offered the rest to Web, who devoured them and one of her muffins as though his last meal had been days ago. When he was done, he sat back and studied her. "What now?" he asked softly.

"You're still hungry?"

"What now...for us? Will you stay a while?"

She'd been debating that one the whole time she'd been making breakfast. "I...think I'd better head home. A lot has happened. Too quickly. I need a little time."

He nodded. More than anything he wished she'd

stay, but he understood her need for time alone to think. He could only hope it would be to his benefit.

She began to clean up the kitchen. "Will you be okay...your hand, and all?"

"I'll be fine.... Marni, what say we try for that picture again on Tuesday? If you can manage it with your schedule, I can make all the other arrangements."

She finished rinsing the frying pan, then reached for the dish towel. "Do you really think you'll be up for it?"

"I've got another shoot set for Monday. It has to go on, no matter what. I'll be up for it.... But that's not the real question here." Not wanting to put undue pressure on her, he remained where he was at the island. "Are you willing to give it another try?"

Her head was bowed. "You really think it's the cover we need?"

"I do. But more than that, I *want* to do it. You have no idea how much it means to me to photograph you and put your face out there for the world to see. I'm proud of you, Marni. Some men might want to keep you all to themselves, and I do in a lot of respects, but I'm a photographer, and you happen to mean more to me than any other subject I've ever photographed. I want you to be on the premier cover of *Class* because I feel you belong there, and because I feel that I'm the only one who can see and capture on film the beauty you are, inside and out." When she simply stood with her back to him, saying nothing, he grew more beseechful. "I know that may sound arrogant, but it's the way I feel. Give me a chance, Marni. Don't deny me this one pleasure."

"It's not only your eyes that get to me, Brian Webster," she muttered under her breath, "it's your tone of voice. How, can you prey on my *vulnerability* this way?"

He knew then that he'd won. Rising, he crossed to the sink and gave her waist a warm squeeze. "Because I know that it's right, Marni. It's right all the way."

MARNI STILL HAD her doubts. She left him soon after that and returned to her apartment. She had errands to run that afternoon—food shopping, a manicure, stockings to buy—and she would have put them all off in a minute if she'd felt it wise to stay longer with Web. But she did need to be alone, and she did need to think. At least, that was what she told herself. Then she did everything possible to avoid being alone, to avoid thinking.

She dallied in the supermarket, spent an extra hour talking with the woman whose manicure followed hers, and whom she'd come to know for that reason, then browsed through every department of Bloomingdale's before reaching the hosiery counter. When she finished her shopping, she returned home in time to put her purchases away, then shower and dress for the cocktail party she'd been invited to. It was a business-related affair, and when she got there she threw herself into it, so much so that when she finally got home she was exhausted and went right to bed.

When she woke up the next morning, though, Web was first and foremost on her mind. She thought back to the same hour the day before, remembering being on his bed, on the verge of making love with him. Her body throbbed at the memory. She took a long shower, but it didn't seem to help. Without considering the whys and wherefores, she picked up the phone and dialed his number.

"Webster, here," was the curt answer.

She hesitated, then ventured cautiously, "Web?"

He paused, then let out a smiling sigh. "Marni. How are you, sunshine?"

"I'm okay.... Am I disturbing you?"

"Not on your life."

"You sounded distracted."

"I was sitting here feeling sorry for myself. Just about to drag out the old morgue book."

"Why feeling sorry for yourself?"

"Because I'm here and you're there, and because my hand hurts and I'm wondering how in hell I'm going to manage tomorrow."

"It's still really bad?"

"Nah. It's a little sore, but self-pity always makes things seem worse."

She grinned. "Then, by all means, drag out the old morgue book."

"I won't have to, now that you've called.... I tried you last night."

She'd been wondering about that, worrying ... hoping. "I had to go to a cocktail party. It was a business thing. Pretty dry." In hindsight that was exactly what it had been, though she'd convinced herself otherwise at the time. No, not really dry, but certainly not as exciting as it might have been had Web been there.

"I sat here alone all night thinking of you," he said without remorse.

"That's not fair."

"I'll say it's not. You're out there munching on scrumptious little hors d'oeuvres while I dig into the peanut butter jar—"

"It's not fair that you're making me feel guilty," she corrected him, but she was grinning. If he'd spent last night with a gorgeous model, she'd have been jealous as hell.

He feigned resignation with an exaggerated sigh. "No need to feel guilty. I'm used to peanut butter—"

"Web..." she warned teasingly.

"Okay. But I really did miss you. I do miss you. Yesterday at this time we were having breakfast together."

"I know." There was a wistfulness to her tone.

"Hey, I could pick you up in an hour and we could go for brunch."

"No, Web. I have work to do. I promised myself I'd stay in all day and get it done."

"Work? On the weekend?"

She knew he was mocking her, but she didn't mind. "I always bring a briefcase home with me. Things get so hectic at the office sometimes that I need quiet time to reread proposals and reports."

"I wouldn't keep you more than an hour, hour and a half at most."

"I...I'd better not."

"You still need time to think."

"Yes."

He spoke more softly. "That I can accept.... We're on for Tuesday, aren't we?"

"I'll have to work it out with my secretary when I go in tomorrow, but I don't think I have anything that can't be shifted around."

"I've already called Anne. She'll have Marjorie get some clothes ready, but I said that I wanted as few people there for the actual shoot as possible. That'll go for my staff, too, and you can leave Edgar and Steve behind at the office."

"I will. Thank you."

He paused, his tone lightening. "Can I call you tomorrow night, just to make sure you don't get cold feet and back out on me at the last minute?"

"I won't back out once all the arrangements are made."

"Can I call you anyway?"

She smiled softly. "I'd like that."

"Good." He hated to let her go. Her voice alone warmed him, not to mention the visual picture he'd formed of her auburn hair framing her face, her cheeks bright and pink, her lips soft, the tips of her breasts peaking through a nightgown, or a robe, or a blouse— it didn't matter which, the effect was the same. "Well," he began, then cleared his throat, "take care, Marni."

"I will." She hated to let him go. His voice alone thrilled her, not to mention the visual picture she'd formed of his dark hair brushing rakishly over his brow, his lean, shadowed cheeks, his firm lips, the raw musculature of his torso. She took an unsteady breath. "Are you sure you can manage everything with your hand?" If he'd said that he was having trouble, she would have rushed to his aid in a minute.

He was tempted to say he was having trouble, but he'd never been one to lie. "I'm sure.... Bye-bye, sweetheart."

"Bye, Web."

MARNI WOULD INDEED HAVE TRIED to back out on the photo session had it not been for the arrangements that had been made. Through all of Sunday, while she tried to concentrate first on the Sunday *Times*, then on her work, she found herself thinking of her relationship with Web. She was no longer seventeen and in that limbo between high school, college and the real world. She was old enough to have serious thoughts about the future, and she knew that with each additional minute she spent with Web those thoughts would grow more and more serious.

Though she wasn't sure exactly what he wanted, she knew from what he'd said that he envisioned some kind of future relationship with her. But there were problems—actually just one, but it was awesome. Her family.

It was this that weighed heavily on her when she arrived at Web's studio Tuesday morning. As he'd promised, Web had called the evening before. He'd been gentle and encouraging, so that when she'd hung up the phone she'd felt surprisingly calm about posing again. Then her mother had called.

"Marni, darling, why didn't you tell me! I had no idea what had happened until Tanya called a little while ago!"

Icy fingers tripped up Marni's spine. What did her mother know? She hadn't sounded angry.... What could *Tanya* know...or was it Marni's own guilty conscience at work? "What is it, Mother? What are you talking about?"

"That little business you witnessed on Friday night. Evidently there was a tiny notice in the paper yesterday. I missed it completely, and if it hadn't been for Tanya—"

Marni was momentarily stunned. She hadn't expected any of that episode to reach the press, much less with her name printed...and, she assumed, Web's. She moistened her lips, unsure as to how much more her mother knew. All she could say was a slightly cryptic, "Tanya reads the paper?"

"Actually it was Sue Beacham—you know, Tanya's friend whose husband is a state senator? They say he's planning to run for Congress, and he'll probably make it. He has more connections than God. Of course, Jim Heuer had the connections and it didn't help. He didn't get Ed Donahue's support, so he lost most of the liberal vote. I guess you can never tell about those things."

Marni took a breath for patience. Her mother tended to run on at the mouth, particularly when it came to name-dropping. "What was it that Sue saw?"

"There was a little article about how you and that photographer were instrumental in interrupting a rape."

"It wasn't a rape," Marni countered very quietly. "It was a mugging."

"But it could have been a rape if you hadn't come along, at least that was what the paper said. I'd already thrown it out, but Tanya had the article and read it to me."

Marni forced herself to relax. It appeared that Adele Lange hadn't made the connection between Brian Webster, the photographer, and the notorious Web. "It was really nothing, Mother. We happened to be walking down the street and heard the woman's cries. By the time we got to her, her assailant was already on his way."

"But this photographer you were with—it said he was injured."

"Just his hand. He's fine."

"Who is he, Marni? You never mentioned you were seeing a photographer, and such a renowned one, at least that's what Tanya says. She says that he's right up there with the best, and I'm sure I've seen his work but I've probably repressed the name. Webster." Her voice hardened. "I don't even like to say it."

Marni's momentary reprieve was snatched away. It didn't matter that her mother hadn't actually connected the two. What mattered was that the ill will lingered.

"Are you seeing him regularly?" Adele asked when Marni remained quiet.

"He's doing the cover work for the new magazine. There were some things we had to work out."

"Do you think you *will* be seeing him? Socially, that is? A photographer." Marni could picture her mother pursing her lips. "I think you should remember that a man in a field like his is involved with many, many women, and glamorous ones at that. You'll have to be careful."

The "many, many women" Marni's mother mentioned went along with the stereotype. Marni felt no threat on that score. Indeed, it was the least of her worries.

"Mother," she sighed, "you're getting a little ahead of yourself."

"It doesn't hurt to go into things with both eyes open."

"I've *got* both eyes open."

"All right, all right, darling. You needn't get riled up. I only called because I was concerned. I know incidents like that aren't uncommon, but witnessing it on the street can be a traumatic experience for a woman."

"It was traumatic for the victim. I'm okay."

"Are you sure? You sound tired."

"After a full day at the office, I am tired."

"Well, I guess you have a right to that. I'll let you rest, darling. Talk with you soon?"

"Uh-huh." Marni had hung up then, but she'd spent a good part of the night brooding, so she was tired and unsettled when Web came to greet her at the reception area of the studio. His smile was warm and pleasure-filled, relaxing her somewhat, but he was quick to see that something was amiss.

"Nervous?" he asked her as he guided her into the studio.

"A little."

"It'll be easier this time."

"I hope so."

"Is…everything all right?"

"Everything's fine."

"Why won't you look at me?"

She did then. "Better?"

He shook his head. "Smile for me."

She did then. "Better?"

He gestured noncommittally, but she was looking beyond him again, so he didn't speak. "See? It's almost quiet here."

Indeed it was. Anne, who appeared to be the only one present from *Class*, waved to her from the other side of the room, where she was in conference with the makeup artist. Marni recognized the hairstylist and, more vaguely, several of Web's assistants.

"Lee?" Web called out. A man turned from the group and, smiling, approached. "Lee, I'd like you to meet Marni. Formally. Marni, my brother, Lee."

Marni's smile was more genuine as she shook Lee's warm hand. He was pleasant-looking, though no-where near as handsome or tall as Web. Wearing a suit, minus its tie, he was more conservatively dressed than the other men in the room, but his easy way made up for the difference. Marni liked him instantly.

"I'm pleased to meet you, Lee. Web's had only good things to say about you."

Lee shot Web a conspiratorial glance. "I'd have to say the same about you. I've heard about nothing else for the past week." He held up his hand. "Not that he's telling everyone, mind you, but—" he winked "—I think the old man needs an outlet."

Marni wondered just how much Lee knew, then realized that it didn't matter. He was Web's brother. The physical resemblance may have been negligible, but there was something deeper, an intangible quality the two men shared. She knew she'd trust Lee every bit as much as she trusted Web. Of course, trust wasn't really the problem....

"Enough," Web was saying with a smile. "We'd better get things rolling here."

Marni barely had time to squeeze Lee's arm before Web was steering her off toward the changing rooms. Once again she was "done over," this time more aware of what was happening. She asked questions—how the hairstylist managed such a smooth sweep from her crown, what the makeup artist had done for her eyes to make them seem so far apart—but she was simply making conversation, perhaps in her way apologizing for having spoiled these people's efforts the week before. And diverting her mind from the worry that set in each time she looked at Web.

If the villain of the previous Tuesday had been the shock and pain of memory, now it was guilt. Marni saw Web's face, so open and encouraging, then the horror-filled ones of her parents when they learned she was seeing him again. She heard his voice, so gentle in instruction, then the harsh, bitter words of her family when they knew she was associating with the enemy.

Web tried different poses from the week before, used softer background music. He tried different lights and different cameras—the latter mostly on his tripod, which he could more easily manage, but in the end holding the camera in his hand with his splinted pinkie sticking straight out.

Halfway through the session, he called a break, shooing everyone else away after Marni had been given a cool drink.

"What do you think?" she asked hesitantly. The face she made suggested that she had doubts of her own but needed the reassurance. "Any better than last week?"

"Better than that, but still not what I want. It's a little matter of...this...spot." With his forefinger, he lightly stroked the soft skin between her brows. "No amount of makeup is going to hide the creases when you frown."

"But I thought I was smiling, or doing whatever it was you asked me to do."

"You were. But those little creases creep in there anyway. When I ask for a tiny smile, the overall effect is one of pleading. When I ask for a broad smile, you look like you're in pain. When I ask you to wet your lips and leave them parted, you look like you're holding your breath."

"I am," she argued, throwing up a hand in frustration. "I'm no good at this. I told you, Web. This isn't my thing."

She was leaning against the arm of a director's chair. He stood close by, looking down at her. "It can't be the crowd, because there's no crowd today. It can't be the music, or the posing. And it can't be shock. Not anymore.... You're worried about something. That's what the creases tell me."

"I'm worried that I'll never be able to give you what

you want, that you won't get your picture and you'll be disappointed and angry."

"Angry? Never. Disappointed? Definitely. But I'm not giving up yet. I'm going to get this picture, Marni. One way or another, I'm going to get it."

He spoke with such conviction, and went back to work with such determination, that Marni began to suspect he'd have her at it every day for a month, if that's what it took. She did her best to concentrate on relaxing her facial muscles, but found it nearly impossible. She'd get rid of the creases, but then her mouth would be wrong, or the angle of her head, or her shoulders.

The session ended not in a burst of tears as it had last time, but in sighs of fatigue from both her and Web. "Okay," he said resignedly as he handed his camera to one of his assistants, "we'll take a look at what we've got. There may be something." He ran his fingers through his hair. "God only knows I've exposed enough film."

Marni whirled around and stalked off toward the dressing room.

"Marni!" he called out, but she didn't stop. So he loped after her, enclosing them in the privacy of the small room. "What was that about? You walked out of there like I'd insulted you."

"You did." She removed the chunky beads from around her neck and put them on a nearby table. Two oversized bracelets soon followed. "You're disgusted with me. You never have to go through this with normal models. 'God only knows I've exposed enough film.' Did you have to say that, in that tone, for everyone in the room to hear?"

"It was a simple comment."

"It was an indictment."

"Then it was as much an indictment of me as it was of you. I'm the photographer! Half of my supposed skill is in drawing the mood and the look from a model!"

She was swiftly unbuttoning her blouse, heedless of Web's presence. "I'm the model. A rank amateur. You're the renowned photographer. If anyone's at fault, we both know who it is."

"Then you're angry at yourself, but don't lay that trip on me!"

"See? You agree!" She'd thrown the blouse aside and was fumbling with the waistband of her skirt. Her voice shook as she released the button and tugged down the zipper. "Well, I'm sorry if I've upset your normal pattern of success, but don't say I didn't warn you. Right from the beginning I knew this was a mad scheme. You need a *model*, an *experienced* model." She stumbled out of the skirt, threw it on top of the blouse, then grabbed for her own clothes and began to pull them on. "I can't be what you want, Web, no matter how much you want to think otherwise. I am what I am. I do what I do, and I do it well, and if there's baggage I carry—like little creases between my eyes—I can't help it." She'd stepped into her wool dress, but left it unbuttoned. Suddenly drained from her outburst, she lifted a hand to rub at those creases.

Web remained quiet. He'd reached the end of his own spurt of temper minutes ago and was simply waiting for her to calm down enough to listen to what he had to say. When she sighed and slumped into a nearby chair, he slowly approached and squatted beside her.

"Firstly, I'm not angry at you. If anything I'm angry

at me, because there's something I'm missing and I don't know how to get at it. Secondly, I'm not really angry, just tired." He flexed his unbound fingers. "My left hand is stiff because I'm not used to working this way." He put his hand down on her knee. "Thirdly, and most importantly, it *is* you I want. I'm not looking for something you're not. I'm not trying to make you into someone else. You're such a unique and wonderful person Marni—it's *that* that I'm trying to capture on film.... Look at me," he said softly, drawing her hand from her face. "You're right. It is much easier photographing a 'normal model,' but only because there isn't half the depth, because I can put there what I want. Creating a mood, a look, is one thing. Bringing out feeling, *individual* feeling is another. Don't you see? That's what's going to make this issue of *Class* stand out on the shelves. Not only are you beautiful to look at, but you'll have all those other qualities shining out from you. The potential reader of *Class* will say to herself, 'Hmmm, this looks interesting.'"

Marni was eyeing him steadily. Her expression had softened, taking on a glimmer of helplessness. He brushed the backs of his fingers against her cheek, thinking how badly he wanted to reach her, to soothe her.

"But what happened this morning," he went on in a whisper-soft tone, "what we've been arguing about in here is really secondary. You've got something on your mind that you haven't been able to shake. Share it with me, Marni. If nothing more, talking about it will make you feel better. Maybe I can help."

She only wished it were so. How could she say that she was falling in love with him again, but that her parents would never accept it? That they hated him, that she'd spent the last fourteen years of her life trying to make up for Ethan's death by being what he might have been if he'd lived, and that she didn't know if she had the strength to shatter her parents' illusion?

"Oh, Web," she sighed, slipping her arms over his shoulders and leaning forward to rest her cheek against his. "Life is so complicated."

He stroked her hair. "It doesn't have to be."

"But it is. Sometimes I wish I could turn the clock back to when I was seventeen and stop it there. Ethan would be alive, and you and I would be carrying on without a care in the world."

"We had cares. There was the problem of where to go so that we could be alone to love each other. And there was the problem of your parents, and what would happen if they found out about us."

Marni's arms tightened around him, and she rubbed her cheek against his jaw, welcoming the faint roughness that branded him man and so very different from her. She loved the smell of him, the feel of him. If only she could blot out the rest of the world...

"It's still a problem, isn't it, Marni?" She went very still, so he continued in the same gentle tone. "I'm no psychologist, but I've spent a lot of time thinking the past week, especially the past few days, about us and the future. Your parents despised me for what I was, and wasn't, and for what I'd done. They'd be a definite roadblock for us, wouldn't they?"

Just then a knock sounded at the door. Web twisted around and snapped, "Yes?"

The door opened, and a slightly timid Anne peered in. Uncomfortably, she looked from Web to Marni. "I'm sorry. I didn't mean to interrupt. I just wanted to know if there was anything I could do to help."

"No. Not just now," Marni said. "You can go back to the office. I'll be along later."

"I'll take a look at the contact sheets as soon as possible and let you know what I think," Web added quietly.

Anne nodded, then shut the door, at which point Web turned back to Marni.

She was gnawing on her lower lip. "Did you know that there was an article in the newspaper about the incident last Friday night?" she asked.

His jaw hardened. "Oh, yes. I got several calls from friends congratulating me on my heroism. Of all the things I'd like to be congratulated on, that isn't one. I could kick myself for not instructing the cops to leave our names off any report they might hand to the press. Neither of us needs that kind of publicity." He frowned. "You didn't mention the article when I spoke with you last night."

"I didn't know about it."

"Then…?"

"My mother called right after you did."

He blinked slowly, lifted his chin, then lowered it. He might have been saying, "Ahhhhhh, that explains it."

"If you can believe it, my sister Tanya brought it to her attention." Marni's voice took on a mildly hysterical note. "Neither of them made the connection, Web. Neither one of them associated Brian Webster, the photographer, with you."

"But you thought at first they might have," he surmised gently, "and it scared the living daylights out of you."

Apologetically Marni nodded, then slid forward in the chair and buried her face against his throat. Her thighs braced his waist, but there was nothing remotely sexual about the pose. "Hold me, Web. Just hold me...please?"

She sighed when he folded his arms around her, knowing in that instant that this would be all she needed in life if only the rest of humanity could fade away.

"Do you love me, Marni?" he asked hoarsely.

"I think I do," she whispered in dismay.

"And I love you. Don't you think that's a start?"

She raised her head. "You love me?"

"Uh-huh."

"When did you... You didn't before..."

He knew she was referring to that summer in Maine. "No, I didn't before. I was too young. You were too young. I didn't know where I was going, and the concept of love was beyond me."

"But when...?"

"Last weekend. After you left me, I realized that I didn't want anyone but you pushing aspirin down my throat."

She pinched his ribs, but she wasn't smiling. "Don't tease me."

"I'm not. No one's ever taken care of me before. I've always wanted to be strong and in command. But somehow being myself with you, being able to say that I'm tired or that I hurt, seemed right. Not that I want to do it all the time—I'm not a hypochondriac. But I want to be able to take care of you like you did me. TLC, and for the first time, the L means something."

Marni lowered her head and pressed closer to him, feeling the strong beat of his heart as though it and her own were all that existed. "I do love you, Web. The second time around it feels even stronger. If only...if only we could forget about everything else."

"We can."

"It's not possible."

"It is, for a little while, if we want."

She raised questioning eyes to his urgent ones.

"Come to Vermont with me this weekend. Just the two of us, alone and uninterrupted. We can talk everything out then and decide what to do, but most importantly we can be with each other. I think we need it. I think we deserve it.... What do you say?"

She sighed, feeling simultaneously hopeless and incredibly light-headed. "I say that it's crazy.... The whole thing's crazy, because the problems aren't going to go away...but how can I refuse?" A slow grin spread over her face, soon matched by his. He hugged her again, then kissed her. It was a sweet kiss, deep in emotion rather than physicality. When it ended, she clung to him for a long time. "I feel a little like I'm seventeen again and we've just arranged an illicit rendezvous. There's something exciting about stealing away, knowing my parents would be furious if they knew, but doing it all the same."

He took her face in his hands and spoke seriously. "We're adults now. Independent, consenting adults. In the end, it doesn't matter what your parents think, Marni."

Theoretically speaking, he was right, she knew. Idealistically she couldn't have agreed with him more. Practically speaking, though, it was a dream. But then, Web hadn't grown up in her house, with her parents. He hadn't gone into her family's business. He hadn't been in her shoes when Ethan had died, and he wasn't in her shoes now. "Later," she whispered. "We'll discuss it later. Right now, let's just be happy…"

MARNI WAS HAPPY. She blocked out all thoughts except one—that she loved Web and he loved her. And she was *very* happy. Business took her to Richmond on Wednesday morning, but she called Web that night, and he was at the airport to meet her when she returned on Thursday evening. Her suitcase had been emptied and repacked, and was waiting by her door when he came to pick her up late Friday afternoon.

"I hope you know I've shocked everyone at the office," she quipped, shrugging into her down jacket. "They've never known me to leave work so early."

He arched a brow. "Did you tell them where you were going?"

"Are you kidding? And spoil the sense of intrigue?"

Web was more practical. It wasn't that he wanted any interruptions during the weekend, but neither did he want the police out searching for her. "What if there's an emergency? What if someone needs to reach you and can't? Shouldn't you leave my number with someone?"

"Actually, I did. Just the number. With my administrative assistant. If anyone wants me that badly, they'll know to contact her. She'll be able to tell from the area code that I'm in Vermont, but that's about it."

Web was satisfied. He felt no fondness for her parents, but regardless of her age, they might worry if she seemed to have disappeared from the face of the earth. He knew that *he*'d be sick with worry if he tried to reach her and no one knew where she was.

"Good girl," was all he said before grabbing her suitcase and leading her to the waiting car.

The drive north was progressively relaxing. The tension of the day-to-day world, embodied by the congestion of traffic, thinned out and faded. Marni's excitement grew. Her eyes brightened, her cheeks took on a natural rosy glow. She had only to look to her left and see Web for her heart to feel lighter and lighter until she felt she was floating as weightlessly as those few snowflakes that drifted through the cold Vermont night air.

Web suggested that they stop for supplies at the village market near his house, so that they wouldn't have to go out again if the weather got bad. Marni was in full agreement.

"So where is your place?" she asked when they'd left the market behind. "I see houses and lots of condominium complexes—"

"They're sprouting up everywhere. Vacation resort areas, they're called. You buy your own place, then get the use of a central facility that usually includes a clubhouse, a restaurant or two, a pool, sometimes a lake or even a small ski slope. Not exactly my style, and I'm not thrilled with all the development. Pretty soon the place will be overrun with people. Fortunately where I am is off the beaten track."

"Where *are* you?"

He grinned and squeezed her knee. "Coming soon, sunshine. Be patient. Coming soon."

Not long after, he turned off the main road onto a smaller dirt one. The car jogged along, climbing steadily until at last they reached a clearing.

Marni caught her breath. "It's a log cabin," she cried in delight. "And you're on your own mountain!"

"Not completely on my own, but the nearest neighbor is a good twenty-minute trek through the trees."

He pulled into the shelter of an oversized carport on the far side of the house.

"This is great! What a change from the city!"

"That's why I like it." He turned off the engine and opened his door. "Come on. It'll be cold inside, but the heat'll come up pretty quickly."

"Heat? That *has* to be from an old Franklin stove."

He chuckled. "I'm afraid I'm more pampered than that. It's baseboard heating. But I do have a huge stone fireplace...if that makes you feel better."

"Oh, yes," she breathed, then quickly climbed from the car and tugged her coat around her. The air was dry, with a sharp nip to it. Snow continued to fall, but it was light, enchanting rather than threatening. Marni wondered if anything could threaten her at that moment. She felt bold and excited and happy.

She looked at Web and beamed. She was in love, and in this place, so far from the city, she felt free.

6

TO MARNI'S AMAZEMENT, what had appeared to be a log cabin was, from within, like no log cabin she'd ever imagined. Soon after Web had bought the place, he'd had it gutted and enlarged. Rich barnboard from ceiling to floor sealed in the insulation he'd added. The furniture was likewise of barnboard, but plushly cushioned in shades of hunter green and cocoa. Though there was a hall leading to the addition that housed Web's bedroom and a small den, all Marni saw at first was the large living area, with the kitchen and dining area at its far end. Oh, yes, there was a huge stone fireplace. But rather than being set into a wall as she'd pictured, it was a three-hundred-and-sixty-degree one with steel supports that would cast its warm glow over the entire room.

Like the apartment above Web's studio, there was a sparseness to the decor, a cleanness of line, though it was very clearly country rather than city, and decidedly cozy.

After Marni had admired everything with unbounded enthusiasm, she helped Web stow the food they'd bought. Then he opened a bottle of wine, poured them each a glass and led her to the living area, where he set to work building a fire. The kindling caught and burned, and the dried logs were beginning to flame when he came to sit beside her on the sofa, opening an arm in an invitation she accepted instantly.

"I'm so happy I'm here with you," she whispered, rubbing her cheek against the wool of his sweater as she snuggled close to him.

He tightened his arm and pressed a slow kiss to her forehead. "So am I. This has always been my private refuge. Now it's *our* private refuge, and nothing could seem righter."

She tipped her head back. "Righter? Is that a word?"

"It is now," he murmured, then lowered his head and took her lips in a slow, deep, savoring kiss that left Marni reeling. Dizzily she set her wine on the floor and shifted, with Web's eager help, onto his lap, coiling her arms around his neck, closing her eyes in delight as she brushed her cheek against his jaw.

"I love you," she whispered, "love you so much, Web."

He set his own wine down and framed her face with his hands. His mouth breezed over each of her features before renewing acquaintance with her mouth. A deep, moist kiss, a shift in the angle of his head, a second deep, moist kiss. The exchange of breath in pleasured sighs. The evocative play of tongues, tips touching, circling, sliding along each other's length.

Marni hadn't had more than a sip of her wine, but she was high on love, high on freedom. She was breathing shallowly, with her head resting on his shoulder, when he began to caress her. She held her breath, concentrating on the intensity of sensation radiating from his touch. He spread his large hands around her waist, moved them up over her ribs and around to her back in slow, sensitizing strokes.

"I love you, sunshine," he whispered hoarsely,

deeply affected by her sweet scent, her softness and warmth, her pliance, her emotional commitment. He brought his hands forward and inched them upward, covering her breasts, kneading them gently as she sighed against his neck.

Everything was in slow motion, unreal but exquisitely real. He caressed her breasts while she stroked the hair at his nape. He stroked her nipples while she caressed his back. They kissed again, and it was an exchange of silent vows, so deep and heartfelt that Marni nearly cried at its beauty.

"I was going to give you time," Web whispered roughly. His body was taut with a need he couldn't have hidden if he tried. "I was going to give you time…I hadn't intended an instant seduction."

"Neither had I," she breathed no less roughly. Her eyes held the urgency transmitted by the rest of her body. "I'm so pleased just to be here with you…but I want you…want to make love to you."

As much as her words inflamed him, he couldn't forget the last time they'd tried. "Are you sure? No doubts? Or guilt?"

She was shaking her head, very sure. "Not here. Not now." She pulled at his sweater. "Take this off. I want to touch you."

He whipped the sweater over his head, and she started working at the buttons of his shirt. When they were released, she spread the fabric wide, gave a soft sigh of relief and splayed her fingers over his hair-covered chest.

"You're so beautiful," she whispered in awe. Her hands moved slowly, exploring the sinewed swells of him, delving to the tight muscles of his middle before rising again and seeking the flat nipples nested amid whirls of soft, dark hair. She rubbed their tips until they stood hard, and didn't take her eyes from her work until Web forced her head up and hungrily captured her mouth.

His kiss left her breathless, and forehead to forehead they panted until at length he reached for the hem of her sweater and slowly drew it up and over her head. Slowly, too, he released one button, then the next, and in an instant's clear thought Marni reflected on the leisure of their approach. Fourteen years ago, when they'd come together for the first time, it had been in a fevered rush of arms and legs and bodies. Last Saturday the fever had been similar, as though they'd had to consummate their union before either of them had had time to think.

This time was different. They were in love. They were alone, in the cocoon of a cabin whose solid walls, whose surrounding forest warded off any and every enemy. This time there was a beauty in discovering and appreciating every inch of skin, every swell, every sensual conduit. This time it was heaven from the start.

Entranced, Marni watched as Web pushed her blouse aside. He unhooked her bra and gently peeled it from her breasts, then with a soft moan he very slowly traced her fullness, with first his fingertips, then the flat of his fingers, then his palm. She was swelling helplessly toward him, biting her lip to keep from crying out, when he finally took the full weight of her swollen flesh and molded his hands to it. His thumbs brushed over her nipples. Already taut, they puckered all the more, and she had to press her thighs together to still what was too quickly becoming a raging inferno.

Web didn't miss the movement. "Here..." He raised her for an instant, brought her leg around so that she straddled him, and settled her snugly against his crotch. With that momentary comfort, he returned his attention to her breasts.

"Web...Web..." she breathed. Her arms were looped loosely around his neck, her forehead hot against his shoulder. He was stroking her nipples again, and the action sent live currents through her body to her womb. Helplessly, reflexively, she began to slowly undulate her hips. "What you do to me—it's so...powerful...."

"It's what I feel for you, what you feel for me that makes it so good."

She was shaking her head in amazement. "I used to think it was good back then...because we do have this instant attraction...but I can't *believe* what...I'm feeling now."

"Then feel, sunshine." He slipped his hands to her shoulders and pushed her blouse completely off, then her bra. "I want you to feel this..." He cupped her breasts and brought them to his chest, rubbing nipple to nipple until she wasn't the only one to moan. "And this..." He sought her lips and kissed her hotly, while his fingers found the snap of her jeans, lowered the zipper and slid inside.

He was touching her then, opening her, stroking deeper and deeper until she was moving against his hand, taking tiny, gasping breaths, instinctively stretching her thighs apart in a need for more.

Her control was slipping, but she didn't want it to. She wanted the beauty to last forever, no, longer. Putting a shaky hand around Web's wrist, she begged him, "Please...I want to touch you, too...I need to..."

"But I want you to come," he said in a hushed whisper by her ear.

"This way, later. The first time—now—I want you inside. Please...take off your pants, Web..."

His fingers stopped their sweet torment and slowly, reluctantly, withdrew. He didn't move to take off his clothes until he'd kissed her so thoroughly that she thought she'd disintegrate there and then. But she didn't, and he shifted her from his lap, sat forward to rid himself of his shirt, then stood and peeled off the rest of his clothes. For a moment, just before lowering his jeans, he suddenly wished he hadn't been as adept at building that fire and that it was still pitch-black in the room. The last thing he wanted was to spoil the mood by having Marni see his scars. But they were there; he couldn't erase them, and if she loved him...

Marni sat watching, enthralled as more and more of his flesh was revealed. It was a long minute before she even saw his leg, so fascinated had she been with what else was now bare. But inevitably her gaze fastened on the multiple lines, some jagged, others straight, that formed a frightening pattern along the length of his right thigh.

"Web?" She caught her breath and, eyes filling with tears, looked up at him. "You didn't tell me... I didn't know...."

Quickly he knelt by her side and took both of her hands tightly in his. "Forget them, sweetheart. They're part of the past, and the past has no place here and now."

"But so many—"

"And all healed. No pain. No limp. Forget them. They don't matter." When she remained doubtful, he began to whisper kisses over her face. "Forget them," he breathed against her eyelids, then her lips. "Just love me...I need that more than anything..."

More than anything, that was what Marni needed, too. So she forgot. She pushed all thought of his scars and what had caused them from her mind. He was right. The past had no place here and now, and she refused to let it infringe on her present happiness. There would be a time to discuss scars she assured herself dazedly, but that time wasn't now, when the tender kisses he was raining over her face and throat, when the intimate sweep of his hands on her breasts was making clear thought an impossibility.

Her already simmering blood began to boil when he stood and reached for her hands to draw her up. She resisted, instead flattening her palms on his abdomen, moving them around and down. Gently, wonderingly, she encircled him and began a rhythmic stroking.

If he'd had any qualms about her reaction to his forty-year-old body, or fears that the sight of his leg would dull her desire, they were put soundly to rest by her worshipful ministration. He was digging his fingers into her shoulders by the time she leaned and pressed soft, wet kisses to his navel. Her hands, holding him, were between her breasts. Tucking in her chin, she slid her lips lower.

He was suddenly forcing her chin up, a pained smile on his face. "You don't play fair," he managed tightly. "I'm not made of stone."

"But I want you to—"

"This way, later," he whispered, repeating her earlier words. "For now, though, you were right..." When he reached for her hands this time, she stood, then with his help took off the rest of her clothes. They looked at each other, drenched in the pale orange glow of the fire. Then they came together, bare bodies touching for the first time in fourteen years, and it was so strangely new yet familiar, so stunningly electric yet right, that once again tears filled Marni's eyes and this time trickled down her cheeks.

Web felt them against his chest, and his arms tightened convulsively around her. "Oh, no..."

"Just joy, Web," she said as she laughed, then sniffled. "Tears of joy." She had her arms wrapped around his neck and held on while he lowered them both to the woven rug before the fire. Bracing himself on his elbows, he traced the curve of her lips with the tip of his tongue. She tried to capture him, but he eluded her, so she raised her head and tried again. Soon he was thrusting his tongue into her welcoming mouth, thrusting and retreating only to thrust again when she whimpered in protest at the momentary loss.

She welcomed the feel of his large body over hers. She felt sheltered, protected, increasingly aroused by everything masculine about him. Her hands skated over the corded swells of his back, glided to his waist and spread over his firm buttocks. She arched up to the hand he'd slipped between their bodies and offered him her breasts, her belly, the smoldering spot between her legs.

They touched and caressed, whispered soft words of love, of pleasure, of urging as their mutual need grew. It was as if nothing in the world could touch them but each other, as if that touch was life-giving and life-sustaining to the extent that their beings were defined by it. Web's lips gave form and substance to each of Marni's features, as his hands did to her every feminine curve. Her mouth gave shape and purpose to his, as her hands did to his every masculine line.

Finally, locked in each other's gaze, they merged fully. Web filled her last empty place, bowed his back and pressed even more deeply until he touched the entrance to her womb.

"I love you," he mouthed, unable to produce further sound.

The best she could do was to brokenly mouth the words back. Her breath seemed caught in her throat, trapped by the intensity of the moment. She'd never felt as much of a person, as much of a woman as she did now, with Web's masculinity surrounding her, filling her, completing her. Fourteen years ago they'd made love, and it had been breathtaking, too, but so different. Now she was old enough to understand and appreciate the full value of what she and Web shared. The extraordinary pleasure was emotional as well as physical, a total commitment on both of their parts to that precious quality of togetherness.

Web felt it, too. As he held himself still, buried deep inside Marni, he knew that he'd never before felt the same pleasure, the same satisfaction with another woman. The pleasure, the satisfaction, encompassed not only his body but his mind and heart as well, and the look of wonder on Marni's face told him the feeling was shared.

Slowly he began to move, all the while watching her. Waves of bliss flowed over her features as he thrust gently, then with increasing speed and force as she moved in tempo beneath him. The act he'd carried through so many times before seemed to have taken on an entirely new and incredible intimacy that added fuel to the flame in his combustive body.

Harder and deeper he plunged, his ardor matched by her increasing abandon. Before long they were both lost in a world of glorious sensation, a world that grew suddenly brilliant, then blinding. Marni caught her breath, arched up and was suspended for a long moment before shattering into paroxysms of mindless delight. The air left her lungs in choked spurts, but she was beyond noticing, as was Web, whose own body tensed, then jerked, then shuddered.

Only when the spasms had ended and his limbs grew suddenly weak did he collapse over her with a drawn-out moan. "Marni...my God! I've never... never..." He buried his face in the damp tendrils of hair at her neck and whispered, "I love you...so much..."

Marni was as limp and weak, but nothing could have kept the broad smile from her face. Words seemed inadequate, so she simply draped her arms over his shoulders, closed her eyes...and smiled on.

It was some time later before either of them moved, and then it was Web, sliding to her side, bringing her along to face him. He brushed the wayward fall of hair from her cheeks and let his hand lightly caress her earlobe.

"You give so much, so much," he whispered. "I almost feel as though I don't deserve it."

She pressed her fingers to his lips, then stroked them gently. "I could say the same to you."

He smiled crookedly. "So why don't you?"

"Because you know how I feel."

"Tell me anyway. My ego needs boosting, since the rest of me is totally deflated."

She grinned, but the grin mellowed into a tender smile as she spoke. "You're warm and compassionate, incredibly intelligent and sensitive. And you're sexy as hell."

"Not right now."

"Yes, right now." She raked the hair from his brow

and let her fingers tangle in its thickness. "Naked and sweaty and positively gorgeous, you'd bring out the animal in me—" she gave a rueful chuckle "—if I had the strength."

"S'okay," he murmured, rolling to his back and drawing her against him, "a soft, purring kitten is all I can handle right about now. You exhaust me, sunshine, inside and out."

"The feeling's mutual, Brian Webster," she sighed, but it was a happy sigh, in keeping with the moment.

They lay quietly for a time, listening to the beat of each other's heart, the lazy cadence of their breathing, the crackling of the fire behind them.

"It's funny, hearing you call me that," he mused, rubbing his chin against her hair. "Brian. It sounds so formal."

"Not formal, just…strange. I keep trying to picture your mother calling you that when you were a little boy. 'Brian! Come in the house this minute, Brian!' When did they start calling you Web?"

"My mother never did, or my stepfather, for that matter. But the kids in school—you know how kids are, trying to act tough calling each other by their last names, then when they're a little older finding nicknames that fit. Web just seemed to fit. By the time I'd graduated from high school, I really thought of myself as Web."

"Did you consciously decide to revert to Brian when you got into photography?"

"It was more a practical thing at that point. I had to sign my name to legal forms—model releases, magazine contracts, that kind of thing. People started calling me Brian." He gave a one-shouldered shrug. "So Brian I became. Again."

"We'll call our son Brian."

He jerked his head up and stared at her. "Our son?"

She put her fingers back on his lips. "Shhh. Don't say another word. This is a dream weekend, and I'm going to say whatever I feel like saying without even thinking of 'why' or 'if' or 'how.' I intend to give due consideration to every impulse that crosses my mind, and the impulse on my mind at this particular moment is what we'll name our son. Brian. I do like it."

Once over the initial shock of Marni's blithe reference to "our son," Web found that he liked her impulsiveness. He grinned. "You're a nut. Has anyone ever told you that?"

"No. No one. I'm not usually prone to nuttiness. You do something to my mind, Web. Or maybe log cabins do something to me. Or mountains."

He propped himself on an elbow and smiled down at her. "Tell me more. What other impulses would you like to give due consideration to?"

"Dinner. I'm starved. Maybe *that*'s why I'm momentarily prone to nuttiness. I didn't eat lunch so I could leave the office that much earlier, and I can't remember breakfast, it was that long ago. I think I'm running on fumes."

Web nuzzled her neck. "I love these fumes. Mmmm, do I love these fumes."

Light-headed and laughing, Marni clung to him until, with a final nip at her neck, he hauled himself to his feet and gave her a hand up. He cleared his throat. "Dinner. I think I could use it, too." He ran his eyes the length of her flushed and slender body. "Did you bring a robe?"

"Uh-huh."

"Think you could get it?"

"Uh-huh."

"...Well?"

She hadn't moved. Her eyes were on his leanly muscled frame. "Have *you* got one?"

"Uh-huh."

"Think you could get it?"

"Uh-huh."

"...Well?"

Their gazes met then, and they both began to smile.
If they'd been back in New York, they'd probably have
made love again there and then, lest they lose the opportunity. But they were in Vermont, with the luxury
of an entire weekend before them. There was something to be said for patience, and anticipation.

With a decidedly male growl, Web dragged her to
his side and started off toward the bedroom, where
he'd left their bags. Moments later, dressed in terry velour robes that were coincidentally similar in every respect but color—Web's was wine, Marni's white—they
set to the very pleasant task of making dinner together.
When Web opted out of chores such as slicing toma-
toes and mushrooms for a salad, claiming that he was
hampered by his injured hand, Marni mischievously
remarked that his injured hand hadn't hampered his
amorous endeavors. When Marni opted out of putting
a match to the pilot light of the stove, claiming that she
didn't like to play with fire, Web simply arched a dev-
ilish brow in silent contradiction.

They ate by the fire, finishing the wine they'd barely
sipped earlier. Then, leaving their dishes on the floor
nearby, they made sweet, slow love again. This time
each touched and tasted the spots that had been denied
earlier; this time they both reached independent peaks
before their bodies finally joined. The lack of urgency

that resulted made the coming together and the leisurely climb and culmination all the more meaningful. Though their bodies would give out in time, they knew, their emotional desire was never-ending.

After talking, then listening to soft music for a while as they gazed into the fire, they finally retired to Web's big bed. When they fell asleep in each other's arms, they felt as satisfied as if they'd made love yet again.

Saturday was a sterling day, one to be remembered by them both for a long time to come. They slept late, awoke to make love, then devoured a hearty brunch in the kitchen. Though the snow had stopped sometime during the night, the fresh inch or two on top of the existing crust gave a crispness, a cleanness to the hilly woodlands surrounding the cabin.

Bundled warmly against the cold, they took a long walk in the early afternoon. It didn't matter that Marni couldn't begin to make out a path; Web knew the woods by heart, and she trusted him completely.

"So beautiful..." Her breath was a tiny cloud, evaporating in the dry air as she looked around her. Tall pines towered above, their limbs made all the more regal by the snowy epaulets they wore. Underfoot the white carpet was patterned, not only by the footprints behind them and the tracks of birds and other small forest creatures, but by the swish of low-hanging branches in the gentle breeze and the fall of powdery clumps from branches. The silence was so reverent across the mountainside that she felt intrusive even when she murmured in awe, "Don't you wish you had a camera?"

It had been a totally innocent question, an unpremeditated one. Realizing the joke in it, Marni grinned up at Web. "That was really dumb. You *do* have a camera...cameras. I'd have thought you'd be out here taking pictures of everything."

He smiled back at her, thoroughly relaxed. "It's too peaceful."

"But it's beautiful!"

"A large part of that beauty is being here with you."

She gave a playful tug at the arm hers was wrapped around. "Flattery, flattery—"

"But I'm serious. Look around you now and try to imagine that you were alone, that we didn't have each other, that you were here on the mountain running away from some horrible threat or personal crisis.... How would you feel?"

"Cold."

"Y'see? People see things differently depending on where they're coming from. Right now I'm exactly where I want to be. I don't think I've ever felt as happy or content in my life. So you're right, this scene is absolutely beautiful."

Standing on tiptoe, she kissed his cheek, then tightened her arm through his. "Do you ever photograph up here?"

He shrugged. "I don't have a camera up here."

"You're kidding."

"Nope. This is my getaway. I knew from the first that if I allowed myself to bring a camera here, it wouldn't be a true escape."

"But you love photography, don't you?"

"I love my work, but photography in and of itself has never become an obsession with me. I've met some colleagues, both men and women, whose cameras are like dog tags around their necks. It gives them their identity. I've never wanted that. The camera is the tool of my trade, much like a calculator or computer is for an accountant, or a hammer is for a carpenter. Have you ever seen a carpenter go away for the weekend with his tool belt strapped around his waist just in case he sees a nail sticking out on someone's house or on the back wall of a restaurant?"

Marni grinned. "No, I guess I haven't.... Why are you looking at me that way?"

"You just look so pretty, all bundled up and rosy-cheeked. You look as happy and content as I feel. I almost wish I did have a camera, but I'm not sure I could begin to capture what you are. Some things are better left as very special images in the mind." He grew even more pensive.

"What is it?" she asked softly.

"Impulse time. Can I do it, too?"

"Sure. What's your impulse?"

"To photograph you out here in the woods. In the summer. Stark naked."

She quivered in excitement. "That's a naughty impulse."

"But that's not all." His blue eyes were glowing. "I'd like to photograph you in bed right after we've made love. You're all rosy-cheeked then too, and naked, but bundled up in love."

She draped her arms over his shoulders. "Mmmm. I like that one."

"But that's not all."

"There's more?"

"Uh-huh." His arms circled her waist. "I'd like to photograph you in bed right after we've made love. You're naked and rosy and wrapped in love. And you're pregnant. You're breasts are fuller, with tiny veins running over them, and your belly is round, the skin stretched tightly, protectively over our child."

Marni sucked in her breath and buried her face against the fleece lining of his collar. "That's... beautiful, Web."

"But that's not all."

She gave a plaintive moan. "I'm not sure I can take much more of this. My legs feel like water."

"Then I'll support you." True to his words, he tightened his arms around her. "I'd like to photograph you with our child at your breast. It could be a little Brian, or a little girl named Sunshine or Bliss or Liberty—"

She looked sharply up in mock rebuke. "You wouldn't."

"Wouldn't photograph you breast-feeding our child? You bet your sweet—"

"Wouldn't name the poor thing Sunshine or Bliss or Liberty. Do you have any idea what she'd go through, saddled with any one of those names?"

"Then you choose the name. Anything your heart desires."

Marni thought for a minute. "I kind of like Alana, or Arielle, or Amber—no, not Amber. It doesn't go well with Webster."

"You're partial to *A*'s?"

She tipped up her chin. "Nope. Just haven't gotten to the *B*'s yet."

She never did get to the *B*'s because he hugged her, and she was momentarily robbed of breath. When he released her long enough to loop his arm through hers again and start them along the path once more, he was thinking of things besides children. "We could keep your place if you'd like. Mine above the studio wouldn't be as appropriate for the entertaining you have to do."

"I don't know about that. It might spice things up. If

we were really doing something big, we could use the studio itself, or rent space at a restaurant. I think I'd like the idea of knowing you'd be there whenever I came home from work."

"Would you have to travel much?"

"I could cut it down."

"I'd feel lonely when you were away."

"Maybe you could come." Her eyes lit up. "I mean, if I knew far enough in advance so that you could re-arrange your schedule, we could take care of my busi-ness and have a vacation for ourselves."

"With Brian or Arielle or whoever?"

"By ourselves. Two adults doing adult things. We'd leave the baby with a sitter.... Uh-oh, that could be one drawback about living above your studio. You wouldn't get much work done with a squalling baby nearby."

"Are you kidding? I'd love it! I mean, we would hire someone to take care of the baby, and no baby of ours is going to be squalling all the time. I'd be able to see him or her during breaks or when the sitter was pass-ing through the studio going out for walks. I'd be proud as punch to show off my child. And I'd be right there in case of any problem or emergency."

"But you shoot on location sometimes."

"Less and less in the last year or so, and I've reached the stage where I could cut it out entirely if I wanted to. Just think of it. It'd be an ideal situation." His cheeks were ruddy, and his blue eyes sparkled.

"You really mean that, don't you?"

"You bet. I never knew my own father. I want to know my children and have them know me."

"Child*ren*? Oh, boy, how many are we having?"

"Two, maybe three. More if you'd like, but I'd hate

to think of your being torn between your work and a whole brood of kids. I'm told that working mothers suffer a certain amount of guilt even with one child."

He was right, but she couldn't resist teasing him. "Who told you that?"

He shrugged. "I read."

"What?"

"Oh...lots of things."

She couldn't contain a grin. His cheeks were a dead giveaway, suddenly redder in a way that couldn't be from the cold. "Women's magazines?"

"Hell, my photographs are in them. Okay, sometimes one article or another catches my eye."

"And how long have you been reading about working mothers?"

"One article, Marni, that's it. It was—I don't know— maybe six or seven months ago."

"Did you know then that you wanted to have kids?"

"I've known for a long time, and when I read the article it was simply to satisfy an abstract curiosity." Smoothly, and with good humor, he took the offensive. "And you should be grateful that I *do* read. I'm thinking of you, sweet. Anything I've learned will make things easier for you."

"I'm not worried," she hummed, with a smile on her face.

They continued to walk, neither of them bothered by the cold air, if even aware of it. They were wrapped up in their world of dreams, a warm world where the sun was shining brightly. They talked of what they'd do in their leisure time, where they'd travel for vacations, what their children might be when they grew up.

The mood continued when they returned to the cabin. Marni sat on a barrel in the carport watching

Web split logs for the fire. He sat on a stool in the kitchen watching her prepare a chicken-and-broccoli casserole. They sat by the fire talking of politics, the economy and foreign affairs, dreaming on, kissing, making love. Arms and legs entwined, they slept deeply that night—a good thing, because Sunday morning they awoke with the knowledge that before the day was through they'd be back in the real world facing those problems neither of them had been willing to discuss before.

Web lay in bed, staring at the ceiling. Marni was in a nearly identical position by his side. They'd been awake for a while, though neither had spoken. A thick quilt covered them, suddenly more necessary than it had seemed all weekend, for now they were thinking of an aspect of the future that was chilling to them both.

"What are we going to do about your parents, Marni?" Web asked. He'd contemplated approaching the topic gradually, but now he saw no point in beating around the bush.

She didn't twist her head in surprise, or even blink. "I don't know."

"What will they say if you announce that we're getting married?"

"Married. Funny...we haven't used that word before."

He tipped his head to look at her. "It was taken for granted, wasn't it?"

She met his gaze and spoke softly. "Yes."

"And you want it, don't you?"

"Yes."

"So—" his gaze drifted away "—what will they say?"

"They'll hit the roof."

He nodded, then swallowed. "How will you feel about that?"

"Pretty sick."

"It bothers you what they think?"

"Of course it does. They're my parents."

"You're not a child. You're old enough to make your own decisions."

"I know that, and I do make my own decisions every day of the week. This, well, this is a little tougher."

"Many adults have differences with their parents."

"But there are emotional issues here, very strong emotional issues."

"They blame me for Ethan's death."

"They blame you for everything that happened that summer."

"But mostly for Ethan's death." He sat up abruptly and turned to her, feelings he'd held in for years suddenly splintering outward. "Don't they know it was an accident? Those two cars collided and began spinning all over the road. There was no possible way I could have steered clear. Hell, we were wearing helmets, but a motorcycle didn't have any more of a chance against either of those monsters than Ethan's neck had against that tree."

Marni was lying stiffly, determined to say it all now. "It was your motorcycle. They felt that if Ethan had been with anyone else he would have been in a car and survived."

Frustrated, Web thrust his fingers through his hair. "I didn't force Ethan to come with me. For that matter, I didn't force Ethan to become my friend."

"But you were friends. My parents blame that on you, too."

"They saw their son as wasting his time with a no-good bum like me. Well, they were wrong, damn it! They were wrong! My friendship with Ethan was good for *both* of us. Ethan got a helluva lot more from me than he was getting from those other guys he hung around with, and I got more from him than you could ever believe. My, God! He was my friend! Do you think I wasn't crushed by his death?"

Tears glistened on his lower lids. Marni saw them and couldn't look away. She wanted to hold him, to comfort him, but at the moment there was a strange distance between them. She was a Lange. She was one of *them*.

"Y'know, Marni," he began in a deep voice that shook, "I lay in that hospital room bleeding on the inside long after they'd stitched me up on the outside. I hurt in ways no drug could ease. Yes, I felt guilty. It was my motorcycle, and I was driving, and if I'd been going a little faster or a little slower we would have missed that accident and been safe.... I called your father from the hospital. Did you know that?"

Eyes glued to his, she swallowed. "No."

"Well, I did. The day after the accident, when I'd been out from under the anesthetic long enough to be able to lift the phone. It was painful, lifting that phone. I had three cracked ribs, and my thigh was shattered into so many pieces that it had taken five hours of surgery to make some order out of it—and that's not counting the two operations that followed. But nothing, *nothing* I felt physically could begin to compare with the pain your father inflicted on me. He didn't ask how I was, didn't stop to think that I was hurting or that I was torn up by the knowledge that Ethan had died and I was alive. No, all he asked was whether I was satisfied, whether I was pleased I'd destroyed a life that would have been so much more meaningful, so much more productive than mine had ever been or could be."

An anger rose in Marni, so great that she could no longer bear the thought of presenting her parents' side of the story. She sat up and moved to Web, her own eyes flooding as she curled her hands around his neck. "He had no right to say that! It *wasn't* your fault! I told him that over and over again, but he wouldn't listen to me. I was an irresponsible seventeen-year-old who'd been stupid to have been involved with you, he said. That showed how much *I* knew."

Web dragged in a long, shaky breath. He was looking at her, but not actually seeing her. His vision was on the past. "I cried. I lay there holding the phone and cried. The nurse finally came in and took it out of my hand, but I kept on crying until I was so tired and in so much pain that I just couldn't cry anymore."

She brushed at the moisture in the corners of his eyes, though his face was blurred to her gaze. "I'm so sorry, Web," she whispered. "So sorry. He was wrong, and cruel. There was nothing you could have done to prevent that accident. It wasn't your fault!"

"But I felt guilty. I still do."

"What about me?" she cried. "If it hadn't been for me—for my pestering the two of you to take me along—you would have been in Ethan's car as you'd originally planned. Don't you think that's haunted me all these years? I tried to tell that to my father, too, because it hurt so much when he put the full blame on you, but he wouldn't listen. All he could think of was that Ethan, his only son and primary heir, was gone.

And my mother seconded everything he said, especially when he forbade me to see you again."

"What about Tanya? Didn't she come to your defense?"

"Tanya, who'd been itching for you from the first moment she knew we were involved with each other? No, Tanya didn't come to my defense. She told my mother everything she knew, about the times I'd said I was out with friends but was actually out with you. She was legitimately upset about Ethan, I have to say that much for her. But she did nothing to help me through what was a double devastation. She sided with my parents all the way."

Marni hung her head. Tears stained her cheeks, and her hands clutched Web's shoulders for the solace that his muscled strength could offer. "I wanted to go to you, Web." Her voice was small and riddled with pain. "I kept thinking of you in that hospital, even when we returned to Long Island for the funeral. I wanted to go back to Maine to see you, because I needed to know you were okay and I needed your comfort. You'd meant so much to me that summer. I'd been in love with you, and I felt that you might be the only one to help me get over Ethan's death."

"But they wouldn't let you come."

"They said that if I made any move to contact you, they'd disinherit me. That if I tried to see you, they'd know that they'd failed as parents."

He smoothed her hair back around her ears, then said softly, "I waited. I was hoping you'd come, or call, because I thought maybe you could make me feel a little better about what had happened. I was in that godforsaken small-town hospital for two months—"

"How could I go against them?" she cried, trying

desperately to justify what she'd done. "Regardless of how wrong they were about you, they were grief-stricken over Ethan. It wasn't the threat of being disinherited that bothered me. It wasn't a matter of money. But they'd given me everything for seventeen years. You'd given me other things, but for barely two months." She took a quick breath. "You said that you thought I was headstrong in my way even then, but I wasn't really, Web. I couldn't stand up for something I wanted. I'd already disappointed my parents. I couldn't do it again. They were going through too rough a time. Dad was never the same after the accident."

Web's expression had softened, and his voice was tinged with regret. "None of us were. That accident was the turning point in my life." His words hung, heavy and profound, in the air for a minute. Then he turned, propped the pillows against the headboard and settled Marni against him as he leaned back. "My leg kept getting infected and wouldn't heal, so I was transferred to a place in Boston. The specialist my stepfather found opened the whole thing up and practically started from scratch again, and between that and a second, less extensive operation, I was hospitalized for another six weeks. I had lots of time to think. Lots of time.

"Ethan and I, I realized, each represented half of an ideal world. He had financial stability, but though many of the things he had told me about in those hours we spent together sounded wonderful, they didn't come free. I had freedom and a sense of adventure, but without roots or money I was limited as to what I could do in life. As I lay there, I thought a lot about my father and about why I'd been running, and it was then I realized I wanted something more in life. Your parents thought I was dirt, and I felt like it after the accident. But I didn't want to be dirt. I wanted to be *someone*, not just a jock moving from job to job and place to place." He stroked her arm as though needing to reassure himself that he'd found a measure of personal stability at last.

"What happened to Ethan made me think about my own mortality," he went on in a solemn voice. "If I'd died then and there, no one—well, other than my immediate family—would have missed me, and it was questionable as to whether they'd really miss me, since I'd never been around all that much." He took a deep breath. "So I hooked onto that dig in New Mexico. It was the first time I'd ever done something with an eye toward the future. By the time I realized I'd never make it as a writer, my pictures were selling. I was on my way. I don't think anything could have stopped me from pushing ahead full steam at that point."

Marni, who'd been listening quietly, raised her face to his. "You've done Ethan proud. He gave you the motivation, and you worked your way up from scratch to become very successful."

Web was studying her tenderly. "And what about you? You've done much of what you have for him, too, haven't you?"

"For him...and my parents." She rushed on before he could argue. "I grieved so long after the accident, for both Ethan and you, and the sadness and guilt I felt were getting me nowhere. I decided that the only way I could redeem myself was to make my parents proud of me. Yes, I've tried to fill Ethan's shoes. I'm sure I haven't done it in the same way he would have, but I do think I've filled a certain void for my parents. After

Ethan's death, Dad began to lose interest in the business. My decision to enter it was like a shot in the arm for him. Of course shots wear off after a while, and he eased away from the corporation earlier than he might have, but by then I was trained and ready to take over."

"You felt you were making up to your parents for having played a small part in Ethan's death."

Her whispered "Yes" was barely audible, but a shudder passed through Web, and he held her tightly to him.

"We've both suffered. We paid the fine for what we'd done, or thought we'd done, but the suffering isn't over if your parents are going to stand between us." They'd come full stride. "What are we going to do about them, Marni?"

"I don't know," she murmured, teeth gritted against the helplessness that assailed her. "I don't know."

"We'll have to tell them. We'll have to present ourselves and our best arguments to them—"

"Not 'we.' It'd never work that way, Web. They'd never listen. Worse, they'd kick you out of the house. It'd be better if I spoke with them first. I could break it to them gently."

"God, it's like we've committed some kind of crime."

"In their minds we have. What I've done will be tantamount to treason in their minds."

"They'll just have to change their way of thinking."

"That's easier said than done."

"What other choice will they have? They can't very well kick their own grown-up daughter out of the house. And then there's the matter of the corporation presidency. Your father may be chairman of the board, but no board worth its salt is going to evict its president simply because she falls in love with someone her father doesn't like. You've done a good job, Marni. You're invaluable to the corporation."

"Not invaluable. Certainly not indispensable. But I'm not really worried about anything happening at work. Dad wouldn't go *that* far. What I fear most is what will happen at home. Ethan's death left a gaping hole. Every time the family got together, we were aware of his absence. If Mom and Dad push us away because of my relationship with you, the unit will be that much weaker. If they could only reconcile themselves to gaining a son, rather than losing a daughter..."

"Reconcile. A powerful word."

Marni was deep in thought. "Mmmm.... What if I break it to them gently? Mother hasn't made the connection between you and that other Web. Apparently neither has Dad, since he didn't make a peep over the plans to use you as cover photographer for *Class*. What if I were to tell them that we were dating, that I was seeing the photographer and that we were pretty serious about each other?"

"They'd want to meet me. One look and they'd know."

"We could stall them. After all, I'm busy, and so are you, which would make it hard to arrange a meeting. In the meantime I could tell them all about Brian Webster, show them examples of your work and snow them with lists of your credits. I could create a picture in their minds of everything you are and everything you mean to me."

"And they won't ask about my background?" He knew very well they would.

"I could fudge it, be as vague as I like. Then, when they've got this super image in their minds, when they're as favorably inclined as possible, I could tell them the rest."

He raised her chin with his forefinger. "A super image can shatter with a few short words. What if, in spite of the advance hype, they go off the deep end?"

His eyes were a mirror of hers. Marni saw there the same trepidation, the same worry that was making her insides knot. "Then I'll have to make a choice," she said at last.

The trepidation, the worry were transferred to his voice, which came out in a tremulous whisper. Once before Marni had had a choice to make, and she'd made it in favor of her family. Web felt that his very life was on the line. "What will you choose?" he asked in a raw whisper.

Neither her eyes, lost in his, nor her voice faltered. "You're my future, Web. I'm grateful for everything they've given me, and I do love them, but you're my future. The love I feel for you is so strong that there's really no choice at all."

Web closed his eyes. His sigh fanned her brow, and his arms tightened convulsively around her. "Oh, baby..." He said nothing more but held her, rocking her, savoring the moment, the joy, the intense relief he felt.

Inevitably, though, the ramifications of what she'd said loomed before him. "It's going to be hard. You'll be upset."

"Yes. It's sad that I have to risk alienating them by telling them that I'm—"

"—marrying the guy who killed their son."

Her head shot up, eyes flashing in anger. "You *didn't* kill Ethan. Don't ever say that again!"

He felt compelled to prepare her. "They'll say it."

"And they'll be wrong again. They may have used you for a scapegoat that summer, they may be doing it still, and I suppose it's only natural that parents try to find someone to blame, some reason to explain a tragedy like that. But, damn it, you've been their scapegoat long enough!"

"You're apt to take over that role, if it comes down to an estrangement."

"Oh, Web, Web, let's not assume the worst until we come to it...please?"

THEY LEFT THE DISCUSSION on that pleading note, but the rest of the day was nowhere near as carefree as the day before had been. They breakfasted, walked again through the woods, packed their bags and closed up the house, all the while struggling to elude the dark cloud hovering overhead.

An atmosphere of apprehension filled the car during the drive back to the city. Web clutched her hand during most of the trip, knowing the dread she was feeling and in turn being swamped by helplessness and frustration. At the door of her apartment, he hugged her with a kind of desperation.

"I'm so afraid of losing you, sunshine...so afraid. I was a fool fourteen years ago for not realizing what I had, but I'm not a fool anymore. I'm going to fight, Marni. I'm going to fight, if it's the last thing I do!"

Those words, and the love behind them, were to be a much-needed source of strength for Marni in the days to come.

7

MARNI HAD HAD every intention on Monday of calling her mother about the wonderful weekend she'd had with Brian Webster, but she didn't seem to find the time. When, as prearranged, Web came to take her to dinner that night, she explained that something had come up in the computer division, demanding her attention for most of the day. She'd had little more than a moment here or there to think of making the call.

On Tuesday it was a problem with the proposed deal in Richmond, one she thought she'd ironed out when she'd gone down there the week before. On Wednesday it was a lawsuit, filed against the corporation's publishing division by one of its authors.

"You're hedging," Web accused when he saw her that night.

"I'm not! These things came up, and I need a free mind when I call her."

"Things are always coming up. It's the nature of your work. You can put off that call forever, but it's not going to solve our problem."

"Speaking of problems, what are we going to do about the cover of *Class*?" She knew the second batch of pictures had been better than the first, but that Web was still not fully satisfied.

"You're changing the subject."

"Maybe, but it is a problem, and we both do have a deadline on that one."

"We've got a deadline on both, if you look at it one way. The longer you put off breaking the news about us to your parents, the longer it'll be before we can get married."

"I know," she whispered, looking down at the fingernail she was picking. "I know."

Web knew she was torn, that she loved him and wanted to marry him, but that she was terrified of what her parents' reaction was going to be. He sympathized, but only to a point.

"I'll make a deal with you," he sighed. "I'll study all the proofs and decide what to do about them, if you call your mother.... Sound fair?"

"Of course it's fair," she snapped. He was right. She was only prolonging the inevitable. "I'll call her tomorrow."

SHE DID BETTER than that. Fearful that she'd lose her nerve when the time came, she called her mother that night and invited her to lunch. It was over coffee and trifle, the latter barely touched on her plate, that Marni broached the subject.

"Mother, do you remember that photographer I was with that night we witnessed the assault?"

Adele Lange, a slender woman with a surprisingly sweet tooth, was relishing every small forkful of wine-soaked sponge cake, fruit, nuts and whipped cream that made up the trifle. She held her fork suspended. "Of course I remember." She smiled. "He's the famous one everyone knows about but me."

Marni forced her own smile as she launched into the

speech she'd mentally rehearsed so many times. "Well, we've been dating. I think it's getting serious."

Adele stared at her, then set down her fork. "But I thought you said it was a business thing."

"It started out that way, but it's evolved into something more." So far, the truth. Marni kept her chin up.

"Marni! It's been—how long—a week since that incident? How many times could you have seen this man to know that it's getting serious?"

"I'm thirty-one, Mom. I know."

"Does he? Remember what I told you about photographers?"

"You're hung up on the stereotype. You've never met Brian."

"Then tell me. What's he like?" Slowly Adele returned to her trifle, but she was clearly distracted.

"He's tall, dark and handsome, for starters."

"Aren't they all?"

"No. Some are squat and wiry-haired—"

"And wear heavy gold jewelry, have their eyes on every attractive woman in sight and can't make it through a sentence without a 'darling' or 'sweetie' or 'babe.'"

Marni grinned. "Brian doesn't use any of those words. He doesn't wear any jewelry except a watch, which is slim and unobtrusive, and he may have the same appreciation that any other man his age has for a beautiful woman, but he's never looked at another woman the way he looks at me." Nicely put, Marni thought, almost poetic. She'd have to remember that one.

"How old is he?"

"Forty."

"And he's never married?"

"No."

"That's something strange to think about. Why hasn't he married? A man who's got looks and a name for himself...maybe he's queer."

If Marni had had a mouthful of coffee, she would have choked on it. It was all she could do to keep a straight face. "Would he be interested in me if he was?"

Adele's lips twitched downward in disdain. "Maybe he goes both ways."

"He doesn't. Take my word for it."

"And you take his word that he doesn't have an ex-wife or two to support?"

"He's never been married," Marni stated unequivocally, then took a sip of her coffee. She knew her mother. The questions were just beginning. She only wished they would all be as amusing.

"Where does he come from?"

"Pennsylvania, originally."

Adele took another tiny forkful of trifle. "What about his parents?"

"His mother is dead. His father is an insurance broker." She'd anticipated the question and had thought about the answer she'd give. To say "stepfather" would only be to invite questions. Web had never known his biological father, hence Marni felt justified in responding as she did.

Adele was chewing and swallowing each bit of information along with the trifle. "How long has he been a photographer?"

"He's been at it since his mid-twenties."

"I assume, given the reputation Tanya claims he has, that he earns a good living."

"What kind of a question is that, Mother?"

"It's a mother's kind of question."

"I'm an independent adult. I earn a more than comfortable salary for myself. Why should it matter what W—what Brian earns?" The sudden skip of her heart hadn't been caused by her indignation. She'd nearly slipped. Brian was a safe name; Web was not. She'd have to be more careful.

Adele scolded her gently. "Don't get upset, darling. For the first time in your adult life, you've told me that you're serious about a man. Your father and I have waited a long time for this. It's only natural that we be concerned about whether he's right for you. Realistically speaking, you're a wealthy woman. We wouldn't want to think that some man was interested in you for your money."

Farcical. That was what it was, and Marni couldn't help but laugh. "No, Brian is *not* interested in my money. Not that it matters, but he's far from being a pauper. He has an extremely lucrative career, he owns the building that houses his studio and his apartment and he's got a weekend home on acres of woodland in Vermont." She hesitated, wondering just how much to say, then decided to throw caution aside. "We were there last weekend. It's beautiful."

Adele's eyes widened fractionally, and she pursed her lips, but said nothing about Marni's having spent the weekend with her photographer. Marni was, after all, thirty-one, and these were modern times. It was too much to expect that her daughter was still a virgin. "Vermont. A little…backwoodsy, isn't it?"

Marni rolled her eyes. "Vermont has become the vacation place of most of New York, or hadn't you noticed? Some of the finest and wealthiest have second homes there. Times have changed, Mother. It doesn't have to be Camden, or South Hampton, or Newport anymore."

"I know that, darling," Adele said gruffly. She scowled at what was left of her dessert, then abandoned it in favor of her coffee.

"I want you to be *pleased*," Marni said softly. "Brian is a wonderful man. He's interesting and fun to be with, he's serious about his work and he respects mine, and he treats me like I'm the best thing that's ever happened to him."

"I am pleased. I just want to make sure you know what you're doing before you get in over your head."

Marni might have said that she was already in over her head, but it wouldn't have served her purpose. "I know what I'm doing," she said with quiet conviction. "I'm happy. That's the most important thing...don't you think?"

"Of course, dear. Of course.... So, when will we be able to meet this photographer of yours?"

"Soon."

"When?"

"When I get up the courage to bring him out."

"Courage? Why would you need courage?"

"Because you and Dad can be intimidating in the best of circumstances. I'm not sure I'm ready to inflict you on Brian yet." Her words had been offered in a teasing tone and accompanied by a gentle smile. Adele was totally unaware of the deeper sentiment behind them.

"Very funny, Marni. We don't bite you know."

"You could send Brian running if you grill him the way you've grilled me. No man likes to have his background, his social standing and his financial status probed."

"Social standing. We haven't even gotten into that."

"No need. He's well-liked and respected, he's the good friend of many well-placed people and he chews with his mouth closed."

"That's a relief," was Adele's sardonic retort. "I wouldn't want to think you were going with some crude oaf."

"Brian can hold his own with any crowd. He'll charm your friends to tears."

"Well, *your father and I* would like to meet him before we introduce him to our friends. Why don't you bring him out to the house on Sunday?"

Marni shook her head. "We're not up to a showing just yet."

"If you're so afraid that we'll scare the man off, maybe you're not so sure about him yourself."

"Oh, I'm sure. But it's still a little early for introductions," she explained with impeccable nonchalance. "When the time's right, I'll let you know."

"YOU WOULD HAVE BEEN proud of me, Web," Marni declared when she arrived at the studio that night. Web had kissed her thoroughly. She was feeling heavenly. "I was cool and relaxed, I followed the script perfectly and I didn't lie once."

"How did she take it?"

"Hesitantly, at first. She asked questions, just as I'd expected." She told him some of them, and they shared a chuckle over the one about money. "I planted the bug in her ear. If I know my mother, she's already on the phone trying to find out whatever she can about you." A sudden frown crossed her brow. Web picked up on it instantly.

"Don't worry. There's nothing she could learn that

will connect me with who I was fourteen years ago. Lee is about the only one who knows anything about what I did during those years, and even if someone called him, which they wouldn't, he'd be tight-lipped as hell."

"He must think my parents are awful."

"Not awful. Just…prejudiced."

"Mmmm. I guess that says it." Her eyes clouded. "It remains to be seen whether they're vengeful as well."

"Don't even think it," Web soothed. "Not yet. We've got more pressing things to consider."

"More pressing?" she asked, worried. But Web was grinning, drawing her snugly against him. "Ahhh. More pressing…"

His lips closed over hers then, and soon he was leading her to the bedroom, where he proceeded to set her priorities straight. It was what she needed, what they both needed—a reaffirmation of all they meant to each other. Passion was a ready spark between them, had always been a ready spark between them, but it was love that dominated the interplay of mouths and hands and bodies, and it was love that transported them to an exquisite corner of paradise.

MARNI'S FATHER DROPPED BY her office on Friday morning. She was surprised to see him, because there wasn't a board meeting scheduled and he rarely came in for anything else. But deep down inside she'd been awaiting some form of contact.

They talked of incidental things relating to the corporation, and Marni indulged him patiently. In his own good time, Jonathan Lange broached the topic that had brought him by. His thick brows were low over his eyes.

"Your mother tells me that you have a special man...this photographer...Brian Webster?"

"Uh-huh." Her pulse rate had sped up, but she kept her eyes and her voice steady and forcefully relaxed her hands in her lap.

"I know your mother has some reservations," he went on in his most businesslike tone, "and I hope you take them seriously. People today get married, then divorced, married, then divorced. Your sister is a perfect example."

"I'm not Tanya," Marni stated quietly.

"Exactly. You're the president of this corporation. I hope you keep that in mind when you go about choosing a husband."

She had to struggle to contain a surge of irritation. "I know who I am, Dad, and I think I have a pretty good grasp of what's expected of me."

"Just so you do. This fellow's a photographer, and big-name photographers often live in the fast lane. I wouldn't want you—or him—to do anything to embarrass us."

Embarrassment had never been among Marni's many worries. "I think you're jumping the gun," she said slowly. "In the first place, you've adopted the same stereotype Mom has. There's nothing fast about Brian. He lives quietly, and his face hasn't been plastered all over the papers, with or without women." Web had assured her of that. All she'd needed was for her mother or Tanya to do a little sleuthing and come up with a picture that would identify Web instantly. "Furthermore, I don't believe I said anything to Mom about marriage."

Jonathan's frown was one of reproof. "Then you'd

move in with the man, without a thought to your image?"

"Come on, Dad. These are enlightened times. No one cares if two adults choose to live together."

"Is that what *you* choose?"

"No! I've never even considered it."

"But you haven't talked marriage with this photographer?"

That one was harder to fudge. She bought a minute's time. "His name is Brian. You can call him Brian."

"All right. Brian. Have you talked marriage with Brian?"

She held his gaze. "I think we'd both be amenable to the idea."

"Then it *is* serious."

"Yes."

"We'll have to meet him. That's all there is to it."

Marni bit her lower lip, then let it slide from beneath her teeth. "You know, Dad, I am a big girl. Technically, I don't need your approval. You may hate him, but that wouldn't change my feelings for him."

Jonathan's gaze sharpened. "If he's as wonderful as you say, why would we hate him?"

"Different people see things differently. You and Mom aren't keen on his profession to begin with."

"That's true. But we'd still like to meet him, and soon, if you're as serious as you say about him."

"Okay, soon. You will meet him soon."

THERE WAS SOON, and there was soon. Marni had no intention of running out to Long Island that Sunday as her mother had originally suggested. Not only did she have more subtle PR to do, but she and Web were go-

ing back to Vermont for the weekend, and not for the
world would she have altered their plans.

They had a relaxed, quiet, loving weekend and returned to New York refreshed and anticipating the
next step in Marni's plan. On Monday she sent her parents tear sheets of the best of Web's work. Each piece
was identified as to where it had appeared; it was an
impressive collection of credits. She also sent along
copies of blurbs and articles praising Web's work.

On Monday night she and Web took in a movie. On
Tuesday they went out to dinner. On Wednesday
morning she called her mother as a follow-up to the
package she'd sent. Yes, Adele had received it, and,
yes, it was an impressive lot. Yes, Marni was planning
to bring him out to the house, but, no, it couldn't be this
week because they were both swamped with work.

Marni and Web spent a quiet Wednesday night at
her place, then a similarly quiet Thursday night at his.
After the full days they put in at their respective jobs,
they found these private times to be most precious.

Friday night, though, they had a party to attend. It
was given by the most recently named vice-president
at Lange, Heather Connolly, whom Marni had personally recruited from another company four years before.

Had the party been an official corporate function,
Marni might have thought twice about bringing Web
along. She felt she was progressing well with her parents and wouldn't have done anything to jeopardize
her plan. But the party was a personal one, a gathering
of the Connollys' friends. Marni was looking forward
to it; it was the first time she would be introducing
Web to any of her own friends.

They had fun dressing up, Web in a dark, well-
tailored suit, Marni in a black sequined cocktail dress.

It was a miracle they noticed anyone else at the party, so captivated were they by each other's appearance. But they did manage to circulate, talking easily with Heather and Fred's friends, their spouses and dates.

At ten o'clock, though, the unthinkable happened. A couple arrived: the man a tennis partner of Fred's, the woman none other than Marni's sister, Tanya.

Marni was the first to see them. She and Web were chatting with another couple when they entered the room. Her heart began to pound, and she stiffened instantly. Instinctively she reached for Web's arm and dug in her fingers. He took one look at her ashen face, followed her gaze and stared.

"Tanya?" he whispered in disbelief. It had been fourteen years, but he would have recognized her even had Marni's reaction not been a solid clue. Clearing his throat, he turned smoothly back to the couple. "Would you excuse us? Marni's sister has just come. We hadn't expected to see her." Without awaiting more than nods from the two, he guided Marni toward the back of the room, ostensibly to circle the crowd toward Tanya.

Marni's whisper was as frantic as she felt. "What are we *going to do*? She'll recognize you! She's *sure* to recognize you, and she's trouble! Oh, God, Web, what do we do?"

He positioned himself so that his large body was a buffer between Marni and the rest of the crowd, then curved his fingers around her arms. "Take it easy. Just relax. There's not much we can do, Marni. If we try to slip out without being seen, our disappearance will cause an even greater stir. Tanya's not dumb. She'll put two and two together, and if she's the troublemaker you say, she'll run right back to your parents. The damage will be done anyway." He paused. "The best thing, the *only* thing we can do is to walk confidently up and say hello."

Marni's eyes were wide with dismay. "But she'll *recognize* you."

"Probably."

"But...that'll be awful!"

"It'll just bring things to a head a little sooner."

"Web, I don't want this...I don't want this!"

He slipped to her side, put his arm around her shoulder and spoke very gently. "Let's get it over with. The sooner the better. Take a deep breath...atta girl...now smile."

She tried, but the best she could muster was a feeble twist of her lips.

Web gave a tight smile of his own. "That'll have to do." He took his own deep breath. "Let's go."

Tanya and her date were talking with Heather and Fred when they approached. "Marni," Heather exclaimed, "look who's here! I never dreamed Tony would be bringing Tanya. Do you and Brian know Tony? Tony Holt, Marni Lange and Brian Webster."

Marni forced a smile in Tanya's direction. "Hi, Tanya." She clutched Web's arm. "I don't think you know Brian."

Tanya hadn't taken her eyes from Web since she'd turned at their approach. Her face, too, had paled, and there was a hint of shock in her eyes, but otherwise her expression was socially perfect. She extended a formal hand. "Brian...Webster, is it?"

If she'd put special emphasis on his last name, only Marni and Web were aware of it. Two things were instantly clear—first, that she did *indeed* know Brian and, second, that she was momentarily going along with the game.

Web took her hand in his own firm one. "It's a pleasure to meet you, Tanya."

"My pleasure entirely," was Tanya's silky response. The underlying innuendo was, again, obvious only to Web and Marni.

Web shook hands with Tony Holt, who, it turned out, was a plastic surgeon very familiar with his photographic work. Reluctantly, since he'd rather have been helping Marni, Web was drawn into conversation with the man. Heather and Fred moved off. Tanya seized Marni's arm. "We'll be in the powder room, Tony." She winked at her date. "Be right back."

Before Marni could think of a plausible excuse, she was being firmly led around the crowd and up the stairs to the second floor of the townhouse. Tanya said nothing until she'd found a bathroom and closed its door firmly behind them. Then she turned on Marni, hands on hips, eyes wide in fury.

"How could you! How could you *think* to do something like this to us! When I talked with Mom the other day, she told me you were serious about this Brian Webster. She didn't make the connection. *None* of us made the connection."

Marni refused to be intimidated. "The connection's unimportant."

"Unimportant? Have you lost your marbles?" Tanya raised a rigid finger and pointed to the door. "That man killed our brother, and you don't think the connection's important?"

"Brian did not...kill...Ethan," Marni stated through gritted teeth, her own fury quickly rising to match her sister's. "That accident was carefully documented by the police. Brian was in no way at fault."

Tanya sliced the air with her hand. "It doesn't matter

what the police said. He was a bad influence on Ethan. If he hadn't come along that summer, Ethan would still be alive. Your *own brother*. How could you insult his memory by doing this?"

"Ethan liked and respected Web," Marni countered angrily. Quite unconsciously she'd reverted to calling Brian Web, but even if she'd thought about it, she'd have realized that there was no longer any need for pretense. "If he'd survived the accident, he'd have been the first one to say that Web wasn't at fault. And given the age that I am now, he'd have been the first to bless my relationship with Web."

"So you're desperate, is that it? You're thirty-one and single, and *that* man is your only hope?"

"Yes, that man is my only hope, but not because I'm thirty-one. I happen to love him. He fills needs I never realized I had."

"Very touching. Is that what you're going to say to Mom and Dad when they finally learn the truth? And when were you planning to tell them anyway? They're going to be thrilled, absolutely thrilled."

"Do you think I don't know that? Do you think I've been evasive simply to amuse myself? I'm finding no pleasure in this, Tanya, and the worst of it is that you people are making me feel guilty when I've got nothing to feel guilty about. I'd planned to tell Mom and Dad when the time was right. I was hoping that they'd form an image of what Brian Webster is like today, to somehow counter the image they've held of him all these years."

"You're dreaming, little sister—"

"Don't call me little sister," Marni said in a warning tone. "We're both adults now. It doesn't seem to me...." She closed her mouth abruptly. She'd been about to say that Tanya hadn't done anything with her life that would give her the right, or authority, to look down on Marni, but she realized that insults would get her nowhere. Yes, Tanya would go to their parents with what she'd learned, and maybe Marni *was* dreaming, but there was always that chance, that slim chance Tanya could be an ally.

Marni took a deep breath and raised both hands in a truce. "What I could use, Tanya, is your help. It's going to be very difficult for Mom and Dad, because I know they share your feelings that Web was responsible for Ethan's death. They're older, and Ethan was their child. I was hoping you could see things more objectively."

Tanya's eyes flashed. "You are *not* going to marry that man."

"And it matters that much to you who I marry?" Marni asked softly.

"You can marry anyone you please as long as it's not him."

Marni looked down at her hands and chose her words with care. "Fourteen years ago, you wanted Web for yourself. Could that be coloring your opinion?"

"Of course not. I didn't want him for myself. I knew what kind of a person he was from the start."

Marni bit back a retort concerning both Tanya's erstwhile interest in Web and the character of her two ex-husbands. "Do you know what kind of a person he is now?" she asked quietly.

"It doesn't matter. When I look at him I can only remember what he did. Mom and Dad are going to do the same."

"But think. He has a good career. He's successful

and well-liked. He doesn't have the slightest blemish on his record. Can you still stand there and claim he's a killer?"

Before Tanya could answer, a light knock came at the door, then Web's voice calling, "Marni?" Marni quickly opened the door. Web looked from one sister to the other, finally settling a more gentle gaze on Marni. "Is everything okay here?"

"No, it's not," Tanya answered in a huff. "If you had any sense, you'd get out of my sister's life once and for all."

Marni turned to her with a final plea. "Tanya, I could really use your help—"

"When hell freezes over. I wouldn't—"

"That's enough," Web interrupted with quiet determination. His voice softened, and he reached for Marni's hand. "We've got to run, Marni. I've already explained to Heather that I have to be up early tomorrow. She understands."

With all hope that Tanya might aid her dashed, Marni didn't look at her sister again. She took Web's hand and let him lead her down the stairs and quietly out of the townhouse. She leaned heavily against him as they began to walk. Yes, Web had to be up early tomorrow. So did she. They were heading for Vermont, where she wouldn't be able to hear her phone when it began to jangle angrily.

8

MARNI'S PARENTS weren't put off by the fact that she wasn't home to answer her phone. They quickly called her administrative assistant, who gave them Web's Vermont number.

It was shortly after two in the afternoon. Marni and Web had left New York early, had stopped at their usual market for food and were just finishing lunch. When the phone rang, they looked up in surprise, then at each other in alarm. In all the time they'd spent at the cabin, the phone hadn't rung once.

"Don't answer it," Marni warned. Neither of them had moved yet.

"It may not be them."

The phone rang a second time. "It is. We both know it is."

"It may be a legitimate emergency. What if one of them is sick?" He began to rise from his seat. The only phone was in the den.

Marni clutched his wrist, her eyes filled with trepidation. "Let it ring," she begged.

"They'll only keep trying. I won't have the weekend spoiled. If we let it ring, we'll keep wondering. But if we answer it, at least we'll know one way or another."

"The weekend will be spoiled anyway.... Web!"

He was on his way toward the den. She ran after him.

He lifted the receiver and spoke calmly. "Hello?"

A slightly gruff voice came from the other end of the line. "Marni Lange, please."

"Who's calling?"

"...Her father."

As if Web hadn't known. He would have recognized that voice in any timbre. He'd last heard it when he'd been lying, distraught, in a hospital room.

"Mr. Lange—" Web began, not knowing what he was going to say, only knowing that he wanted to deflect from Marni the brunt of what was very obviously anger. He was curtly interrupted.

"My daughter, please."

Marni was at Web's elbow, trying to take the phone from him, but he resisted. "If this is something that concerns—"

"I'd like to *speak to my daughter!*"

Hearing her father's shout, Marni tugged harder on the phone. "Web, please..."

He held up his free hand to her, even as he spoke calmly into the receiver. "If you're angry, Mr. Lange, you're angry at me. Perhaps you ought to tell me what's on your mind."

"Are you going to put my daughter on the line?"

"Not yet."

Jonathan Lange hung up the phone.

Web heard the definitive click and took the phone from his ear, whereupon Marni snatched it to hers. "Dad? Hello? Dad?" She scowled at the receiver, then slammed it down. "Damn it, Web. You should have let me talk! What good does it do if he's hung up? Now nothing's accomplished!"

"Something is. Your father knows that I have no intention of letting you face this alone. You faced it alone fourteen years ago. I like to think I'm more of a man now."

"Then it's a macho thing?" she cried. "You're trying to show him who wears the pants around here?"

"Don't be absurd, Marni! Our relationship has been one of equals from the start. I simply want your father to know that we're standing together, that if he thinks he can browbeat you, he'll be browbeating both of us. And I don't take to being browbeaten."

"Then you'll shut every door as soon as it's opened. He *called. You* were the one who insisted on answering the phone. Now you've hung up on him—"

"He hung up on me!"

"Same difference—"

"No, it's not," Web argued angrily. "*He* shut the door. I was perfectly willing to talk."

"But he wouldn't talk with you, so now he's not talking with either of us."

"He'll call back. If he went to the effort of getting this number, he won't give up so easily."

"Then I'll answer it next time."

"And he'll bully you mercilessly. You've got to be firm with him, Marni! You've got to let him know that you're not a child who can be pushed around!"

"I'm *not* a child, and I don't like your suggestion that I am."

"I didn't suggest—"

"You don't trust me! You think I'm going to crumble. You think that I'll submit to every demand he makes. I told you I wouldn't, Web! I *told* you that my choice was made!"

"But you're torn, because you don't want to hurt them. Well, what about me? Don't I have a right to stand in my own defense? If he's going to call me a killer, it's my *right* to tell him where to get off!"

"But that won't accomplish anything!" she screamed, then caught her breath and held it. The silence was deafening, coming on the heels of their heated exchange. "Oh, God," she whimpered at last. She clutched his shoulders, then threw her arms around his neck and clung to him tightly. "Oh, God, he's doing it already. He's putting a wedge between us. Do you see what's happening? Do you see it, Web?"

His own arms circled her slowly, then closed in. Eyes squeezed shut, he buried his face in her hair. "I see, sweetheart. I see, and it makes me sick. If we start fighting about this, we'll never make it. And if *we* don't, *I* won't."

"Me neither," she managed shakily. "I love you so much, Web. It tears me up that you have to go through this, when you've already paid such a high price for something that wasn't your fault."

He rubbed soothing circles over her back. "That's neither here nor there at this point. I'm more than willing to go through hell if it means I'll get you in the end." His voice grew hoarse. "I don't know how I could have yelled at you that way. You're not responsible for the situation any more than I am."

The phone rang again. A jolt passed from one body to the other. Marni raised her face and looked questioningly at Web, who held her gaze for a minute before stepping back and nodding toward the phone.

Marni lifted the receiver. "Hello?"

"Marni!" It was her mother. "Thank goodness it's you this time! Your father is ready to—"

Cutting her off, Jonathan came on the line. "What do

you think you're doing, Marni?" he demanded harshly. "Do you know who that man is?"

She felt surprisingly calm. Anticipation had prepared her well. With the moment at hand, she was almost relieved. "I certainly do. He's the man I'm going to marry." She reached for Web's hand and held it to her middle.

"Over my dead body!" came the retort. "Do you have any idea what this has done to your mother and me? You were very cagey, telling us everything about this Brian Webster of yours but his real identity. If Tanya hadn't called—"

"Everything I told you was the truth."

"Don't interrupt me, Marni. You may be the president of the corporation, but in this house you're still the baby."

"I am not still in that house, and I am *not* still the baby! I'm a grown woman, Dad. Isn't it about time you accepted that?"

"I had, until you pulled this little stunt. Are you out of your mind? Do you have any *idea* how I feel about this?"

Marni took a deep breath in a bid for calm. She had to be able to think clearly and project conviction. A glance at Web gave her strength a boost. "Yes, I think I do. I also think that you're wrong. But I won't be able to convince you of it over the phone."

"Damned right you won't. I'd suggest you get *that* man to drive you right back down here. He can drop you at the door and then leave. I won't have him in this house."

"Listen to yourself, Dad. You sound irrational. The facts are that Web and I are here in Vermont for the weekend, and that when we do come by to see you, we'll be together. Now, you can shut the door on us both, but that would be very sad, because I am your daughter and I do love you."

"I'm beginning to doubt that, young lady."

It was a low blow, and one she didn't deserve after all she'd done for her parents' sake in the past fourteen years. Clenching her jaw against the anger that flared, she went on slowly and clearly. "We'll be heading back to New York tomorrow afternoon. We'll stop by at the house sometime around seven. We can talk this all out then."

"Do *not* bring *him*."

"He'll be with me, and if you refuse to see me, we'll be married by the end of the week. Think about it, Dad. I'll see you tomorrow." Without awaiting his answer, she quietly put down the phone.

Web sucked in a deep breath, then let it out in a stunned whoosh. "You are quick, lady. I never would have dreamed up that particular threat, but you've practically guaranteed that he'll see us."

"Practically," she said without pride. Then she muttered, "He *is* a bastard."

Web drew her against him. "Shhhh. He's your father, and you love him."

"For that, yes, but as a person..."

"Shhhh. The door's open. Let's let it go at that."

THE DOOR WAS INDEED OPEN when Marni and Web arrived Sunday evening at the handsome estate where she'd grown up. Fourteen years before, Web would have been taken aback by the splendor of the long, tree-lined drive and the majesty of the huge Georgian colonial mansion. Now he could admire it without awe or envy.

They were greeted in the front hall by Duncan, Cook's husband, who'd served as handyman, chauffeur and butler for the Langes for as long as Marni could remember. "Miss Marni, it's good to see you. You're looking fine."

"Thank you, Duncan," she said quietly. "I'd like you to meet my fiancé, Mr. Webster."

"How are you, Duncan?" Web extended his hand. He, like Marni, was unpretentious when it came to hired help. He'd always treated the most lowly of his own assistants as important members of the crew. Whereas Marni was softhearted and compassionate, Web was understanding as only one who'd once been "hired help" himself could be.

Duncan pumped his hand, clearly pleased with the offering. "Just fine, Mr. Webster. And my congratulations to you both. I had no idea we'd be having a wedding coming up here soon."

Marni cleared her throat and threw what might have been an amused glance at Web had she not been utterly incapable of amusement at that moment. "We, uh, we haven't made final plans." She paused. "My parents are expecting me, I think."

"That's right," Duncan returned with the faintest hint of tension. "They're in the library. They suggested you join them there."

The library. Warm and intimate in some homes, formal and forbidding in this one. It had been the scene of many a reprimand in Marni's youth, and that knowledge did nothing to curb her anxiety now. There were differences of course. She was no longer in her youth, and Web was with her...

Head held high, she led the way through the large front hall and down a long hallway to the room at the very end. The door was open, but the symbolism was deceptive. Marni knew what she would find even before she entered the room and nodded to her parents.

Jonathan Lange was sitting in one corner of the studded leather sofa. His legs were crossed at the knees, and one arm was thrown over the back of the sofa while the other hand held his customary glass of Scotch. He was wearing a suit, customary as well; he always wore a suit when discussing serious business.

Adele Lange sat on the sofa not far from him. She wore a simple dress, nursed an aperitif and looked eminently poised.

"Thank you for seeing us," Marni began with what she hoped was corresponding poise. "I think you remember Brian."

Neither of the Langes looked at him. "Sit down," Jonathan said stiffly, tossing his head toward one of two leather chairs opposite the sofa. That particular symbolism did have meaning, Marni mused. The two chairs were well separated by a marble coffee table.

Marni took the seat near her father, leaving the one closer to her mother for Web. She sat back, folded her hands in her lap and spoke softly. "Brian and I are planning to get married. We'd like your support."

"Why?" Jonathan asked baldly.

"Because we feel that what we're doing is right and we'd like you to share our happiness."

"Why now? It's been fourteen years since you were first involved. Fourteen years is a long time for an engagement. Why the sudden rush to marry?"

Marni was confused. "We haven't been seeing each other all that time. I hadn't seen him since the day of the accident until three weeks ago when I went to his studio to be photographed."

"But you've carried a torch for him all these years."

"No! After the accident you forbade me to see him, so I didn't. I forced myself to forget about him, to put what we had down to a seventeen-year-old's infatuation, just as you said. It wasn't a matter of carrying a torch, and I never dreamed he'd be the photographer when I stepped foot in that studio—"

"I was wondering about that, too," Jonathan interrupted scornfully. "You were in favor of this magazine thing from the start—" his eyes narrowed "—and then to suddenly come up with the photographer who just happened to be the man you'd imagined yourself in love with—"

"It wasn't that way at all!"

Web, who'd been sitting quietly, spoke for the first time. "Marni's right. She had no idea I was—"

"I'm not talking to you," Jonathan cut in, his eyes still on Marni.

Web wasn't about to be bullied. "Well, I'm talking to you, and if you have *anything* to say to me, you can look me in the eye."

Marni put out a hand. "Web, please..." she whispered.

He softened his tone, but that was his only concession. His eyes were sharply focused on Marni's father. "I have pictures from that first photo session, one after the other showing the shock on Marni's face. She knew nothing of the past identity of Brian Webster the photographer. No one does except your family and mine."

Though Jonathan still refused to look at him, Adele did. Instinctively Web met her gaze. "Marni hadn't been pining away for me any more than I'd been pining away for her. In hindsight I can see that she was special even back then. But it's the woman I know today whom I've fallen in love with. And it's the man I am today whom I think you should try to understand."

"There's not much to understand," Adele returned. Her voice wasn't quite as cold as her husband's had been, but it was far from encouraging. "We firmly believe that had it not been for you our son would be alive today. Can you honestly expect us to let our daughter marry you, knowing that every time we look at you we'll remember what you did?"

Web sat back. "Okay, let's get into that. Exactly what *did* I do?"

"You were recklessly driving that motorcycle," Jonathan snapped, eyes flying to Web's for the first time.

Web felt a small victory in that he'd been acknowledged as a person at last. "Is that what the police said after the investigation?"

"Ethan would never have *been* on a motorcycle had it not been for you."

"I didn't force him to get on it. He wasn't some raw kid of fourteen. He was a man of twenty-five."

"You were a bad influence that entire summer!"

"That's what you assumed, since I was only an employee at the Inn. Did Ethan ever tell you what we did together? Did he tell you that we spent hours talking politics, or philosophy, or psychology? Or that we discussed books we'd both read, or that we played chess? I loved playing chess with Ethan. I beat him three times out of four, but he took it with a grin and came back for another game more determined than ever to win. There was nothing irresponsible about what we did, and I was probably a better influence on him than the spoiled and self-centered characters he would have been with otherwise. You really should have been proud of him. He chose to be with me because the time we spent together was intellectually productive."

Marni wanted to applaud, but her fingers were too tightly intertwined to move.

Jonathan wasn't about to applaud either. Choosing to ignore what Web had said, he turned his attention back to Marni. "What were you intending with the song and dance you've been doing for the past two weeks? Did you hope to pull the wool over our eyes? Did you think we were that foolish?"

"I had hoped that you'd see Brian as he is today. Aside from his profession, which you're unfairly biased against, he's everything I'd have thought you'd want in the man I decided to marry." She turned to her mother. "What did you find out? I'm sure you made calls."

"I did," Adele sniffed. "It appears he's fooled the rest of the world, but we know him as he is."

Marni scowled. "You don't know him at all. You may have met him in passing once or twice that summer, but you never spent any time talking with him, and you certainly never invited him to the house. Don't you think it's about time you faced the fact that Ethan's death just *happened*?"

"You wouldn't say that if you were a mother, Marni. You'd be angry and grief-stricken, just like we were, like we are."

"For God's sake, it's been fourteen years!"

"Have *you* forgotten?" Adele cried.

Marni sagged in her seat. "Of course not. I adored Ethan. I'll never forget him. And I've never forgotten the sense of injustice, the anger I felt that those two cars had to collide right in Web's path. But you can't live your life feeding on anger and grief. Ethan would

never have wanted it. Have you ever stopped to consider that? Web was his friend. Whether you like it or
not, he was. He suffered in that accident, both physically and emotionally." She suddenly sat forward and
rounded on her father. "Your response when Web
called you from the hospital was *inexcusable*! How
could you have done something like that? He's a human being, for God's sake, a human being!" She took a
quick breath and sat straighter. "Web mourned Ethan
just as we did, and he suffered through his share of
guilt, though God only knows he had nothing to feel
guilty for. But that's all in the past now. There's nothing any of us can do to bring Ethan back, and I refuse to
live my life any longer trying to make up to you for his
loss!"

"What are you talking about, girl?" Jonathan
snarled.

"Marni," Web began, "you don't have to—"

"I do, Web. It's about time the entire truth came
out." She faced her parents, looking from one to the
other. "I felt guilty because I'd loved both Ethan and
Web. Ethan was dead. Web was as good as dead to me
because you never let up on the fact that he was to
blame, and if he was to blame, *I* was to blame, too." She
focused on her father. "Do you think I wasn't aware
that you'd been grooming Ethan for the corporation
presidency? And that you practically lost interest in
the business after he died? Why do you think I buckled
down and whipped through Wellesley, then Columbia? Didn't it ever occur to you that I was trying to be
what Ethan would have been? That I felt I could somehow make things easier for you if I joined the corporation myself?" She tempered her tone, though her voice
was shaky. "I'm not saying that I'd had my heart set on

something else, or that I'm unhappy being where I am, but I think you should both know that what I did I did for you, even more than for me."

"Then you were a fool," was Jonathan's curt response.

"Maybe so, but I don't regret it for a minute. I did make things easier for you. You won't admit it, any more than you'll admit that I've done a good job. You never did that, Dad. Do you realize?" Her eyes had grown moist and her knuckles were white as she gripped the arms of the chair. "I tried so hard, and you promoted me and gave me more and more responsibility until finally I became president. But not once, *not once* did you tell me you were proud of me. Not once did you actually praise my work—"

Her voice cracked, and she stopped talking. She was unaware that Web had risen from his seat to stand behind hers until she felt his comforting touch on her shoulder. Her hands left the arms of the chair and found his instantly.

Jonathan's expression was as tight as ever, though his voice was quieter. "I assumed that actions spoke louder than words."

"Well, they don't! I beat my tail to the ground trying to win your approval, but I failed, I failed. And now I'm tired." Her voice reflected it. "I'm tried of trying to please someone else. I'm thirty-one years old, and it's about time I see to *my* best interests. I have every intention of continuing on as Lange's president, and I'll continue to do the best job I can, but for me now, and for Web. I'm going to marry him, and we're going to have children, and if you can't find it in your hearts to forgive, or at least forget, then I guess you'll miss out on the happiness. It's your choice. I've already made mine."

There was a moment's heavy silence in the room before Jonathan spoke in a grim voice. "I guess there's not much more to say, then, is there." It wasn't a question but a dismissal. Pushing himself from the sofa, he turned his back on them and walked toward the window.

Web addressed Adele. "There's one last thing I'd like to say," he ventured quietly. "I'd like you to consider what would have happened if Marni—or Tanya—had had Ethan for a passenger when her car crashed, killing him but only injuring her. Would you have ostracized one of your daughters from the family? Would you have held a permanent grudge? You know, that's happened in families, where two members were in an accident, one killed and the other survived. I don't know how those families reacted. Regardless of guilt or innocence, it's a tragic situation.

"Ethan and I were innocent victims of that accident fourteen years ago. Once those cars started spinning all over the road, the motorcycle didn't have a chance in hell of escaping them. If I had been the son of one of your oldest and dearest friends, would you still feel the way you do now?"

"You are *not* the son of one of our oldest and dearest friends," Jonathan said without turning. "And I thank God for it!"

MARNI AND WEB left then. They'd said what they'd come to say and had heard what they'd suspected they'd hear. They felt disappointed and saddened, hurt and angry.

"That's it, Web," Marni stated grimly as they began

the drive into the city. "We know how they feel, and they're not going to change. I think we should get married, and as soon as possible."

Web kept his eyes on the road, his hands on the wheel. "Let's not do anything impulsively," he said quietly.

Her gaze flew to his face in dismay. "Impulsively? I thought marriage was what we both wanted! Weren't you the one who said that the longer we put off telling my parents the truth, the longer it would be before we got married? I thought *you* were the one who wanted to get married soon!"

"I do." His voice was even, and he didn't blink. "But we're both upset right now. It's not the ideal situation in which to be starting a marriage."

"Then what do we do? Wait forever in the hope that they'll do an about-face? They won't, Web!"

"I know. I know." He was trying to sort out his thoughts, to find some miraculous solution to their problem. "But if we rush into something, they'll be all the more perverse."

"I can't believe you're saying this! You were the one who felt so strongly that we were adults and didn't need their permission!"

He held the car steady in the right-hand lane. "We don't. And we are adults. But they're your parents, and you do love them. It'd still be nice if they came around. This all has to be a shock to them. Two days, Marni, that's all they've had."

"It wouldn't matter if it were two months!"

"It might. We presented our arguments tonight, and they were logical. I think your mother was listening, even if your father tried hard not to. Don't you think we owe them a little time to mull it over? They may never come fully around to our way of thinking, but it's possible they might decide to accept what they can't change."

Marni didn't know what to think, particularly about Web's sudden reluctance to get married. "Do you really think that could happen?" Her skepticism was nearly palpable.

"I don't know," he said with a sigh. "But I do think it's worth the wait. To rush and get married now will accomplish nothing more than throwing our relationship in their faces."

"It would accomplish much more. We'd be *married!* Or doesn't that mean as much to you as it does to me?"

"You're upset, Marni, or you wouldn't be saying that—"

"And why shouldn't we throw our relationship in their faces? We're in love. We want to get married. We asked for their support, and they refused it. They couldn't have been more blunt. I don't understand you, Web," she pleaded. "Why are you suddenly having reservations?"

He glanced at her then and saw the fear on her face. Reaching for her hand, he found it cold and stiff, so he enclosed it in his own, warmer hand and brought it to his thigh. "I'm not having reservations, sweetheart," he said gently. "Not about what I feel for you, or about getting married, or about doing all those things we've been dreaming about. If you know me at all, you know how much they mean to me. It's just that I'm trying to understand your parents, to think of what they must be feeling."

She would have tugged her hand away had he not held it firmly. "How can you be so generous after everything they've done to you?"

"Generosity has nothing to do with it," he barked. "It's selfishness from the word go."

"I don't understand."

Unable to concentrate on the road, he pulled over onto its shoulder and killed the engine. Then he turned to her and pressed her hand to his heart. "It's for *us*, Marni," he stated forcefully. "You're right. They've done a hell of a lot to me—and to you, too—and for that they don't deserve an ounce of compassion. I'd like to ignore them, to pretend they don't exist, and in the end that may be just what we'll have to do. In the meantime, though, I refuse to let them dictate any of our actions, and that includes when we'll be getting married." His voice gentled, but it maintained its urgency, and his gaze pierced Marni's through the dark of night.

"Don't you see? Our rushing to get married just because of what happened tonight would be a kind of shotgun wedding in reverse. I won't have that! We'll plan our wedding, maybe for a month or two from now, and we'll do it right. I want you wearing a beautiful gown, and I want flowers all over the place, and I want our friends there to witness the day that means so much to us. I will *not* sneak off and elope behind someone's back. I won't have our marriage tainted in any way!"

Through her upset, Marni felt a glimmer of relief. She'd begun to think that Web would put off their marriage indefinitely. A month or two she could live with. And he did have a point; the only purpose of rushing to get married in three days would be to spite her parents. "In a month or two they'll still be resisting," she warned, but less caustically.

"True, but at least we'll know that we've given them

every possible chance. If we've done our best, and still they refuse to open up their minds, we'll have nothing to regret in the future." He raised her hand to his lips and gently kissed her palm. "I want it to be as perfect as it can be, sweetheart. Everything open and above-board. We owe that to ourselves, don't you think?"

9

DURING THE DAY following the scene with Marni's parents, Web convinced himself that he'd been right in what he'd said to Marni. Deep in his heart he suspected that her parents would never accept their marriage, and he regretted it only in terms of Marni's happiness. He had cause to think of his own, though, when he received a call from a friend on Tuesday morning.

Cole Hammond wrote for New York's most notorious gossip sheet parading as a newspaper. The two men had met in a social context soon after Web had arrived in New York, and though Web had no love for Cole's publication, he'd come to respect the man himself. When Cole asked if he could meet with Web to discuss something important, Web promptly invited him over.

"I received an anonymous call today," Cole began soon after Web had tossed him a can of beer. They were in Web's living room. The studio was still being cleaned up from the morning's shoot. "It was from a woman. She claimed that she had a sensational story about you. Something to do with an accident in Maine fourteen years ago?"

Web had had an odd premonition from the moment he'd heard Cole's voice on the phone, which was the main reason he'd had him come right over. "Yes," he agreed warily. "There was an accident."

"This woman said that you were responsible for a man's death. Any truth to it?"

Curbing his anger against "this woman" and her allegations, Web looked his friend in the eye. "No."

"She gave me dates and facts. It was a rainy night, very late, and you were speeding along on a motorcycle with a fellow named Ethan Lange on the back."

"Not speeding. But go on."

"You skidded and collided with a car. Lange was thrown and killed."

"...Is that it?"

"She said you'd been drinking that night and that you had no business being on the road."

"What else?"

Cole shrugged. "That's it. I thought I'd run it by you before I did anything more with it."

"I'm glad you have, for your sake more than mine." Web's entire body was rigid with barely leashed fury. "If you're hoping to get a story out of this, I'd think twice. In the first place, she had the facts wrong. In the second place, the police report will bear that out. And in the third place, if you print something like this, you'll have a hefty lawsuit on your hands. I will not stand by and let you—"

"Hold on, pal," Cole interrupted gently, raising a hand, palm out. "I'd never print a thing without getting the facts straight, which is why I'm here. I know you don't trust the paper, but this is *me*. We've talked about situations like this many times. If the facts don't merit a story, there won't *be* a story." He sat back. "So. Why don't you tell me what happened that night?"

Web took a deep breath and forced himself to calm down. Very slowly and distinctly, he outlined the facts of the accident. By the time he was done, he was back on the edge of fury. "You're being used, Cole. I don't know who the caller was, but I've got a damned good idea.... Is this off the record now, just between us?"

"We're friends. Of course it is."

Web trusted him. He also knew that nothing he was about to say wouldn't come out eventually, and that if Cole chose to print it, friend or no, Web would have even greater grounds for a lawsuit. He knew that Cole knew it, too.

"I'm engaged to marry Marni Lange. It was her brother who died that night. Her parents have always blamed me for the accident, regardless of the facts or the police report. Needless to say, they're totally against our marriage. I suspect that it was her sister who called you, and that her major purpose was vengeance."

Cole ingested the possibility thoughtfully. "It's not a unique motive."

"You should be livid."

The other shrugged. "One out of four may be done for vengeance, but even then there's often a story that will sell."

"Well, there isn't one here. It's history. It may be tragic, but it's not spectacular. Hey, go ahead and check out my story. Get that police report. You can even interview the drivers of the other two cars. They were the first ones to say that there wasn't anything I could have done, that both of them had passed me on the road right before the accident, and that I wasn't weaving around or driving recklessly. The bartender at the tavern we'd been to said we'd been stone sober when we'd left. The first car skidded. The second one collided with it and started spinning. I braked, but the road was wet. I might even have been able to steer clear if one of those cars hadn't careened into me." He took a quick breath, then sagged. "It's all there in black and white. An old story. Not worth fiddling with."

"If you were a nobody, I'd agree with you." When Web bolted forward, he held up his hand again. "Listen, what you say makes sense. I'm just doing my job."

"Your job sucks. This isn't *news*, for God's sake!"

"I agree."

"Do you trust me?"

"I always have."

"Do you believe that what I've told you is the truth?"

Cole paused. "Yes, I believe you."

"Then...you'll forget you got that call?"

Another pause, then a nod. "I will." And a sly grin. "But will you?"

"Not on your life! Someone's going to answer for it!"

"Watch what you do," Cole teased. "You may give me a story yet. Though come to think of it, you've got my news editor wrapped around your little finger. I'm not sure she could bear to print anything adverse about you."

Web's answering grin was thin and dry. "If it'd sell, she'd do it.... Give her a kiss for me, will you?"

"My pleasure."

MARNI'S GUESS AS TO WHO the caller had been matched Web's, and her anger was as volatile as his had initially been. Fortunately he'd had time to calm down.

"Tanya! That bitch! How could she *dare* try to pull something like this?"

Web put his arm around her and spoke gently. "Maybe she's trying to score points with your parents."

"She's starting at zero, so it won't get her very far," Marni scoffed, then her voice rose. "Maybe my parents put her up to it!"

"Nah. I don't think so, and you shouldn't either, sweetheart. They wouldn't sink that low, would they? I mean, voicing their disapproval to us is one thing, dirty tricks another. And besides, if the whole story came out, particularly the part about our relationship, they'd be as embarrassed as anyone. They wouldn't knowingly hurt themselves."

"I'm not sure 'knowingly' has anything to do with it. They seem to be incapable of rational thought. That's the problem." She pulled away from Web and reached for the phone. "I'm calling Tanya."

His hand settled over hers, preventing further movement. "No. Don't do it."

"She may contact another paper. For that matter, how do we know she hasn't already?"

"Because Cole's is the sleaziest. It's the only one that would have considered touching the story. I'm sure she knew that."

Marni marveled at Web's composure. "Aren't you angry?"

"This morning I would have willingly rung Tanya's neck if I'd seen her. But that wouldn't accomplish anything. It's over, Marni. Cole won't write any story, and confronting Tanya will only make her more determined to do something else."

"What else could she do?" Marni asked with a hysterical laugh.

As IT HAPPENED, it wasn't Tanya, but Marni's father who had something else in mind. The first Marni got wind of it was in a phone call she received on Wednesday afternoon from one of the corporation's directors. He was an old family friend, which eased Marni's indignation somewhat when he suggested that her father was disturbed about her relationship with Brian Webster, and that he hoped she wasn't making a mistake. She calmly assured him that she wasn't, and that no possible harm could come to the corporation from her marriage to Web.

The second call, though, wasn't as excusable. It came on Thursday morning and was from another of the directors. This one was not a family friend and therefore, theoretically, had no cause to question her private life. Livid, she hung up the phone after talking with him, then stewed at her desk for a time, trying to decide on the best course of action. Indeed, action was called for. If her father was planning to undermine her authority by individually calling each member of the board, she wasn't about to take it sitting down.

She promptly instructed her administrative assistant to summon the board members for a meeting the following morning.

"Your father, too?" Web asked incredulously when she called him to tell him what had happened.

"Yes, my father, too. You were right. Everything should be open and aboveboard. He can hear what I'm going to say along with everyone else."

"What *are* you going to say?"

Her voice dropped for the first time. "I'm not sure." With the next breath, her belligerency resurfaced. "But I'm taking the offensive. Dad's obviously been planting seeds of doubt about me. The only thing I can do is nip it in the bud." She paused, knowing that for all the conviction she might project, she'd called Web because she desperately needed his support.

He didn't let her down. "I agree, sweetheart. I think you've made the right decision. One thing I've learned from talking with you about the corporation is that you haven't gotten where you are by sitting back and waiting for things to happen. You're doing the right thing, Marni. I know it."

She sighed. "I hope so. If Dad has an argument with what I say, he can voice it before the board. Maybe *they* can talk some sense into him."

"Will they?" Web asked very softly. "Will they stand up for you instead of him? How strong is his hold over them?"

"I'll know soon enough, won't I?" she asked sadly.

MARNI STAYED LATE at the office, working with her administrative assistant and secretary to gather, copy and assemble for distribution an armada of facts, figures and reports.

She spent the night with Web at his place, but a pall hung over them, one they couldn't begin to shake. They both sensed that the outcome of Marni's meeting would be telling in terms of her future with the corporation. While on the one hand it was absurd to think that she'd be ousted simply because she married Web, on the other hand neither of them had dreamed Jonathan Lange would do what he already had.

"And if it happens, sweetheart?" Web asked. They were lying quietly curled against each other in bed. Sleep eluded them completely. "What if they side with your father? What will you do then?"

She'd thought about that. "My choice has been made, Web. I told you that. I love you. Our future together is the most important thing to me."

"But you love your work—"

"And I have no intention of giving it up. If the board goes against me, I'll submit my resignation and look for another position. Corporate executives often jump around. We keep the headhunters in business."

"Would you be happy anywhere else but at Lange?"

She smiled up at him, very sure about what she was going to say. "If it meant that I could have both you and my own peace of mind, I'd be happy. Yes, I'd be happy."

AT TEN O'CLOCK the following morning, Marni entered the boardroom. She'd chosen to wear a sedate white wool suit with a navy blouse and accessories. Her hair was perfect, as was her makeup. She knew that no one in the room could fault her appearance. She represented Lange well.

Twelve of the fourteen members of the board were present, talking quietly among themselves until she took her seat at one end of the long table. Her father was at the other. He stood stiffly, and the room was suddenly quiet.

"I will formally call this meeting to order, but since my daughter was the one who organized it, and since I am myself in the dark as to its purpose, I will turn it over to her."

Ignoring both his glower and his very obvious impatience, Marni stood. She rested her hands lightly on the alternating stacks of papers that had been set there for her by her assistant. "Thank you all for coming," she said with quiet confidence, looking from one face to the next, making eye contact wherever possible. "I appreciate the fact that many of you have had to cancel other appointments on such short notice, but I felt the urgency was called for." Pausing, she lifted the first pile of papers from the stack, divided it and sent one half down each side of the table. "Please help yourselves. These are advance copies of our latest production figures, division by division, subsidiary by subsidiary. I don't expect you to read through them now, but I think when you do you'll see that the last quarter was the most productive one Lange has had to date. We're growing, ladies and gentlemen, and we're healthy."

She went to the next pile of papers and passed them around in like fashion. "These are proposals for projects we hope to launch within the next few months. Again, read them at your leisure. I believe that you'll find them exciting, and that you'll see the potential profit in each." She waited until the last of the papers had been distributed, using the time to bolster herself for the tougher part to come. When she had the attention of all those present once more, she went on quietly.

"It is important to me that the board knows of everything that is happening at Lange, and since I'm its president, and as such more visible than our other employees, I want you to be informed and up-to-date on what is happening to me personally." As she spoke her gaze skipped from one member to the next, though she studiously avoided her father's face. He would either intimidate or infuriate her, she feared, and in any case would jeopardize her composure.

"At some point within the next two months, I'll be getting married. My fiancé's name is Brian Webster. Perhaps some of you have heard of him. If not, you'll read about him in the papers I've given you. He's been chosen as the cover photographer for *Class*, the new magazine our publishing division will be putting out. Let me say now that, although Mr. Webster and I knew each other many years ago, the decision to hire him was made first and foremost by the publishing division. At the time I didn't realize that the man I knew so long ago was the same photographer New York has gone wild for. We met, and I realized who he was only after the contracts had been signed and he'd begun to work for us."

There were several nods of understanding from various members of the group, so she went on. "The fact of my marriage will in no way interfere with the quality of work I do for Lange. I believe you all know of my dedication to the corporation. Mr. Webster certainly knows of it. My father built this business from scratch, and I take great pride in seeing that it grows and prospers." She dared a glance at her father then. He was sitting straight, his eyes hard, his lips compressed into a thin line. She quickly averted her gaze to more sympathetic members of the group.

"You may be asking yourself why I felt it so important to call you here simply to tell you of my engagement. I did it because I wanted to assure you that I intend to continue as president of Lange. But there was another reason as well. There is," she said slowly, "a very important matter concerning Brian Webster and my family that some of you may already know about, but which I wanted all of you to hear about first hand. There is apt to be speculation, and perhaps some ill will, but I'm counting on you all to keep that in perspective."

She lifted her hand from the last pile of papers and sent them around the table. "Fourteen years ago Brian Webster and my brother Ethan were good friends. Brian was the one driving the motorcycle on the night Ethan was killed."

Barely a murmur surfaced among those present, which more than anything told Marni that her father had been busier than she'd thought. The knowledge made her all the more determined to thwart his efforts to discredit both her and Web.

"What you have before you are copies of the police report from that night. You'll learn that Mr. Webster was found entirely without fault in the accident. I've also included excerpts from articles about Brian and his work. They were gathered by the publishing division when it cast its vote for him as the *Class* photographer. I don't think any of us can fault either his qualifications or his character."

She took a deep breath and squared her shoulders. "There are some who will claim that Brian was responsible for Ethan's death, and that I am therefore acting irresponsibly by thinking of marrying him. Once you've read what I've given you, I feel confident that you'll agree with me that this is not the case. In no way could Brian Webster embarrass this corporation, or me, and in no way could he adversely affect the job I plan to do as your continuing president."

She looked down, moistened her lips, then raised her chin high. "Are there any questions I might answer? If any of you have doubts as to my moral standing, I'd appreciate your airing them now." Her gaze passed from one director to another. There were shrugs, several headshakes, several frighteningly bland expressions. And then there was her father.

With both hands on the edge of the table, he pushed himself to his feet. "I have questions, and doubts, but you've already heard them."

"That's right. I have. I'd like to know if any of the other members of the board share your opinion. If a majority of the others agree with you, I'll submit my resignation as of now and seek a position elsewhere."

That statement did cause a minor stir, but it consisted of gasps and grunts, the swiveling of heads and a shifting in seats, so that in the end Marni wasn't sure whether the group was in her favor or against. Her gaze encompassed all those who would sit in judgment on her.

"I truly believe that what we have here is a difference of opinion between my father and myself." She purposely didn't include mention of her mother or Tanya. "It should have remained private, and would have, had it not been for calls that were made to several of you that I know of, perhaps all of you—which is why I've asked you here today. It's not your place to decide who I should or shouldn't marry, but since it is in your power to decide whether or not I remain as president of this corporation, I felt that my interests, and Brian's, should be represented.

"As it is, someone tried to plant a story in one of the local papers." She was staring at her father then and was oblivious to the other eyes that widened in dismay. "It would have been a scandal based on nothing but sleazy headlines. Fortunately, Brian is well enough respected in this community that the writer who received the anonymous tip very quickly dismissed it as soon as he heard the truth. Now—" her eyes circled the room again "—do any of you have questions I can answer before I leave?"

Emma Landry spoke up, smiling. "When's the wedding?"

Marni smiled in return. She knew she had one ally. "We haven't set the date yet."

"Will we all be invited?" asked Geoffrey Gould.

"Every one of you," she said, seeking out her father's gaze and holding it for a minute before returning her attention to the group. There were several stern faces among them, several more meek. All she could do was to pray she'd presented her case well.

"If there are no further questions," she said, taking a breath, "I'll leave you to vote on whether I'll be staying on as president. If you say 'yes,' I'll take it as a vote of confidence in what I've done at Lange during the past seven years. If you say 'no,' I'll accept it with regret and move on." Her voice lowered and was for the first time less steady as she looked at her father a final time. "I'll be at my mother's awaiting your decision."

That, too, had been a studied decision. Marni had felt that it would be a show, albeit false, of some support from her family. But she did want to tell Adele what she'd done. If she failed with this group, her mother would witness firsthand her pain. If she succeeded, it would be a perfect opportunity to try to swing Adele to her way of thinking.

Marni had no idea that Web was a full step ahead of her.

"I APPRECIATE your seeing me, Mrs. Lange," Web said after he was shown into the solarium at the back of the house. "I would have called beforehand, but I didn't want to be turned down on the phone. I know that your husband is in the city at a meeting of the board of directors."

"That's right," Adele said quietly. She was sitting in a high-backed wicker chair, with her elbows on its broad arms and her hands resting in her lap.

"You're probably wondering why I'm here, and, to tell you the truth—" he rubbed the tense muscles at the back of his neck "—part of me is, too. It was obvious at our last meeting that you agree with your husband in your opinion of me, and I'm not sure I could change it if I wanted to." He sighed and sat forward, propping his elbows on his thighs. He studied his hands, which hung between his knees, then frowned.

"Perhaps this is a sexist thing to say, but I thought I might appeal to your softer side. All women have a softer side. I know Marni does. Right about now it's not showing, because she's addressing the board of directors, and I'm sure she's making as businesslike a pitch as she can for their understanding. But the softer side's there, not very far from the surface. Marni loves me. She's aching because she loves you both, too, and it hurts her that she's had to make a choice between us."

"She chose you," Adele stated evenly. "I'd think you would be pleased."

He looked up. "Pleased, yes. I'm pleased, and relieved, because I don't think I could make it through a future without her. But I don't feel a sense of victory, if that's what you're suggesting. There's no victory when a family is torn apart, particularly one that has already suffered its share of loss."

Adele arched a brow. "Do *you* know about loss, Mr. Webster?"

"No. At least, not as you know it. One can't lose things one has never had. I never had a father. Did you know that?"

"No. No, I didn't."

"There's a lot you don't know about me. I'd like to tell you, if I may."

Adele paused, then nodded. Though she maintained an outer semblance of arrogance, there was a hint of curiosity in her eyes. Web wasn't about to pass that up.

"I never knew my father. He and my mother didn't marry. When I was two my mother married another man, a good man, a hard worker. I'm afraid I didn't make things terribly easy for him. For reasons I didn't understand at the time, I was restless. I hated school, but I loved to learn. I spent my nights reading everything I could get my hands on, but during the days I felt compelled to move around. Instead of going to college, I took odd jobs where I could find them. I traveled the world, literally, working my way from one place to the next.

"Then I met Ethan. We shared a mutual respect. Through him, I realized I had to settle down, that I wouldn't get anywhere if I didn't focus in on one thing and try to be good at it. I was a jack of all trades, master of none. And I was tired of it."

He gazed at his thumbnail, pressed it with his other thumb. "Maybe I'd simply reached an age where it was time to grow up. After Ethan died, I did a lot of thinking. There were many unresolved feelings I had, about my father and about myself. I don't know who my father is, so those feelings will remain unresolved to a point. But fourteen years ago I realized that I couldn't let them affect my life, that I didn't really need to be running around to escape that lack of identity. That if I stayed in one place and built a life, a reputation for myself, I could make up for it."

He raised his eyes to Adele's intent ones and wondered if she realized the extent of her involvement with his story. "I think I have. But there's more I want, and it involves Marni." He sat up in the chair. "I adore that woman, Mrs. Lange. You have no idea how much. I want to marry her, and we want children."

"You've already told us that," Adele pointed out, but the edge was gone from her voice.

"Yes, but I'm not sure if you realize how much Marni wants our family to encompass you and your husband. Do you want her to be happy, Mrs. Lange?"

"Of course. I'm her mother. What mother wouldn't want that for her daughter?"

"I don't know," he said slowly. "That's what I'm trying to understand."

"Are you accusing me of being blind to what Marni needs, when she sat here herself last Sunday night and announced that she'd go ahead with her plans regardless of what we said or did?"

He kept his tone gentle. "I'm not accusing you of anything. What I'm suggesting is that maybe you don't fully understand Marni's needs. I'm not sure I did myself until I heard what she said to you the other night. She badly wants your approval. You're right, she and I will go ahead and get married even if you continue to hold out. We'll have our home and our children, and we'll be happy. But there will always be a tiny part of Marni that will feel the loss of her parents, and it will be such a premature and unnecessary loss that it will be all the sadder." He paused. "How will *you* feel about such a loss? You lost your son through a tragedy none of us could control. This one would be a tragedy of your own making."

"Ethan would have been alive if it hadn't been—"

"Do you honestly believe that? *Honestly?* Am I a killer, Mrs. Lange? Look at me and tell me if you think I am truly a killer."

Scowling, she shifted in her seat. "Well, not in the sense of a hardened criminal..."

"Not in any sense. I think in your heart you agree.

Otherwise you never would have let me talk with you today."

"My husband's out. That's why I'm talking with you today."

"Then he's the one who dictates your opinion?"

"We've been married for nearly forty years, Mr. Webster. I respect what my husband feels strongly about."

"Even when he's wrong?"

"I...I owe him my loyalty."

"But what about the loyalty you owe your children? You had a choice when it came to picking your husband. Your children had no choice about being born. You gave them life and brought them into this world. They had no say in the matter. Marni didn't *choose* you to be her mother, any more than she chose to be Ethan's sister. And she didn't choose to have him killed in that accident, yet she's spent the past fourteen years trying to make up to you for it. Don't you owe her some kind of loyalty for that?"

"Now you're asking me to make a choice between my daughter and my husband."

"No. I'm simply asking you to decide for yourself whether Marni's marrying me would be so terrible, and if you decide that it wouldn't be, that you try to convince your husband of it. We're not asking for an open-armed welcome. We'll very happily settle for peaceful coexistence. You don't have to love me, Mrs. Lange, but if you love your daughter you'll respect the fact that *she* loves me."

"Web!"

Both heads in the room riveted toward its door, where Marni was standing in a state of utter confusion. Web came instantly to his feet.

"What are you doing here?" she asked, her brows knitting as she looked from him to her mother and back.

"We were just talking." He approached her quickly, ran his hands along her arms and spoke very softly. "How did it go?"

"I don't know. I left before they took a vote. Then I needed a little time to myself, so I took the roundabout way getting here." Apprehension was written all over her face. "There's been no word?"

Web hesitated, then shook his head.

Adele frowned. "A vote? What vote?"

"As to whether I should remain as president. I tendered my resignation, pending the board's decision."

Adele, too, was on her feet then. "You didn't! What a foolish thing to do, Marni! You've been a fine president! You can't be replaced!"

"Oh, I can. No one's indispensable."

"But we always intended that the presidency should remain in the family!"

"Maybe Tanya should give it a try," Marni suggested dryly, only to be answered by an atypical and distinctly unladylike snort from her mother.

"Tanya! That's quite amusing." Her head shot up. "Jonathan! When did *you* get here?"

Web had seen the man approach, but Marni, with her back to the door, had had no such warning. Turning abruptly, her heart in her throat, she faced the tired and stern face of her father.

10

AT ONE TIME Marni might have run to Jonathan Lange. Too much had passed between them in recent days, though, and she grew rigid as he approached. Web dropped his hands to his sides but stayed close, offering his silent support as they both waited to hear what her father had to say.

The older man ran a hand through his thinning gray hair, then glanced at his wife. "I could use a drink."

"Duncan? Duncan!" Adele's voice rang out, and the butler promptly appeared. "Mr. Lange will have his usual. I'll have mine with water." She turned to Marni and Web, her brows raised. When they both shook their heads, she nodded to Duncan. "That will be all."

Jonathan walked past them, deeper into the solarium. He stopped before one glass expanse, thrust his hands in his pockets and, stiff-backed, stood with his feet apart as he gazed at the late March landscape.

Marni stared after him. She knew he had news, but whether it was good or bad she had no idea. In that instant she realized how very much she did want to stay on as president of Lange.

Adele looked from Marni to her husband, then back.

Web, standing close behind Marni, put his hands lightly at her waist. "Do you want to sit down?" he asked softly.

She shook her head, but her eyes didn't leave her father's rigid back. "Dad? What happened?"

Jonathan didn't answer immediately. He raised a hand and scratched his neck, then returned the hand to his pocket. Duncan entered the solarium, offered Adele her drink from a small silver tray, then crossed the room to offer Jonathan his. Only when the butler had left did Jonathan turn. He held the drink in both hands, watching his thumbs as they brushed against the condensation beginning to form on the side of the glass.

"I didn't know she'd done that, Marni," he began solemnly. "I had no idea Tanya had called that reporter—"

"What reporter?" Adele interrupted fearfully. "What has Tanya done?"

There was sadness, almost defeat in the expression Jonathan turned on his wife. "Tanya tried to plant a story in the newspaper about the accident and Webster's role in it."

Adele clutched her glass to her chest. "Tanya did *that?*"

Jonathan's gaze met Marni's. "I have no proof that it was Tanya, but no one else would have had cause except perhaps your mother and I. But I never would have condoned something like that. I'll have a thing or two to say to your sister when I call her later."

Marni couldn't move. Her heart was pounding as she waited, waited. "It's not important. What happened at the meeting? Was a vote taken?"

He took a drink. The ice rattled as he lowered his glass. "Yes."

"And...?"

Jonathan studied the ice, but it was Marni who felt

its chill. "You'll be staying on as president of Lange. There was an easy majority in your favor."

Marni closed her eyes in a moment's prayerful thanks. Web's hands tightened on her waist when she swayed. It was his support, and the warmth of his body reaching out to her, that gave her the strength to open her eyes and address her father again.

"And you, Dad? How did you vote?"

Jonathan cleared his throat. "I exercised my right to abstain."

It was better than a flat-out "no," but it left major questions unanswered. "May I ask why?"

He tipped his head fractionally in a gesture of acquiescence. "I felt that I was too emotionally involved to make a rational decision."

"Then you do question my ability as president?"

He cleared his throat again. As before, it brought him an extra few seconds to formulate his response. "No. I simply question my own ability to see the truth one way or the other."

Such a simple statement, Marni mused, yet it was a powerful concession. Up to that point, Jonathan had refused to see anything but what he wanted to see. The fact that he could admit his view might be jaded was a major victory.

Web felt the release of tension in Marni's body. He, too, had immediately understood the significance of Jonathan's statement, and he shared her relief and that small sense of triumph, even hope. Lowering his head, he murmured, "Perhaps we should leave your parents alone now. I think both you and your father have been through enough today."

She knew he was right. It was a matter of quitting while she was ahead. If she stayed and forced her father to say more, she might well push him into a corner. He was a proud man. For the present it was enough to leave with the hope that one day he might actually join her in *her* corner.

Mutely she nodded. Under Web's guiding hand, she left the solarium and walked back through the house to the front door. Only when she reached it did she realize that her mother had come along.

"Darling..." Adele began. Her hand clutched the doorknob, and she seemed unsure of herself. Marni had turned, surprised and slightly wary. "I...I'm pleased things worked out for you with the board."

"So am I," Marni answered quietly. "I never really wanted to leave Lange."

Adele's voice was a whisper. "I know that." She gave an awkward smile, reached up as if to stroke Marni's hair, but drew her hand back short of physical contact. "Perhaps...perhaps we can get together for lunch one day next week?"

Marni wasn't about to look a gift horse in the mouth. She was pleased, and touched. "I'd like that, Mom. Will you call?"

Adele nodded, her eyes suspiciously moist. She did touch Marni then, wrapping an arm around her waist and pressing a cheek to hers in a quick hug. "You'd better leave now," she whispered. "Drive safely."

Marni, too, felt the emotion of the moment. She nodded and smiled through her own mist of tears, then let Web guide her out the door and down the front steps to their cars.

"I DON'T BELIEVE THESE!" Marni exclaimed in delight. She was sitting cross-legged on Web's bed, wearing nothing but the stack of photographs he'd so nonchalantly tossed into her lap moments before. "They're incredible!"

He came to sit behind her, fitting his larger body to hers so that he could look over her shoulder at the pictures he'd taken three days before. "They're *you*. Exactly what I wanted for the premier cover of *Class*."

Astonished, Marni flipped from one shot to the next. "They're all so good, Web! How are you ever going to decide which one to use? For that matter, how did you ever get so many perfect ones?"

He nipped at her bare shoulder, then soothed the spot with his chin. "I had a super model. That's all there is to it. As for which one to use, I've got my personal preference, but your people will have some say in that." He curled one long arm around hers and extracted a print from the pile. "I sent a duplicate of this one to your parents yesterday."

She met his gaze at her shoulder. "You didn't."

"I did. It's beautiful, don't you think? Every parent should have a picture like this of his daughter."

"But…isn't that a little heavy-handed? I mean, Mom and I have just begun to talk things through." Two weeks had passed since the board meeting, and she'd met with her mother as many times during that stretch.

"You said yourself that she's softening up. And if anything will speed up the process, this will. Look at it, Marni. Look at your expression here. It's so…*you*. The determined set of chin, the little bit of mischief at the mouth, the tilt of the eyebrows with just a hint of indignation, and the eyes, ah, the eyes…"

"Filled with love," she whispered, but she wasn't looking at the picture. Her own eyes were reflected in Web's, and the love flowing between them was awesome.

Web caught his breath, then haphazardly scattered the pictures from Marni's lap and turned her so she was straddling his legs. His fingers delved into her hair, and he held her face steady. "I love you, sunshine. Ohhh, do I love you." When she smiled, he ran his tongue over the curve. Then he caught her lower lip between his own lips and sipped at it.

Marni was floating wild and free, with Web as her anchor, the only one she'd ever truly need. She slipped her arms around his neck and tangled her fingers in the hair at his nape, fighting for his lips, then his tongue, then the very air he breathed.

"Where did you ever...get that passion?" he gasped. His hands had begun a questing journey over the planes and swells of her soft body.

"From you, my dear man," she breathed, greedily bunching her fingers over the twisting muscles of his back. "You taught me...fourteen years ago...and I haven't been the same since...ahhh, Web..." He'd found her breasts and was taunting them mercilessly. "Will it always...be this way?"

"Always." He rolled her nipples between his thumb and forefinger and was rewarded by her gasp.

"Promise?" She spread her hand over his flat middle and let it follow the tapering line of dark hair to that point where it flared.

"Sunshine...mmmmmmm...ah, yesss..." What little thought her artful stroking left him was centered in his fingers, which found the tiny nub of pleasure between her legs and began to caress it as artfully. "Ahhhh, sweet...so moist, soft..."

They were both breathing shallowly, and Marni's body had begun to quiver in tune with his.

"C'mere," he ordered. Cupping her bottom, he drew

her forward, capturing her mouth and swallowing her rapturous moan as he entered her.

Knees braced on either side of his hips, she moved in rhythm with him. Her breasts rubbed against his with each forward surge, and their mouths mated hungrily. They rose together on passion's ladder, reaching the very highest rung before Web held her back.

"Watch," he whispered. He lowered his gaze to the point of their joining, then, when her head too was bowed, he slowly withdrew, as slowly filled her again, then repeated the movement.

It was too much for Marni. She cried his name once, then threw back her head and closed her eyes tight upon the waves of pulsing sensation that poured through her.

Web held himself buried deep inside her, hoping to savor each one of her spasms, but their very strength was his undoing. Without so much as another thrust, he gave a throaty moan and exploded. Arms trembling, he clutched her tightly to him. She was his anchor in far more than the storm of passion. He could only thank God that she was his.

ON A BRIGHT, SUNNY MORNING in early June, Marni and Web were married. The ceremony was held beneath the trees in the backyard of the Langes' Long Island estate and was followed by a lavish lawn luncheon for the two hundred invited guests.

Marni's mother was radiant, exuding the air of confidence that was her social trademark. Marni's father was gracious, if stoical, accepting congratulations with the formality that was his professional trademark.

Marni was in seventh heaven. Her mother had been the one to insist that the wedding be held there, and she'd personally orchestrated every step of the affair. While her father hadn't once vocally blessed the marriage, Marni had seen the tears in his eyes in those poignant moments when he'd led her down the rose-strewn aisle and to the altar, then given her away. She'd whispered a soft "I love you" to him as she'd kissed him, but after that her eyes had been only for Web.

"I now pronounce you man and wife," the minister had said, and she'd gone into Web's arms with a sense of joy, of fulfillment and promise that had once only been a dream.

In the years to come, they'd have their home, their careers and their children. Most important, though, they'd have each other. Their ties went back to when they'd both been young. They'd weathered personal storms along the way, but they'd emerged as better people, and their love was supreme.

GRANITE MAN

by Elizabeth Lowell

One

Forcing herself to let out the breath she had been holding, Mariah MacKenzie fumbled with the brass door knocker, failed to hang on to it, and curled her trembling fingers into a fist.

Fifteen years is a long time. I should have telephoned. What if my brother doesn't remember me? What if he throws me off the ranch? Where will I go then?

Using her knuckles, Mariah rapped lightly on the door frame of the ranch house. The sound echoed like thunder, but there was no response. She lifted her hand again. This time she managed to hold on to the horseshoe-shaped knocker long enough to deliver several staccato raps.

"Keep your shirt on! I'm coming!"

The voice was deep, impatient, unmistakably masculine. Mariah's heartbeat doubled even as she nervously took a backward step away from the door. A few instants later she was glad she had retreated.

The man who appeared filled the doorway. Literally. Mariah started to say her brother's name, only to find that her mouth was too dry to speak. She retreated again, unable to think, unable to breathe.

Cash McQueen frowned as he stared down at the slender girl who was backing away from him so quickly he was afraid she would fall off the porch. That would be a pity. It had been years since he had seen such an appealing female. Long legs, elegant breasts, big golden eyes, tousled hair that was the color of bittersweet chocolate, and an aura of vulnerability that slid past his hard-earned defenses.

"Can I help you?" Cash asked, trying to soften the edges of his deep voice. There was nothing he could do to gentle the rest of his appearance. He was big and he was strong and no amount of smiling could change those facts. Women usually didn't mind, but this one looked on the edge of bolting.

"My car b-boiled," Mariah said, the only thing she could think of.

"The whole thing?"

Cash's gentle voice and wry question drew a hesitant smile from Mariah. She stopped inching backward and shook her head. "Just the part that held water."

A smile changed Cash's face from forbidding to handsome. He walked out of the house and onto the front porch. Clenching her hands together, Mariah looked up at the big man who must be her brother. He had unruly, thick hair that was a gleaming chestnut brown where it wasn't streaked pale gold by the sun. He was muscular rather than soft. He looked like a man who was accustomed to using his body for hard physical work. His eyebrows were wickedly arched, darker than his hair, and his eyes were—

"The wrong color."

"I beg your pardon?" Cash asked, frowning.

Mariah flushed, realizing that she had spoken aloud.

"I'm—that is—I thought this was the Rocking M," she managed to stammer.

"It is."

All other emotions gave way to dismay as Mariah understood that the unthinkable had happened: the MacKenzie ranch had been sold to strangers.

Of the many possibilities she had imagined, this had not been among them. All her plans for coming back to the lost home of her dreams, all her half-formed hopes of pursuing a lost mine over the landscape of her ancestors, all her anticipation of being reunited with the older brother whose love had been the bright core of her childhood; all that was gone. And there was nothing to take its place except a new understanding of just how alone she was.

"Are you all right?" Cash asked, concerned by her sudden pallor, wanting to fold her into his arms and give her comfort.

Comfort? he asked himself sardonically. *Well, that too, I suppose. God, but that is one sexy woman looking like she is about to faint at my feet.*

A big, callused hand closed around Mariah's upper arm, both steadying her and making her tremble. She looked up—way up—into eyes that were a dark, smoky blue, yet as clear as a mountain lake in twilight. And, like a lake, the luminous surface concealed depths of shadow.

"Sit down, honey. You look a little pale around the edges," Cash said, urging her toward the old-fashioned porch swing. He seated her with a restrained strength that allowed no opposition. "I'll get you some water. Unless you'd like something with more kick?"

"No. I'm fine," Mariah said, but she made no move to stand up again. Her legs wouldn't have cooperated. Without thinking, she wrapped her fingers around a powerful, hairy wrist. "Did Luke MacKenzie—did the former owner leave a forwarding address?"

"Last time I checked, Luke was still the owner of the Rocking M, along with Tennessee Blackthorn."

Relief swept through Mariah. She smiled with blinding brilliance. "Are you Mr. Blackthorn?"

"No, I'm Cash McQueen," he said, smiling in return, wondering what she would do if he sat next to her and pulled her into his lap. "Sure you don't want some water or brandy?"

"I don't understand. Do you work here?"

"No. I'm visiting my sister, Luke's wife."

"Luke is married?"

Until Cash's eyes narrowed, Mariah didn't realize how dismayed she sounded. He looked at her with cool speculation in his eyes, a coolness that made her realize just how warm he had been before.

"Is Luke's marriage some kind of problem for you?" Cash asked.

Dark blue eyes watched Mariah with a curiosity that was suddenly more predatory than sensual. She knew beyond a doubt that any threat to his sister's marriage would be taken head-on by the big man who was watching her the way a hawk watched a careless field mouse.

"No problem," Mariah said faintly, fighting the tears that came from nowhere to strangle her voice. She felt her uncertain self-control fragmenting and was too tired to care. "I should have guessed he would be married by now."

"Who are you?"

The question was as blunt as the rock hammer hanging from a loop on Cash's wide leather belt. The cold steel tool looked softer than his narrowed eyes. The almost overwhelming sense of being close to hard, barely restrained masculinity increased the more Mariah looked at Cash—

wide, muscular shoulders, flat waist, lean hips, long legs whose power was hinted at with each supple shift of his weight. Cash was violently male, yet his hand on her arm had been gentle. Keeping that in mind, she tried to smile up at him as she explained why she was no threat to his sister's marriage.

"I'm Mariah MacKenzie. Luke's sister." Still trying to smile, Mariah held out her hand as she said, "Pleased to meet you, Mr. McQueen."

"Cash." The answer was automatic, as was his taking of Mariah's hand. "You're Luke's *sister?*"

Even as Cash asked the question, his senses registered the soft, cool skin of Mariah's hand, the silken smoothness of her wrist when his grip shifted, and the racing of her pulse beneath his fingertips. Hardly able to believe what he had heard, he looked again into Mariah's eyes. Only then did he realize that he had been so struck by her sexual appeal that he had overlooked her resemblance to Luke. He, too, had tawny topaz eyes and hair so brown it was almost black.

But Mariah's resemblance to her brother ended there. All five feet, eight inches of her was very definitely female. Beneath the worn jeans and faded college T-shirt were the kinds of curves that made a man's hands feel both empty and hungry to be filled. Cash remembered the smooth resilience of her arm when he had steadied her, and then he remembered the warmth beneath the soft skin.

"What in hell brings you back to the Rocking M after all these years?"

There was no way for Mariah to explain to Cash her inchoate longings for a lost home, a lost family, a lost childhood. Each time she opened her mouth to try, no words came.

"I just wanted to—to see my brother," she said finally.

Cash glanced at his wrist. His new black metal watch told the time around the globe, was guaranteed to work up to a hundred and eighty feet underwater and in temperatures down to forty below zero. It was his third such watch in less than a year. So far, it was still telling time. But then, he hadn't been out prospecting yet. The repeated shock of rock hammer or pickax on granite had done in the other watches. That, and panning for gold in the Rocking M's icy mountain creeks.

"Luke won't be in from the north range until dinner, and probably not even then," Cash said. "Carla is in Cortez shopping with Logan. They aren't due back until late tomorrow, which means that unless the Blackthorns get in early from Boulder, there won't be anyone to cook dinner except me. That's why I don't expect Luke back. Neither one of us would walk across a room to eat the other's cooking."

Mariah tried to sort out the spate of names and information, but had little success. In the end she hung on to the only words that mattered: Luke wouldn't be back for several hours. After waiting and hoping and dreaming for so many years, the hours she had left to wait seemed like an eternity. She was tired, discouraged and so sad that it was all she could do not to put her head on Cash's strong shoulder and cry. Her feelings were irrational, but then so was her whole hopeful journey back to the landscape of her childhood and her dreams.

It will be all right. Everything will work out fine. All I have to do is hang on and wait just a little longer. Luke will be here and he'll remember me and I'll remember him and everything will be all right.

Despite the familiar litany of reassurance Mariah spoke in the silence of her mind, the tears that had been making her throat raspy began to burn behind her eyelids. Knowing it was foolish, unable to help herself, she looked out across the ranch yard to MacKenzie Ridge and fought not to cry.

"Until then, someone had better go take a look at your car," Cash continued. "How far back down the road did it quit?"

He had to repeat the question twice before Mariah's wide golden eyes focused on him.

"I don't know."

The huskiness of Mariah's voice told Cash that she was fighting tears. A nearly tangible sadness was reflected in her tawny eyes, a sadness that was underlined by the vulnerable line of her mouth.

Yet even as sympathy stirred strongly inside Cash, bitter experience told him that the chances were slim and none that Mariah was one-tenth as vulnerable as she looked sitting on the porch swing, her fingers interlaced too tightly in her lap. Helpless women always found some strong, willing, stupid man to take care of them.

Someone like Cash McQueen.

Mariah looked up at Cash, her eyes wide with unshed tears and an unconscious appeal for understanding.

"I guess I'll wait here until…" Mariah's voice faded at the sudden hardening of Cash's expression.

"Don't you think your time would be better spent trying to fix your car?" Cash asked. "Or were you planning on letting the nearest man take care of it for you?"

The brusque tone of Cash's voice made Mariah flinch. She searched his eyes but saw none of the warmth that had been there before she had told him who she was.

"I hadn't thought about it," she admitted. "I didn't think about anything but getting here."

Cash grunted. "Well, you're here."

His tone made it clear that he was less than delighted by her presence. Fighting tears and a feeling of being set adrift,

Mariah told herself that it was silly to let a stranger's disapproval upset her. She looked out toward the barn, blinked rapidly, and finally focused on the building. Its silhouette triggered childhood memories, Luke playing hide-and-seek with her, catching her and lifting her laughing and squirming over his head.

"Yes, I'm here," Mariah said huskily.

"And your car isn't."

"No." She banished the last of the memories and faced the big man who was watching her without pleasure. "I'll need something to carry water."

"There's a plastic water can in the barn."

"Is there a car I could drive?"

Cash shook his head.

Mariah thought of the long walk she had just made and was on the edge of suggesting that she wait for her brother's return before she tried to cope with her car. Cash's coolly appraising look put an end to that idea. She had received that look too many times from her stepfather, a man who took pleasure only in her failures.

"Good thing I wore my walking shoes," Mariah said with forced cheerfulness.

Cash muttered something beneath his breath, then added, "Stay here. I'll take care of it for you."

"Thank you, but that's not necessary. I can—"

"The hell you can," he interrupted abruptly. "You wouldn't get a hundred yards carrying two gallons of water. Even if you did, you wouldn't know what to do once you got there, would you?"

Before Mariah could think of a suitable retort, Cash stepped off the porch and began crossing the yard with long, powerful strides. He vanished behind the barn. A few minutes later he reappeared. He was driving a battered Jeep.

As he passed the porch she realized that he didn't mean to stop for her.

"Wait!" Mariah called out, leaping up, sending the swing gyrating. "I'm going with you!"

"Why?" Cash asked, watching with disfavor as Mariah ran up to the Jeep.

"To drive the car back, of course."

"I'll tow it in."

It was too late. Mariah was scrambling into the lumpy passenger seat. Without a word Cash gunned the Jeep out of the yard and headed toward the dirt road that was the Rocking M's sole connection to the outer world.

The Jeep's canvas cover did little to shield the occupants from the wind. Hair the color of bittersweet chocolate flew in a wild cloud around Mariah's shoulders and whipped across her face. She grabbed one handful, then another, wrestling the slippery strands to a standstill, gathering and twisting the shining mass into a knot at the nape of her neck. As the wind picked apart the knot, she tucked in escaping strands.

Cash watched the process from the corner of his eye, intrigued despite himself by the glossy, silky hair and the curve of Mariah's nape, a curve that was both vulnerable and sexy. When he realized the trend of his thoughts, he was irritated. Surely by now he should have figured out that the more vulnerable a girl appeared, the greater the weapon she had to use on men such as himself—men who couldn't cure themselves of the belief that they should protect women from the harshness of life.

Stupid men, in a word.

"Luke didn't say anything about expecting you."

Although Cash said nothing more, his tone made it plain that he thought the ranch—and Luke—would have been better off without Mariah.

"He wasn't expecting me."

"What?" Cash's head swung for an instant toward Mariah.

"He doesn't know I'm coming."

Whatever Cash said was mercifully obliterated by the sudden bump and rattle as the Jeep hurtled over the cattle guard set into the dirt road. Mariah made a startled sound and hung on to the cold metal frame. The noise of wheels racing over the cattle guard, plus the smell of nearby grass and the distant tang of evergreens, triggered a dizzying rush of memories in Mariah.

Eyes the color of my own. Clever hands that made a doll whole again. Tall and strong, lifting me, tossing me, catching me and laughing with me. Dark hair and funny faces that made me smile when I wanted to cry.

There were other memories, too, darker memories of arguments and sobbing and a silence so tense Mariah had been afraid it would explode, destroying everything familiar. And then it had exploded and her mother's screams had gone on and on, rising and falling with the howling December storm.

Shivering in the aftermath of a storm that had occurred fifteen years ago, Mariah looked out over the hauntingly familiar landscape. She had recognized MacKenzie Ridge before she had seen the ranch buildings at its base. The rugged silhouette was burned into her memory. She had watched her home in the rearview mirror of her grandparents' car, and when the ranch buildings had vanished into a fold of land, she had sobbed her loss.

It hadn't been the house she mourned, or even the father who had been left behind. She had wept for Luke, the brother who had loved her when their parents were too consumed by private demons to notice either of their children.

That's all in the past. I've come home. Everything will be all right now. I'm finally home.

The reassuring litany calmed Mariah until she looked at the hard profile of the man who sat within touching distance of her. And she wanted to touch him. She wanted to ask what she had done to make him dislike her. Was it simply that she was alive, breathing, somehow reminding him of an unhappy past? It had been that way with her stepfather, an instant masculine antagonism toward another man's child that nothing Mariah did could alter.

What would she do if Luke disliked her on sight, too?

has worn off the print. The tires know the roads you
so diligently avoid," Cash said.

The reasoning there, turned relaxed, until the headrests
the far portion of the rear seat came booming into play
to last. And just ordered to touch both ends a weight of
what ain't had the faintest imprint, Rather use. Was it really
that difficult once, Mariah wondered, somehow a hidden point or
to comfort past? It had been that way with her everything
in history, mounting more people served another through
came that rush so whole and could sleep on.

What wouldn't he do if I let him find her on him. took

Two

Arms aching, Mariah held up the rumpled hood of her car
while Cash rummaged in the engine compartment, muttering choice phrases she tried very hard not to overhear. A
grimy, enigmatic array of parts was lined up on the canvas
cloth that Cash had put on the ground nearby. Mariah
looked anxiously from the greasy parts to the equally
greasy hands of the big man who had taken one look at her
sedan's ancient engine and suggested making a modern
junk sculpture of it.

"When was the last time you changed the oil?"

The tone of voice was just short of a snarl. Mariah closed
her eyes and tried to think.

"I can't remember. I wrote it in the little book in the
glove compartment, but I needed paper for a grocery list
so I—"

The rest of what Mariah said was lost beneath a rumble

of masculine disgust. She caught her lower lip between her teeth and worried the soft flesh nervously.

"When was the last time you added water to the radiator?"

That was easy. "Today. Several times. Then I ran out."

Slowly Cash's head turned toward Mariah. In the shadow of the hood his eyes burned like dark, bleak sapphire flames. "What?"

Mariah swallowed and spoke quietly, calmly, as though gentleness and sweet reason was contagious.

"I always put water in the radiator every day, sometimes more often, depending on how far I'm going. Naturally I always carry water," she added, "but I ran out today. After that little town on the way in—"

"West Fork," Cash interrupted absently.

"That's the one," she said, smiling, encouraged by the fact that he hadn't taken her head off yet.

Cash didn't return the smile.

Mariah swallowed again and finished her explanation as quickly as possible. "After West Fork, there wasn't any place to get more water. I didn't realize how long it would take to get to the ranch house, so I didn't have enough water. Every time I stopped to let things cool off, more water leaked out of the radiator and I couldn't replace it, so I wouldn't get as far next time before it boiled and I had to stop. When I recognized MacKenzie Ridge I decided it would be faster to walk."

Shaking his head, muttering words that made Mariah wince, Cash went back to poking at the dirty engine. His hands hesitated as he was struck by a thought.

"How far did you drive this wreck?"

"Today?"

"No. From the beginning of your trip."

"I started in Seattle."

"Alone?"

"Of course," she said, surprised. Did he think she'd hidden a passenger in the trunk?

Cash said something sibilant and succinct. He backed out from beneath the hood, wiped his hands on a greasy rag and glared at the filthy engine; but he was seeing Mariah's lovely, uncertain smile, her clean-limbed, sexy body and her haunting aura of having been hurt once too often. He guessed that Mariah was a bit younger than his own sister, Carla, who was twenty-three. It made Cash furious to think of a girl who seemed as vulnerable as Mariah driving alone in a totally unreliable car from Seattle to the Rocking M's desolate corner of southwestern Colorado.

Cash took the weight of the hood from Mariah's hands and let the heavy metal fall into place with a resounding crash.

"What in hell were you thinking of when you set off across the country in this worthless piece of crud?"

Mariah opened her mouth. Nothing came out. She had driven the best vehicle she could afford. What was so remarkable about that?

"That's what I thought. You didn't think at all." Disgusted, Cash threw the greasy rag on top of the useless parts. "Well, baby, this wreck is D.O.R."

"What?"

"Dead on Road," Cash said succinctly. "I'll tow it to the ranch house, but the only way you'll get back on the road is with a new engine and you'd be a fool to spend that kind of money on this dog. From the wear pattern on the tires I'd guess the frame is bent but good. I know for damn sure the body is rusted through in so many places you could use it as a sieve. The radiator *is* a sieve. The battery is a pile of corrosion. The spark plugs are beyond belief. The carburetor—'' His hand slashed the air expressively. "It's a miracle you got this far."

Mariah looked unhappily at the rumpled sedan. She started to ask if Cash were sure of his indictment, took one look at the hard line of his jaw and said nothing. Silently she watched while he attached her dead car to the Jeep. In spite of her unhappiness, she found herself appreciating the casual strength and coordination of his movements, a masculine grace and expertise that appealed to her in a way that went deeper than words.

Unfortunately, it was obvious to Mariah that the attraction wasn't mutual. After several attempts, she gave up trying to make small talk as she and Cash bumped down the one-lane dirt road leading toward the ranch house. Rather quickly the wind pulled apart the knot she had used to confine her hair. The silky wildness seethed around her face, but she didn't notice the teasing, tickling strands or the occasional, covert glances from Cash.

Mariah's long trip from Seattle in her unreliable car, her disappointment at not seeing Luke, her attraction to a man who found her aggravating rather than appealing—everything combined to drain Mariah's customary physical and mental resilience. She felt tired and bruised in a way she hadn't since her mother had died last year and she had been left to confront her stepfather without any pretense of bonds between them. Nor had her stepfather felt any need to pretend to such bonds. Immediately after the funeral, he had put a frayed cardboard carton in Mariah's hands and told her, *Your mother came to me with this. Take it and go.*

Mariah had taken the carton and gone, never understanding what she had done to earn her stepfather's coldness. She had returned to her tiny apartment, opened the carton, and found her MacKenzie heritage, the very heritage that her mother had refused ever to discuss. Holding a heavy necklace of rough gold nuggets in one hand, turning the pages of a huge family Bible with the other, Mariah had wept until she had no more tears.

Then she had begun planning to get back to the only home she had ever known—the Rocking M.

The Jeep clattered over the cattle guard that kept range cows from wandering out of the Rocking M's huge home pasture. Shrouded by dark memories, Mariah didn't notice the rattling noise the tires made as they hurtled over pipe.

Nor did Cash. He was watching Mariah covertly, accurately reading the signs of her discouragement. No matter how many times he told himself that Mariah was just one more female looking for a free ride from a man, he couldn't help regretting being so blunt about the possibilities of fixing her car. The lost look in her eyes was a silent remonstration for his lack of gentleness. He deserved it, and he knew it.

Just as Cash was on the verge of reaching for Mariah and stroking her hair in comfort, he caught himself. In silent, searing terms he castigated himself for being a fool. A child learned to keep its hands out of fire by reaching out and getting burned in the alluring dance of flames. A man learned to know his own weaknesses by having them used against himself.

Cash had learned that his greatest weakness was his bone-deep belief that a man should protect and cherish those who weren't as strong as himself, especially women and children. The weakest woman could manipulate the strongest man simply by using this protective instinct against him. That was what Linda had done. Repeatedly. After too much pain, Cash had finally realized that the more vulnerable a woman appeared, the greater was her ability to deceive him.

If the pain had gone all the way to the bone, so had the

lesson. It had been eight years since Cash had trusted any woman except Carla, his half sister, who was a decade younger than he was and infinitely more vulnerable. From the day of her birth, she had returned his interest and his care with a generous love that was uniquely her own. Carla gave more than she received, yet she would be the first one to deny it. For that, Cash loved and trusted Carla, exempting her from his general distrust of the female of the species.

Wrapped in their separate thoughts, sharing a silence that was neither comfortable nor uneasy, Cash and Mariah drove through the home pasture and up to the ranch buildings. When he parked near the house, she stirred and looked at him.

"Thank you," she said, smiling despite her own weariness. "It was kind of you to go out of your way for a stranger."

Cash looked at Mariah with unfathomable dark eyes, then shrugged. "Sure as hell someone had to clean up the mess you left. Might as well be me. I wasn't doing anything more important than looking at government maps."

Before Mariah could say anything, Cash was out of the Jeep. Silently she followed, digging her keys from her big canvas purse. She unlocked the trunk of her car and was reaching for the carton her stepfather had given her when she sensed Cash's presence at her back.

"Planning on moving in?" he asked.

Mariah followed Cash's glance to the car's tightly packed trunk. Frayed cardboard cartons took up most of the space. A worn duffel crammed as full as a sausage was wedged in next to the scarred suitcase she had bought at a secondhand shop. But it wasn't her cheap luggage that made her feel ashamed, it was Cash's cool assumption that she had come to the Rocking M as a freeloader.

Yet even as Mariah wanted fiercely to deny it, she had to admit there was an uncomfortable core of truth to what Cash implied. She did want to stay on at the Rocking M, but she didn't have enough money to pay for room and board and fix her car, too.

The screen door of the ranch house creaked open and thudded shut, distracting Cash from the sour satisfaction of watching a bright tide of guilt color Mariah's face.

"Talk about the halt leading the lame," said a masculine voice from the front porch. "Are you towing that rattletrap or is it pushing your useless Jeep?"

"That's slander," Cash said, turning toward the porch. He braced his hands on his hips, but there was amusement rather than anger in his expression.

"That's bald truth," the other man retorted. "But not as bald as those sedan's tires. Surprised that heap isn't sitting on its wheel rims. Where in hell did you—" The voice broke off abruptly. "Oh. Hello. I didn't see you behind Cash. I'll bet you belong to that, er, car."

Mariah turned around and looked up and felt as though she had stepped off into space.

She was looking into her own eyes.

"L-Luke?" she asked hoarsely. "Oh, Luke, after all these years is it really you?"

Luke's eyes widened. His pupils dilated with shock. He searched Mariah's face in aching silence, then his arms opened, reaching for her. An instant later she was caught up in a huge bear hug. Laughing, crying, holding on to her brother, Mariah said Luke's name again and again, hardly able to believe that he was as glad to see her as she was to see him. It had been so long since anyone had hugged her. She hadn't realized how long until this instant.

"Fifteen years," Mariah said. "It's been fifteen years. I thought you had forgotten me."

"Not a chance, Muffin," Luke said, holding Mariah tightly. "If I had a dime for every time I've wondered where you were and if you were happy, I'd be a rich man instead of a broke rancher."

Hearing the old nickname brought a fresh spate of tears to Mariah. Wiping her eyes, smiling, she tried to speak but was able only to cry. She clung more tightly to Luke's neck, holding on as she had when she was five and he was twelve and he had comforted her during their parents' terrifying arguments.

"Without you, I don't know what would have happened to me," she whispered.

Luke simply held Mariah tighter, then slowly lowered her back to the ground. Belatedly she realized how big her brother had become. He was every bit as large as Cash. In fact, she decided, looking from one man to the other, they were identical in size.

"We're both six foot three," Luke said, smiling, reading his sister's mind in the look on her face. "We weigh the same, too. Just under two hundred pounds."

Mariah blinked. "Well, I've grown up, too, but not that much. I'm a mere five-eight, one twenty-six."

Luke stepped back far enough to really look at the young woman who was both familiar and a stranger. He shook his head as he cataloged the frankly feminine lines of her body. "Couldn't you have grown up ugly? Or at least skinny? I'll be beating men back with a whip."

Mariah swiped at tears and smiled tremulously. "Thanks. I think you're beautiful, too."

Cash snorted. "Luke's about as beautiful as the south end of a northbound mule. Never could understand what Carla saw in him."

Instantly Mariah turned on Cash, ready to defend her big brother. Then she realized that Luke was laughing and Cash was watching him with a masculine affection that was like nothing she had ever encountered. It was as though the men were brothers in blood as well as in law.

"Ignore him, Muffin," Luke said, hugging Mariah again. "He's just getting even for my comments about his ratty, unreliable Jeep." He looked over Mariah's head at Cash. "Speaking of ratty and unreliable, what's wrong with her car?"

"Everything."

"Um. What's right with it?"

"Nothing. She started in Seattle. It's a damned miracle she got this far. Proves the old saying—God watches over fools and drunks."

"Seattle, huh?" Luke glanced at the open trunk, accurately assessed its contents and asked, "Did you leave anything you care about behind?"

Mariah shook her head, suddenly nervous.

"Good. Remember the old ranch house where we used to play hide-and-seek?"

She nodded.

"You can live there."

"But…" Mariah's voice died.

She looked from one large man to the other. Luke looked expectant. Cash wore an expression of barely veiled cynicism. She remembered his words: *Planning on moving in?* Unhappily she looked back at Luke.

"I can't just move in on you," she said.

"Why not?"

"What about your wife?"

"Carla will be delighted. Since Ten and Diana started living part-time in Boulder, there hasn't been a woman for Carla to talk to a lot of the time. She hasn't said anything, but I'm sure she gets a little lonely. The Rocking M is hard on women that way."

Though Luke said nothing more, Mariah sensed all that he didn't say, their mother's tears and long silences, their father's anger at the woman who couldn't adjust to ranch life, a woman who simply slipped through his fingers into a twilight world of her own making.

"But I can't—" Mariah's voice broke. "I can't pay my way. I only have enough money for—"

Luke talked over her stumbling words. "Don't worry. You'll earn your keep. Logan needs an aunt and Carla sure as hell will need help a few months down the road. Six and a half months, to be exact."

The cynical smile vanished from Cash's mouth as the implication of Luke's words sank in.

"Is Carla pregnant?" Cash demanded.

Luke just grinned.

Cash whooped with pleasure and gave Luke a bone-cracking hug.

"It better be a girl, this time," Cash warned. "The world needs more women like Carla."

"I hear you. But I'll be damned grateful for whatever the good Lord sends along. Besides," Luke added with a wolfish smile, "if at first we don't succeed..."

Cash burst out laughing.

Mariah looked from one grinning man to the other and felt a fragile bubble of pleasure rise and burst softly within her, showering her with a feeling of belonging she had known only in her dreams. Hardly able to believe her luck, she looked around the dusty, oddly luminous ranch yard and felt dreams and reality merge.

Then Mariah looked at the tall, powerful man whose eyes were the deepest blue she had ever seen, and she decided that reality was more compelling than any dream she had ever had.

Three

———

"**A**re you sure you're a MacKenzie?" Cash asked Mariah as he removed another slab of garlic pork from the platter. "No MacKenzie I know can cook."

"Carla can," Luke pointed out quickly.

"Yeah, but that's different. Carla was born a McQueen."

"And Mariah was born a MacKenzie," Nevada Blackthorn said matter-of-factly as he took two more slices of meat off the platter Mariah held out to him. "Even a hardrock miner like you should be able to figure that out. All you have to do is look at her eyes."

"Thanks," Mariah said.

She smiled tentatively at the dark, brooding man whose own eyes were a startlingly light green. Nevada had been introduced to her as the Rocking M's *segundo*, the second in command. When his brother Ten was gone, Nevada was the foreman, as well. He was also one of the most unnerving men Mariah had ever met. Not once had she seen a smile flash behind his neatly trimmed beard. Yet she had no feeling that he disliked her. His reserve was simply part of his nature, a basic solitude that made her feel sad.

Cash watched Mariah smile at Nevada. Irritation pricked at Cash even as he told himself that if Mariah wanted to stub her toe on a hard piece of business like Nevada, it wasn't Cash's concern.

Yet no sooner had Cash reached that eminently reasonable decision when he heard himself saying, "Don't waste your smiles on Nevada. He's got no more heart than a stone."

"And you've got no more brain," Nevada said matter-of-factly. Only the slight crinkling at the corners of his eyes betrayed his amusement. "Like Ten says—Granite Man."

"Your brother was referring to my interest in mining."

"My brother was referring to your thick skull."

Cash grinned. "Care to bet on that?"

"Not one chance in hell. After a year of watching you play cards, I know why people nicknamed you Cash." Nevada glanced sideways at Mariah. "Never play cards with a man named Cash."

"But I like to play cards," she said.

"You do?" Cash asked, looking at her sharply.

Mariah nodded.

"Poker?"

Dark hair swung as Mariah nodded again.

"I'll be damned."

Nevada lifted one black eyebrow. "Probably, but not many men would brag about it."

Luke snickered.

Cash ignored the other men, focusing only on Mariah. It was easy to do. There was an elegance to her face and a subtle lushness to the curves of her body that caught Cash anew each time he looked at her. Even when he reminded himself that Mariah's aura of vulnerability was false, he remained interested in the rest of her.

Very interested.

"Could I tempt you into a hand or two of poker after dinner?" he asked.

"No!" Luke and Nevada said simultaneously.

Mariah looked at the two men, realized they were kidding—sort of—and smiled again at Cash. "Sure. But first I promised to show the MacKenzie family Bible to Luke."

An unreasonable disappointment snaked through Cash.

"Maybe after that?" Mariah asked hesitantly, looking at Cash with an eagerness she couldn't hide, sensing his interest despite his flashes of hostility. Though she had never been any man's lover, she certainly knew when a man looked at her with masculine appreciation. Cash was looking at her that way right now.

When Mariah passed the steaming biscuits to Cash, the sudden awareness of him that made her eyes luminous brought each of his masculine senses to quivering alert. Deliberately he let his fingertips brush over Mariah's hands as he took the warm, fragrant food from her. The slight catch of her breath and the abrupt speeding of the pulse in her throat told Cash how vividly she was aware of him as a man.

Covertly, Cash glanced at Luke, wondering how he would react to his sister's obvious interest in his best friend. Luke was talking in a low voice with Nevada about the cougar tracks the *segundo* had seen that morning in Wildfire Canyon. Cash looked back to Mariah, measuring the sensual awareness that gave her eyes the radiance of candle flames and made the pulse at the base of her soft throat beat strongly.

Desire surged through Cash, shocking him with its speed and ferocity, hardening him in an aching torrent of blood.

He fought to control his torrential, unreasonable hunger for Mariah by telling himself that she was no better looking than a lot of women, that he was thirty-three, too old to respond this fast, this totally, to his best friend's sister. And in any case Mariah was just one more woman hungry for a lifetime sinecure—look at how quickly she had moved in on the Rocking M. Her token protests had been just that. Token.

"You're a good cook," Nevada said, handing Mariah the salt before she had time to do more than glance in the direction of the shaker. "Hope Luke can talk you into staying. From what Ten has told me, the Rocking M never had a cook worth shooting until Carla came along. But by January, Carla won't feel much like cooking."

"How did you know?" Luke asked, startled. "Dr. Chacon just confirmed it today."

Nevada shrugged. "Small things. Her skin. Her scent. The way she holds her body."

Cash shook his head. "Your daddy must have been a sorcerer. You have the most acute perceptions of anyone I've ever met."

"Chalk it up to war, not sorcery," Nevada said, pouring himself a cup of coffee. "You spend years tracking men through the night and see what happens to your senses. The Blackthorns come from a long line of warriors. The slow and the stupid didn't make the cut."

Nevada set the coffeepot aside and glanced back at Luke. "If you want, I'll check out that new cougar as soon as Ten gets back. I couldn't follow the tracks long enough to tell if it was male or female. Frankly, I'm hoping the cat is a young male, just coming out of the high country to mate and move on."

"I hope so, too. Wildfire Canyon can't support more than one or maybe two adult cats in a lean season. Long about

February, some of the cattle in the upland pastures might get to looking too tasty to a big, hungry cat.'' Luke sipped coffee and swore softly. ''I need to know more about cougars. The old ranchers say the cats are cow killers, the government says the cats only eat rabbits and deer....'' Frowning, Luke ran a hand through his hair. ''Check into the new tracks when Ten comes back, but I can't turn you loose for more than a day or two. Too damned short-handed.''

''Need me?'' Cash asked, trying and failing to keep the reluctance from his voice. He had been planning on getting in at least a week of prospecting in the Rocking M's high country. He no longer expected to find Mad Jack's lost mine, but he enjoyed the search too much to give it up.

''Maybe Luke needs you, but I don't,'' Nevada said. ''When it comes to cows you make a hell of a good ranch mechanic.''

Mariah looked at Cash and remembered his disgust with the state of her car's engine. ''Are you a mechanic?''

Luke snickered. ''Ask his Jeep. It runs only on alternate Thursdays.''

''The miracle is that it runs at all,'' Nevada said. ''Damned thing is even older than Cash is. Better looking, too.''

''I don't know why I sit and listen to this slander,'' Cash complained without heat.

''Because it's that or do dishes. It's your turn, remember?'' Luke asked.

''Yeah, but I was hoping you'd forget.''

''That'll be the day.'' Luke pushed back from the table, gathered up his dishes and headed for the kitchen. ''Nevada, you might want to stick around for the MacKenzie family show-and-tell. After all, some of them are your ancestors, too.''

Nevada's head turned toward Luke with startling speed. "What?"

There was a clatter of dishes from the kitchen, then Luke came back to the big "mess hall" that adjoined the kitchen. He poured himself another cup of potent coffee before he looked down at Ten's younger brother with an odd smile.

"Didn't Ten tell you? The two of us finally figured it out last winter. We share a pair of great-great-grandparents—Case and Mariah MacKenzie."

"Be damned."

"No doubt," Cash said slyly, "but no man wants to brag about it, right?"

Nevada gave him a sideways glance that would have been threatening were it not for the telltale crinkling around Nevada's eyes. Luke just kept on talking, thoroughly accustomed to the masculine chaffing that always accompanied dinners on the Rocking M.

"Case was the MacKenzie who started the Rocking M," Luke explained as he looked back at Cash. "Actually, Mariah should have been one of your ancestors. Her granddaddy was a gold prospector."

"He was? Really?" Mariah said eagerly, her voice lilting with excitement. "I never knew that Grandpa Lucas was a prospector."

Luke blinked. "He wasn't."

"But you just said he was."

Simultaneously Nevada spoke. "I don't remember my parents talking about any MacKenzie ancestors."

"No, I didn't," Luke said to Mariah. Then, to Nevada, "I'm not surprised. It wasn't the kind of relationship that families used to talk about."

When Nevada and Mariah began speaking at once, Cash stood up with a resigned expression and began carrying dirty dishes into the kitchen. No one noticed his comings and goings or his absence when he stayed in the kitchen. Once he glanced through the doorway, saw Luke drawing family trees on a legal tablet and went back to the dishes. The next time Cash looked out, Mariah was gone. He was irrationally pleased that Nevada had remained behind. The bearded cowhand was too good-looking by half.

Cash attacked the counters with unusual vigor, but before he had finished, he heard Mariah's voice again.

"Here it is, Nevada. Proof positive that we're kissing kin."

The dishrag hit the sink with a distinct smack. Wiping his hands on his jeans, Cash moved silently across the kitchen until he could see into the dining room. Mariah stood next to Luke. She was holding a frayed cardboard carton as though it contained the crown jewels of England.

"What's that?" Luke asked, eyeing the disreputable box his sister was carrying so triumphantly to the cleared table.

"This is the MacKenzie family Bible," she said in a voice rich with satisfaction and subdued excitement.

There was a time of stretching silence ended by the audible rush of Luke's breath as Mariah removed the age-worn, leather-bound volume from the box. The Bible's intricate gilt lettering rippled and gleamed in the light.

Nevada whistled softly. He reached for the Bible, then stopped, looking at Mariah.

"May I?" he asked.

"Of course," she said, holding the thick, heavy volume out to him with both hands. "It's your family, too."

While Cash watched silently from the doorway, Nevada shook his head, refusing to take the book. Instead, he moved his fingertips across the fragile leather binding, caressing it as though it were alive.

The sensuality and emotion implicit in that gesture made conflicting feelings race through Cash—irritation at the softness in Mariah's eyes as she watched the unsmiling man touch the book, curiosity about the old Bible itself, an aching sense of time and history stretching from past to present to future; but most of all Cash felt a bitter regret that he would never have a child who would share his past, his present or his future.

"How old is this?" Nevada asked, taking the heavy book at last and putting it on the table.

"It was printed in 1867," Mariah said, "but the first entry isn't until the 1870s. It records the marriage of Case MacKenzie and Mariah Elizabeth Turner. I've tried to make out the date, but the ink is too blurred."

As she spoke, Mariah turned to the glossy pages within the body of the Bible where births, deaths and marriages were recorded. Finger hovering just above the old paper, she searched the list of names quickly.

"There it is," she said triumphantly. "Matthew Case MacKenzie, our great-grandfather. He married a woman called Charity O'Hara."

Luke looked quickly down the page of names, then pointed to another one. "And there's your great-granddaddy, Nevada. David Tyrell MacKenzie."

Nevada glanced at the birthdate, flipped to the page that recorded marriages and deaths, and found only a date of death entered. David Tyrell MacKenzie had died before he was twenty-six. Neither his marriage nor the births of any of his children had been recorded.

"No marriage listed," Nevada said neutrally. "No children, either."

"There wasn't a marriage," Luke said. "According to my grandfather, his uncle David was a rover and a loner. He spent most of his time living with or fighting various Indian tribes. No woman could hold him for long."

Nevada's mouth shifted into a wry line that was well

short of a smile. "Yeah, that's always been a problem for us Blackthorns. Except for Ten. He's well and truly married." Nevada flipped the last glossy pages of the register, found no more entries and looked at Luke. "Nothing here. What makes you think we're related?"

"Mariah—no, not you, Muffin, the first Mariah. Anyway, she kept a journal. She mentioned a woman called Winter Moon in connection with her son David. Ten said your great-grandmother's name was Winter Moon."

Nevada nodded slowly.

"There was no formal marriage, but there was rumor of a child. A girl."

"Bends-Like-the-Willow," Nevada said. "My grandmother."

"Welcome to the family, cousin," Luke said, grinning and holding out his hand.

Nevada took it and said, "Well, you'll have no shortage of renegades in the MacKenzie roster now. The Blackthorns are famous for them. Bastards descended from a long line of bastards."

"Beats no descent at all," Luke said dryly.

Only Mariah noticed Cash standing in the doorway, his face expressionless as he confronted once again the fact that he would never know the sense of family continuity that other people took for granted. That, as much as his distrust of women, was the reason why he hadn't married again.

And why he never would.

Four

Cash turned back to the kitchen and finished cleaning it without taking time out for any more looks into the other room. When he was finished he poured himself a cup of coffee from the big pot that always simmered on the back of the stove and walked around the room slowly, sipping coffee. Finally he sat down alone at the kitchen table. The conversation from the dining room filtered through his thoughts, sounds without meaning.

His dark blue eyes looked at the kitchen walls where Carla had hung kitchen utensils that had been passed down through generations of MacKenzies and would be passed on to her own children. Cash's eyes narrowed against the pain of knowing that he would leave no children of his own when he died.

For the hundredth time he told himself how lucky he was to have a nephew whose life he was allowed to share. When he traced Logan's hairline and the shape of his jaw,

Cash could see his own father and himself in his half-sister's child. If Logan's laughter and curiosity and stubbornness made Cash ache anew to have a child of his own, that was too bad. He would just have to get over it.

"...real gold?"

"It is. The nuggets supposedly came from Mad Jack's mine."

Nevada's question and Mariah's answer were an irresistible lure for Cash. He set aside his cooled cup of coffee and went into the room that opened off the kitchen.

Mariah was sitting between Luke and Nevada, who was looking up from the handful of faded newspaper clippings and letters he had collected from the Bible. Despite his question, Nevada spared only a moment's glance for the gold that rippled and flowed between Mariah's hands like water. The necklace of nuggets linked by a long, heavy gold chain didn't interest Nevada as much as the faded, smudged marks on the brittle paper he held.

"Cash?" Luke called out without looking up. "What the hell is taking you so—oh, there you are. Remember the old jewelry I thought was lost? Look at this. Mother must have taken the chain when she left Dad. Muffin brought it back."

Cash's large, powerful hand reached over Mariah's shoulder. Her breath came in swiftly when his forearm brushed lightly against the curve of her neck and shoulder. His flesh was hard, radiating vitality, and the thick hair on his arm burned with metallic gold highlights. When he turned his hand so that it was palm up, Mariah saw the strong, raised, taut veins centered in his wrist, silent testimony to the times when his heart had had to beat strongly to feed the demands he made on his muscular body.

The sudden desire to trace the dark velvet branching of Cash's life was so great that Mariah had to close her eyes before she gave in to it.

"May I?" Cash asked.

Too shaken by her own reaction to speak, Mariah opened her eyes and handed the loops of chain over to Cash. She told herself it was an accident that her fingertips slid over his wrist, but she knew she lied. She also knew she would never forget the hard strength of his tendons or the alluring suppleness of the veins beneath the clean, tanned skin.

Silently Mariah watched Cash handle the necklace, testing its weight with his palm and the hardness of random nuggets with his fingernail. Very faint marks appeared on the rough gold, legacy of his skillful probing.

"High-test stuff," Cash said simply. "Damn few impurities. I couldn't tell without a formal assay, but I'd guess this is about as pure as gold gets without man's help."

"Is it from Mad Jack's mine?" Mariah asked.

Cash shrugged, but his eyes were intent as he went from nugget to nugget on the old necklace, touching, probing, measuring the malleable metal against his own knowledge and memories. Then, saying nothing, he took Mariah's hand and heaped the necklace in it. Gold chain whispered and moved in a cool fall over both sides of her palm, but the weight of the nuggets that remained in her palm kept the necklace from falling to the table.

Cash pulled a key from his jeans pocket. Dangling from the ring was a hollow metal cylinder about half the size of his thumb. With a deftness that was surprising for such big hands, he unscrewed the cylinder.

"Hold out your other hand," he said to Mariah.

She did, hoping that no one else sensed the sudden race of her heart when Cash's hand came up beneath hers, steadying it and cupping her fingers at the same time. Holding her with one hand, he upended the cylinder over her palm. She made a startled sound when a fat gold nugget dropped into her hand. The lump was surprisingly heavy for its size.

Carefully Cash selected a strand of chain and draped it over her palm so that one of the necklace nuggets rested next to the nugget he had taken from the cylinder. There was no apparent difference in the color of the gold, or in the texture of the surface. Both lumps of gold were angular and rough rather than rounded and smooth. Both were of a very deep, richly golden hue.

"Again, without an assay it's impossible to be sure," Cash said, "but…" He shrugged.

Mariah looked up at Cash with eyes the color of gold. "They're from Mad Jack's mine, aren't they?"

"I don't know. I've never found the mine." Cash looked down into Mariah's eyes and thought again of golden heat, golden flames, desire like a knife deep in his loins. "But I'd bet my last cent that these nuggets came from the same place, wherever that is."

"You mentioned that Case kept a journal," Mariah said, her voice a husky rasp that made Cash's blood thicken.

"Yes," Luke answered, though his sister hadn't looked at him, having eyes only for the gold in her hands—and for Cash, the man who hunted for gold.

"Didn't he say where the mine was?" she asked.

"No. All we know for sure was that Case had saddlebags full of gold from Mad Jack's mine."

"Why?"

"He was going to give it to Mad Jack's son. Instead he gave it to Mariah, Mad Jack's granddaughter."

That caught Mariah's attention. "You mean it's really true?" she asked, turning quickly toward Luke. "You weren't just joking? We're really related to Mad Jack?"

"Sure. Where else do you think the nuggets in that necklace came from? It used to be a man's watch chain. Mariah had it made for Case as a wedding gift. The chain came down through the family, staying with whichever son held the Rocking M. Until Mother left.'' Luke shrugged. ''I guess she thought she had earned it. Maybe she had. God knows she hated every minute she ever spent on the ranch.''

Mariah looked at the gold heaped on her palm, shining links infused with a legacy of both love and hatred. Yet all she said was ''That explains the modern clasp. I assumed the old one had fallen apart, but watch chains don't need clasps, do they?'' Without hesitation she poured the long, heavy chain and bulky nuggets into a heap in front of Luke. ''Here. It belongs to you.''

He looked startled. ''I didn't mean—''

''I know you didn't,'' she interrupted. ''It's still yours. It belongs with the man who holds the Rocking M. You.''

''I've been thinking about that. Half of what I inherited should be—''

''No.'' Mariah's interruption was swift and determined. ''The ranch was meant to be the inheritance of whichever MacKenzie son could hold it. Mariah's letters made that quite clear.''

''That might have been fair in the past, but it sure as hell isn't fair now.''

''It wasn't fair that our parents couldn't get along or that Mother had a nervous breakdown or that Dad drank too much or that I was taken away from the only person who really loved me. You.'' Mariah touched Luke's hand. ''Lots of life isn't fair. So what?'' Her smile was a bittersweet curve of acceptance. ''You offered me a home when I had none. That's all I hoped for and more than I had any right to expect. Or accept.''

''You'll by God accept it if I have to nail your feet to the floor,'' Luke said, squeezing Mariah's hand.

She laughed and tried to blink away the sudden tears in her eyes. "I accept. Thank you."

Luke picked up the gold chain and dumped it back in Mariah's hand. She tilted her palm, letting the heavy, cool gold slide back to the table.

"Mariah," he began roughly. "Damn it, it's yours."

"No. Make it back into a watch chain and wear it. Or give it to Logan. Or to your next child. Or to whichever child holds the Rocking M. But," Mariah added, speaking quickly, overriding the objections she saw in her brother's tawny eyes, "that doesn't mean I wouldn't like a gold necklace of my own. So, with your permission, I'll go looking for Mad Jack's mine. I've always believed I would find a lost gold mine someday."

Luke laughed, then realized that Mariah was serious. Smiling crookedly, he said, "Muffin, Cash has been looking for that mine for—how many years?"

"Nine."

Startled, Mariah looked up at Cash. "You have?"

He nodded slightly.

"And if a certified, multi-degreed geologist, a man who makes his living finding precious metals for other people—" began Luke.

"You do?" interrupted Mariah, still watching Cash with wide golden eyes.

He nodded again.

"—can't find Mad Jack's lost mine," Luke continued, talking over his sister, "then what chance do you have?"

Mariah started to speak, then sighed, wondering how she could explain what she barely understood herself.

"Remember how you used to put me to bed and tell me stories?" she asked after a few moments.

"Sure. You would watch me all wide-eyed and fascinated. Nobody ever paid that much attention to me but you. Made me feel ten feet tall.''

She smiled and said simply, "You were. I would lie in bed and forget about Mother and Dad yelling downstairs and I'd listen to you talking about the calves or the new colts or some adventure you'd had. Sometimes you'd sneak in with cookies and a box full of old pictures and we would make up stories about the people. And sometimes you'd talk about Mad Jack and his mine and how we would go exploring and find it and buy everything the ranch didn't have so Mother would be happy on the Rocking M. We used to talk about that a lot.''

In silent comfort Luke squeezed Mariah's hand. "I remember.''

She leaned forward with an urgency she couldn't suppress. "I've always believed I can find that mine. I'm Mad Jack's own blood, after all. Please, Luke. Let me look. What harm can there be in that?'' Despite the need driving her, Mariah smiled teasingly and added, "I'll give you half of whatever I find, cross my heart and hope to die.''

Luke laughed, shaking his head, unable to take her seriously. "Muffin, this is a big damned ranch. It's a patchwork quilt of outright ownership, plus lease lands from three government agencies, plus water rights and mineral rights and other things only a land lawyer or a professional gold hunter like Cash would understand.''

"I'll learn.''

"Oh hell, honey, if you found anything in Rocking M's high country land but granite and cow flops, I'd give it to you without hesitation and you know it, but—''

"Sold!'' Mariah crowed, interrupting before Luke could say anything she didn't want to hear. She looked at Nevada and Cash. "You heard him. You're my witnesses.''

Nevada looked up, nodded, and returned his attention to one of the old pieces of paper he held.

Cash was much more attentive to Mariah. "I heard," he said, watching her closely. "But just what makes you so sure that mine is on the Rocking M?"

"Mariah said it was. It's in her letter to the son who inherited the ranch."

Luke looked up at Cash. "You were right. Damn. I was hoping that mine would never..." He shrugged and said no more.

Silently Cash took the single nugget from Mariah's hand. A few deft movements returned the gold to its cylinder.

"What do you mean, Cash was right?" she asked. "And why were you hoping he was wrong?"

There was a pause before Luke said anything. When he finally did speak, he answered only her first question.

"When Mother cleaned out the family heirlooms, she overlooked a fat poke of gold, all that was left from Case's saddlebags. I showed the poke to Cash. He took one look and knew the gold hadn't come from any of the known, old-time strikes around here."

"Of course," Mariah said. "The MacKenzie gold wasn't found in placer pockets."

Cash looked at Mariah with renewed interest. "How did you know?"

"I did my homework." She held up her hand, ticking off names with her fingers. "The strikes at Moss Creek, Hard Luck, Shin Splint, Brass Monkey, Deer Creek, and Lucky Lady were all placer gold. Some small nuggets, a lot of dust. Everything was smooth from being tumbled in water." Mariah gestured toward the necklace. "For convenience we call those lumps of gold 'nuggets,' but I doubt they spent any real time in the bottom of a stream. If they had, they would be round or at least rounded off. But they're rough and asymmetrical. The longer I thought about it, the more certain I was that the lumps came from 'jewelry rock.'"

"What's that?" Luke asked.

Cash answered before Mariah could. "It's an old miner's term for quartz that is so thickly veined with pure gold that the ore can be broken apart in your bare hands. It's the richest kind of gold strike. Veins of gold like that are the original source of all the big nuggets that end up in placer pockets when the mother lodes are finally eroded away and washed by rain down into streams."

"Is that what you think Mad Jack's mine is?" Luke persisted. "A big strike of jewelry rock?"

"I wasn't sure. Except for the chunk you gave me—" Cash flicked his thumbnail against the cylinder "—the poke was filled with flakes and big, angular grains, the kind of thing that would come from a crude crushing process of really high-grade ore." Thoughtfully Cash stirred the chain with a blunt fingertip. Reflected light shifted and gleamed in shades of metallic gold. "But if these nuggets all came from Mad Jack's mine, it was God's own jewelry box, as close to digging pure gold as you can get this side of Fort Knox."

Luke said something unhappy and succinct beneath his breath.

Mariah looked at her brother in disbelief. "What's wrong with that? I think it's fantastic!"

"Ever read about Sutter's Mill?" he asked laconically.

"Sure. That was the one that set off the California gold rush in 1849. It was one of the richest strikes in history."

"Yeah. Remember what happened to the mill?"

"Er, no."

"It was trampled to death in the rush. So was a lot of other land. I don't need that kind of grief. We have enough trouble keeping pothunters out of the Anasazi ruins on Wind Mesa and in September Canyon."

"What ruins?" Mariah asked.

"They're all over the place. Would you like to see them?" Luke asked hopefully, trying to sidetrack her from the prospect of gold.

"Thanks, but I'd rather look for Mad Jack's mine."

Cash laughed ruefully. When he spoke, his voice was rich with certainty. "Forget it, Luke. Once the gold bug bites you, you're hooked for life. Not one damn thing is as bright as the shine of undiscovered gold. It's a fever that burns out everything else."

Luke looked surprised but Mariah nodded vigorously, making dark brown hair fly. She knew exactly what Cash meant.

Looking from Cash to Mariah, Nevada raised a single black eyebrow, shrugged, and returned his attention to the paper he was very gently unfolding on the table's surface.

"Smile," Mariah coaxed Luke. "You'd think we were talking about the Black Death."

"That can be cured by antibiotics," he shot back. "What do you think will happen if word gets out that there's a fabulous lost mine somewhere up beyond MacKenzie Ridge? A lot of our summer grazing is leased from the government, but the mineral rights *aren't* leased. There are rules and restrictions and bureaucratic papers to chase, but basically, when it comes to prospecting, it's come one, come all. Worst of all, mineral rights take precedence over other rights."

Mariah looked to Cash, who nodded.

"So we get a bunch of weekend warriors making camp-fires that are too big," Luke continued, "carrying guns they don't know how to use, drinking booze they can't hold, and generally being jackasses. I can live with that if I have to. What I can't live with is when they start tearing up the fences and creeks and watersheds. This is a cattle ranch, not a mining complex. I want to keep it that way."

"But…" Mariah's voice faded. She began worrying her lower lip between her teeth. "Does this mean I can't look for Mad Jack's mine?"

Luke swiped his fingers through his hair in a gesture of frustration. "No. But I want you to promise me two things. First, I don't want you telling anyone about Mad Jack's damned missing mine. That goes for Nevada, too. And I mean no one. Cash didn't even tell Carla."

"No problem," Nevada said. He looked at Cash with blunt approval. "You've been looking for nine years, huh? I like a man who can keep his mouth shut."

Cash's lips made a wry line and he said not one word.

"No problem for me, either," Mariah said, shrugging. "I don't have anyone to tell but you and you already know. What's the second thing?"

"I don't want you going out alone and looking for that damned mine," Luke said. "That's wild, rough country out there."

Mariah was on the verge of agreeing when she stopped. "Wait a minute. I can't tell anyone, right?"

Luke nodded.

"And you, Nevada and Cash are the only other ones who know. Right?"

"Carla knows," Luke said. "I told her myself."

"So five people know, including me."

"Right."

"Tell me, older brother—how much time do you have to spend looking for lost mines?"

"None," he said flatly.

"Nevada?"

He looked toward Luke, but it was Cash who spoke first.

"Nevada has cougar tracking duty. That takes care of his spare time for the summer."

The satisfaction in Cash's voice was subtle but unmistakable. Luke heard it. His smile was so small and swift that only Nevada saw it.

Mariah didn't notice. She was looking at Cash with hopeful eyes, waiting for him to volunteer. He didn't seem to notice her.

"No one prospects the high country in the winter," Luke said unhelpfully.

Mariah simply said, "Cash?"

"Sorry," he said. "That country is too rough for a tenderfoot like you."

"I've camped out before."

Cash grunted but was obviously unimpressed.

"I've hiked, too."

"Who carried your pack?"

"I did."

He grunted again. The sound wasn't encouraging.

Inspiration struck Mariah. "I'll do the cooking. I'll even do the dishes, too. Please?"

Cash looked at her luminous golden eyes and the graceful hand resting on his bare forearm in unconscious pleading. Desire shot through him at the thought of having her pleading with him for his skill as a lover rather than his expertise in hunting for gold.

"*No,*" Cash said, more roughly than he had intended.

Mariah flinched as though she had been slapped. Hastily she withdrew her hand from his arm.

For an instant Luke's eyes widened, then narrowed with a purely male assessment. Soon his mouth shifted into a smile that was both sympathetic and amused as he realized what Cash's problem was.

"If I were you, Granite Man," Nevada drawled calmly, "I'd change my mind."

Cash shot the other man a savage look. "You're not me."

"Does that mean you're volunteering to go gold hunting?" Mariah said to Nevada, hoping her voice didn't sound as hurt as she felt by Cash's harsh refusal.

"Sorry, Muffin," Luke said, cutting across anything Nevada might have wanted to say. "I'm too shorthanded as it is. I can't afford to turn loose of Nevada."

"Damn shame," Nevada said without heat. "Hate to see a good treasure map go to waste."

"What?" Luke and Cash said together.

Silently Nevada pushed a piece of paper toward Mariah. Cash bent over her shoulder, all but holding his breath so that he wouldn't take in her fragile, tantalizing scent.

"I'm a warrior, not a prospector," Nevada said, "but I've read more than one map drawn by a barely literate man. Offhand, I'd guess this one shows the route to Mad Jack's mine."

Five

With a harshly suppressed sound of disgust and anger, Cash looked from the age-darkened, brittle paper to Mariah's innocent expression.

No wonder she was so eager to trade her nonexistent rights of inheritance in exchange for Luke's permission to prospect on the Rocking M—she has a damned map to follow to Mad Jack's mine!

Yet Mariah had looked so vulnerable when she had pleaded with Cash for his help.

Sweet little con artist. God. Why are men so stupid? And why am I so particularly stupid!

Mariah glanced from the paper to Nevada and smiled wryly. "I got all excited the first time I looked at it, too. Then I looked again. And again. I stared until I was cross-eyed, but I still couldn't make out two-thirds of the chicken scratches. Even if I assume Mad Jack drew this—and that's by no means a certainty—he didn't even mark north or south in any way I can decipher. As for labeling any of the landmarks, not a chance. I suspect the old boy was indeed illiterate. There's not a single letter of the alphabet on the whole map.''

''He didn't need words. He read the land, not books.'' Nevada turned the map until the piece of paper stood on one chewed corner. ''That's north,'' he said, indicating the upper corner.

''You're sure?'' she asked, startled. ''How can you tell?''

''He's right,'' Cash said an instant later. He stared at the map in growing excitement. ''That's Mustang Point. Nothing else around has that shape. Which means…yes, there. Black Canyon. Then that must be Satan's Bath, which leads to the narrow rocky valley, then to Black Springs…'' Cash's voice trailed off into mutterings.

Mariah watched, wide-eyed, as local place names she had never heard of were emphasized by stabs of Cash's long index finger. Then he began muttering words she had heard before, pungent words that told her he had run into a dead end. She started to ask what was wrong, but held her tongue. Luke and Nevada were standing now, leaning over the map in front of her, tracing lines that vanished into a blurred area that looked for all the world as though someone long ago had spilled coffee on the paper, blotting out the center of the map.

''Damn, that's enough to peeve a saint,'' Cash said, adding a few phrases that were distinctly unsaintly. ''Some stupid dipstick smudged the only important part of the map. Now it's useless!''

''Not quite,'' Luke said. ''Now you know the general area of the ranch to concentrate on.''

Cash shot his friend a look of absolute disgust. ''Hell,

Luke, where do you think I've been looking for the past two years?''

"Oh. Devil's Peak area, huh?''

Cash grunted. "It's well named. It has more cracks and crannies, rills and creeks than any twelve mountains. It looks like it's been shattered by God's own rock hammer. I've used the line shack at Black Springs for my base. So far, I've managed to pan the lower third of a single small watershed.''

"Find anything?''

"Trout,'' Cash said succinctly.

Mariah licked her lips. "Trout? Real, free-swimming, wild mountain trout?''

A smile Cash couldn't prevent stole across his lips. "Yeah. Sleek, succulent little devils, every one of them.''

"Fresh butter, a dusting of cornmeal, a pinch of—''

"Stop it,'' groaned Cash. "You're making me hungry all over again.''

"Does Black Springs have watercress?'' she asked, smiling dreamily.

"No, but the creek does farther down the valley, where the water cools. Black Springs is hot.''

"Hot? Wonderful! A long day of prospecting, a hot bath, a meal of fresh trout, camp biscuits, watercress salad....'' Mariah made a sound of luxuriant anticipation.

Luke laughed softly. Cash swore, but there was no heat in it. He had often enjoyed nature's hard-rock hot tub. The meal Mariah mentioned, however, had existed only in his dreams. He was a lousy cook.

"Then you'll do it?'' Mariah asked eagerly, sensing that Cash was weakening. "You'll help me look for Mad Jack's mine?''

"Don't push, Muffin,'' Luke said. "Cash and I will talk it over later. Alone.''

"I'll give you half of my half," she said coaxingly to Cash, ignoring her older brother.

"Mariah—" began Luke.

"Who's pushing?" she asked, assuming an expression of wide-eyed innocence. "*Moi?* Never. I'm a regular door-mat."

Nevada looked at Cash. "You need this map?"

"No."

"Then if nobody minds, I'd like to pass it along to some people who are real good at making ruined documents give up their secrets."

Cash started to ask questions, then remembered where—and for whom—Nevada had worked before he came to the Rocking M.

"Fine with me," Cash said. "The map belongs to Luke and Mariah, though."

"Take it," said Luke.

"Sure. Who are you sending it to?" Mariah asked.

"Don't worry. They'll take good care of it," Nevada said, folding the map delicately along age-worn creases.

"But where are you sending it?"

Mariah was talking to emptiness. Nevada had simply walked away from the table. The back door opened and closed quietly.

"I didn't mean to make him mad."

"You didn't," Luke said, stretching. "Nevada isn't long on social niceties like smiling and saying excuse me. But he's a damned good man. One of the best. Just don't ever push him," Luke added, looking directly at Cash. "Even you. Nevada doesn't push worth a damn."

Cash smiled thinly. "My mother didn't hatch any stupid chicks. I saw Nevada fight once. If I go poking around in that lion's den, it will be with a shotgun."

"But where is Nevada taking the map?" Mariah asked in a plaintive voice.

"I don't know," Luke admitted. "I do know you'll get it back in as good shape as it was when Nevada took it. Better, probably."

"Then you must know where he's taking it."

"No, but I can make an educated guess."

"Please do," Mariah said in exasperation.

Luke smiled. "I'd guess that map will end up in an FBI lab on the east coast. Or some other government agency's lab. Nevada wasn't always a cowboy." Luke stretched and yawned again, then looked at Mariah. "Did you get everything moved into the old house?"

"Yes."

"All unpacked?"

"Well, not quite."

"Why don't you go finish? I'll be along in a few minutes to make sure you have everything you need."

"Why do I feel like I'm being told to leave?"

"Because you are."

Mariah started to object before she remembered that Luke wanted to talk with Cash in private about going prospecting with her.

"I'm not six years old anymore," she said reasonably. "You can talk in front of me."

It was as though she hadn't spoken.

"Don't forget to close the bathroom window," Luke said, "unless you want a battle-scarred old tomcat sleeping on your bed."

Mariah looked at Cash. "Why do you let him insult you like that?"

There was a two-second hesitation before Cash laughed out loud, but the sudden blaze in his eyes made Mariah's heart beat faster.

Shaking his head, Luke said, "Good night, Muffin."

"Don't forget to bring my cookies and milk," she retorted sweetly, "or I'll cry myself to sleep."

Luke grabbed Mariah, hugged her and ruffled her hair as though she were six years old again. Laughing, she stood on tiptoe and returned the favor, then found herself suddenly blinking back tears.

"Thank you, Luke," she said.

"For what?"

"Not throwing me out on my ear when I turned up without warning."

"Don't be silly. This is your home."

"No," she whispered, "it's yours. But I'm grateful to share it for a while."

Before Luke could say anything else, she kissed his cheek and walked quickly from the dining room. Cash stood and watched the outer door for a long, silent moment, admiring the perfection with which Mariah played the role of vulnerable child-woman. She was very good. Even better than Linda had been, and Linda had fooled him completely. Of course, Linda had had a real advantage. She had told him something he would have sold his soul to believe—that she was carrying his child.

What he hadn't known until too late was that Linda had been sleeping with another man. That was another thing women were good at—making each man feel like he was the only one.

"You don't have to worry about Nevada," Luke said calmly.

Startled, Cash turned toward his friend. "What do you mean?"

"Oh, he's a handsome son, but it's you Mariah keeps looking at." Deadpan, Luke added, "Which proves that there's no accounting for taste."

"Despite the beard, Nevada isn't a prospector," Cash pointed out coolly, "and the lady's heart is obviously set on gold."

"The lady was looking at you before she knew you were a prospector. And you were looking at her, period."

Cash's eyes narrowed into gleaming slits of blue. Before he could say anything, Luke was talking again.

"Yeah, yeah, I know, it puts a man between a rock and a hard place when he wants his best friend's little sister. Hell, I ought to know. I spent a lot of years wanting Carla."

"Not as many as she spent wanting you."

Luke smiled crookedly. "So I was a prize fool. If it weren't for her matchmaking older brother, I'd still be waking up alone in the middle of the night."

"Is that what you're doing now? Matchmaking? Is that why you want me to go prospecting with Mariah? You figure we'll find something more valuable and permanent than gold?"

Wincing at Cash's sardonic tone, Luke raked his fingers through his hair as he said, "The area around Devil's Peak is damned wild country."

Cash looked at the ceiling.

"I can't let her go alone," Luke continued.

Cash looked at his hands.

"I can't take her myself."

Cash looked at the floor.

"I need every cowhand I've got, and five more besides."

Cash looked at the table.

Luke swore. "Forget it. I'll get Nevada to—"

"*Hell,*" Cash interrupted fiercely, angered by the thought of throwing Mariah and Nevada together in the vast, lonely reaches of the Rocking M's high country. Cash pinned Luke with a black look. "All right, I'll do it. But

I'm usually gone for weeks at a time. Have you thought about that?''

''Mariah said she was a camper. Besides, there's always the Black Springs line shack.''

''Damn it, that's not what I mean and you know it! Your sister is one very sexy female.''

Luke cocked his head to one side. ''Interesting.''

A snarl was Cash's only answer.

''No, I mean it,'' Luke continued. ''Not that I think Mariah is a dog, but sexy wouldn't be the word I'd use to describe her. Striking, maybe, with those big golden eyes and lovely smile. Warm. Quick. But not sexy.''

''I wouldn't describe Carla as sexy, either.''

''Then you're blind.''

''No. I'm her brother.''

''Point taken,'' Luke said, grinning.

There was silence, then Cash spoke in a painfully reasonable tone of voice. ''Look. It takes half a day just to get to the Black Springs line shack by horseback. From there, it's a hard scramble up boulder-choked creeks and steep canyons. There's no way we can duck in, poke around for a few hours, and duck out. We'll be spending a lot of nights alone.''

''I trust you.''

''Then you are a damned fool,'' Cash said, spacing each word carefully.

''You trusted me in the wilds of September Canyon with Carla,'' Luke pointed out.

''Yeah. Think about it. Carla ended up pregnant and alone.''

Luke grimaced. ''You're not as big a fool as I was.''

''Damn it—''

''Mariah is twenty-two,'' Luke continued over Cash's words, ''college educated, a consenting adult in every sense of the word. I trust you in exactly the same way you trusted me, and for the same reason. You may be hardheaded as hell and not trust women worth a damn, but you would never touch a girl unless she wanted you to. Mariah will never be safer in that way than when she is with you. Beyond that, whatever happens or doesn't happen between the two of you is none of my business."

For a minute there was no sound in the dining room. Cash stood motionless, his hands jammed in his back pockets, his mind racing as he assessed the situation and the man he loved more than most men loved their blood brothers. In the end, there was only one possible conclusion: Luke meant every word he had said.

Well, at least I won't have to worry about getting Mariah pregnant the way Luke did Carla.

But Cash's bitterly ironic thought remained unspoken. It wasn't the sort of thing a man talked about.

"I'll hold you to that," Cash said finally.

Luke nodded, then smiled widely and gave Cash an affectionate whack on his shoulder. "Thanks for getting me off the hook. I owe you one."

"Like hell. I spend more time here than I do in my apartment in Boulder."

"So move here. You can build at the other end of the big pasture, just across the stream from Ten and Diana. Plenty of space."

"One of these days you're going to say that and I'm going to take you up on it."

"Why do you think I keep saying it?" Luke stretched and yawned. "Damn, I wish Carla were home. I never sleep as well when she's gone."

"You're breaking my heart. Go to bed."

"Mariah's waiting for me."

"I'll tell her what we decided," Cash said. "With luck,

she'll change her mind when she finds out Nevada won't be her trusty wilderness guide.''

"Are you deaf as well as blind? I keep telling you, it's not Nevada she's looking at!"

Cash turned on his heel and left the room without saying another word, but he let the outside door close behind him hard enough to make a statement about his temper.

Outside, the cool summer darkness was awash with stars and alive with the murmur of air sliding down from the highlands to the long, flat valley that was the Rocking M's center. Lights burned in the bunkhouse and in the old ranch house. Cash moved with the swift, ground-covering strides of a man who has spent much of his adult life walking over wild lands in search of the precious metals that fed civilization's endless demands. Though he wore only a shirt and jeans, he didn't notice the crisp breeze. He knocked on the front door of the old ranch house with more force than courtesy.

"Come in, Luke. It's open."

"It's Cash. Is it still open?"

Mariah looked down at her oversize cotton nightshirt and bare feet. For an instant she wished she were wearing Spanish lace, Chinese silk and French perfume. Then she sighed. As angry as Cash sounded, she could be naked and it wouldn't make a speck of difference.

What is it about me that irritates him?

There was no answer to the question, other than the obvious one. He wasn't wild about the idea of being saddled with her out in the backcountry, just as he hadn't been wild about helping her with her car. He looked at her as a helpless, useless burden. That shouldn't surprise her. Her stepfather had felt precisely the same way.

Mariah opened the door and stifled an impulse to slam it shut before Cash could come in. He towered over her,

looming out of the darkness like a mountain, and his eyes
were black with anger.

"Come in, or would you rather bite my head off out in
the yard?"

The sound Cash made could most politely be described
as a growl. He stepped forward. Mariah retreated. A gust
of wind sucked the door shut.

Cash looked at the nightshirt that should have concealed
Mariah's curves but ended up teasing him by draping softly
over her breasts and hips. Desire tightened his whole body,
hammering through him with painful intensity. The thought
of being alone with her night after night was enough to
make him slam his fist into the wall from sheer frustration.

"What do you know about wild country?" Cash asked
savagely.

"It's where gold is found."

He hissed a single word, then said, "This won't be a
trendy pseudo-wilderness trek along a well-beaten path
maintained by the National Park Service. Can you even ride
a horse?"

"Yes."

"Can you ride rough country for half a day, then scramble over rocks for another half day?"

"If I have to."

"The line shack leaks and it rains damn near every night.
The only privy is a short-handled shovel. At the end of a
hard day you have to gather firewood, haul water, wash out
your socks so you won't blister the next day, eat food
you're too tired to cook properly, sleep on a wood floor
that has more drafts than bare dirt would and—"

"You make it sound irresistible," Mariah interrupted. "I
accept."

"Damn it, you aren't even listening!"

"You aren't telling me anything I don't already know."

"Then you better know this. We'll be alone out there, and I mean *alone*."

Mariah met Cash's dark glance without flinching and said, "I've been alone since I was dragged off the Rocking M fifteen years ago."

Cash jammed his hands into his back pockets. "That's not what I meant, lady. Up on Devil's Peak you could scream your pretty head off and no one would hear."

"You would."

"What if I'm the one making you scream? Have you thought about that?"

"Frankly, you're making me want to scream right now."

There was a charged silence.

Mariah smiled tentatively and put her hand out in silent appeal. "I know what you're trying to say, Cash, but let's be honest. I don't have the kind of looks that drive a man crazy with desire and we both know it. Just as we both know you don't want to take me across the road, much less spend a few weeks in the wild with me. But I'm going to Devil's Peak. I've been dreaming of looking for Mad Jack's mine as long as I can remember. Come hell or high water, that's what I'm going to do."

Cash looked down at the pale, graceful hand held out to him in artful supplication. He remembered how cool and silky Mariah's fingers had felt when they had rested on his bare forearm. He remembered how quickly her hand had warmed at his touch. He wondered if all of her would catch fire that fast.

The thought made him burn.

"I'll take care of packing the supplies and horses," Cash said coldly, "because sure as hell you won't know how. We leave in five hours. If you aren't ready, I'll leave without you."

"I'll be ready."

Cash turned and left the house before Mariah could see just how ready he was right now.

Six

Five hours later Mariah pulled open the front door before Cash could knock. Silently he stared at her, noting the lace-up shoes, faded jeans, an emerald turtleneck T-shirt beneath a black V-necked sweater and a long-sleeved man's flannel shirt that ended at her hips. The arms of a windbreaker were tied casually around her neck. The outfit should have made her look as appealing as a mud post, but it was all he could do not to run his hands over her to find the curves he knew waited beneath the sensible trail clothes.

"Here," Cash said, holding out a pair of cowboy boots. "Luke said to wear these if they fit. They're Carla's."

While Mariah tried on the boots, Cash glanced around. She had packed a lot less gear than he had expected. A military surplus backpack was stuffed tightly and propped against the wall. Other military surplus items were tied to the backpack—canteen, mess kit and the like. Extra blankets had been rolled up and tied with thongs.

"Where's your sleeping bag?" he asked.

"I don't have one."

"What the hell are you planning to sleep on?"

"My side, usually. Sometimes my stomach."

Cash clenched his jaw. "What about hiking boots?"

"My shoes are tougher than they look." Mariah stood and stamped her feet experimentally. "They're long enough, but they pinch in the toes."

"That's how you know they're cowboy boots," Cash retorted.

Mariah glanced at Cash's big feet. He was wearing lace-up, rough-country hiking boots that came to just below his knees. The heels were thick enough to catch and hold the edge of a stirrup securely. She had priced a similar pair in Seattle and decided that she would have to find Mad Jack's mine before she could afford the boots.

She bent down, tied her shoes to the backpack, and picked it up. "Ready."

Cash's long, powerful arm reached out, snagged Mariah's impromptu bedroll, and stuffed it none too gently into her hands. "Don't forget this."

"You're too kind," she muttered.

"I know."

Empty-handed, Cash followed Mariah to the corral. Four horses waited patiently in the predawn darkness. Two of them were pack animals. The other two were saddled. Cash added Mariah's scant baggage to one of the existing packs and lashed everything securely in place. Moments later he stepped into the saddle of a big, rawboned mountain horse, picked up the lead rope of the pack animals and headed out into the darkness without so much as a backward look.

"It won't work," Mariah said clearly. "I don't need your help to carry my stuff. I don't need your help to get on a horse. I don't need your help for one damned thing except to make Luke feel better!''

If Cash heard, he didn't answer.

Mariah went to the remaining horse, untied it and mounted a good deal less gracefully than Cash had. It had been six years since she had last ridden, but the reflexes and confidence were still there. When she reined the small mare around and booted it matter-of-factly in the ribs, it quickly trotted after Cash's horse. The mare was short-legged and rough-gaited, but amiable enough for a child to ride.

An hour later Mariah would have traded the mare's good temperament for a mean-spirited horse with a trot that didn't rattle her teeth. The terrain went up and down. Steeply. If there was a trail, Mariah couldn't make it out in the darkness, which meant that she spent a lot of time slopping around in the saddle because there was no way for her to predict her horse's next movements. She would be lucky to stand up at the end of three more hours of such punishment, much less hike with a backpack up a steep mountain and look for gold until the sun went down.

Don't forget the bit about hauling water and washing your socks, Mariah advised herself dryly. *On second thought, do forget it. No socks could be that dirty.*

When dawn came, it was a blaze of incandescent beauty that Mariah was too uncomfortable to fully appreciate. Whichever way she turned in the saddle, her body complained.

Even so, she felt the tug of undiscovered horizons expanding away in all directions. It was exciting to be in a place where not so much as a glimpse of man was to be seen. For all that she could tell, she and Cash might have been the first people ever to travel the land. Wild country rolled away from her on all sides in pristine splendor, shades of green and white and gray, evergreens and granite.

Mixed in with the darker greens of conifers was the pale green of aspens at the higher elevations, a green that was subtly repeated by grassy slopes at the lower elevations and occasional meadows in between. Ahead, Devil's Peak loomed in black, shattered grandeur, looking like the eroded ruins of a volcano rather than the granite peak Mariah had expected.

I wonder why Cash is searching for gold on a volcano's flanks? All the strikes I've read about were in granite, not lava.

Mariah would have asked Cash to explain this reasoning to her, but she had promised herself that she wouldn't speak until he did. Not even to ask for a rest break. Instead, she just hooked one leg around the saddle horn and rode side-saddle for a time. She prayed there would be enough strength left in her cramped muscles to keep her upright after she dismounted.

As the sun rose, its heat intensified until it burned through the high country's crystalline air. The last chill of night quickly surrendered to the golden fire. Mariah began shedding layers of clothing until only the long-sleeved, fitted ski shirt remained. She unzipped the turtleneck collar and shoved up the sleeves, letting the breeze tease as much of her skin as it could reach.

At the end of four hours, Mariah rather grimly reined the mare down a narrow rocky crease that opened into a tiny valley. Although Cash had been only a few minutes ahead of her, he had already unloaded the pack animals and was in the act of throwing his saddle over the corral railing. Even as Mariah resented it, she envied his muscular ease of movement. She pulled her horse to a halt and slowly, carefully, began to dismount.

Two seconds later she was sitting in the dirt. Her legs simply hadn't been able to support the rest of her. She gritted her teeth and was beginning the tedious job of getting to her feet when she felt herself picked up with dizzying speed. The world shifted crazily. When it settled again, she was being carried like a child against Cash's chest.

"I thought you said you could ride," Cash said harshly.

"I can." Mariah grimaced. "I just proved it, remember?"

"And now you won't be able to walk."

"*Quelle* shock. Wasn't that the whole idea? You didn't want me looking for gold with you and now I won't be able to. Not right away, at any rate. I'll be fine as soon as my legs start cooperating again and then you'll be out of luck."

Cash's mouth flattened into a hard line. "How long has it been since you were on a horse?"

"About a minute."

Against his will, Cash found himself wanting to smile. Any other woman would have been screaming at him or crying or doing both at once. Despite the grueling ride, Mariah's sense of humor was intact. Biting, but intact.

And she felt exciting in his arms, warm and supple, soft, fitting him without gaps or angles or discomfort. He shifted her subtly, savoring the feel of her, silently urging her to relax against his strength.

"Sorry, honey," he said. "If I had known how long it had been since—"

"Pull my other leg," Mariah interrupted. Then she smiled wearily. "On second thought, don't. It might fall off."

"How long has it been since you've ridden?" he asked again.

"Years. Six blessed, wonderful years."

Cash said something savage.

"Oh, it's not that bad," Mariah said.

"You sure?"

"Yeah. It's worse."

He laughed unwillingly and held her even closer. She braced herself against the temptation to put her head on the muscular resilience of his chest and relax her aching body. Her head sagged anyway. She sighed and gave herself to Cash's strength, figuring he had plenty to spare.

"A soak in the hot springs will help," he said.

Mariah groaned softly at the thought of hot water drawing out the stiffness of her muscles.

"My swimsuit is in my backpack," she said. "Better yet, just give me a bar of soap and throw me in as is. That way I won't have to haul water to wash my socks."

Laughing soundlessly, shaking his head, Cash held Mariah for a long moment in something very close to a hug. She might be an accomplished little actress in some ways, but she was good company in others. Linda hadn't been. When things didn't go according to her plan—and often even when they did—she pouted and wheedled like a child after candy. At first it had been gratifying to be the center of Linda's world. Gradually it had become tedious to be cast in a role of father to a manipulative little girl who would never grow up.

A long, almost contented sigh escaped Mariah's lips, stirring the hair that pushed up beneath Cash's open collar. A visible ripple of response went through him as he felt her breath wash over his skin. He clenched his jaw and walked toward the corral fence.

"Time to stand on your own two feet," he said tightly.

With the unself-consciousness of a cat, Mariah rubbed

her cheek against Cash's shirt and admitted, "I'd rather stand on yours."

"I figured that out the first time I saw you."

The sardonic tone of Cash's voice told Mariah that the truce was over. She didn't know what she had done to earn either the war or the truce. All she knew was that she had never enjoyed anything quite so much as being held by Cash, feeling the flex and resilience of his body, being so close to him that she could see sunlight melt and run through his hair like liquid gold.

When Cash's left arm released Mariah's legs, everything dipped and turned once more, but slowly this time. Instinctively she put her arms around his neck, seeking a stable center in a shifting world. Held securely more by the hard power of his right arm than by both her own arms, Mariah felt her hips slide down the length of Cash's body with a slow intimacy that shook her. Her glance flew to his face. His expression was as impassive as granite.

"Grab hold of the top rail," Cash instructed.

Mariah reached for the smooth, weathered wood with a hand that trembled. As she twisted in Cash's arms, the fitted T-shirt outlined her breasts in alluring detail, telling of the soft, feminine flesh beneath.

He wondered whether her nipples were pink or dusky rose or even darker, a vivid contrast to the pale satin of her skin. He thought of bending down and caressing her breasts with his tongue and teeth, drawing out the nipples until they felt like hot, hard velvet and she twisted beneath him, crying for release from the passionate prison of their love-making.

Don't be a fool, Cash told himself savagely. *No woman ever wants a man like that. Not really. Not so deep and hard and wild she forgets all the playacting, all the survival calculations, all the cunning.*

Yet, despite the cold lessons of past experience, when Cash looked down at Mariah curled softly in his arms, blood pulsed and gathered hotly, driven by the redoubled beating of his heart, blood surging with a relentless force that was tangible proof of his vulnerability to Mariah's sensual lures. Silently he cursed the fate that gave men hunger and women the instinctive cunning to use men's hunger against them.

"Put both hands on the rails," he said curtly.

When Mariah tried to respond to the clipped command, she found she couldn't move. Cash's arm was a steel band holding her against a body that also felt like steel. Discreetly she tried to put some distance between herself and the man whose eyes had the indigo violence of a stormy twilight. The quarter inch she gained by subtle squirming wasn't enough to allow her left hand to reach across her body to the corral fence. She tried for another quarter inch.

"What the hell do you think you're doing?" Cash snarled.

"I'm trying to follow your orders."

"When did I order you to rub against me like a cat in heat?"

Shock, disbelief and indignation showed on Mariah's face, followed by anger. She shoved hard against his chest. "Let go of me!"

She might as well have tried to push away the mountain itself. All her struggles accomplished were further small movements that had the effect of teaching her how powerful and hard Cash's body was—and how soft her own was by comparison. The lesson should have frightened her. Instead, it sent warmth stealing through her, gentle pulses of heat that came from the secret places of her body. The sensations were as exquisite as they were unexpected.

"C-Cash...?"

The catch in Mariah's voice sent a lightning stroke of desire arcing through Cash. For an instant his arm tightened even more, pinning Mariah to the hungry length of his body. Then he spun her around to face the corral, clamped her left hand over the top rail of the corral and let go of her. When her knees sagged, he caught her around the ribs with both hands, taking care to hold her well away from his body. Unfortunately there was nothing he could do about her breasts curving so close to his fingers, her soft flesh moving in searing caress each time she took a breath.

"Stand up, damn it," Cash said through clenched teeth, "or I swear I'll let you fall."

Mariah took in a shuddering breath, wondering if the jolting ride to Black Springs had scrambled her brains as well as her legs. The weakness melting her bones right now owed nothing to the hours on horseback and everything to the presence of the man whose heat reached out to her, surrounding her. She took another breath, then another, hanging on to the corral fence with what remained of her strength.

"I'm all right," Mariah said finally.

"Like hell. You're shaking."

"I'll survive."

With a muttered word, Cash let go of Mariah. His hands hovered close to her, ready to catch her if she fell. She didn't. She just sagged. Slowly she straightened.

"Now walk," he said.

"What?"

"You heard me. Walk."

A swift look over her shoulder told Mariah that Cash wasn't kidding. He expected her not only to stand on her rubbery legs but also to walk. Painfully she began inching crabwise along the corral fence, hanging on to the top rail with both hands. To her surprise, the exercise helped.

Strength returned rapidly to her legs. Soon she was moving almost normally. She turned to give Cash a triumphant smile, only to discover that he was walking away. She started after him, decided it was a bit too soon to get beyond reach of the corral fence's support, and grabbed the sun-warmed wood again.

By the time Mariah felt confident enough to venture away from the fence, Cash had the horses taken care of and was carrying supplies into the line shack. The closer she walked to the slightly leaning building, the more she agreed that "shack" was the proper term. Tentatively she looked in the front—and only—door.

Cash hadn't been lying when he described the line shack's rudimentary comforts. Built for only occasional use by cowhands working a distant corner of the Rocking M's summer grazing range, the cabin consisted of four walls, a ceiling, a plank floor laid down over dirt, and two windows. The fireplace was rudely constructed of local rocks. The long tongue of soot that climbed the exterior stone above the hearth spoke eloquently of a chimney that didn't draw.

"I warned you," Cash said, brushing by Mariah.

"I didn't say a word."

"You didn't have to."

He dumped her backpack and makeshift bedroll on the floor near the fireplace. Puffs of dust arose.

"If you still want to go to Black Springs, put on your swimsuit," Cash said, turning away. "And wear shoes unless you want to ride there."

"Ride?" she asked weakly. "Uh, no thanks. How far is it?"

"I never measured it."

Mariah's small sigh was lost in the ghastly creaking the door made as it shut. She changed into her swimsuit as quickly as her protesting leg muscles allowed. The inexpensive tank suit was made of a thin, deep rose fabric that fit without clinging when it was dry. Wet, it was another matter. It would cling more closely than body heat. Since Mariah had been dry when she purchased the suit, she hadn't known about its split personality.

"Hey, tenderfoot. You ready yet?"

Groaning, Mariah finished tying her shoelaces and struggled to her feet. "I'm coming."

As she stood, she felt oddly undressed. If she had been barefoot in the bathing suit, she would have had no problem. But somehow wearing shoes made her feel...naked. She grabbed her windbreaker and put it on. The lightweight jacket was several sizes too big. Normally she wore it over a blouse and bulky sweater, so the extra room was appreciated. With only the thin tank suit to take up room, the windbreaker reached almost halfway down her thighs, giving her a comforting feeling of being adequately covered.

When Cash heard the front door creak, he turned around. His first impression was of long, elegant, naked legs. His second impression was the same. He felt a nearly overwhelming desire to unzip the jacket and see what was beneath. Anything, even the skimpiest string bikini, would have been less arousing than the tantalizing impression of nakedness lying just beneath the loose black windbreaker.

Mariah walked tentatively toward Cash, wondering at the harsh expression on his face.

"Which way to the hot tub?" she asked, her voice determinedly light.

Without a word Cash turned and walked around to the back of the cabin. Mariah followed as quickly as she could, picking her way along the clear stream that ran behind the cabin. Even if her legs hadn't been shaky, she would have had a hard time keeping up with Cash's long stride. When

her path took her on a hopscotch crossing of the creek, she
bent and tested the temperature of the water. It was icy.

"So much for my hot tub fantasy," she muttered.

The racing, glittering water came from a narrow gap in
the mountainside that was no more than fifty yards from
the cabin. Inside the gap the going became harder, a scramble along a cascade that hissed and foamed with the force
of its downhill race. The rocks were dark, almost black,
which only added to the feeling of chill. Just when Mariah
was wondering if the effort would be worth it, she realized
that the mist peeling off the water was warm.

A hundred feet later the land leveled off to reveal a series
of graceful, stair-step pools that were rimmed by smooth
travertine and embroidered by satin waterfalls no more than
three feet high. As Mariah stared, a shiver of awe went
over her. The pools could not have been more beautiful if
they had been designed by an artist and built of golden
marble.

The water in the lowest pool was a pale turquoise Mariah
had seen only on postcards of tropical islands. The water
in the next pool was a luminous aquamarine. The water in
the last pool shaded from turquoise to aquamarine to a
clear, very dark blue that was the exact shade of Cash's
eyes. At the far end of the highest pool, the water was so
deep it appeared black but for swirls of shimmering indigo
where liquid welled up from the depths of the earth in silent, inexhaustible pulses that had begun long before man
ever walked the western lands and would continue long
after man left.

Slowly Mariah sank to her knees and extended her hand
toward the jeweled beauty of the pool. Before she could
touch the water, Cash snatched her hand back.

"I've cooked trout at this end of Black Springs. Sometimes the downstream end of the pool is cool enough to

bear touching for a few moments. Most often it isn't. It depends.''

''On what?''

Cash didn't answer her directly. ''You get hot springs when groundwater sinks down until it reaches a body of magma and then flashes into superheated steam,'' he said, absently running his thumb over Mariah's palm as he looked at the slowly twisting depth of Black Springs. ''The steam slams up through cracks in the country rock until the water bursts through to the surface of the land in a geyser or a hot spring. Most often the water never breaks the surface. It simply cools and sinks back down the cracks until it encounters magma, flashes to steam and surges upward again.''

Mariah made a small sound, reflection of the sensations that were radiating up from her captive hand. Cash looked away from the water and realized that his thumb was caressing Mariah's palm in the rhythm of the water pulsing deep within the springs. With a muttered word, he released her hand.

''I can tell you how a hot spring works, but I can't tell you why some days Black Springs is too hot and other days it's bearable. So be careful every day. Even on its best behavior, Black Springs is dangerously hot a foot beneath the surface.''

''Is the water drinkable?'' she asked.

''Once it cools off the trout love it. So do I. It has a flavor better than wine.''

Mariah stared wistfully at the beautiful, intensely clear, searingly hot water. ''It looks so wonderful.''

''Come on,'' Cash said, taking pity on her. ''I'll show you the best place to soak out the aches.'' He led her back to the middle pool. ''The closer you are to the spring, the hotter the water. Start at the lower end and work your way up until you're comfortable.'' He started to turn away, then stopped. "You *do* swim, don't you?''

Mariah glanced at the pool. "Sure, but that water is hardly deep enough for me to get wet sitting down.''

"The pool is so clear it fools your eyes. At the far end, the water is over my head.'' Cash turned away. "If you're not back in an hour, I'll come back and drag you out. I'm hungry.''

"You don't have to wait for me,'' she said, setting shoes and socks aside.

"The hell I don't. You're the cook, remember?''

Seven

Seven

On the fourth day, Mariah didn't have to be awakened by the sound of the front door creaking as Cash walked out to check on the horses. She woke up as soon as sunrise brightened the undraped windows. Silently she struggled out of her tangle of blankets. Although she still ached in odd places and she wished that she had brought a few more blankets to cushion the rough wood floor, she no longer woke up feeling as though she had been beaten and left out in the rain.

Shivering in the shack's chill air, Mariah knelt between her blankets and Cash's still-occupied sleeping bag as she worked over the ashes of last night's fire. As always, she had slept fully clothed, for the high mountain nights were cold even in summer. Yet as soon as the sun shone over the broken ramparts of Devil's Peak, the temperature rose swiftly, sometimes reaching the eighties by noon. So while Mariah slept wearing everything she had brought except her shoes, she shed layers throughout the morning, adding them again as the sun began its downward curve across the sky.

Enough coals remained in the hearth to make a handful of dry pine needles burst into flames after only a few instants. Mariah fed twigs into the fire, then bigger pieces, and finally stove-length wood. Despite the fireplace's sooty front, little smoke crept out into the room this morning. The chimney drew quite well so long as there wasn't a hard wind from the northeast.

When she was satisfied with the fire's progress, Mariah turned to the camp stove that she privately referred to as Beelzebub. It was the most perverse piece of machinery she had ever encountered. No matter how hard or how often she pumped up the pressure, the flame wobbled and sputtered and was barely hot enough to warm skin. When Cash pumped up the stove, however, it put out a flame that could cut through steel.

With a muttered prayer, Mariah reached for the camp stove. A tanned, rather hairy hand shot out of Cash's sleeping bag and wrapped around her wrist, preventing her from touching the stove.

"I'll take care of it."

"Thanks. The thing hates me."

There was muffled laughter as a flap of the partially zipped sleeping bag was shoved aside, revealing Cash's head and bare shoulders. Another big hand closed over Mariah's. He rubbed her hand lightly between his own warm palms. Long, strong, randomly scarred fingers moved almost caressingly over her skin. She shivered, but it had nothing to do with the temperature in the cabin.

"You really *are* cold," he said in a deep voice.

"You're not. You're like fire."

"No, I mean it," Cash said. He propped himself up on

one elbow and pulled Mariah's hands toward himself. "Your fingers are like ice. No wonder you thrash around half the night. Why didn't you tell me you were cold?"

"Sorry." Mariah tugged discreetly at her hands. They remained captive to Cash's enticing warmth. "I didn't mean to keep you awake."

"To hell with that. Why didn't you tell me?"

"I was afraid you'd use it as an excuse to make me go back."

Cash hissed a single harsh word and sat up straight. The sleeping bag slithered down his torso. If he was wearing anything besides the bag, it didn't show. Although Mariah had seen Cash at Black Springs dressed in only cutoff jeans, somehow it just wasn't the same as seeing him rising half-naked from the warm folds of a sleeping bag. A curling, masculine pelt went in a ragged wedge from Cash's collarbones to a hand span above his navel. Below the navel a dark line no thicker than her finger descended into the undiscovered territory concealed by the sleeping bag.

"It's not worth getting upset about," Mariah said quickly, looking away. "Any extra calories I burn at night I replace at breakfast, and then some. Speaking of which, do you want pancakes again? Or do you want biscuits and bacon? Or do you just want to grab some trail mix and go prospecting? I'm going with you today. I'm not stiff anymore. I won't be a drag on you. I promise."

There was a long silence while Cash looked at Mariah and she looked at the fire that was struggling to burn cold wood. Deliberately he cupped her hands in his own, brought them to his mouth, and blew warm air over her chilled skin. Before she had recovered from the shock of feeling his lips brushing over her palms, he was rubbing her hands against his chest, holding her between his palms and the heat of his big body. It was like being toasted between two fires.

"Better?" he asked quietly after a minute.

Mariah nodded, afraid to trust her voice.

With a squeeze so gentle that she might have imagined it, Cash released her hands and began dressing. For a few moments Mariah couldn't move. When she went to measure ingredients for biscuits, her hands were warm, but trembling. She was glad Cash was too busy dressing to notice.

The front door creaked as he went outside. A few minutes later it creaked again when he returned. The smell of dew and evergreen resin came back inside with him.

"If that's biscuits and bacon, make a double batch," Cash said. "We'll eat them on the trail for lunch."

"Sure." Then the meaning of his words penetrated. Mariah turned toward him eagerly. "Does that mean I get to come along?"

"That's what you're here for, isn't it?" Cash asked curtly, but he was smiling.

She grinned and turned back to the fire, carefully positioning the reflector oven. She had discovered the oven in a corner of the shack along with other cooking supplies Cash rarely ever used. Her first few attempts to cook with the oven had been a disaster, but there had been little else for her to do except experiment with camp cooking while Cash was off exploring and she was recovering from the ride to Devil's Peak.

Mariah had been grateful to be able to keep the disasters a secret and pretend that the successes were commonplace. It had been worth all the frustration and singed fingertips to see Cash's expression when he walked into the line shack after a day of prospecting and found fresh biscuits, fried ham, baked beans with molasses and a side dish of fresh watercress and tender young dandelion greens waiting for him.

While the coffee finished perking on the stove and the last batch of bacon sizzled fragrantly in the frying pan, Mariah sliced two apples and piled a mound of bacon on a tin plate. She surrounded the crisp bacon with biscuits and set the plate on the floor near the fireplace, where a squeeze bottle of honey was slowly warming. She poured two cups of coffee and settled cross-legged on the floor in front of the food. The position caused only a twinge or two in her thigh muscles.

"Come and get it," Mariah called out.

Cash looked up from the firewood he had been stacking in a corner of the shack. For a moment he was motionless, trying to decide which looked more tempting—the food or the lithe young woman who had proven to be such good company. Too good. It would have been much easier on him if she had been sulky or petulant or even indifferent—anything but humorous and quick and so aware of him as a man that her hands shook when he touched her.

The tactile memory of Mariah's cool, trembling fingers still burned against his chest. It had taken all of his self-control not to pull her soft hands down into the sleeping bag and let her discover just how hot he really was.

Damn you, Luke. Why didn't you tell me to leave your sister alone? Why did you give me a green flag when you know me well enough to know I don't have marriage in mind? And why can't I look at Mariah without getting hot?

There was no answer to Cash's furious thoughts. There was only fragrance and steamy heat as he pulled apart a biscuit, and then a rush of pleasure as he savored the flavor and tenderness of the food Mariah had prepared for him.

They ate in a silence that was punctuated by the small sounds of silverware clicking against metal plates, the muted whisper of the fire and the almost secretive rustle of clothes as one or the other of them reached for the honey. When Cash could eat no more, he took a sip of coffee, sighed, and looked at Mariah.

"Thanks," he said.

"For what?"

"Being a good cook."

She laughed, but her pleasure in the compliment was as clear as the golden glow of her eyes. "It's the least I could do. I know you didn't want me to come with you."

"And you're used to being not wanted, aren't you." There was no question in Cash's voice, simply the certainty that had come of watching her in the past days.

Mariah hesitated, then shrugged. "Harold—my mother's second husband—didn't like me. Nothing I did in fifteen years changed that. I spent most of those years at girls' boarding schools and summer camps." She smiled crookedly. "That's where I learned to ride, hike, make camp fires, put up a tent, cook, sew, give first aid, braid thin plastic thongs into thick useless cords, make unspeakably ugly things in clay, and identify poisonous snakes and spiders."

"A well-rounded education," Cash said, hiding a grin.

Mariah laughed. "You know, it really was. A lot of girls never get a chance at all to be outdoors. Some of the girls hated it, of course. Most just took it in stride. I loved it. The trees and rocks and critters didn't care that your real father never wrote to you, that your stepfather couldn't stand to be in the same room with you, or that your mother's grip on reality was as fragile as a summer frost."

Cash drained his coffee cup, then said simply, "Luke wrote to you."

"What?"

"Luke has written to you at least twice a year for as long

as I've known him," Cash said as he poured himself more coffee. "Christmas and your birthday. He sent gifts, too. Nothing ever came back. Not a single word."

"I didn't know. I never saw them. But I wrote to him. Mother mailed..." Realization came, darkening Mariah's eyes. "She never mailed my letters. She never let me see Luke's."

The strained quality of Mariah's voice made Cash glance up sharply. Reflected firelight glittered in the tears running down her cheeks. He set aside his coffee and reached for her, brushing tears away with the back of his fingers.

"Hey, I didn't mean to hurt you," Cash said, stroking her cheek with a gentleness surprising in such a big man.

"I know," Mariah whispered. "It's just...I used to lie awake and cry on Christmas and my birthday because I was alone. But I wasn't alone, not really, and I didn't even know it." She closed her eyes and laced her fingers tightly together to keep from reaching for Cash, from crawling into his lap and asking to be held. "Poor Luke," she whispered. "He must have felt so lonely, too." She hesitated, then asked in a rush, "Your sister loves Luke, doesn't she? Truly loves him?"

"Carla has always loved Luke."

Mariah heard the absolute certainty in Cash's voice and let out a long sigh. "Thank God. Luke deserves to be loved. He's a good man."

Cash looked down at Mariah's face. Her eyes were closed. Long, dark eyelashes were tipped with diamond tears. All that kept him from bending down and sipping teardrops from her lashes was the certainty that anything he began wouldn't end short of his becoming her lover. Her sadness had made her too vulnerable right now—and it made him too vulnerable, as well. The urge to comfort her in the most elemental way of all was almost overwhelming. He wanted her far too much to trust his self-control.

"Yes," Cash said as he stood up in a controlled rush of power. "Luke is a good man." He jammed his hands into his back jeans pockets to keep from reaching for Mariah. "If we're going to get any prospecting done, we'd better get going. From the looks of the sky, we'll have a thunderstorm by afternoon."

"The dishes will take only a minute," Mariah said, blotting surreptitiously at her cheeks with her shirttail.

It was longer than a minute, but Cash made no comment when Mariah emerged from the cabin wearing her backpack. He put his hand underneath her pack, hefted it, and calmly peeled it from her shoulders.

"I can carry it," Mariah said quickly.

Cash didn't even bother to reply. He simply transferred the contents of her backpack to his own, put it on and asked, "Ever panned for gold?"

She shook her head.

"It's harder than it looks," he said.

"Isn't everything?"

Cash smiled crookedly. "Yeah, I guess it is." He looked at Mariah's soft shoes, frowned and looked away. "I'm going to try a new area of the watershed. It could get rough, so I want you to promise me something."

Warily Mariah looked up. "What?"

"When you need help—and you will—let me know. I don't want to pack you out of here with a broken ankle."

"I'll ask for help. But it would be nice," she added wistfully, "if you wouldn't bite my head off when I ask."

Cash grunted. "Since you've never panned for gold and we're in a hurry, I'll do the panning. If you really want to learn, I'll teach you later. Come on. Time's a-wasting."

The pace Cash set was hard but not punishing. Mariah

didn't complain. She was certain the pace would have been even faster if Cash had been alone.

There was no trail to follow. From time to time Cash consulted a compass, made cryptic notes in a frayed notebook, and then set off over the rugged land once more, usually in a different direction. Mariah watched the landscape carefully, orienting herself from various landmarks each time Cash changed direction. After half an hour they reached a stream that was less than six feet wide. It rushed over and around pale granite boulders in a silver-white blur that shaded into brilliant turquoise where the water slowed and deepened.

Cash shrugged out of his backpack and untied a broad, flat pan, which looked rather like a shallow wok. Pan in one hand, short-handled shovel in the other, he sat on his heels by the stream. With a deft motion he scooped out a shovel full of gravel from the eddy of water behind a boulder. He dumped the shovel-load into the gold pan, shook it, and picked over the contents. Bigger pieces of quartz and granite were discarded without hesitation, despite the fact that some of them had a golden kind of glitter that made Mariah's heart beat faster and her breath catch audibly.

"Mica," Cash explained succinctly, dumping another handful of rocks back in the stream.

"Oh." Mariah sighed. Her reading on the subject of granite, gold, and prospecting had told her about mica. It was pretty, but it was as common as sand.

"All that glitters isn't gold, remember?" he asked, giving her an amused, sideways glance.

She grimaced.

Cash laughed and scooped up enough water to begin washing the material remaining in the bottom of the gold pan. A deft motion of his wrists sent the water swirling around in a neat circle. When he tilted the pan slightly away from himself, the circular movement of the water lifted the lighter particles away from the bottom of the pan. Water and particles climbed the shallow incline to the rim and drained back into the stream. After a minute or two, Cash looked at the remaining stuff, rubbed it between his fingers, stared again, and flipped it all back into the stream. He rinsed the pan, attached it and the shovel to his backpack again, and set off upstream.

"Nothing, huh?" Mariah said, scrambling to keep up.

"Grit, sand, pea gravel, pebbles. Granite. Some basalt. A bit of chert. Small piece of clear quartz."

"No gold?"

"Not even pyrite. That's fool's gold."

"I know. Pyrite is pretty, though."

Cash grunted. "Leave it to a woman to think pretty is enough."

"Oh, right. That's why men have such a marked preference for ugly women."

Cash hid a smile. For a time there was silence punctuated by scrambling sounds when the going became especially slippery at the stream's edge. Twice Mariah needed help. The first time she needed only a steadying hand as she scrambled forward. The second time Cash found it easier simply to lift her over the obstacle. The feel of his hands on her, and the ease with which he moved her from place to place, left Mariah more than a little breathless. Yet despite the odd fluttering in the pit of her stomach, her brain continued to work.

"Cash?"

The sound he made was encouraging rather than curt, so Mariah continued.

"What are we doing?"

"Walking upstream."

"Why are we walking upstream?"

"It's called prospecting, honey. Long hours, backbreaking work and no pay. Just like I told you back at the ranch house. Remember?"

Mariah sighed and tried another approach.

"We're looking for Mad Jack's mine, right?" she asked.

"Right."

"Mad Jack's gold was rough, which meant it didn't come out of a placer pocket in a stream, right?"

"Right."

"Because placer gold is smooth."

"Right."

The amusement in Cash's tone was almost tangible. It was also gentle rather than disdainful. Knowing that she was being teased, yet beguiled by the method, Mariah persisted.

"Then why are you panning for Mad Jack's nonplacer mine?"

Cash's soft laughter barely rose above the sound of the churning stream. He turned around, made a lightning grab and had Mariah securely tucked against his chest before she knew what was happening. With a startled sound she hung on to him as he crossed the stream in a few strides, his boots impervious to the cold water.

"Wondered when you'd catch on," Cash said.

He set Mariah back on her feet, releasing her with a slow reluctance that was like a caress. His smile was the same. A caress.

"But the truth is," he continued in a deep voice, resolutely looking away from her, "I *am* panning for that mine. Think about it. Gold is heavy. Wherever a gold-bearing formation breaks the surface, gradually the matrix surrounding the gold weathers away. Gold doesn't weather.

That, and its malleability, is what makes it so valuable to man.''

Mariah made an encouraging sound.

''Anyway, the matrix crumbles away and frees the gold, which is heavy for its size. Gravity takes hold, pulling the gold downhill until it reaches a stream and sinks to the bottom. Floods scoop out the gold and beat it around and drop it off farther downstream. Slowly the gold migrates downhill, getting more and more round until the nugget settles down to bedrock in a deep placer pocket.''

''Mad Jack's gold is rough,'' Mariah pointed out.

''Yeah. I'm betting that canny old bastard panned a nameless stream and found bits of gold that were so rough they had to have come from a place nearby. So he panned that watershed, tracking the color to its source—the mother lode.''

Cash looked back at Mariah to see if she understood. What he saw were wisps of dark, shiny hair feathered across her face, silky strands lifted by a cool wind. Before he could stop himself, he smoothed the hair away from her lips and wide golden eyes. Her pupils dilated as her breath came in fast and hard.

''You see,'' he said, his voice husky, ''streams are a prospector's best friend. They collect and concentrate gold. Without them a lot of the West's most famous gold strikes would never have been made.''

''Really?''

The breathless quality of Mariah's voice was a caress that shivered delicately over Cash.

''They're still looking for the mother lode that put Sutter's Mill on the map,'' he murmured, catching a lock of her hair and running it between his fingers.

The soft sound Mariah made could have been a response to his words or to the fragile brush of Cash's fingertips at her hairline. With a stifled curse at his inability to keep his hands off her, Cash opened his fingers, releasing Mariah from silken captivity.

"Anyway," he said, turning his attention back to the rugged countryside, "I'm betting Mad Jack was panning a granite-bottomed stream, because only a fool looks for gold in lava formations, and that old boy was nobody's fool."

"You're not a fool, either," Mariah said huskily, grabbing desperately for a safe topic, because it was that or grab Cash's hand and beg him to go on touching her. "So why were you prospecting the Devil's Peak area before you saw Mad Jack's map? Until we got to this stream, I didn't see anything that looked like granite or quartzite or any of the 'ites' that are usually found with gold. Just all kinds of lava. Granted, I'm no expert on gold hunting, but..."

"This area wasn't my first choice," Cash said dryly. "Almost two years ago I was having a soak in Black Springs when I realized that Devil's Peak is basically a volcano rammed through and poured out over country rock that's largely granite. Where the lava has eroded enough, the granite shows through. And where there's granite, there could be gold." He smiled, gave Mariah a sideways glance, and admitted, "I was glad to see that ratty old map, though. I've been panning up here for two years and haven't gotten anything more to show for it than a tired back."

"No gold at all?"

"A bit of color here and there. Hobbyist flakes, the kind you put in a magnifying vial and show to patient friends. Nothing to raise the blood pressure."

"Darn, I was hoping that—trout!" Mariah said excitedly, pointing toward the stream.

"What?"

"I just saw a trout! Look!"

Smiling down at Mariah, barely resisting the urge to fold

her against his body in a long hug, Cash didn't even glance at the stream that had captured her interest.

"Fish are silver," he said in a deep voice. "We're after gold. We'll catch dinner on the way back."

"How can you be so sure? The fish could be hiding under rocks by then."

"They won't be."

Mariah made an unconvinced sound.

"I bet we'll catch our fill of trout for dinner tonight," Cash said.

"What do you bet?"

"Loser cleans the fish."

"What if there are no fish to clean?"

"There will be."

"You're on," she retorted quickly, forgetting Nevada's advice about never gambling with a man called Cash. "If we don't get fish, you do dishes tonight."

"Yeah?"

"Yeah."

"You're on, lady." Cash laughed softly and tugged at a silky lock of Mariah's hair once more. "Candy from a baby."

"Tell me that while you're doing dishes."

Cash just laughed.

"It's not a bet until we shake on it," she said, holding out her hand.

"That's not how it works between a man and a woman."

He took her hand and brought it to his mouth. She felt the mild rasp of his growing beard, the brush of his lips over her palm, and a single hot touch from the tip of his tongue. She thought Cash whispered *candy* when he straightened, but she was too shaken to be sure.

"Now it's a bet," he said.

Eight

"How's it going?" Cash asked.

Mariah looked up from the last fish that remained to be cleaned. "Better for me than for the trout."

He laughed and watched as she prepared the fish for the frying pan with inexpert but nonetheless effective swipes of his filleting knife.

Cash had expected Mariah to balk at paying off the bet, or at the very least to sulk over it. Instead, she had attacked the fish with the same lack of complaint she had shown for sleeping on the shack's cold, drafty floor. Only her unconscious sigh of relief as she rinsed the last fish—and her hands—in the icy stream told Cash how little she had liked the chore.

"I'll do the dishes," he said as she finished.

"Not a chance. It's the only way I'll get the smell of fish off my hands."

Cash grabbed one of Mariah's hands, held it under his nose and inhaled dramatically. "Smells fine to me."

"You must be hungry."

"How did you guess?"

"You're alive," she said, laughing up at him.

Smiling widely, Cash grabbed the tin plate of fish in one hand. The other still held Mariah's water-chilled fingers. He pulled her to her feet with ease.

"Lady, you have the coldest hands of any woman I've ever known."

"Try me after I've done the dishes," she retorted.

He smiled down at her. "Okay."

Mariah's stomach gave a tiny little flip that became a definite flutter when Cash pulled her fingers up his body and tucked them against the warm curve of his neck. Whether it was his body heat or the increased beating of her own heart, Mariah's fingers warmed up very quickly. She slanted brief, sideways glances at Cash as they walked toward the line shack, but he apparently felt that warming her cold hands on his body was in the same category as helping her over rough spots in the trail—no big deal. Certainly it wasn't something for him to go all breathless over.

But Mariah was. Breathless. Each time Cash touched her she felt strange, almost shaky, yet the sensations shimmering through her body were very sweet. Even as she wondered if Cash felt the same, she discarded the idea. He was so matter-of-fact about any physical contact that it made her response to it look foolish.

"Listen," Cash said, stopping suddenly.

Mariah froze. From the direction of Devil's Peak came a low, fluid, rushing sound, as though there were a river racing by just out of sight. Yet she knew there wasn't.

"What is it?" she whispered.

"Wind. See? It's bending the evergreens on the slope

like an invisible hand stroking fur. The rain is about a quarter mile behind.''

Mariah followed the direction of his pointing finger and saw that Cash was right. Heralded by a fierce, transparent cataract of wind, a storm was sweeping rapidly toward them across the slope of Devil's Peak.

''Unless you want the coldest shower you ever took,'' Cash said, ''stretch those long legs.''

A crack of thunder underlined Cash's words. He grabbed the plate of fish from Mariah and pushed her in the direction of the cabin.

''Run for it!''

''What about you?''

''Move, lady!''

Mariah bolted for the cabin, still feeling the imprint of Cash's hand on her bottom, where he had emphasized his command with a definite smack. She barely beat the speeding storm back to the line shack's uncertain shelter.

Cash, who had the plate of slippery fish to balance, couldn't move as quickly as Mariah. The difference in reaching shelter was only a minute or two, but it was enough. He got soaked. Swearing at the icy rain, Cash bolted through the line shack's open door and kicked it shut behind him. Water ran off his big body and puddled around his feet.

''Put all the stuff that has to stay dry over there,'' Cash said loudly, trying to be heard over the hammering of rain on the roof.

Mariah grabbed bedding, clothes and dry food and started stacking them haphazardly in the corner Cash had indicated. He set aside the fish and disappeared outside again. Moments later he returned, his arms piled high with firewood. The wood dripped as much as he did, adding to the puddles that were appearing magically on the floor in every area of the cabin but one—the corner where Mariah was frantically storing things. Cash dumped the firewood near the hearth and went back outside again. Almost instantly he reappeared, arms loaded with wood once more. With swift, efficient motions he began stacking the wood according to size.

"Don't forget the kindling," he said without looking up.

Quickly Mariah rescued a burlap sack of dry pine needles and kindling from the long tongue of water that was creeping across the floor. Before the puddle could reach the dry corner, gaps in the wooden planks of the floor drained the water away.

"At least it leaks on the bottom, too," Mariah said.

"Damn good thing. Otherwise we'd drown."

Thunder cracked and rolled down from the peak in an avalanche of sound.

"What about the horses?" Mariah asked.

"They'll get wet just like they would at the home corral."

Cash stood up and shook his head, spraying cold drops everywhere.

"We had a dog that used to do that," Mariah said. "We kept him outside when it rained. In Seattle, that was most of the time."

She started to say something else, then forgot what it was. Cash was peeling off his flannel shirt and arranging it on a series of nails over the hearth. The naked reality of his strength fascinated her. Every twist of his body, every motion, every breath, shifted the masculine pattern of bone and muscle, sinew and tendon, making new arrangements of light and shadow, strength and grace.

"Is something wrong?" Cash said, both amused and aroused by the admiration in Mariah's golden eyes.

"Er...you're steaming."

"What?"

"You're steaming."

Cash held out his arms and laughed as he saw that Mariah was right. Heat curled visibly up from his body in the line shack's chilly air.

"I'll get you a shirt before you freeze," Mariah said, turning back to the haphazard mound she had piled in the corner. She rummaged about until she came up with a midnight-blue shirt that was the color of Cash's eyes in the stormy light. "I knew it was here."

"Thanks. Can you find some jeans, too?"

The voice came from so close to Mariah that she was startled. She glanced around and saw bare feet not eight inches away. Bare calves, too. And knees. And thighs. And—hastily she looked back at the pile of dry goods, hoping Cash couldn't see the sudden color burning on her cheeks or the clumsiness of her hands.

But Cash saw both the heat in Mariah's cheeks and the trembling of her fingers as she handed him dry jeans without looking around.

"Sorry," he said, taking the jeans from her and stepping into them. "In these days of co-ed dorms, I didn't think the sight of a man in underwear would embarrass you."

"There's rather a lot of you," Mariah said in an elaborately casual voice, then put her face in her hands. "I didn't mean it the way it sounded. It's just that you're bigger than most men and...and..."

"Taller, too," Cash said blandly.

Mariah made a muffled sound behind her hands, and then another.

"You're laughing at me," he said.

"No, I'm strangling on my feet."

"Try putting them in your mouth only one at a time. It always works for me."

Mariah gave up and laughed out loud. Smiling, Cash listened to her laughter glittering through the drumroll of rain on the roof. He was still smiling when he went down on one knee in front of the fire and stirred it into life.

"What do you say to an early dinner and a game of cards?" Cash asked.

"Sure. What kind of game?"

"Poker. Is there any other kind?"

"Zillions. Canasta and gin and Fish and Old Maid and—"

"Kid games," Cash interrupted, scoffing. He looked over his shoulder and saw Mariah watching him. "We're too old for that."

The gleaming intensity of Cash's eyes made Mariah feel weak.

"I just remembered something," she said faintly.

"What?"

"Never play cards with a man called Cash."

"It doesn't apply. My name is Alexander."

"I'm reassured."

"Thought you would be."

"I'm also broke."

"That's okay. We'll play for things we have lots of."

"Like what?"

"Pine needles, smiles, puddles, kisses, raindrops, that sort of thing." Without waiting for an answer, Cash turned back to the fire. "How hot do you need it for trout? Or do you want to cook them over the camp stove?"

Blinking, Mariah tried to gather her scattered thoughts. Cash couldn't have mentioned kisses, could he? She must have been letting her own longing guide her hearing down false trails.

"Trout," she said tentatively.

"Yeah. You remember. Those slippery little devils you

cleaned.'' He smiled. "The look on your face... Never bet anything you mind losing, honey.''

Abruptly Mariah was certain she had heard his list of betting items very clearly, and kisses had definitely been one of them.

And he had nearly gotten away with it.

"Cash McQueen, you could teach slippery to a fish.''

He laughed out loud, enjoying Mariah's quick tongue. Then he thought of some other ways he would like to enjoy that tongue. The fit of his jeans changed abruptly. So did his laughter. He stood in a barely controlled rush of power and turned his back on Mariah.

"You'll need light to cook,'' he muttered.

He crossed the shack in a few long strides, ignoring the puddles, and yanked a pressurized gas lantern from its wall hook. He pumped up the lantern with short, savage strokes, ripped a wooden match into life on his jeans and lit the lantern. Light pulsed wildly, erratically, until he adjusted the gas feed. The lantern settled into a hard, bright light whose pulses were so subtle they were almost undetectable. He brought the lantern across the room and hung it on one of the many nails that cowhands had driven into the line shack's walls over the years.

"Thank you,'' Mariah said uncertainly, wondering if Cash had somehow been insulted by being called slippery. But his laughter had been genuine. Then he had stopped laughing and that, too, had been genuine.

With a muffled sigh Mariah concentrated on preparing dinner. While she worked, Cash prowled the six-foot-by-nine-foot shack, putting pans and cups and other containers under the worst leaks. Rain hammered down with the single-minded ferocity of a high-country storm. Although it was hours from sunset, the light level dropped dramatically. Except for occasional violent flashes of lightning, the hearth and lantern became isolated islands of illumination in the gloom.

Both Cash and Mariah ate quickly, for the metal camp plates drained heat from the food. Cash stripped the sweet flesh from the fish bones with a deftness that spoke of long practice. Cornbread steamed and breathed fragrance into the chilly air. When there was nothing left but crumbs and memories, Mariah reached for the dishes.

"I'll do them," Cash said. "You've had a hard day."

"No worse than yours."

Cash didn't argue, he simply shaved soap into a pot with his lethally sharp pocketknife, added water that had been warming in the bucket by the hearth and began washing dishes. Mariah rinsed and stacked the dishes to one side to drain, watching him from the corner of her eyes. He had rolled up his sleeves to deal with the dishes. Each movement he made revealed the muscular power of his forearms and the blunt strength in his hands.

When the dishes were over and Cash sat cross-legged opposite Mariah on the only dry patch of floor in the cabin, lantern light poured over him, highlighting the planes of his face, the sensual lines of his mouth, and the sheer power of his body. As Cash quickly dealt the cards, Mariah watched him with a fascination she slowly stopped trying to hide.

The cards she picked up time after time received very little of her attention. As a result, the pile of dried pine needles in front of her vanished as though in an invisible fire. She didn't mind. She was too busy enjoying sitting with Cash in a cabin surrounded on the outside by storm and filled on the inside by the hushed silence of pent breath.

"Are puddles worth more than pine needles?" Mariah asked, looking at the three needles left to her.

"Only if you're thirsty."

"Are you?"

"I've got all the water I can stand right now."

Mariah smiled. "Yeah, I know what you mean. Well, that lets out raindrops, too. I guess I have to fold. I'm busted."

Cash nudged a palm-size pile of needles from his pile over to her side of the "table."

"What's that for?" she asked.

"Your smile."

"Really? All these needles? If that's what a smile is worth, how much for a kiss?"

Abruptly Cash looked up from his cards. His glance moved almost tangibly over Mariah's face, lingering with frank intensity on the curving line of her lips. Then he looked back at his cards, his expression bleak.

"More than either of us has," he said flatly.

Several hands were played in silence but for the hissing of the lantern and the slowly diminishing rush of rain. Cash kept winning, which meant that he kept dealing cards. As he did, the lantern picked out various small scars on his hands.

"How did you get these?" Mariah asked, touching the back of Cash's right hand with her fingertips.

He froze for an instant, then let out his breath so softly she didn't hear. Her fingers were cool, but they burned on his skin, making him burn, as well.

"You pan gold for more than a few minutes in these streams and your hands get numb," Cash said. His voice was unusually deep, almost hoarse, reflecting the quickening of his body. "I've cut myself and never even known it. Same for using the rock hammer during cold weather. Easiest thing in the world to zing yourself. What my own clumsiness doesn't cause, flying chips of rock take care of."

"Clumsy?" Mariah laughed. "If you're clumsy, I'm a trout."

"Then you're in trouble, honey. I'm still hungry."

"I'm a very, very *young* trout."

Cash smiled grimly. "Yeah. I keep reminding myself of that. You're what…twenty-two?"

Startled by the unexpected question, Mariah nodded.

"I teach grad students who are older than you," Cash said, his tone disgusted.

"So?"

"So quit looking at me with those big golden eyes and wondering what it would be like to kiss me."

Mariah's first impulse was to deny any such thoughts. Her second was the same. Her third was embarrassment that she was so transparent.

"You see," Cash said flatly, pinning Mariah with a look, "I'm wondering the same thing about you. But I'm not a college kid. If I start kissing you, I'm going to want more than a little taste of all that honey. I'm going to want everything you have to give a man, and I'm going to want it until I'm too damn tired to lick my lips. I get hard just watching you breathe, so teasing me into kissing you would be a really dumb idea, unless you're ready to quit playing and start screwing around." He watched Mariah's face, muttered something harsh under his breath, and threw a big handful of pine needles into the pot. "Call and raise you."

"I d-don't have that many needles."

"Then you lose, don't you?" he asked. And he waited.

How much is a kiss worth?

Mariah didn't speak the words aloud. She didn't have to. She knew without asking that a kiss would be worth every needle in the whole forest. In electric silence she looked at Cash's mouth with a hunger she had never felt before. The days of beard stubble enhanced rather than detracted from

the smooth masculine invitation of his lips. And he was
watching her with eyes that burned. He had meant his warning. If she teased him into kissing her, she had better be
prepared for a lot more than a kiss.

The thought both shocked and fascinated Mariah. She
had never wanted a man before. She wanted Cash now. She
wanted to be kissed by him, to feel his arms around her,
to feel his strength beneath her hands. But she had never
been a man's lover before. She wasn't sure she was ready
tonight, and Cash had made it very clear that there would
be no way for her to test the water without getting in over
her head.

"I guess I lose," Mariah whispered. "But it isn't fair."

"What isn't?"

"Not even one kiss, when you must have kissed a hundred other women."

"Don't bet on it. I'm very particular about who gets
close to me." Abruptly Cash closed his eyes against the
yearning, tentative flames of desire in Mariah's golden
glance. "The game is over, Mariah. Go to bed. Now."

Without a word Mariah abandoned her cards, rushed to
her feet and began arranging her blankets for the night.
After only a few moments she was ready for bed. She
kicked out of her shoes, crawled into the cold nest she had
made and began shivering. The first few minutes in bed at
night, and the first few out of it in the morning, were the
coldest parts of the day.

Cash stood up and moved around the cabin, listening to
the rain. When he had checked all the pans he turned off
the lantern and knelt to bank the fire. Although Mariah tried
not to watch him, it was impossible. Firelight turned his
hair to molten gold and caressed his face the way she
wanted to. Closing her eyes, shivering, she gripped the

blankets even more tightly, taking what warmth she could from them.

"Here."

Mariah's eyes snapped open. Cash was looming above her. His hands moved as he unfurled a piece of cloth and pulled it over her. One side of the cloth was a metallic silver. The other was black.

"What is it?"

"Something developed by NASA," Cash said. He knelt next to Mariah and began tucking the odd blanket around her with hard, efficient movements. "It works as good on earth as it does in space. Reflects heat back so efficiently I damn near cook myself if I use it. I just bring it along for emergencies. If I'd known earlier how cold you were, I'd have given it to you."

Mariah couldn't have answered if her life depended on it. Even with blankets in the way, the feel of Cash's hands moving down her sides as he tucked in the odd cloth was wonderful.

Suddenly Cash shifted. His hands flattened on the floor on either side of Mariah's head. He watched her mouth with an intensity that left her weak. Slowly his head lowered until he was so close she could taste his breath, feel his heat, sense the hard beating of his heart.

"Cash...?" she whispered.

His mouth settled over hers, stealing her breath, sinking into her so slowly she couldn't tell when the kiss began. At the first touch of his tongue, she made a tiny sound in her throat. A shudder ripped through Cash, yet his gradual claiming of Mariah's mouth didn't hasten. Gently, inevitably, he turned his head, opening soft feminine lips that were still parted over the sighing of his name. The velvet heat of Mariah's mouth made him dizzy. The tiny sounds she made at the back of her throat set fire to him. He rocked his head back and forth until her mouth was completely his, and then he drank deeply of her, holding the intimate kiss until her breathing was as broken and rapid as his own. Only then did he lift his head.

"You're right," Cash said hoarsely. "It isn't fair."

There was a rapid movement, then the sound of Cash climbing fully clothed into his sleeping bag.

It was a long time before either of them got to sleep.

Nine

Mariah sat on a sun-warmed boulder and watched Cash pan for gold in one of the nameless small creeks along the Devil's Peak watershed. Sunlight fell over the land in a silent golden outpouring that belied the chilly summer night to come. Stretching into the warmth, smiling, Mariah relished the clean air and the sun's heat and the feeling of happiness that had grown within her until she found herself wanting to laugh and throw her arms out in sheer pleasure.

The first days at the line shack had been hard, but after that it had been heaven. By the sixth day Mariah no longer awoke stiff every morning from a night on the hard floor and Cash no longer looked for excuses not to take her prospecting. By the eleventh day Mariah no longer questioned the depth of her attraction to Cash. She simply accepted it as she accepted lightning zigzagging through darkness or sunlight infusing the mountains with summer's heat.

Or the way she had accepted that single, incredible kiss.

Since then, Cash had been very careful to avoid touching Mariah but his restraint only made him more compelling to her senses. She had known men who wouldn't have hesitated to push her sexually if they had sensed such a deep response on her part. The fact that Cash didn't press for more was a sign to Mariah that he, too, cherished the glittering emotion that was weaving between the two of them, growing stronger with each shared laugh, each shared silence, drawing them closer and closer each day, each hour, each minute. Their closeness was becoming as tangible as the water swirling in Cash's gold pan, a transparent, fluid beauty stripping away the ordinary to reveal the gleaming gold beneath.

Shivering with a delicious combination of pleasure and anticipation each time she looked at Cash, Mariah told herself to be as patient as he was. When Cash was as certain of the strength of their emotion as she was, he would come to her again, ask for her again.

And this time she would say yes.

"Find anything?" Mariah asked, knowing the answer, wanting to hear Cash's voice anyway.

She loved the sound of it, loved seeing the flash of Cash's smile, loved the masculine pelt that had grown over his cheeks after eleven days without a razor, loved seeing the flex and play of muscles in his arms, loved...*him.*

"Nope. If the mine is up this draw, nothing washed down into the creek. I'll try a few hundred yards farther up, just to be sure."

Before Cash could flip the gritty contents of the pan back into the small creek, Mariah bent over his shoulder, bracing herself against his strength while she stirred through the gold pan with her fingertip. After a time she lifted her hand and examined her wet fingertip. No black flakes stuck to the small ridges on the pad of her finger. No gold ones stuck, either.

Mariah didn't care. She had already found what she sought—a chance to touch the man who had become the center of her world.

"Oh, well," she said. "There's always the next pan."

Cash smiled and watched while Mariah absently dried her fingertip on her jeans. A familiar heat pulsed through him as he looked at her. The desire he had felt the first time he saw her had done nothing but get deeper, hotter, harder. Despite the persistent ache of arousal, Cash had never enjoyed prospecting quite so much as he had in the past week. Mariah was enjoying it, too. He could see it in her smile, hear it in her easy laughter.

And she wanted him. He could see that, too, the desire in her eyes, a golden warmth that approved of everything he did, everything he said, every breath he took. He knew his eyes followed her in the same way, approving of every feminine curve, every golden glance, every breath, everything. He wanted her with a near-violent hunger he had never experienced before. All that kept him from taking what she so clearly wanted to give him was the bitter experience of the past, when he had so needed to believe a woman's lies that he had allowed her to make a fool of him. Yet no matter how closely Cash looked for cracks in Mariah's facade of warmth and vulnerability, so far he had found none.

It should have comforted him. It did not. Cash was very much afraid that his inability to see past Mariah's surface to the inevitable female calculation beneath was more a measure of how much he wanted her than it was a testimony to Mariah's innate truthfulness.

But God, how he wanted her.

Cash came to his feet in a swift, coordinated movement that startled Mariah.

"Is something wrong?"

"No gold here," Cash said curtly. He secured the gold pan to his backpack with quick motions. "We might as well head back. It's too late to try the other side of the rise today."

Mariah looked at the downward arc of the sun. "Does that mean there will be time for Black Springs before dinner?"

The eagerness in Mariah's voice made Cash smile ruefully. He had been very careful not to go to the hot springs with Mariah if he could avoid it. He had enough trouble getting to sleep at night just remembering what she looked like bare-legged and wearing a windbreaker. He didn't need visions of her in a wet bathing suit to keep him awake.

"Sure," he said casually. "You can soak while I catch dinner downstream."

Disappointed at the prospect of going to the springs alone, Mariah asked, "Aren't you stiff after a day of crouching over ice water?"

Cash shrugged. "I'm used to it."

Using a shortcut Cash had discovered, they took only an hour to get back to the line shack. While he picketed the horses in fresh grass, Mariah changed into her tank suit and windbreaker. When she appeared at the door of the cabin, Cash glanced up for only an instant before he lowered his head and went back to driving in picket stakes.

With a disappointment she couldn't conceal, Mariah started up the Black Springs path. After a hundred yards she turned around and headed back toward the cabin. Cash had just finished picketing the last horse when he spotted Mariah walking toward him.

"What's wrong?"

"Nothing. I just decided it would be more fun to learn how to handle a gold pan than it would be to soak in an oversize hot tub."

Cash's indigo glance traveled from the dark wisps of hair caressing Mariah's face to the long, elegant legs that were naked of anything but sunlight.

"Better get some more clothes on. The stream is a hell of a lot colder than Black Springs."

"I wasn't planning on swimming."

"You'll get wet anyway. Amateurs always do."

"But it's hot. Look at you. You're in shirtsleeves and you're sweating."

He didn't bother to argue that the sun wasn't warm. If he had been alone, he would have been working stripped to the waist. But he wasn't alone. He was with a woman he wanted, a woman who wanted him, a woman he was trying very hard to be smart enough not to take.

"If you plan on learning how to pan for gold," Cash said flatly, "you better get dressed for it."

Mariah threw up her hands and went back to the line shack before Cash changed his mind about teaching her how to pan for gold at all. She tore off the windbreaker and yanked on jeans over her shoes. Without looking, she grabbed a shirt off the pile of clothes that covered her blankets. She was halfway out the door before she realized that the shirt belonged to Cash.

"Tough," she muttered, yanking the soft navy flannel into place over her tank suit and fastening the snaps impatiently. "He wanted me to be dressed. I'm dressed. He didn't say whose clothes I had to wear."

There was no point in fastening the shirt's cuffs, which hung down well past her fingertips, just as the shoulders overhung hers by four inches on either side. The shirttails draped to her knees. Yet when Cash wore the shirt, it fit him without wrinkles or gaps.

"Lord, but that man is big," Mariah muttered. "It's a good thing he doesn't bite."

Impatiently she shoved the cuffs up well past her elbows, tied a hasty knot in the tails, grabbed the gold pan and shovel and ran back to where Cash was still working on the horses.

"I'm ready," Mariah said breathlessly.

Cash looked up, blinked, tried not to smile and failed completely. He released the horse's hoof he had been cleaning and stood up.

"Next time, don't wear such a tight shirt," he said, deadpan.

"Next time," Mariah retorted, "don't leave your tiny little shirt on my blankets when I'm in a hurry."

Snickering, Cash shook his head. "Let me get my fishing rod. We'll start in the riffles way up behind the shack. The creek cuts through a nice grassy place just above the willow thicket. Grass will be a lot easier on your knees than gravel."

"Don't you need gravel to pan gold?"

"Only if you expect to find gold. You don't. You're just learning how to pan, remember?"

"Boy, wouldn't you be surprised if I found nuggets in that stream."

"Nope."

Mariah blinked. "You wouldn't be surprised?"

"Hell no, honey. I'd be dead of shock."

Her smile flashed an instant before her laughter glittered in the mountain silence, brighter than any gold Cash had ever found. Unable to resist touching her, he ruffled her hair with a brotherly gesture that was belied by the sudden heat and tension of his body. The reaction came every time he touched her, no matter how casually, which was why he tried not to touch her at all.

Unfortunately for Cash's peace of mind, there was no satisfactory way to teach Mariah how to pan for gold without touching her or at least getting so close to her that not touching was almost as arousing as touching would have been. The soft pad of grass beneath their feet, the liquid murmur of the brook and the muted rustle of nearby willows being stroked by the breeze did nothing to make the moment less sensually charged.

Mariah's own response to Cash's closeness didn't help ease the progress of the lessons at all. When he put his hands next to hers on the cold metal in order to demonstrate the proper panning technique, she forgot everything but the fact that Cash was close to her. Her motions became shaky rather than smooth, which defeated the whole point of the lessons.

"It's a good thing the pan is empty," Cash muttered finally, watching Mariah try to imitate the easy swirling motion of proper panning. "The way you're going at it, any water in that pan would be sprayed from hell to breakfast."

"It looks so easy when you do it," Mariah said unhappily. "Why can't I get the rhythm of it?"

Cursing himself silently, knowing he shouldn't do what he was about to do, Cash said, "Here, try it this way."

Before common sense could prevent him, he stepped behind Mariah, reached around her and put his hands over hers on the pan. He felt the shiver that went through her, bit back a searing word and got on with the lesson.

"You can pan with either a clockwise or counterclockwise motion," Cash said through clenched teeth. "Which do you prefer?"

Mariah closed her eyes and tried to stifle the delicious

shivering that came each time Cash brushed against her. Standing as close as they were, the sweet friction occurred each time either of them breathed.

"Damn it, Mariah, wake up and concentrate! Which way do you want to pan?"

"C-count."

"What?"

"Counter." She dragged in a ragged breath. "Counter-clockwise."

With more strength than finesse, Cash moved his hands in counterclockwise motions, dragging Mariah's hands along. The circles he made weren't as smooth as usual, but they were a great improvement on what she had managed alone. The problem was that, standing as they were, Cash couldn't help but breathe in Mariah's fragile, elementally female fragrance. Nor could he prevent feeling her warmth all the way down to his knees.

And if he kept standing so close to her, there would be a lot less innocent kind of touching that he couldn't—or wouldn't want to—prevent.

Yet brushing against Mariah was so sweet that Cash couldn't force himself to stop immediately. He continued to stand very close to her for several excruciating minutes, teaching her how to pan gold and testing the limits of his self-control at the same time.

"That's it," Cash said abruptly, letting go of Mariah's hands and stepping back. "You're doing much better. I'm going fishing."

"But—how much water do I put in the pan?" Mariah asked Cash's rapidly retreating back.

"As much as you can handle without spilling," he answered, not bothering to turn around.

"And how much gravel?"

There was no answer. Cash had stepped into the willow thicket and vanished.

"Cash?"

Nothing came back to Mariah but the sound of the wind.

She looked at the empty gold pan and sighed. "Well, pan, it's just you and me. May the best man win."

At first Mariah tried to imitate Cash and crouch on her heels over the stream while she panned. The unaccustomed position soon made her legs protest. She tried kneeling. As Cash had predicted, kneeling was more comfortable, but only because of the thick mat of streamside grass. Kneeling on gravel wouldn't have worked.

Alternating between crouching and kneeling, Mariah concentrated on making the water in the pan turn in proper circles. As she became better at it, she used more water. While she worked, sunlight danced across the brook, striking silver sparks from the water and pouring heat over the land.

Patiently Mariah practiced the technique Cash had taught her, increasing the amount of water in the pan by small amounts each time. The more water she used, the greater the chance that she would miscalculate and drench herself with a too-energetic swirl of the pan. So far she had managed to make her mistakes in such a way as to send the water back into the stream, but she doubted that her luck would hold indefinitely.

Just when Mariah was congratulating herself on learning how to pan without accidents, she made an incautious movement that sent a tidal wave of ice water pouring down her front. With a stifled shriek she leaped to her feet, automatically brushing sheets of water from Cash's shirt and her jeans. The motions didn't do much good as far as keeping the clothes dry, but Mariah wasn't particularly worried.

Once the first shock passed, the water felt rather refreshing. Except in her right shoe, which squished.

Mariah kicked off her shoes and socks, relishing the feel of sun-warmed grass on bare feet. Sitting on her heels again, she dipped up more water in the pan. Just as she was starting to swirl the water, she sensed that she wasn't alone any longer. She spun around, spilling water down her front again. She brushed futilely at the drops, shivered at the second onslaught of ice water, and smiled up at Cash in wry defeat.

He was standing no more than an arm's length away, watching her with heavy-lidded eyes and a physical tension that was tangible.

"Cash? What's wrong?"

"I was just going to ask you the same thing."

"Why?"

"You screamed."

"Oh." Mariah gestured vaguely to her front, where water had darkened the flannel shirt to black. "I goofed."

"I can see that."

Cash could see a lot more, as well. His soaked shirt clung lovingly to Mariah's body, doing nothing to conceal the shape of her breasts and much to emphasize them. The frigid water had drawn her nipples into hard pebbles that grew more prominent with each renewed pulse of breeze.

Watching Cash, Mariah shivered again.

"You should go back to the line shack and change out of those wet clothes," he said in a strained voice. "You're cold."

"Not really. The shirt is clammy, but I can take care of that without going all the way back to the cabin."

While Mariah spoke, her hands picked apart the loose knot in the bottom of Cash's shirt. She had undone the bottom two snaps before his fingers closed over hers with barely restrained power.

"What the hell do you think you're doing?" he demanded.

"Giving my bathing suit a chance to live up to its no-drip, quick-dry advertising."

Cash looked down into Mariah's topaz eyes, felt the smooth promise of her flesh against his knuckles and could think of nothing but how easy it would be to strip the clothes from her and find out whether the feminine curves that had been haunting him were as beautiful as he had dreamed.

"Bathing suit?" he asked roughly. "You're wearing a bathing suit under your clothes?"

Mariah nodded because she couldn't speak for the sudden tension consuming her, a tension that was more than equalled in Cash's hard body.

The sound of a snap giving way seemed very loud in the hushed silence, as did Mariah's tiny, throttled gasp. Cash's hands flexed again and another snap gave way.

Mariah made no move to stop him from removing the shirt. She hadn't the strength. It was all she could do to stand beneath the sultry brilliance of his eyes while snap after snap gave way and he watched her body emerge from the dripping folds of his shirt. Where the thin fabric of the tank suit was pressed wetly against her body, everything was revealed.

Cash's breath came out in a sound that was almost a groan. "God, woman, are you sure that suit is legal?"

Mariah looked down. The high, taut curves of her breasts were tipped by flesh drawn tightly against the shock of cold water. Every change from smooth skin to textured nipple was faithfully reflected by the thin, supple fabric. She made a shocked sound and tried to cover her breasts.

It was impossible, for Cash's hands suddenly were holding Mariah's in a vise that was no less immovable for its gentleness. He looked at her breasts with half-closed eyes, too unsure of his own control to touch her. Nor could he give up the pleasure-pain of seeing her. Not just yet. She was much too alluring to turn away from.

There was neither warning nor true surprise when Cash's hands released Mariah's so that he could sweep the wet shirt from her faintly trembling body. Warm, hard palms settled on her collarbones. Long masculine fingers caressed the line of her jaw, the curve of her neck, the hollow of her throat, and the gentle feminine strength of her arms all the way to her wrists.

Too late Mariah realized that the straps of her tank suit had followed Cash's hands down her arms, leaving not even the flimsy fabric between her breasts and the blazing intensity of his eyes.

"You're perfect," Cash said hoarsely, closing his eyes like a man in pain. "So damn perfect."

For long, taut moments there was only the sound of Cash's rough breathing.

"Cash," Mariah said.

His eyes opened. They were hungry, fierce, almost wild. His voice was the same way, strained to breaking. "Just one word, honey. That's all you get. Make damn sure it's the word you want to live with."

Mariah drew in a long, shaking breath and looked at the man she loved.

"Yes," she whispered.

Ten

Cash said nothing, simply bent and took the pink velvet tip of one breast into his mouth. The caress sent streamers of fire through Mariah's body. Her breath came out in a broken sound of pleasure that was repeated when she felt the hot, silky rasp of his tongue over her skin. Cash's warm hands enveloped her waist, kneading the flesh sensuously while his mouth tugged at her breast.

Even as Mariah savored the delicious fire licking through her body, Cash's hands shifted. Instants later her jeans were undone and long, strong fingers were pushing inside the wet denim, sliding over the frail fabric of her bathing suit, seeking the heat hidden between her thighs, finding it, stroking it in the same urgent rhythms of his mouth shaping her breast.

The twin assaults made Mariah's knees weaken, forcing her to cling to Cash's upper arms for balance. The heat and hardness of the flexed muscles beneath her hands surprised her. They were a tangible reminder of Cash's far greater physical power, a power that was made shockingly clear when he lifted her with one arm and with the other impatiently stripped away her wet jeans, leaving only the fragile tank suit between her body and his hands.

"Cash?" Mariah said, unable to control the trembling of her voice as the beginnings of sweet arousal turned to uncertainty.

His only answer was the sudden spinning of the world when he carried her down to the sun-warmed grass. Hungrily he took her mouth and in the same motion pinned her legs beneath the weight of his right thigh, holding her stretched beneath him while his hands plucked at her nipples and his tongue thrust repeatedly into her mouth.

Mariah couldn't speak, could barely breathe, and had no idea of how to respond to Cash's overwhelming urgency. After a few minutes she simply lay motionless beneath his powerful body, fighting not to cry. That, too, proved to be beyond her abilities. When Cash tore his mouth from hers and began kissing and love-biting a path to her ear, the taste of tears was plain on her cheek.

"What the hell...?" he asked.

Baffled, he levered himself up until he could look down into Mariah's eyes. They were huge against the paleness of her skin, shocking in their darkness. Whatever she might have said a few minutes ago, it was brutally clear right now that she didn't want him.

"What kind of game are you playing?" Cash demanded savagely. "If you didn't want sex, why the hell did you say yes?"

Mariah's lips trembled when she tried to form words, but no words came. She no more knew what to say than she had known what to do. Tears came more and more quickly as her self-control disintegrated.

Cash swore. "You're nothing but a little tease whose bluff got called!"

With a searing word of disgust, Cash rolled aside, turning completely away from Mariah, not trusting himself even to look at her. If it weren't for his overwhelming arousal, he would have gotten to his feet and walked off. Bitterly he waited for the firestorm to pass, hating the realization that he had been so completely taken in by a woman. Again.

"I'm not a tease," Mariah said after a moment of struggling to control her tears. "I d-didn't say no."

"You didn't have to," Cash snarled. "Your body said it loud and clear."

There was a long moment of silence, followed by Mariah's broken sigh and a shaky question.

"How was I supposed to respond?"

Cash began to swear viciously; then he stopped as though he had stepped on solid ground only to find nothing beneath his feet but air. He turned toward Mariah and stared at her, unable to believe that he had heard her correctly.

"What did you say?" he asked.

"How was I supposed to respond?" she repeated shakily. "I couldn't even move. What did you want me to do?"

Cash's eyes widened and then closed tightly. An indescribable expression passed over his face, only to be replaced by no expression at all.

"Have you ever had a lover?" Cash asked neutrally.

"No," Mariah whispered. "I never really wanted one until you." She turned her face away from Cash, not able to cope with any more of his anger and contempt. Her eyes closed as her mouth curved downward. "Now I wish I'd had a hundred men. Then I would have known how to give you what you want."

Cash said something appalling beneath his breath, but the words were aimed at himself rather than at Mariah.

Grimly he looked from her slender, half-naked form to the scattered clothes he had all but torn off her body. He remembered his own uncontrolled hunger, his hands on her breasts and between her legs in a wildness that only an experienced, very hungry woman would have been able to cope with. Mariah was neither.

"My fault, honey, not yours," Cash said wearily. He took off his shirt, wrapped it around Mariah like a sheet and gently took her into his arms. "I wanted you so much I lost my head. That's a sorry excuse, but it's all I have. I'm sure as hell old enough to know better."

Mariah looked up at him with uncertain golden eyes.

"Don't be afraid," he said, kissing her forehead. One hand moved down her back in slow, comforting strokes. "It's all right, honey. It won't happen again."

The easy, undemanding hug Cash gave Mariah was like a balm. With a long sigh, she rested her head against his chest. When she moved slightly, she realized that his pelt of curling hair had an intriguing texture. She rubbed her cheek against it experimentally. Liking the feeling, she snuggled even closer.

"I wasn't afraid," Mariah whispered after a moment.

Cash made a questioning sound, telling Mariah that he hadn't heard her soft words.

"I wasn't afraid of you," Mariah said, tilting back her head until she could see Cash's eyes. "It was just…things were happening so fast and I wanted to do what you wanted but I didn't know how."

The soothing rhythm of Cash's hand hesitated, then continued as he absorbed Mariah's words.

"Virginity doesn't guarantee sexual inexperience," he said after a time. "You're both, aren't you? Virgin and inexperienced."

"There's no such thing as a sexually experienced virgin," Mariah muttered against his chest.

He laughed softly. "Don't bet on it, honey. My ex-wife was a virgin, but she had my pants undone and her hands all over me the first time we made out."

Mariah made an indecipherable noise that sounded suspiciously like "Virgin my fanny."

"Say again?" Cash said, smiling and tilting Mariah's face up to his.

She shook her head, refusing to meet his eyes. He laughed softly and bent over her mouth. His lips brushed hers once, twice, then again and again in tender motions that soon had her mouth turning after his, seeking him in a kiss less teasing than he was giving her. He seemed to give in, only to turn partially aside at the last instant and trace her upper lip with his tongue. The sensuous caress drew a small gasp from her.

Very carefully Cash lifted his head, took a slow breath and tucked Mariah's cheek against his chest once more. She gave a rather shaky sigh and burrowed against him. Hesitantly her hands began stroking him in the same slow rhythms that he was stroking her. His chest was hot beneath the silky mat of hair, and his muscles moved sleekly. Closing her eyes, she memorized his strength with her hands, enjoying the changes in texture from silky hair to smooth skin, savoring his heat and the muscular resilience of his torso.

When Mariah's hand slid down to Cash's waist, hovered, then settled on the fastening of his jeans, his breath came in with an odd, ripping sound.

"Would you like having my hands all over you?" Mariah asked tentatively.

A shudder of anticipation and need rippled over Cash, roughening his voice. "Hell yes, I'd like it. But," he added, capturing both her hands in one of his, preventing her from moving, "not unless you'd like it, too."

"There's only one way to find out...."

With a sound rather like a groan, Cash dragged Mariah's hands up to his mouth. "Let's wait," he suggested, biting her fingers gently. "There are other things you might like better at first."

"Like what?"

"Like kissing me."

Cash bent over Mariah's lips, touched the center of her upper lip with the tip of his tongue, then retreated. He returned again, touched, retreated, returned, touched and retreated once more. The slow, sensual teasing soon had Mariah moving restlessly in his arms, trying to capture his lips, failing, trying again and again until with a sound of frustration she took his head between her hands.

The cool, course silk of Cash's growing beard was an intense contrast to the heat and satin smoothness of his lips. The difference in textures so intrigued her that she savored them repeatedly with soft, darting touches of her tongue. When his lips opened, her tongue touched only air...and then the tip of his tongue found hers, touched, retreated, touched, withdrew. The hot caresses lured her deeper and yet deeper into his mouth, seducing her languidly, completely, until finally she was locked with him in an embrace as urgent as the one that had dismayed her a few minutes earlier.

But this time Mariah wasn't dismayed. This time she couldn't taste Cash deeply enough, nor could she be tasted deeply enough by him in turn. She clung to him, surrendering to and demanding his embrace at the same time, wholly lost in the shimmering sensuality of the moment. When he would have ended the kiss, she made a protesting sound and closed her teeth lightly on his tongue. With a hoarse rush of breath, Cash accepted the seductive demand and made one of his own in return, nipping at her lips, her tongue, sliding into the hot darkness behind her teeth until he had total possession of her mouth once more.

Gently Cash urged Mariah over onto her back. When she was lying against the soft grass once more, he settled onto her body in slow motion, easing apart her legs, letting her feel some of his weight while he explored the sweet mouth he had claimed with rhythmic strokes of his tongue.

Mariah made a soft sound at the back of her throat and arched against Cash's hard body. She couldn't imagine what had been wrong with her before, why his weight had frightened and then paralyzed her. The feel of his weight was delicious, maddening, incredibly arousing. Her only dilemma was how to get closer to him, how to ease the sweet aching of her body by pressing against his, soft against hard, fitting so perfectly.

When Cash's hips moved against Mariah, fire splintered in the pit of her stomach. She gasped and arched against him in an instinctive effort to feel the fire again. The sound he made was half throttled need, half triumph at having ignited the passion he had been so certain lay within her. Reluctantly, teasingly, he moved aside, lifting his body and his mouth from hers, releasing her from a sensual prison she had no desire to leave. Smiling, he looked down into her dazed topaz eyes. He was breathing too fast, too hard, but he didn't care. Mariah was breathing as quickly as he was.

"I think we can say with certainty that you like kissing me," Cash murmured.

Mariah's only answer was to capture his face between her hands once more, dragging his mouth back to hers. But he evaded her with an easy strength that told her he had been only playing at being captive before. He took her hands in his, interlacing them and rubbing against the sensitive skin between her fingers at the same time. When he could lace himself no more tightly to her, he flexed his hands, gently stretching her fingers apart. Her eyes widened as fire raced through her in response to the unexpected sensuality of the caress.

Smiling darkly, Cash flexed his hands once more as he bent down to Mariah.

"Want to taste me again?" he asked against her mouth.

Mariah's lips opened on a warm outrush of breath. The tip of her tongue traced his smile. He lifted his head just enough to see the sensual invitation of her parted lips revealing the glistening pink heat that waited for him. He wondered if she would open the rest of her body to him so willingly, and if he would slide into it with such sultry ease. With a throttled groan Cash took what Mariah offered and gave her his own mouth in return.

Slowly he pulled Mariah's hands above her head until she was stretched out beneath him. Each slow thrust of his tongue, each flexing of his hands, each hoarse sound he made was another streamer of fire uncurling deep inside Mariah's body. She twisted slowly, hungrily, trying to ease the aching in her breasts and at the apex of her thighs. When Cash lifted his head and ended the kiss, she felt empty, unfinished. She whimpered her protest and tried to reach for him, but her arms were still captive, stretched above her head in sensual abandon.

Mariah's eyes opened. Cash was watching her body's sinuous, restless movement with eyes that smoldered. Breathless, she followed his glance. The shirt he had used to cover her had long since fallen aside, leaving her bare to the waist once more. Her nipples were tight and very pink. One breast showed faint red marks, legacy of his first, wild hunger.

The memory of Cash's mouth went through Mariah in a rush of fire, tightening her body until her back arched in elemental reflex. When she saw the reaction that went through Cash, shaking his strength, she arched again, watching him, enjoying the heat of his glance and the sun pouring over her naked breasts.

"If you keep that up, I'm going to think you've forgiven me for this," he said in a deep voice, touching the vague mark on her breast caressingly. "Have you forgiven me, honey?"

"Yes."

The sound was more a sigh than a word. Mariah twisted slowly, trying to bring Cash's hand into more satisfying contact with her breast, but she could not. Cash still held her arms stretched above her head, her wrists held in his left hand, her body softly pinned beneath his right hand.

"If I promise to be very gentle, will you let me kiss you again?"

This time Mariah's answer was a sound of anticipation and need that made Cash ache. Slowly he bent down to her. His tongue laved the passionate mark on her breast, then kissed it so gently she shivered.

"I'm sorry," Cash whispered, kissing the mark once more. "I didn't mean to hurt you."

"You didn't, you just surprised me," Mariah said moving restlessly, wanting more than the gentle torment of his lips. "I know you won't hurt me. And I—I liked it. Cash? *Please.*"

Cash wanted to tell Mariah what her trust and sensual pleas did to him, but he couldn't speak for the passion constricting his throat. With exquisite care he caught the tip of first one breast then the other between his teeth. The arching of her body this time was purely reflex, as was the low sound of pleasure torn from her throat when he drew her nipple into his mouth and tugged it into a taut, aching peak. When he released her she made a sound of protest that became a moan of pleasure when he captured her other breast and began drawing it into a sensitive peak, pulling small cries of passion from her.

Mariah didn't know when Cash released her hands. She only knew that the heat of his skin felt good beneath her palms, and the flexed power of his muscles beneath her probing fingers was like a drug. She couldn't get enough of it, or of him.

A lean, strong hand stroked from Mariah's breasts to her thighs and back again while Cash's mouth plucked at her hardened nipple in a sensual teasing that made her breath break into soft cries. Long fingers slid beneath the flimsy tank suit and kneaded her belly, savoring the taut muscles and resilient heat. Gradually, imperceptibly, inevitably, his hand eased down until he could feel the silken thicket concealing her most vulnerable flesh. When he could endure teasing himself no longer, he slid farther down, finding and touching a different, hotter softness.

Mariah's eyes opened and her breath came in with a startled gasp that was Cash's name.

"Easy, honey. That doesn't hurt you, does it?"

"No. It just—" Mariah's breath broke at another gliding caress. "It's so—" Another gasp came, followed by a trembling that shook her.

Mariah looked up at Cash with wide, questioning eyes, only to find that he was watching the slow twisting of her half-clothed body as he caressed her intimately. The stark sensuality of the moment made heat bloom beneath her skin, embarrassment and desire mingling. When his hand slid from between her legs, she made a broken sound of protest. An instant later she felt the fragile fabric of her tank suit being drawn down her legs until she was utterly naked. She saw the heavy-lidded blaze of Cash's eyes memorizing the secrets he had revealed, and she was caught between another rush of embarrassment and passion. He was looking at her as though he had never seen a nude woman before.

"You're beautiful," Cash breathed, shaken and violently aroused by Mariah's smooth, sultry body.

One of his big hands skimmed from her mouth to her knees, touching her reverently, marveling at the sensual contrast between her deeply flushed nipples and the pale cream of her breasts. The soft mound of nearly black curls fascinated him. He returned again and again to skim their promise, lightly seeking the honeyed softness he knew lay within.

Shivering with a combination of uncertainty and arousal, Mariah watched Cash cherish her body with slow sweeps of his hand. The dark intensity of his eyes compelled her, the tender caresses of his fingertips reassured her, the hot intimacy of seeing his hand touching the secret places of her body made her blush.

"Cash?" she asked shakily.

"If it embarrasses you," Cash said without looking up, "close your eyes. But don't ask me to. I've never touched a woman half so beautiful. If you weren't a virgin, I'd be doing things to you right now that would make you blush all the way to the soles of your feet."

"I already am," she said shakily.

A dark, lazy kind of smile was Cash's only answer. "But you like this, don't you?"

His knuckles skimmed the dark curls again, turning Mariah's answer into a broken sigh of pleasure.

"Good," he whispered, bending down to kiss her lips slowly, then rising once more, wanting to watch her. "I like it, too. There's something else I know I'll like doing. I think you'll like it even better."

Cash's fingertips caressed Mariah's thighs, sliding up and down between her knees, making her shiver. Watching her, he smiled and caressed her soft inner thighs again and again, gently easing them apart. When she resisted, he bent and took her mouth in a kiss that was sweet and gentle and deep. The rhythmic penetration and withdrawal of his tongue teased her, as did the sensual forays of his mouth over her breasts.

Soon Mariah's eyelids flickered shut as thrill after thrill of pleasure went through her. She forgot that she was naked and he was watching her, forgot that she was uncertain and he was tremendously strong, forgot her instinctive protection of the vulnerable flesh between her legs. With a moan she arched her back, demanding that he do something to ease the tightness coiling within her body.

The next time Mariah lifted, pleading for Cash, sensual heat bloomed from within the softness no man had ever touched. And then Cash's caress was inside her, testing the depth of her response, his touch sliding into her sleek heat until he could go no farther. Mariah made a low sound that could have been pain or pleasure. Before Cash could ask which, he felt the answer in the passionate melting of her body around his deep caress. The instant, fierce blaze of his own response almost undid him.

With a hoarse groan of male need, Cash sought Mariah's mouth, found it, took it in hungry rhythms of penetration and retreat. She took his mouth in return while her hands moved hungrily over his head, his chest, his back, half-wild with the need he had called from her depths. When he finally tore his mouth away from hers in an agonizing attempt to bring himself under control, Mariah's nails scored heedlessly on his arms in silent protest.

Cash didn't complain. He was asking for all of her response each time he probed caressingly within her softness and simultaneously rubbed the sleek bud that passion had drawn from her tender flesh. Mariah's quickening cries and searing meltings were a fire licking over him, arousing him violently, yet he made no move to take her. Instead, his hands pleasured and enjoyed her with an unbridled sensuality that was as new to him as it was to her, each of his caresses a mute demand and plea that was answered with liquid fire.

Finally Cash could bear no more of the sensuous torment. It was as difficult as tearing off his own skin to withdraw from Mariah's softness, but he did. The lacings of his boots felt harsh, alien, after the silky perfection of her aroused body. He yanked off his boots and socks with violent impatience, wanting only to be inside her. Shuddering with the force of his suppressed need, he fought for control of the passion that had possessed him as completely as it had possessed her.

"Is it—is it supposed to be—like this?" Mariah asked, breathing too hard, too fast, watching Cash with wild golden eyes.

"I don't know," Cash said, reaching for his belt buckle, looking at her with eyes that were black with desire. "But I'm going to find out."

Mariah's eyes widened even more as Cash stripped out of his clothes and turned toward her. Admiration became uncertainty when she looked from the muscular strength of his torso to the blunt, hard length of his arousal. She looked quickly back up to his eyes.

"If it were as bad as you're thinking now," Cash said huskily, drawing her body close to his, "the human race would have died out a long time ago."

Mariah's smile was too brief, too shaky, but she didn't

withdraw from him. When Cash rubbed one of her hands slowly across his chest, she let out a long breath and closed her eyes, enjoying his newly familiar textures. Her fingertips grazed one of his smooth, flat nipples, transforming it into a nail head of desire. The realization that their bodies shared similarities beneath their obvious differences both comforted and intrigued her. She sought out his other nipple with her mouth. A slow touch of her tongue transformed his masculine flesh into a tiny, tight bud.

"You *do* like that," Mariah whispered, pleased by her discovery.

A sound that was both laughter and groan was Cash's only answer. Then her hand smoothed down his torso and breath jammed in his throat, making speech impossible. The tearing instants of hesitation when she touched the dense wedge of hair below Cash's waist shredded his control. Long fingers clamped around her wrist, dragging her hand to his aching flesh, holding her palm hard against him while his hips moved in an agony of pleasure. She made an odd sound, moved by his need. Abruptly he released her, afraid that he had shocked her.

Mariah didn't lift her hand. Her fingers curled around Cash, sliding over him in sweet, repeated explorations that pushed him partway over the brink. When she touched the sultry residue of his desire, she made a soft sound of discovery and wonder. She could not have aroused him more if she had bent down and tasted him.

Cash groaned hoarsely and clenched his teeth against the release that was coiled violently within his body, raging to be free. With fingers that trembled, he pulled Mariah's hand up to his mouth and bit the base of her palm, drawing a passionate sound from her. His hand caressed down the length of her body, sending visible shivers of response through her. When he reached the apex of her thighs, he had only to touch her and she gave way before him, trusting him.

He settled his weight slowly between her thighs, easing them apart even more, making room for his big body. She was sleek, hot, promising him a seamless joining. He pushed into her, testing the promise, savoring the feverish satin of her flesh as it yielded to him.

"Cash."

He forced himself to stop. His voice was harsh with the pain of restraint. "Does it hurt?"

"No. It—" Mariah's breath fragmented as fire streaked through her. "I—"

Even as her nails scored Cash's skin, he felt the passionate constriction and then release of her body. The hot rain of her pleasure eased his way, but not enough. Deliberately he slid his hand between their joined bodies, seeking and finding the velvet focus of her passion. Simultaneously his mouth moved against her neck, biting her with hot restraint. Fire and surprise streaked through Mariah, and then fire alone, fire ripping through her, filling her as Cash did, completely, a possession that transformed her.

Mariah's eyes opened golden with knowledge and desire.

"You feel like heaven and hell combined," Cash said, his voice rough with passion. "Everything a man could want."

Mariah tried to speak but could think of no words to describe the pleasure-pain of having so much yet not quite enough...heaven and hell combined. She closed her eyes and moved her hips in a sinuous, languid motion, caressing Cash as deeply as he was caressing her. Exquisite pleasure pierced her, urging her to measure him again and then again, but it wasn't enough, it was never enough, she was burning. She twisted wildly beneath the hands that would have held her still.

"Mariah," Cash said hoarsely. "Baby, stop. You don't know what you're doing to me. I—"

His voice broke as her nails dug into the clenched muscles of his hips. Sweet violence swept through him, stripping away his control. He drove into her seething softness, rocking her with the force of his need, giving all that she had demanded and then more and yet more, becoming a driving force that was as fast and deep within her as the hammering of her own heart.

At a distance Mariah heard her own voice crying Cash's name, then the world burst and she could neither see nor hear, she was being drawn tight upon a golden rack of pleasure, shuddering, wild, caught just short of some unimaginable consummation, unborn ecstasy raking at her nerves.

For an agonizing moment Cash held himself away from Mariah, watching her, sensing her violent need as clearly as he sensed his own.

"Mariah. Look at me. *Look at me.*"

Her eyelids quivered open. She looked at Cash and saw herself reflected in his eyes, a face drawn by searing pleasure that was also pain.

"*Help me,*" she whispered.

With a hoarse cry that was her name, Cash drove deeply into Mariah once more, sealing their bodies together with the profound pulses of his release. Her body shivered in primal response, ecstasy shimmering through her, burning, bursting in pulses of pleasure so great she thought she would die of them. She clung to Cash, absorbing him into herself, crying as golden fire consumed her once more.

Cash drank Mariah's cries while ecstasy unraveled her, giving her completely to him and unraveling him completely in turn. Passion coiled impossibly, violently, within him once more. The elemental force was too overwhelming to fight. He held her hard and fast to himself, pouring himself into her again and again until there was no beginning, no end, simply Mariah surrounding him with the golden fury of mutual release.

Eleven

Mariah floated on the hot currents at the upstream end of the middle pool, keeping herself in place with languid motions of her hands. The sky overhead was a deep, crystalline blue that reminded her of Cash's eyes when he looked at her, wanting her. A delicious feeling shimmered through her at the memories of Cash's body moving over hers, his shoulders blocking out the sky, his powerful arms corded with restraint, his mouth hungry and sensual as it opened to claim her.

If only they had been able to leave the cellular phone behind, they would have remained undisturbed within Black Springs's sensual silence. But their peace was disturbed by the phone's imperious summons. It woke them from their warm tangle of blankets on the shack's wooden floor. Mariah appreciated the emergency safeguard the phone represented, but she resented its intrusion just the same.

Cash had picked up the phone, grunted a few times and hung up. Mariah had fallen asleep again, not awakening until Cash had threatened to throw her in the stream. He had taken one look at the slight hesitation in her movements as she crawled out of his sleeping bag and had sent her to Black Springs to soak. When she had tried to tell him that she wasn't really sore from the long, sweet joining of their bodies, he hadn't listened.

But she wasn't sore. Not really. She was just deliciously aware of every bit of herself, a frankly female awareness that was enhanced by the slight tenderness he deplored.

"Have I ever told you how lovely you are?"

Mariah's eyes opened and she smiled.

Cash was standing at the edge of the pool, watching her with dark blue eyes and a hunger that was more unruly for having been satisfied so completely. He knew beyond doubt what he was missing. He had sent her to the hot springs because he was afraid he wouldn't be able to keep his hands off her if she stayed in the cabin. Now he was certain he wouldn't be able to keep his hands to himself. The thin, wet fabric of her suit clung to every lush line of her body, reminding him of how good it had felt to take complete possession of her softness.

The cutoff jeans Cash wore in Black Springs didn't conceal much of his big body. Certainly not the desire that had claimed him as he stood watching Mariah.

"I'm not sure lovely is the right word for you," Mariah said, smiling. "Potent, certainly."

The shiver of desire that went over his skin as she looked at Cash did nothing to cool his body.

"Kiss me?" Mariah asked softly, holding a wet, gently steaming hand toward him.

"You're hard on my good intentions," he said in a deep voice, wading into the pool.

"Should that worry me?"

"Ask me this afternoon, when you're two hours into a half-day ride back to the ranch house."

"We have to go back so soon again?" Mariah asked, unable to hide her dismay. "Why?"

"I just got a ten-day contract in Boulder. Then I'll be back and we can go gold hunting again."

"Ten days…"

The soft wail wasn't finished. It didn't need to be. Mariah's tone said clearly how much she would miss Cash.

"Be grateful," Cash said thickly. "It will give you time to heal. I'm too damn big for you."

"I don't need time. I need…you."

The sound Cash made could have been laughter or hunger or both inextricably mixed. The water where Mariah was floating came to the middle of his thighs, not nearly high enough to conceal what her honest sensuality did to him. His former wife had used sex, not enjoyed it. At least not with him. Maybe Linda had liked sex with the father of her child.

I should be grateful that I can't get Mariah pregnant. Holding back would be impossible with her.

"Cash? Is something wrong?"

"Just thinking about the past."

"What about it?"

Without answering, Cash pulled Mariah into his arms and gave her a kiss that was hotter than the steaming, gently seething pool.

Discreetly Mariah shifted position in the saddle. After she had recovered from the initial trip to the line shack, Cash had insisted that she ride every day no matter where she was. Thanks to that, and frequent rest breaks, she wasn't particularly sore at the moment. She was very tired of her horse's choppy gait, however. Next time she would insist on a different horse.

"Are you doing okay?" Cash asked, reining in until he came alongside Mariah.

"Better than I expected. My horse missed her calling. She would have made a world-class cement mixer."

"You should have said something sooner. We'll trade."

Mariah looked at Cash and then at the small mare she rode. "Bad match. You're too big."

"Honey, I've seen Luke ride that little spotted pony all day long."

"Really? Is he a closet masochist?"

Cash smiled and shook his head. "He saves her for the roughest country the ranch has to offer. She's unflappable and surefooted as a goat. That's why Luke gave her to you. But the rough country is behind us, so there's no reason why we can't switch horses."

Before Mariah could object any more, Cash pulled his big horse to a stop and dismounted. Moments later she found herself lifted out of the saddle and into his embrace.

"You don't have to do this," she said, putting her arms around Cash's neck. "I was finally getting the hang of that spotted devil's gait."

"Call it enlightened self-interest. Luke will peel me like a ripe banana if I bring you back in bad shape. I'm supposed to be taking care of you, remember?"

"You're doing a wonderful job. I've never felt better in my life."

Mariah's smile and the feel of her fingers combing through his hair sent desire coursing through Cash. The kiss he gave her was hard and deep and hungry. His big hands smoothed over her back and hips until she was molded to him like sunlight. Then he tore his mouth away from her alluring heat and lifted her onto his horse. He stood for a moment next to the horse, looking up into Mariah's golden eyes, his hand absently stroking the resilience of her thigh while her fingertips traced the lines of his face beneath the growth of stubble.

"What are you thinking?" Mariah asked softly.

Cash hesitated, then shrugged. "Even though we'll sleep separately on the ranch, a blind man could see we're lovers."

It was Mariah's turn to hesitate. "Is that bad?"

"Only if Luke decides he didn't mean what he said about you and me."

"What did he say?"

"That you wanted me," Cash said bluntly. "That you were past the age of consent. That whatever the two of us did was our business."

Mariah flushed, embarrassed that her attraction to Cash had been so obvious from the start.

"I hope Luke meant it," Cash continued. "He and Carla are the only home I'll ever have. But what's done is done. We might as well have the pleasure of it because sure as hell we'll have the pain."

The bleak acceptance in Cash's voice stunned Mariah. Questions crowded her mind, questions she had just enough self-control not to ask. Cash had never said anything to her about their future together beyond how long he would be gone before he came back to the Rocking M and the two of them could go gold hunting again.

I haven't said anything about the future, either, Mariah reminded herself. *I haven't even told him that I love him. I keep hoping he'll tell me first. But maybe he feels the same way about speaking first. Maybe he's waiting for me to say something. Maybe…*

Cash turned, mounted the smaller horse, picked up the pack animals' lead ropes and started down the trail once more. Mariah followed, her thoughts in a turmoil, questions ricocheting in her mind.

By the time the ranch house was in sight, Mariah had decided not to press Cash for answers. It was too soon. The feelings were too new.

And she was too vulnerable.

It will be all right, Mariah told herself silently. *Cash just needs more time. Men aren't as comfortable with their emotions as women are, and Cash has already lost once at love. But he cares for me. I know he does.*

It will be all right.

As they rode up to the corral, the back door of the ranch house opened and Nevada came out to meet them. At least Mariah thought the man was Nevada until she noticed the absence of any beard.

"It's about time you got back!" Cash called out. "If I don't see Carolina more often, she won't recognize me at all."

The man took the bridle of Mariah's horse and smiled up at her. "With those eyes, you've got to be Luke's little sister, Mariah. Welcome home."

Mariah grinned at the smiling stranger who was every bit as handsome as his unsmiling younger brother. "Thanks. Now I know what Nevada looks like underneath that beard. You must be Tennessee."

"You sure about that?" Ten asked.

"Dead sure. With those shoulders and that catlike way of walking, you've got to be Nevada's older brother."

Ten laughed. "It's a shame Nevada's not the marrying kind. You'd make a fine sister-in-law."

Cash gave Ten a hard glance. Ten had no way of knowing that Mariah's gentle interest in Nevada was a raw spot with Cash. No matter how many times he told himself that Mariah had no sexual interest in Nevada, Cash kept remembering his bitter experience with Linda. It had never occurred to him that she was sleeping with another man. After all, she had come to him a virgin.

Like Mariah.

"Put your ruff down," Ten drawled to Cash, amused by his response to the idea of Nevada and Mariah together. "Nevada was the one who told me the lady was already taken."

"See that he remembers it."

Ten shook his head. "Still the Granite Man. Hard muscles and a skull to match. You sure you didn't just buy your Ph.D. from some mail-order diploma mill?"

Laughing, Cash dismounted. When Ten offered his hand to help Mariah dismount, Cash reached past the Rocking M's foreman and lifted her out of the saddle. When Cash put her down, his arm stayed around her.

"Not that I don't trust you, ramrod," Cash said dryly to Ten. "It's just that you're handsome as sin and twice as hard."

The left corner of Ten's mouth turned up. "That's Nevada you're thinking of. I'm hard as sin and twice as handsome."

Cash snickered and shook his head. "Lord, what are we going to do if Utah comes home to roost?"

Mariah blinked. "Utah?"

"Another Blackthorn," Cash explained.

"There are a lot of them," Ten added.

"Don't tell me," Mariah said quickly. "Let me guess. Fifty, right? Who got stuck being called New Hampshire?"

The two men laughed simultaneously.

"My parents weren't that ambitious," Ten said. "There are only eight of us to speak of."

"To speak of?" Mariah asked.

"The Blackthorns don't run to marriage, but kids have

a way of coming along just the same." Ten smiled slightly, thinking of his own daughter.

"Is Carolina awake?" Cash asked.

"I hope not. She'll be hungry when she wakes up and Diana isn't due back from our Spring Valley house for another hour. She and Carla are measuring for drapes or rugs or some darn thing." Ten shook his head and started gathering up reins and lead ropes. "Life sure was easier when all I had to worry about was a blanket for my bedroll."

"Crocodile tears," Cash snorted. "You wouldn't go back to your old life and you know it. Hell, if a man even looks at Diana more than once, you start honing your belt knife."

"Glad you noticed," Ten said dryly.

"Not that you need to," Cash continued, struck by something he had never put into words. "Diana is a rarity among females—a one-man woman."

"And I'm the lucky man," Ten said with tangible satisfaction as he led the horses off. "You two go on up to the big house and watch Carolina sleep. I'll take care of the horses for you."

When Cash started for the house, Mariah slipped from his grasp. "I've got to clean up before Carla gets back. I don't want to get off on the wrong foot with Luke's wife."

"Carla won't care what you look like. She's too damn happy that Logan finally shook off that infection and both of them can stay on the ranch again instead of in my apartment in Boulder. Besides, I happen to know Carla's dying to meet you."

"You go ahead," Mariah urged. "I'll catch up as soon as I've showered."

He tipped up Mariah's chin, kissed her with a lingering heat that made her toes curl, and reluctantly released her.

"Don't be long," Cash said huskily.

She almost changed her mind about going at all, but the thought of standing around in camp clothes while meeting Carla stiffened Mariah's determination. As her brother's wife and the sister of the man she loved, Carla was too important to risk alienating. Bitter experience with Mariah's stepfamily had taught her how very important first impressions could be.

Putting the unhappy past out of her mind, Mariah hurried toward the old ranch house. She had her blouse half-unbuttoned when she opened the front door, only to encounter Nevada just inside the living room. He was carrying a huge carton.

"Don't stop on my account," he said, appreciation gleaming in his eyes.

Hastily Mariah fumbled with a button, trying to bring her décolletage under some control.

"Relax," he said matter-of-factly. "I'm just a pack animal."

"Funny," she muttered, feeling heat stain her cheeks. "To me you look like a man called Nevada Blackthorn."

"Optical illusion. Hold the door open and I'll prove it by disappearing."

"What are you hauling?" she asked, reaching for the door, opening it only a few inches.

"Broken crockery."

"What?"

"Ten and Diana are finally moving the Anasazi artifacts out of your way. I'm taking the stuff to their new house in Spring Valley."

"That's not necessary," Mariah said. "I don't want to be a bother. I certainly don't need every room in the old house. Please. Put everything back. Don't go to any trouble because of me."

The fear beneath Mariah's rapid words was clear. Even if Nevada hadn't heard the fear, he would have sensed it in the sudden tension of her body, felt it in the urgency of the hand wrapped around his wrist.

"You'll have to take that up with Ten and Diana," Nevada said calmly. "They were looking forward to having all this stuff moved into their new house where they could work on it whenever they wanted." He saw that Mariah didn't understand yet. "Diana is an archaeologist. She supervises the September Canyon dig. Ten is a partner in the Rocking M. He owns the land the dig is on."

Slowly Mariah's fingers relaxed their grip on Nevada's wrist, but she didn't release him yet.

"You're sure they don't mind moving their workroom?" she asked.

"They've been looking forward to it. Would have done it sooner, but Carolina came along a few weeks early and upset all their plans."

Mariah smiled uncertainly. "If you're sure..."

"I'm sure."

"Just what are you sure of?" Cash's voice asked coldly, pushing the door open. Bleak blue eyes took in Mariah's partially unbuttoned blouse and her hand wrapped around Nevada's wrist.

"I was just telling her that Diana and Ten don't mind clearing out their stuff," Nevada said in a voice as emotionless as the ice-green eyes measuring Cash's anger. "Your woman was afraid she'd be kicked off the ranch if she upset anyone."

"My woman?"

"She lit up like a Christmas tree when she heard your voice. That's as much a man's woman as it gets," Nevada said. "Now if you'll get out of my way, I'll get out of yours."

There was a long silence before Cash stepped aside. Nevada brushed past him and out the front door. Only then did Mariah realize she was holding her breath. She closed her eyes and let out air in a long sigh.

When she opened her eyes again, Cash was gone.

Twelve

Mariah showered, dried her hair, dusted on makeup and put on her favorite casual clothes—a tourmaline green blouse and matching slacks. She checked her appearance in the mirror. Everything was tucked in, no rips, no missing buttons, no spots. Satisfied, she turned away without appreciating the contrast of very dark brown hair, topaz eyes and green clothes. She had never seen herself as particularly attractive, much less striking. Yet she was just that—tall, elegantly proportioned, with high cheekbones and large, unusually colored eyes.

Mentally crossing her fingers that everything would go well with Carla, Mariah grabbed a light jacket and headed for the big house. No one answered her gentle tapping on the front door. She opened it and stuck her head in.

"Cash?" she called softly, not wanting to wake Carolina if she were still sleeping.

"In here," came the soft answer.

Mariah opened the door and walked into the living room. What she saw made her throat constrict and tears burn behind her eyelids. A clean-shaven Cash was sitting in an oversize rocking chair with a tiny baby tucked into the crook of his arm. One big hand held a bottle that looked too small in his grasp to be anything but a toy. The baby was ignoring the bottle, which held only water. Both tiny hands had locked onto one of Cash's fingers. Wide, blue-gray eyes studied the man's face with the intensity only young babies achieved.

"Isn't she something?" Cash asked softly, his voice as proud as though he were the baby's father rather than a friend of the family. "She's got a grip like a tiger."

Mariah crept closer and looked at the smooth, tiny fingers clinging to Cash's callused, much more powerful finger.

"Yes," Mariah whispered, "she's something. And so are you."

Cash looked away from the baby and saw the tears magnifying Mariah's beautiful eyes.

"It's all right," she said softly, blinking away the tears. "It's just...I thought men cared only for their own children. But you care for this baby."

"Hell, yes. It's great to hold a little girl again."

"Again?" Mariah asked, shocked. "Do you have children?"

Cash's expression changed. He looked from Mariah to the baby in his arms. "No. No children." His voice was flat, remote. "I was thinking of when Carla was born. It was Dad's second marriage, so I was ten years old when Carla came along. I took care of her a lot. Carla's mother was pretty as a rosebud, and not much more use. She married Dad so she wouldn't have to support herself." Cash shrugged and said ironically, "So what else is new?

Women have lived off men since they got us kicked out of Eden."

Although Mariah flinched at Cash's brutal summation of marriage and women, she made no comment. She suspected that her mother's second marriage had been little better than Cash's description.

Cash looked back to the baby, who was slowly succumbing to sleep in his arms. He smiled, changing the lines of his face from forbidding to beguiling. Mariah's heart turned over as she realized all over again just how handsome Cash was.

"Carla was like this baby," Cash said softly. "Lively as a flea one minute and dead asleep the next. Carla used to watch me with her big blue-green eyes and I'd feel like king of the world. I could coax away her tears when no one else could. Her smile...God, her smile was so sweet."

"Carla was lucky to have a brother like you. She was even luckier to keep you," Mariah whispered. "Long after my grandparents took me from the Rocking M, I used to cry myself to sleep. It was Luke I was crying for, not my father."

"Luke always hoped that you were happy," Cash said, looking up at Mariah.

"It's in the past." Mariah shrugged with a casualness that went no deeper than her skin. "Anyway, I was no great bargain as a child. The man my mother married was older, wealthy, and recently widowed. I met him on Christmas Day. I had been praying very hard that the special present my mother had been hinting at would be a return trip to the Rocking M. When I was introduced to my new 'father' and his kids, I started crying for Luke. Not the best first impression I could have made," Mariah added unhappily. "A disaster, in fact. Harold and his older kids resented being saddled with a 'snot-nosed, whining seven-year-old.' Boarding schools were the answer.''

Cash muttered something savage under his breath.

''Don't knock them until you've tried them,'' Mariah said with a wry smile. ''At least I was with my own kind. And I had it better than some of the other outcasts. I got to see Mother most Christmases. And I got a good education.''

The bundle in Cash's arm shifted, mewing softly, calling his attention back from Mariah. He offered little Carolina the bottle again. Her face wrinkled in disgust as she tasted the tepid water.

''Don't blame you a bit,'' Cash said, smiling slightly. ''Compared to what you're used to, this is really thin beer.''

Gently he increased the rhythm of his rocking, trying to distract the baby from her disappointment. It didn't work. Within moments Carolina's face was red and her small mouth was giving vent to surprisingly loud cries. Patiently Cash teased her lips with his fingertip. After a few more yodels, the baby began sucking industriously on the tip of his finger.

''Sneaky,'' Mariah said admiringly. ''How long does it last?''

''Until she figures out that she's working her little rear end off for nothing.''

Car doors slammed out in the front yard. Women's voices called out, to be answered from the vicinity of the barn.

''Hang in there, tiger,'' Cash said. ''Milk is on the way.''

Mariah smoothed her clothes hastily, tucked a strand of hair behind her ear and asked, ''Do I look all right?''

Cash looked up. ''It doesn't matter. Carla isn't so shallow that she's going to care what you look like.''

Mariah heard the edge in Cash's voice and knew he was

still angry about finding her with Nevada. But before she could say anything, the front door opened and a petite, very well built woman hurried in.

"Sorry I'm late. I—oh, hello. What gorgeous eyes. You must be Luke's sister. I'm Diana Blackthorn. Excuse me. Carolina is about to do her imitation of a cat with its tail in a wringer. Thanks, Cash. You have a magic touch with her. Even Ten would have had a hard time keeping the lid on her this long."

Diana whisked the small bundle from Cash's arms and vanished up the staircase, speaking to Carolina in soothing tones at every step.

Mariah blinked, not sure that she had really seen the honey-haired woman at all. "That was an archaeologist?"

"Um," Cash said tactfully.

"Ten's wife?"

"Um."

"Whew. No wonder he smiles a lot."

"Ask Diana and she'll tell you that she'd trade it all for four more inches of height."

"She can have four of mine if I can have four of hers," Mariah said instantly.

Cash came out of the rocking chair in a fluid motion and pulled Mariah close. His hands slid from her hips to her waist and on up her body, stopping at the top of her rib cage. Watching her, he eased his hands underneath her breasts, taking their warm weight into his palms, teasing her responsive nipples with his thumbs, smiling lazily.

"You're too damn sexy just the way you are," Cash said, his voice gritty, intimate, as hot as the pulse suddenly speeding in Mariah's throat. "I've never seen anything as beautiful as you were this morning in that pool wearing nothing but steam. *You watched me take you.* The sweet sounds you made then almost pushed me over the edge. Just thinking about it now makes me want to—''

"Hi, Nevada. Is that another box of shards? Good. Put them in Diana's car. Here, Logan, chew on this instead of Nosy's tail. Even if the cat doesn't mind it, I do.''

The voice from the front porch froze Cash. He closed his eyes, swore softly, and released Mariah. He turned toward the front door, blocking Mariah's flushed face with his body.

"Where's my favorite nephew?'' Cash called out.

"Your only nephew,'' Carla said, smiling as she walked into the living room. "He's a one hundred percent terror again. How's my favorite brother?''

"Your only brother, right?'' Cash bent down and scooped up Logan in one arm. "Lord, boy. What have you been eating—lead? You must have gained ten pounds.''

As a toddler, Logan wasn't exactly a fountain of conversation. Action was more his line. Laughing, he grabbed Cash's nose and tried to pull it off.

"That's not the way to do it,'' Cash said, grabbing Logan's nose gently. Very carefully Cash pulled and made a sucking, popping noise. Moments later he triumphantly held up his hand. The end of his thumb was pushed up between his index and second finger to imitate Logan's snub nose. "See? Got it! Want me to put it back on?''

With an expression of affection and amusement, Carla watched her brother and her son. Then she realized that someone was standing behind Cash. She looked around his broad shoulders and saw a woman about her own age and height hastily tucking in her blouse.

"Hello?''

Mariah bit her lip and gave up trying to straighten her clothes. "Hi, I'm—''

"Mariah!'' Carla said, smiling with delight. She stepped

around Cash and gave Mariah a hug. "I'm so glad you came home at last. When the lawyer told Luke his mother was dead, there was no mention of you at all. We had no way to contact you. Luke wanted so much to share Logan with you. And most of all he wanted to know that you were happy."

Mariah looked into Carla's transparent, blue-green eyes and saw only welcome. With a stifled sound, Mariah hugged Carla in return, feeling a relief so great it made her dizzy.

"Thank you," Mariah said huskily. "I was so afraid you would resent having me around."

"Don't be ridiculous. Why would anyone resent you?" Carla stared into Mariah's huge, golden-brown eyes. "You mean it. You really were worried, weren't you?"

Mariah tried to smile, but it turned upside down. "Families don't like outsiders coming to live with them."

Cash spoke without looking up from screwing Logan's nose back into place. "As you might guess from that statement, Mariah's mother didn't pick a winner for her second husband. In fact, he sounds like a real, um, prince. Kept her in boarding schools all year round."

"Why didn't he just send you back to the Rocking M?" Carla asked Mariah.

"Mother refused. She said the Rocking M was malevolent. It hated women. She could feel it devouring her. Just talking about it upset her so much I stopped asking." Mariah looked past Carla to the window that framed MacKenzie Ridge's rugged lines. "I never felt that way about the ranch. I love this land. But as long as Mother was alive, I couldn't come back. She simply couldn't have coped with it."

"You're back now," Carla said quietly, "and you're staying as long as you want."

Mariah tried to speak, couldn't, and hugged her sister-in-law instead.

Cash watched the two women and told himself that no matter why Mariah had originally come to the Rocking M, she was genuinely grateful to be accepted into Luke's family. And, Cash admitted, he couldn't really blame Mariah for wanting a place she could call home. He felt the same way. The Rocking M, more than his apartment in Boulder, was his home. Only on the Rocking M were there people who gave a damn whether he came back from his field trips or died on some godforsaken granite slope.

Almost broodingly Cash watched Mariah and his sister fix dinner. With no fuss at all they went about the business of cooking a huge meal and getting to know one another. As he looked at them moving around the kitchen, Cash realized that the two women were similar in many ways. They were within a year of each other in age, within an inch in height, graceful, supremely at home with the myriad tools used to prepare food, willing to do more than half of any job they shared; and their laughter was so beautiful it made him ache.

Linda never wanted to share anything or do any work. I thought it was just because she was young, but I can see that wasn't it. She was the same age then as Mariah is now. Linda was just spoiled. Mariah may have come here looking for room and board—and a crack at Mad Jack's mine—but at least she's not afraid to work for it.

Best of all, Mariah doesn't whine.

No. Not best of all. What was best about Mariah, Cash conceded, was her incandescent sensuality. After Linda, he had never found it difficult to control himself where women were concerned. Mariah was different. He wanted her more, not less, each time. It was just as well that he was going to Boulder. He needed distance from Mariah's fire, distance and the coolness of mind to remember that a woman didn't have to be spoiled in order to manipulate a man. She simply had to be clever enough to allow him to deceive himself.

Cash was still reminding himself of how it had been with Linda when he let himself into the old house in the hour before dawn. He knew he should be on the road, driving away, putting miles between himself and Mariah. Yet he couldn't bring himself to leave without saying goodbye to her.

The front door of the old house closed softly behind Cash. An instant later he heard a whispering, rushing sound and felt Mariah's soft warmth wrapping around him, holding him with a woman's surprising strength. His arms came around her in a hard hug that lifted her feet off the floor.

Her tears were hot against his neck.

"Mariah?"

She shuddered and held on to Cash until she could trust her voice. "I couldn't sleep. I heard you loading the Jeep. I thought you weren't even going to say goodbye to me. Please don't be angry with me over Nevada. I like him but it's nothing to what I feel about you. I—"

But Cash's mouth was over hers, sealing off her words. The taste of him swept through her, making her tremble. His arms shifted subtly, both molding and supporting her body, stroking her over his hard length, telling her without a word how perfectly they fit together, hard against soft, key against lock, male and female, hunger and fulfillment.

It took an immense amount of willpower for Cash to end the kiss short of taking Mariah down to the floor and burying himself in her, ending the torment that raked him with claws of fire.

"Don't leave me," Mariah whispered when Cash lowered her feet back to the floor. "Not yet. Hold me for just a little longer. Please? I—oh, Cash, it's so cold without you."

She felt the tremor that went through Cash, heard his faint groan, and then the world tilted as he picked her up once more. Moments later he put her on the bed, grabbed the covers and pulled them up beneath her chin. She struggled against the confining sheet and comforter, trying to get her arms free, but it was impossible.

"Warm enough?" he asked. "I don't want you getting sick." His voice was too deep, too thick, telling of the heavy running of his blood. "You didn't get much sleep last night, I couldn't keep my hands off you in the pool, it was a long ride back and then you cooked a meal for twelve."

"Carla did most of the work and—"

"Bull. I was watching, honey."

"—and I loved your hands on me in the pool," Mariah said quickly, talking over Cash's voice. "I love your mouth. I love your body. I love—"

His mouth came down over hers again, ending the husky flow of words that were like tiny tongues of fire licking over him.

"I shouldn't have taken you this morning," Cash said when he managed to tear himself away from Mariah's sweet, responsive mouth. "Damn it, honey, you're not used to having a man yet, and you make me so hard and hungry."

"The pool must have magic healing properties," Mariah whispered, looking up at Cash with wide golden eyes. In the vague golden illumination cast by the night-light, Cash was little more than a dense man-shadow, a deep voice and powerful hands holding her imprisoned within the soft cocoon of bed covers. "And when I couldn't sleep tonight I took a long soak in the tub. I'm not sore, not even from

the ride back. If you don't believe it, touch me. You'll see
that I'm telling the truth. I know you want me, Cash. I felt
it when you hugged me. Touch me. Then you'll know I
want you, too.''

''Mariah,'' he whispered.

Cash kissed her again and again, tiny, fierce kisses that
told of his restraint and need. When she made soft sounds
of response and encouragement, he deepened the kiss. As
their tongues caressed, hunger ripped through him, loosening his hold on the bedclothes for a few moments.

It was all Mariah needed. She kicked aside the soft, enfolding covers even as she reached for Cash. He groaned
when he saw her elegant, naked legs and the cotton nightshirt that barely came below her hips. Then she took his
hand in hers and began smoothing it down her body.

He could have pulled away and they both knew it. He
was far stronger than she was, more experienced, more able
to control the hot currents of hunger that coursed through
his body. But Mariah's abandoned sensuality disarmed him
completely. When her breasts tightened and peaked visibly
beneath cloth, he remembered how it felt to hold her in his
mouth, shaping and caressing her while cries of pleasure
shivered from her lips.

Even before Mariah guided Cash's hand to the sultry
well of her desire, he suspected he was lost. When he
touched the liquid heat that waited for him, he knew he
was. He tried not to trace the soft, alluring folds and failed.
He skimmed them again, probing delicately, wishing that
his profession hadn't left his fingertips so scarred and callused. She deserved to be caressed by something as silky
and unmarked as her own body.

''Baby?'' Cash whispered. ''Are you sure?''

The answer he received was a broken sound of pleasure
and a sensual melting that took his doubts and his breath

away. When he started to lift his hand, Mariah's fingers tightened over his wrist, trying to hold him.

"Cash," Mariah said urgently, "don't leave yet. Please stay with me for a little more. I—"

"Hush, honey," Cash said, kissing away Mariah's words. "I'm not going far." He laughed shakily. "I couldn't walk out of here right now if I had to. Don't you know what you do to me?"

"No," she whispered. "I only know what you do to me. I've never felt anything close to it. I didn't even know it was possible to feel so much. It's like I've been living at night all my life and then the sun finally came up."

The words were more arousing than any caress Cash had ever received. His hands shook with the force of the hunger pouring through him.

Mariah watched while Cash stripped away his clothes with careless, powerful motions that were very different from the tender caresses he had given to her just moments before. The nebulous glow of the tiny night-light turned Cash's skin to gold and the hair on his body to a dark, shimmering bronze. Each movement he made was echoed by the black velvet glide of shadows over his muscular body.

Cash watched Mariah as he kicked aside the last of his clothes and stood naked before her. Mariah's eyes were heavy lidded, the color of gold, shining, and they worshiped all of him, even the full, hard evidence of his desire. Still looking at him, she reached for the bottom button on her nightshirt with fingers that trembled.

Cash rested one knee on the mattress, making it give way beneath his weight. One long finger traced from the instep of Mariah's foot, up the calf, behind the knee, then slowly up the inside of her thighs. When her leg flexed in response, he smiled slowly.

"That's it, little one. Show me you want me," Cash whispered. "Make room for me between those beautiful legs."

Mariah's long legs shifted and separated. He followed each movement with dark, consuming eyes and light caresses. Slowly he knelt between her legs, watching her, seeing the same sensual tension in her that had taken his body and drawn it tight on wires of fire.

For a moment Cash didn't move, couldn't move, frozen by the beauty of Mariah's body and the trust implicit in her vulnerable position. Slowly, irresistibly, his hands pushed aside her unbuttoned nightshirt, smoothing it down over her shoulders and arms, stopping at her wrists, for he had become distracted by the rose-tipped, creamy invitation of her breasts.

Mariah made a murmurous sound of pleasure that became a soft cry as his mouth found one nipple and pulled it into a tight, shimmering focus of pleasure. When she arched up in sensual reflex, the nightshirt slid down beneath her back to her hips, stopping there, holding her hands captive. She didn't notice, for Cash's hands were smoothing up her legs, making her tremble in anticipation of the pleasure to come. When he touched her very lightly, she shivered and cried out.

"It occurred to me," Cash said, his voice deep and slow, "that something as soft as you shouldn't have to put up with hands as callused as mine."

Mariah would have told Cash how much she loved his hands, but couldn't. The feel of his tongue probing silkily into her navel took her breath away. Glittering sensations streaked through her body at the unexpected caress.

"You should be touched by something as hot and soft as you are," Cash said. He sampled the taut skin of Mariah's belly with his tongue, smiling to feel the response

tightening her. His tongue flicked teasingly as he slid down
her body. "Since it's too late for you to go out and find
some soft gentleman to be your lover, we'll just have to do
the best we can with what we've got, won't we?"

Mariah didn't understand what Cash was talking about.
As far as she was concerned he was perfect as a lover. She
was trying to tell him just that when she felt the first sultry
touch of his tongue. The intimacy of the kiss shocked her.
She tried to move, only to find her legs held in her lover's
gentle, immovable hands and her wrists captive to the tangled folds of her nightdress.

"Cash—you shouldn't—I—"

"Hush," he murmured. "I've always wondered what a
woman tastes like. I just never cared enough to find out.
But I do now. I want you, honey. And that's what you are.
Honey."

Cash's voice was like his mouth, hungry, hot, consuming. The words Mariah had been trying to speak splintered
into a pleasure as elemental as the man who was loving her
in hushed, wild silence. For long moments she fought to
speak, to think, to breathe, but in the end could only give
herself to Cash, twisting slowly, drawn upon a rack of exquisite fire.

By the time Cash finally lifted his head, Mariah was
shaking and crying his name, balanced on the jagged break-
point of release. He sensed that the lightest touch would
send her over the edge. Knowing he should release her from
her sensual prison, Cash still held back, loving the sound
of her voice crying for him, loving the flushed, petal-
softness of her need, loving the raggedness of her breathing
matching his own.

At last he bent down to her once more, seeking the satin
knot of sensation he had called from her, touching it with
the tip of his tongue.

With a husky cry that was his name, Mariah was overcome by an ecstasy that convulsed her with savage delicacy. Cash held her and smiled despite the shudders of unfulfilled need that were tearing him apart. Caressing her softly, he waited for her first, wild ecstasy to pass. Then he gently flexed her legs, drawing them up her body until she was completely open to him. With equal care he fitted his body to hers, pressing very, very slowly into her.

When he looked up, he saw Mariah watching him become a part of her. He felt the shivering, shimmering ripples of pleasure that were consuming her all over again, ecstasy renewed and redoubled by his slow filling of her body. The knowledge that she welcomed the deep physical interlocking as much as he did raced through Cash, sinking all the way into him, calling to him at a profound level, luring him so deeply into Mariah that he couldn't tell where she ended and he began, for there was no difference, no separation, no boundary, nothing but their shared body shuddering in endless, golden pulses of release.

And in the pauses between ecstasy came Mariah's voice singing a husky litany of her love for Cash.

Thirteen

Kiss me goodbye, honey. The sooner I go, the sooner I'll be back.

Mariah had heard those same words of parting from Cash many times in the five months since she had come to the Rocking M, including the one time she had declared her love. Cash's goodbyes were woven through her days, through her dreams, a pattern of separations and returns that had no end in sight. Even though Cash was no longer teaching at the university, his consulting work rarely allowed him to spend more than two weeks at a time at the Rocking M. More often, he was free for only a handful of incandescent days, followed by several weeks of loneliness after he left. Each time Mariah hoped that he would invite her to Boulder, but he hadn't.

Nor had Cash told Mariah that he loved her.

He must love me. Surely no man could make love to a woman the way Cash does to me without loving her at least a little. Carla and Luke assume Cash loves me. So does everyone else on the Rocking M. He just can't say the words. And is that so important, after all? His actions are those of a man in love, and that's what matters.

Isn't it?

Mariah had no doubt about her own feelings. She had never expected to love anyone the way she loved Cash—no defenses, nothing held back, an endless vulnerability that would have terrified her if Cash hadn't been so clearly happy to see her each time he came back to the ranch.

He was gone for only four days this time and he called every night and we talked for hours about nothing and everything and we laughed and neither one of us wanted to hang up. He loves me. He just doesn't say it in so many words.

It will be all right. If he hadn't wanted children he would have used something or seen that I did. But he never even mentioned it.

The emotional fragility that had plagued Mariah for too many weeks sent tears clawing at the back of her eyes. It had been more than four months since her last period. Soon she wouldn't be able to hide the life growing within her by leaving her pants unbuttoned and wearing her shirts out. Cash had noticed the new richness in the curves of her body but hadn't guessed the reason. Instead, he had teased her about the joys of regular home cooking.

He loves children and kids love him. He'll be a wonderful father.

It will be all right.

Fighting for self-control, unconsciously pressing one hand against her body just below her waist, Mariah stood on the small porch of the old house and stared out through the pines at the road that wound through the pasture. She thought she had seen a streamer of dust there a moment ago, the kind of boiling rooster tail of grit that was raised by Cash's Jeep when he raced over the dirt road to be with her again.

"Are you going to tell him this time?"

Mariah started and turned away from the road. Nevada Blackthorn stood a few feet away, watching her with his uncanny green eyes.

"Tell who what?" she asked, off balance.

"Tell Cash that he's going to be a daddy sometime next spring." Nevada swore under his breath at the frightened look Mariah gave him. "Damn it, woman, you're at least four months along. You should be going to a doctor. You should be taking special vitamins. If you don't have sense enough to realize it, I do. Have you ever seen a baby that was too weak to cry? Babies don't have any control over their lives," he continued ruthlessly. "They're just born into a world that's more often cruel than not, and they make the best of it for as long as they can until they either die or grow up. Too often, they die."

Mariah simply stared at Nevada, too shocked to speak. The bleakness of his words was more than matched by his eyes, eyes that were looking at her, noting each telltale difference pregnancy had made.

"You must have decided to have the baby," Nevada said, "or you would have done something about it months ago. A woman who has guts enough to go through with a pregnancy should have guts enough to tell her man about it."

"I've tried." Mariah made a helpless gesture. "I just can't find the right time or the right words."

Because Cash has never said he loves me. But she couldn't say that aloud. She could barely stand to think it.

"The two of you go off looking for gold at least twice a month, but there's never enough time or words for you to say 'I'm pregnant'?" Nevada hissed a word beneath his breath. "If you don't have the guts to tell Cash this time, I'll take you into Cortez after he leaves. Dr. Chacon is a good man. He'll tell you what the baby needs and I'll make damn sure you get it."

Mariah looked at Nevada and knew he meant every word. He was as honest as he was hard. If he said he would help her, he would. Period.

"You're a good man," she said softly, touching his bearded jaw with her fingertips. "Thank you."

"You can thank me by telling Cash." Despite the curtness of Nevada's voice, he took Mariah's hand and squeezed it encouragingly. "You've got about twenty seconds to find the right words."

"What?"

"He's here."

Mariah spun to face the road. When she saw that Cash's battered Jeep had already turned into the dusty yard of the old house, her face lit up. She ran to the Jeep and threw herself into Cash's arms as he got out.

Cash lifted her, held her close, and looked at Nevada over Mariah's shoulder. Nevada returned the cool stare for a long moment before he turned and walked toward the bunkhouse without a backward glance.

"What did Nevada want?" Cash asked.

Mariah stiffened. Cash's voice was every bit as hard as Nevada's had been.

"He just—he was wondering when you would get here," she said hurriedly.

It was a lie and both of them knew it.

Cash's mouth flattened at the surprise and the pain tearing through him. Somehow he hadn't expected Mariah to lie. Not to him. Not about another man.

A freezing fear congealed in Cash as he realized how dangerously far he had fallen under Mariah's spell.

"Nevada wanted something else, too," Mariah said quickly, hating having told the lie. "I can't tell you what. Not yet. Before you leave, I'll tell you. I promise. But for now just hold me, Cash. Please hold me. I've missed you so!"

Cash closed his eyes and held her, feeling her supple warmth, a warmth that melted the ice of her half lie, leaving behind a cold shadow of memory, a forerunner of the betrayal he both feared and expected.

"Did you miss me?" Mariah asked. "Just a little?"

The uncertainty in her voice caught at Cash's emotions. "I always miss you. You know that."

"I just—just wanted to hear it."

Cash pulled away from Mariah until he could look down into her troubled golden eyes. The unhappiness he saw there made his heart ache despite his effort to hold himself aloof. "What is it, Mariah? What's wrong?"

She shook her head, took a deep breath and smiled up at the man she loved. "When you hold me, nothing is wrong. Come to the big house with me. Let me lust after you while I make dinner."

His expression changed to a lazy kind of sensuality that sent frissons of anticipation over Mariah's nerves. Smiling, Cash dipped his head until he could take her mouth in a kiss that left both of them short of breath.

"I'd rather you lusted after me in the old house where we can do something about it," Cash said, biting Mariah's lips with exquisite care, wanting her even more than he feared wanting her.

"So would I. But then I'd never get around to cooking dinner and the cowhands would rebel."

Laughing despite the familiar hunger tightening his body,

Cash slowly released Mariah, then put his arm around her waist and began walking toward the big house. The time of reckoning and payment would come soon enough. Anticipating it would only diminish the pleasure of being within reach of Mariah's incandescent sensuality.

"I don't want to be responsible for a Rocking M rebellion," he said.

"Neither do I," Mariah answered, putting her arm around Cash's lean waist. "I tried to do as much of dinner as possible ahead of time, but Logan and Carolina decided they didn't want a nap."

Cash looked down at Mariah questioningly. "Where are Diana and Carla?"

"I'm watching the kids during the morning so Diana and Carla can work on the artifacts that keep coming in from September Canyon."

"And you're cooking six nights a week for the whole crew."

"I love to cook."

"And Diana is making an archaeologist out of you three nights a week."

"She's a very good teacher."

"And you're taking correspondence courses in commercial applications of geology. And technical writing."

Mariah nodded. "I have my first job, too," she said proudly. "The Four Corners Regional Museum wants to do a splashy four-color book about the history of the area. They commissioned specialists for each section of the book, then discovered that having knowledge isn't the same thing as being able to communicate knowledge through writing."

Ruefully Cash smiled. Despite the fact that his profession required writing reports of his fieldwork, he knew his shortcomings in that department. In fact, he had begun writing all his reports on the Rocking M. Not only did it give him more time with Mariah, he had discovered that she had a knack for finding common words to describe esoteric scientific data. He had been the one to suggest that Mariah pursue technical writing, since she obviously had a flair for it.

"So," Mariah continued, "I'm translating the geology and archaeology sections into plain English. If they like my work, I have a chance to do the whole book for them."

Cash stopped, caught Mariah's face between his hands, kissed her soundly and smiled down at her. "Congratulations, honey. When did you find out?"

"This morning. I wanted to call, but you were already on the road. I thought you would never get here. It's such a long drive. And in the winter..."

Mariah's voice trailed off. They both knew that driving to the Rocking M from Boulder was tedious under good conditions, arduous during some seasons and impossible when storms turned segments of the ranch's dirt roads into goo that even Cash's Jeep couldn't negotiate.

The difficulty of getting to the Rocking M wasn't a subject Cash wanted to pursue. If Mariah hadn't been Luke's sister, Cash would have asked her to stay with him in Boulder months ago. But that was impossible. It was one thing to go gold hunting with Mariah or to steal a few hours alone with her in the old house before both of them went to sleep in separate beds under separate roofs. It was quite another thing to set up housekeeping outside of marriage with his best friend's little sister.

The obvious solution was marriage, but that, too, was impossible. Even if Cash brought himself to trust Mariah completely—especially if he did—he wouldn't ask her to share a childless future with him. Even so, he found himself coming back to the idea of marriage again and again.

Maybe Mariah wouldn't mind. Maybe she would learn

to be like me, accepting what can't be changed and enjoying Logan and Carolina whenever possible. Maybe...

And maybe not. How can I ask her to give up so much? No matter how much she thinks she loves me, she wants children of her own. I can see it every time she looks at Logan and then looks at me with a hunger that has nothing to do with sex. She wants my baby. I know it as surely as I know I can't give it to her.

But God, I can't give her up, either. I'm a fool. I know it. But I can't stop wanting her.

There wasn't any answer to the problem that circled relentlessly in Cash's mind, arguments and hopes repeated endlessly with no solution in sight. No matter how many times Cash thought about Mariah and himself and the future, he had no answer that he wanted to live with. So he did what he had always done since he had realized what being effectively sterile meant. He put the future out of his mind and concentrated on the present.

"Come on," Cash said, kissing Mariah's forehead. "I'll peel potatoes while you tell me all about your new job."

If he noticed the uncertainty in her smile, he didn't mention it, any more than she mentioned the fact that he was gripping her hand as though he expected her to run away.

Motionless, aware only of his own thoughts, Cash let himself into the old ranch house in the velvet darkness that comes just before dawn. Mariah didn't expect him. They had decided to spend the day at the ranch and not leave for Black Springs until the following dawn.

But Cash hadn't been able to stay away. He had awakened hours before, fought with himself, and finally lost. He had just enough self-control not to go into Mariah's bedroom and wake her up by slowly merging their bodies. Fighting the need that never left him even when he had just taken her, Cash went into the house and sat in what had once been Diana's workroom and gradually had evolved into an office for him and a library for Mariah's increasing collection of books.

He didn't even bother to turn on the light. He just pulled out one of the straightback chairs, faced it away from the table, and tried to reason with his unruly body and mind. His body ignored him. His mind supplied him with images of a night at the line shack when Mariah had teased him because his body steamed in the frosty autumn air. He had teased her, too, but in other ways, drawing from her the sweet cries of desire and completion that he loved to hear. The thought of hearing those cries again was a banked fire in Cash's big body, and the fire was no less hot for being temporarily controlled.

The sound of the bedroom door opening and Mariah's light footsteps crossing the living room sent a wave of desire through Cash that was so powerful he couldn't move. A light in the living room came on, throwing a golden rectangle of illumination onto the workroom floor. None of the light reached as far as Cash's feet.

"Cash?"

"Sorry, honey. I didn't mean to wake you up."

Mariah was silhouetted in the doorway. The shadow of her long flannel nightshirt rippled like black water.

"I'm here."

"What are you doing sitting in the dark?"

"Watching the moonlight. Thinking."

The huskiness of Cash's deep voice made Mariah's heartbeat quicken. She walked through the darkened room and stood in front of Cash.

"What are you thinking about?" she asked softly.

"You."

Big hands came up and wrapped around Mariah's wrists.

She whispered his name even as he tugged her down into his lap. He kissed her deeply, shifting her until she sat astride his legs and he could rock her hips slowly against his body. The heavy waves of his need broke over her, sweeping away everything but the taste and feel and heat of the man she loved. When his hands found and teased her breasts, she made rippling sounds of hunger and pleasure.

When Mariah unfastened her nightshirt to ease his way, Cash followed the wash of moonlight over her skin with his tongue until she moaned. Soon her nightshirt was undone and he was naked to the waist and his jeans were open and her hands were moving over him, loving the proof of his passion, making him tighten with desire.

"If you don't stop, we'll never make it to bed," Cash said, his voice hoarse.

"But you feel so good. Better each time. You're like Black Springs, heat welling up endlessly."

Cash's laugh was short and almost harsh. "Only since I've known you."

Without warning he lifted Mariah off his lap.

"Cash?"

"Honey, if I don't move now, I won't be able to stand up at all. I want you too much."

Despite Cash's words, he made no move to get up. When Mariah's hands pushed at his jeans, tugging them down until she had the freedom of his body, he didn't object. He couldn't. He could hardly breathe for the violence of the need hammering through him. When she touched him, the breath he did have trickled out in a groan that sounded as though it had been torn from his soul.

Mariah's eyes widened and her breath caught in a rush of sensual awareness that was as elemental as the power of the man sitting before her. Her fingertips traced Cash gently

again. Closing his eyes, he gave himself to her warm hands.
When the caressing stopped a few moments later, he
couldn't prevent a hoarse sound of protest. He heard a rustling sound, sensed Mariah's nightshirt sliding to the floor,
and shuddered heavily. When he opened his eyes she was
standing naked in front of him.

"Can people make love in a chair?" Mariah asked
softly.

Before the words were out of her mouth, Cash's hand
was caressing her inner thighs, separating them, seeking the
sultry heat of her. She shivered and melted at the caress.
When his touch slid into her, probing her softness, her
knees gave way. Swaying, she grabbed his shoulders for
balance.

"Cash?" she whispered. "Can we?"

"Sit on my lap and find out," he said, luring her closer
and then closer still, easing her down until she was a balm
around his hard, aching flesh and her name was a broken
sigh on his lips. "Each time—better."

For Mariah, the deep rasp of Cash's voice was like being
licked by loving fire. She leaned forward to wrap her arms
around his neck. The movement caused sweet lightning to
flicker out from the pit of her stomach. She moved again,
seeking to recapture the stunningly pleasurable sensation.
Again lightning curled through her body.

"That's right," Cash said huskily, encouraging Mariah's
sensual movements. "Oh, yes. Like that, honey. Just...
like...that."

Shivering, moving slowly, deeply, repeatedly, giving and
taking as much as she could, Mariah fed their mutual fire
with gliding movements of her body. When the languid
dance of love was no longer enough for either of them,
Cash's hands fastened onto her hips, quickening her move-

ments. Her smile became a gasp of pleasure when he flexed hard against her, enjoying her as deeply as she did him.

He watched her, wanting all of her, breathing dark, hot words over her until control was stripped away and he poured himself into her welcoming softness. Mariah held herself utterly still, drinking Cash's release, loving him, feeling her own pleasure beginning to unravel her in golden pulses that radiated through her body, burning gently through to her soul.

And then there was a savage flaring of ecstasy that swept everything away except her voice calling huskily to Cash, telling him of her love and of their baby growing within her womb....

For an instant Cash couldn't believe what he was hearing.

"What?"

"I'm pregnant, love," she whispered, leaning forward to kiss him again.

Suddenly Cash believed it, believed he was hearing the depth of his own betrayal from lips still flushed with his kisses. He had thought he was prepared for it, thought that a woman's treachery had nothing new to teach him.

He had been wrong. He sat rigid, transfixed by an agony greater than any he had ever known...and in its wake came a rage that was every bit as deep as the passion and the pain.

"You're pregnant," Cash repeated flatly, a statement rather than a question.

He could control his voice, but not the sudden, violent rage snaking through his body, a tension that was instantly transmitted to the woman who was so intimately joined with him.

"Yes," Mariah said, trying to smile, failing, feeling the power of Cash's fingers digging into her hips. "Didn't you want this? You never tried to prevent it and you like children and I thought…"

Her voice died into a whisper. She swallowed, but no ease came to her suddenly dry throat. In the moonlight Cash looked like a man carved from stone.

"No, I never tried to prevent it," Cash said. "I never spend time trying to make lead into gold, either."

He heard his own words as though at a vast distance, an echo from a time when he could speak and touch and feel, a time when betrayal hadn't spread like black ice through his soul, freezing everything.

"I don't understand," Mariah whispered.

"I'll just bet you don't."

With bruising strength Cash lifted Mariah from his lap, kicked out of his entangling clothes and stood motionless, looking through her as though she weren't there. She had the dizzying feeling of being trapped in a nightmare, unable to move, unable to speak, unable even to cry. She had imagined many possible reactions to her pregnancy, even anger, but nothing like this, an absolute withdrawal from her.

"Cash?" Mariah whispered.

He didn't answer. In electric silence he studied the deceptively vulnerable appearance of the woman who stood with her face turned up to him, moonlight heightening both the elegance and the fragility of her bone structure.

She's about as fragile as a rattlesnake and a hell of a lot more dangerous. She's one very shrewd little huntress. No one will believe that I'm not the father of her baby. I could go to the nearest lab and get back the same result I got years ago, when Linda told me she was pregnant—a chance I was the father, but not much of one.

But Cash had wanted to believe in that slim chance. He

had wanted it so desperately that he had blinded himself to any other possibility.

Luke would feel the same way this time. Rather than believe that his beloved Muffin was a liar, a cheat and a schemer, Luke would believe that Mariah was carrying Cash's baby. If Cash refused to marry Mariah, it would drive a wedge between himself and Luke. Perhaps even Carla. Then there would be nothing left for Cash, nowhere on earth he could call home. He had no choice but to accept the lie and marry the liar.

It was as nice a trap as any woman had ever constructed for a foolish man.

Except for one thing, one detail that could not be finessed no matter how accomplished a huntress Mariah was. There was one way to prove she was lying. It would take time, though. Time for the baby to be born, time for its blood to be tested, time for the results to be compared with Cash's own blood. Then, finally, it would be time for truth.

"When is it due."

Cash didn't recognize his own voice. There was no emotion in it, no resonance, no real question, nothing but a flat requirement that Mariah give him information.

"I d-don't know."

"What does the doctor say."

"I haven't been to one." Mariah interlaced her fingers and clenched her hands in order to keep from reaching for Cash, touching him, trying to convince herself that she actually knew the icy stranger standing naked in the darkness while he interrogated her. "That's—that's what Nevada wanted. He said he'd take me into see Dr. Chacon if I didn't tell you this time."

So that's who fathered her bastard. I should have known. God, how can one man be such a fool?

Suddenly Cash didn't trust his self-control one instant

longer. Too many echoes of the past. He had known the
trap. He had taken the bait anyway.

So be it.

Mariah watched as Cash dressed. Though he said nothing
more, his expression and his abrupt handling of his clothes
said very clearly that he was furious. Uncertainly Mariah
tried to dress, but her trembling fingers forced her to be
satisfied with simply pulling her nightshirt on and leaving
it unfastened. When she looked up from fumbling with the
nightshirt, Cash was standing at the front door watching
her as though she were a stranger.

"Congratulations, honey. You just got a name for your
baby and a free ride for the length of your pregnancy."

"What?"

"We're getting married. That's what you wanted, isn't
it?"

"Yes, but—"

"We'll talk about it later," Cash said, speaking over
Mariah's hesitant words. "Right now, I'm not in the mood
to listen to any more of your *words*."

The door opened and closed and Mariah was alone.

Fourteen

It will be all right. He just needs some time to get used to the idea. He must care for me. He wouldn't have asked me to marry him if he didn't care for me, would he? Lots of men get women pregnant and don't marry them.

It will be all right.

The silent litany had been repeated so often in Mariah's mind during the long hours after dawn that the meaning of the words no longer really registered with her. She kept seeing Cash's face when he had told her that she would have a free ride and a name for the baby.

When we're married I'll be able to show Cash how much I love him. He must care for me. He doesn't have to marry me, but he chose to. It will be all right.

The more Mariah repeated the words, the less comfort they gave. Yet the endless, circling words of hope were all she had to hold against a despair so deep that it terrified her, leaving sweat cold on her skin, and a bleak, elemental cry of loss vibrating beneath her litany of hope.

Cash would marry her, but he did not want the child she was carrying. He would marry her, but he didn't believe in her love. He would marry her, but he thought she wanted only his name and the money to pay for her pregnancy. He would marry her, but he believed he had been caught in the oldest trap of all.

And how can I prove he's wrong? I have no money of my own. No home. No job. No profession. I'm working toward those things, but I don't have them yet. I have nothing to point to and say, "See, I don't need your apartment, your food, your money. I just need you, the man I love. The only man I've ever loved."

But she could not prove it.

"Mariah? You awake?"

For a wild instant she thought the male voice belonged to Cash, but even as she spun toward the front door with hope blazing on her face, she realized that it was Nevada, not Cash. She went to the front door, opened it, and looked into the pale green eyes that missed not one of the signs of grief on her face.

"Are you feeling all right?" Nevada asked.

Mariah clenched her teeth against the tears that threatened to dissolve her control. Telling Nevada what had happened would only make things worse, not better. Cash had always resented the odd, tacit understanding between Nevada and Mariah.

Nor could she tell Luke, her own brother, because telling him would in effect force him to choose between his sister and Cash, the man who was closer to him than any brother could be. No good could come of such a choice. Not for her. Not for Cash. And most of all, not for Luke, the brother who had opened his arms and his home to her after a fifteen-year separation.

"I'm...just a little tired." Mariah forced a smile. She noticed the flat, carefully wrapped package in Nevada's hand and changed the subject gratefully. "What's that?"

"It's yours. It came in yesterday, but I didn't have time to get it to you."

Automatically Mariah took the parcel. She looked at it curiously. There was no stamp on the outside, no address, no return address, nothing to indicate who the package was for, who had sent it or where it had come from.

"It's yours, all right," Nevada said, accurately reading Mariah's hesitation.

"What's underneath all that tape?"

"Mad Jack's map."

"Oh. I suppose they found where the mine was."

Nevada's eyes narrowed. There was no real curiosity in Mariah's voice, simply a kind of throttled desperation that was reflected in her haunted golden eyes.

"I didn't ask and they didn't tell me," Nevada said after a moment. "They just sent it back all wrapped up. I'm giving it to you the same way I got it."

Mariah looked at the parcel for a long moment before she set it aside on a nearby table. "Thank you."

"Aren't you going to open it?"

"I'll wait for...Cash."

"Last time I saw him, he was in the kitchen with Carla." Nevada looked closely at Mariah, sensing the wildness seething just beneath her surface. "You told Cash about the baby."

Mariah shivered with pent emotion. "Yes. I told him."

Without another word Mariah stepped off the porch and headed for the big house. She couldn't wait for a moment longer. Maybe by now Cash had realized that she hadn't meant to trap him. Maybe by now he understood that she loved him.

It will be all right.

Mariah was running by the time she reached the big house. She raced through the back door and into the kitchen, but no one was around. Heart hammering, she rushed into the living room. Cash was there, standing next to Carla. His hand was over her womb and there was a look of wonder on his face.

"It's moving," he said, smiling suddenly. "I can feel it moving!"

The awe in Cash's voice made Mariah's heart turn over with relief. Surely a man who was so touched by his sister's pregnancy could accept his own woman's pregnancy.

"Moving? I should say so." Carla laughed. "It's doing back flips."

A healthy holler from the second-floor nursery distracted Carla. "Logan just ran out of patience." She hurried out of the room. "Hi, Mariah. The coffee is hot."

"Thank you," Mariah said absently.

She walked up to Cash, her face suffused with hope and need. She took his hand and pressed it against her own womb.

"I think I've felt our baby moving already. But you have to be very still or you won't—"

Mariah's words ended in a swift intake of breath as Cash jerked his hand away, feeling as though he had held it in fire. The thought of what it might be like to actually feel his own child moving in the womb was a pain so great it was all he could do not to cry out.

"I can't feel a damned thing," Cash said roughly. "I guess my imagination isn't as good as yours."

He spun away, clenching his hands to conceal their fine trembling. When he spoke, his voice was so controlled as to be unrecognizable.

"I'll leave tomorrow to make the arrangements. After

we're married, you'll stay here.''

Mariah heard the absolute lack of emotion in Cash's voice and felt ice condense along her spine.

"What about you?" she asked.

"I'll be gone most of the time."

Tears came to Mariah's eyes. She could no more stop them than she could stop the spreading chill in her soul.

"Why?" she asked. "You never used to work so much."

"I never had a wife and baby to take care of, did I."

The neutrality of Cash's voice was like a very thin whip flaying Mariah's nerves. She swallowed but it did nothing to relieve the aching dryness of her mouth or the burning in her eyes.

"If you don't want me to be your wife," Mariah said in a shaking voice, "why did you ask me to marry you?"

Cash said something savage beneath his breath, but Mariah didn't give up. Anything, even anger, was better than the frigid lack of emotion he had been using as a weapon against her.

"Other men get women pregnant and don't marry them," she said. "Why are you marrying me?"

"I could hardly walk out on my best friend's sister, could I? And you have Carla wrapped around your little finger, too. They would think I was a real heel for knocking you up and then not marrying you."

"That's why…?" Mariah shuddered and felt the redoubling of the chill despair that had been growing in the center of her soul.

"Carla and Luke are the only family I have or ever will have," Cash continued with savage restraint.

"That's not true," Mariah said raggedly. "You have me! You have our baby!"

She went to Cash in a rush, wrapping her arms around

him, holding him with all her strength. It was like holding granite. He was unyielding, rigid, motionless but for the sudden clenching of his hands when Mariah's soft body pressed against his.

"We'll be a family," she said. Her lips pressed repeatedly against his cheek, his neck, his jaw, desperate kisses that said more than words could about yearning and loneliness, love and need. "Give us a chance, Cash. You enjoyed being with me before, why not again?"

While Mariah spoke, her hands stroked Cash's back, his shoulders, his hair, the buttons of his shirt; and then her mouth was sultry against his skin. When she felt the involuntary tremor ripping through his strong body, she made a small sound in the back of her throat and rubbed her cheek against his chest.

"You enjoyed my kisses, my hands, my body, my love," Mariah said, moving slowly against Cash, shivering with the pleasure of holding him. "It can be that way again."

Cash moved with frightening power, pushing Mariah away at arm's length, holding her there. Black fury shook him as he listened to his greatest dream, his deepest hungers, his terrifying vulnerability used as weapons by the woman he had trusted too much.

"I'll support you," he said through his clenched teeth. "I'll give your bastard a name. But I'll be damned if I'll take another man's leavings to bed."

Shock turned Mariah's face as pale as salt.

"What are you saying?" she whispered hoarsely. "This baby is yours. You must know that. I came to you a virgin. You're the only man I've ever loved!"

Cash's mouth flattened into a line as narrow as the cold blaze of his eyes.

"A world-class performance, right down to the tears trembling in your long black eyelashes. There's just one thing wrong with your touching scenario of wounded innocence. I'm sterile.''

Mariah shook her head numbly, unable to believe what she was hearing. Cash kept talking, battering her with the icy truth, freezing her alive.

"When I was sixteen," Cash said, "Carla came down with mumps. So did I. She recovered. So did I…after a fashion. That's why I never worried about contraceptives with you. I couldn't get you pregnant."

"But you did get me pregnant!"

"You're half right." Cash's smile made Mariah flinch. "Settle for half, baby. It's more than I got."

"Listen to me," Mariah said urgently. "I don't care what you had or when you had it or what the doctors told you afterward. They were wrong. Cash, you have to believe me. I love you. I have never slept with another man. *This baby is yours.*"

For an instant Cash's fingers dug harshly into Mariah's shoulders. Then he released her and stepped back, not trusting himself to touch her any longer.

"You're something else." He jammed his hands into the back pockets of his jeans. "Really. Something. For the first time in my life I'm grateful to Linda. If she hadn't already inoculated me against your particular kind of liar, I'd be on my knees begging your forgiveness right now. But she did inoculate me. She stuck it in and then she broke it off right at the bone."

"I—"

Cash kept right on talking over Mariah's voice.

"Virginity is no proof of fidelity," he said flatly. "Linda was a virgin, too. She told me she loved me, too. Then she told me she was pregnant. Sound familiar?" He measured Mariah's dismay with cold eyes. "Yeah, I thought it would. The difference was, I believed her. I was so damned hungry to believe that I'd gotten lucky, hit that slim, lucky chance and had gotten her pregnant. We hadn't been married five months when she came and told me she was leaving. Seems her on-again, off-again boyfriend was on again, and this time he was willing to pay her rent.''

Mariah laced her fingers together in a futile attempt to stop their trembling.

"You loved her," Mariah whispered.

"I loved the idea of having gotten her pregnant. I was so convinced she was carrying my baby that I told her she couldn't have a divorce until after the baby was born. Then she could leave, but not with the baby. It would stay with me. Well, she had the baby. Then she had a blood test run on it. Turns out I hadn't been lucky. The baby wasn't mine. End of story.''

Cash made a short, thick sound that was too harsh to be a laugh. "Want to know the really funny part? I never believed Linda loved me, but I was beginning to believe that you did. You got to me in a way Linda never did." He looked at Mariah suddenly, really looked at her, letting her see past the icy surface to the savage masculine rage beneath. "Don't touch me again. You won't like what happens.''

Mariah closed her eyes and swayed, unable to bear what she saw in Cash's face. His remoteness was as terrifying as her own pain.

Suddenly she could take no more. She turned and ran from the house. The chilly air outside settled the nausea churning in her stomach. Walking swiftly, shivering, she headed for the old ranch house. The pines surrounding the old house were shivering, too, caressed by a fitful wind.

When the front door closed behind Mariah, she made a

stifled sound and swayed, hugging herself against a cold that no amount of hope could banish. Slowly she sank to her knees, wishing she could cry, but even that release was beyond her.

It will be all right. It has to be. Somehow I'll make him believe me.

Slim chance, isn't that what you said? But it came true, Cash. It came true and now you won't believe in it. In my love. In me. And there's nothing I can do. Nothing!

Mariah swayed and caught her balance against the table that stood near the front door. A small, flat package slid off. Automatically she caught it before it hit the floor.

Slim chance.

Almost afraid to believe that hope was possible, Mariah stripped off paper and tape until Mad Jack's map fell into her hands. With it was a cover letter and a copy of the map. There was no blank area on the copy, no ancient stain, no blur, nothing but a web of dotted lines telling her that she and Cash had been looking at the wrong part of Devil's Peak.

Will you believe I love you if I give you Mad Jack's mine? Will that prove to you that I'm not after a free ride like your stepmother and your wife? Will you believe me if...

With hands that trembled Mariah refolded the copy and put it in her jeans. Silently, quickly, she went to the workroom cupboard and changed into her trail clothes. When she was ready to leave, she pulled out a sheet of notepaper and wrote swiftly.

I have nothing of value to give you, no way to make you believe. Except one. Mad Jack's mine. It's yours now. I give it to you. All of it.

I'll find the mine and I'll fill your hands with gold
and then you'll have to believe I love you. When you
believe that, you'll know the baby is yours.

Slim chance.
But it was the only chance Mariah had.

Fifteen

The memory of Mariah's lost, frightened expression rode Cash unmercifully as he worked over his Jeep. No matter how many times he told himself she was an accomplished little liar, her stricken face contradicted him, forcing him to think rather than to react from pain and rage.

And reason told Cash that no matter how good an actress Mariah was, she didn't have the ability to make her skin turn pale. She didn't have the ability to make the black center of her eyes dilate until all the gold was gone. She didn't have the ability...but those things had happened just the same, her skin pale and her eyes dark and watching him as though she expected him to destroy her world as thoroughly as she had destroyed his.

With a savage curse Cash slammed shut the Jeep's hood and went to the old house. The instant he went through the front door, he knew the house was empty. He could feel it.

"Mariah?"

No one answered his call. With growing unease, Cash walked through the living room. Shreds of wrapping paper and tape littered the floor. On the table near the door was a typed note and what looked like Mad Jack's faded old map. Cash read the note quickly, then once more.

There was no mistake. A copy of the map had been in the package, a clean copy that supposedly showed the way to Mad Jack's mine. Automatically Cash glanced out the window, assessing the weather. Slate-bottomed clouds were billowing over the high country.

Mariah wouldn't risk it just for money. She would count on Luke to support her even if I refused.

Yet even as the thought came, Cash discarded it. Mariah had been very careful to take nothing from Luke that she didn't earn by helping Carla with Logan and the demands of being a ranch wife. That was one of the things Cash had admired about Mariah, one of the things that had gotten through his defenses.

As he turned away from the small table, he saw another piece of paper that had fallen to the floor. He picked it up, read it, and felt as though he were being wrenched apart.

It can't be true. It...can't...be.

Cash ran to the workroom and wrenched open the cupboard that held Mariah's camping clothes. It was empty.

That little fool has gone after Mad Jack's mine.

Cash looked at his watch. Three hours since Mariah had tried to seduce him and his treacherous body had responded as though love rather than lies bound him to her. Three hours since he had told her that he was sterile. Three hours since she had looked at him in shock and had tried to convince him that the baby was his. Three hours since she had looked at his face and fled.

Three hours, a treasure map, and a high-country storm coming down.

Cursing under his breath, Cash began yanking drawers open, pulling out cold-weather gear he hadn't used since the past winter. After he changed clothes, he started cramming extra clothing into a backpack. Then he remembered the Rocking M's cellular telephones. When Mariah and Cash weren't hunting gold, one of those phones was kept in the old house's tiny kitchen.

The phone was missing from its place on the kitchen counter. Cash ran out to his Jeep, opened the glove compartment and pulled out his own battery-operated unit. He punched in numbers, praying that Mad Jack's map kept Mariah out of canyons that were too steep and narrow for the signal to get in or out. Cellular phones worked better than shortwave radio, but the coverage wasn't complete. Twentieth-century technology had its limitations. The Rocking M's rugged terrain discovered every one of them.

The ringing stopped. No voice answered.

"Mariah? It's Cash."

Voiceless sound whispered in response, a rushing sense of space filled with something that was both more and less than silence.

"Mariah, turn around and come back."

There was a long, long pause before her answer came.

"No. It's my proof. When I find it you'll know I love you and then maybe, just maybe, you'll…"

Cash strained to hear the words, but no more came.

"Mariah. Listen to me. I don't want the damned mine. Turn around and head back to the ranch before it starts snowing."

"It already did. Then it rained a little and now it's just sort of slushy. Except for the wind, it's not too cold."

But Mariah was shivering. He could hear it in the pauses between words, just as he could hear the shifting tone of her voice when she shivered.

"Mariah, you're cold. Turn around and come back."

"No. The mine is here. It has to be. I'll find it and then I'll have p-proof that slim chances are different from none. Life's a lottery and you're one of the l-luckiest men alive. I'm going to find your mine, Cash. Then you'll have to b-believe me. Then everything will be all right. Everything will be…"

The phone went dead.

Quickly Cash punched up the number again, ignoring the first chill tendrils of fear curling through his gut.

It can't be.

Mariah didn't answer the phone. After ten rings Cash jammed the phone into his jacket pocket, zipped the pocket shut and ran to the corral.

Slim chance.

Ice crystallized in the pit of Cash's stomach, displacing the savagery that had driven him since the instant Mariah had told him she was pregnant.

In three hours it would be freezing up in the high country. Mariah didn't have any decent winter gear. She didn't even have enough experience in cold country to know how insidious hypothermia could be, how it drained the mind's ability to reason as surely as it drained the body's coordination, cold eating away at flesh until finally the person was defenseless.

Three hours. Too much time for the cold to work on Mariah's vulnerable body. Doubly vulnerable. Pregnant.

Slim chance.

Oh God, what if I was wrong?

Trying not to think at all, Cash caught and bridled two horses. He saddled only one. Leading one horse, riding the other, Cash headed out of the ranch yard at a dead run. Mariah's trail was clear in the damp earth and slanting autumn light. Holding his mount at a hard gallop, Cash fol-

lowed the trail she had left, forcing himself to think of
nothing but the task in front of him. After half an hour he
stopped, switched his saddle to the spare horse and took
off again at a fast gallop, leading his original mount.

Although the dark, wind-raked clouds rained only fitfully, the ground was glistening with cold moisture. In the
long afternoon shadows, puddles wore a rime of ice gran-
ules left by the passage of a recent hailstorm. The horses'
breaths came out in great soft plumes, only to be torn away
by the rising wind.

Except for the wind, it's not too cold.

Mariah's words haunted Cash. He tried not to think of
how cold it was, how quickly wind stripped heat from even
his big body. Even worse than the cold was the fitful rain.
He would have preferred snow. In an emergency, dry snow
could be used as insulation against the wind, but the only
defense from rain was shelter. Otherwise wind simply
sucked out all body heat through the damp clothes, leaving
behind a chill that drained a person's strength so subtly yet
so completely that most people didn't realize how close
they were to death until it was too late; they thought they
stopped shivering because their bodies had miraculously
become warm again.

Mariah looked at the map once more, then at the dark
lava slope to her right. There was a pile of rocks that looked
rather like a lizard, but there was no lightning-killed tree
nearby. Shrugging, she reminded herself that more than a
century had passed since Mad Jack drew the map. In that
amount of time, a dead tree could have fallen and been
absorbed back into the land. Carefully Mariah reined her
mount around until the lizard was at her back. The rest of
the landmarks fit well enough.

Shivering against the chill wind, she urged her horse

downhill, checking every so often in order to keep the pile of rocks at her back. The horse was eager to get off the exposed slope. It half trotted, half slid down the steep side of a ravine. The relief from the wind was immediate.

With a long sigh, Mariah gave the horse its head and tucked her hands into the huge pockets of her jacket. Once in the ravine, the only way to go was downhill, which was exactly the way Mad Jack had gone. Her fingers were so cold that she barely felt the hard weight of the cellular phone she had jammed into one of the oversize pockets and forgotten.

I'll count to one hundred. If I don't see any granite by then, I'll get out of the ravine and head for Black Springs. It can't be more than twenty minutes from here, just around the shoulder of the ridge. It will be warm there.

Mariah had counted to eighty-three when she saw a spur ravine open off to the right. The opening was too small and too choked with stones for the horse to negotiate. Almost afraid to breathe, much less to believe, she dismounted and hung on to the stirrup until circulation and balance returned to her cold-numbed body. Scrambling, falling, getting up again, she explored the rocky ravine.

When Mariah first saw the granite, she thought it was a patch of snow along the left side of the ravine. Only as she got closer did she realize that it was rock, not ice, that gleamed palely in the fading light. The pile of rubble she crawled over to reach the granite had been made by man. The shattered, rust-encrusted remains of a shovel proved it.

Breathing quickly, shivering, Mariah knelt next to the small hole in the mountainside that had been dug by a man long dead. Inside, a vein of quartz gleamed. It was taller than she was, thicker, and running through it like sunlight through water was pure gold.

Slowly Mariah reached out. She couldn't feel the gold

with her chilled fingers, but she knew it was there. With both hands she grabbed a piece of rocky debris and used it as a hammer. Despite her clumsiness, chunks of quartz fell away. Pure gold gleamed and winked as she gathered the shattered matrix in both hands. She shoved as much as she could in her oversize jacket pockets, then stood up. The weight of the rocks staggered her.

Very slowly Mariah worked her way back down the side ravine to the point where she had left her horse. It was waiting patiently, tail turned toward the wind that searched through the main ravine. Mariah tried to mount, fell, and pulled herself to her feet again. No matter how she concentrated, she couldn't get her foot through the stirrup before she lost her balance.

And her pocket was jeering at her again. It had jeered at her before, but she had ignored it.

Mariah realized that it was the cellular phone that was jeering. With numb fingers she groped through the pieces of rock and gold until she kept a grip on the phone long enough to pull it from her pocket and answer. The rings stopped, replaced by the hushed, expectant sound of an open line.

"Mariah? Mariah, it's Cash."

The phone slid through Mariah's fingers. She made a wild grab and caught the unit more by luck than skill.

"Mariah, talk to me. Where are you? Are you warm enough?"

"Clumsy. Sorry." Mariah's voice sounded odd to her own ear. Thick. Slow.

"Where are you?"

"Devil's Peak. But isn't hell warm? I'm warm, too. I think. I was cold after the rain. Now I'm tired."

The words were subtly slurred, as though she had been drinking.

"Are you on the north side of Devil's Peak?" Cash asked, his voice as hard and urgent as the wind.

Mariah frowned down at the phone as she struggled with the concept of direction. Slowly a memory of the map formed in her mind.

"And...west," she said finally.

"Northwest? Are you on the northwest side?"

Mariah made a sound that could have meant anything and leaned against her patient horse. The animal's warmth slowly seeped into her cold skin.

"Are you above timberline?" Cash asked.

"No."

"Are there trees around you?"

"Rocks, too. Gray. Looked like snow. Wasn't."

"Look up the mountains. Can you see me?"

Mariah shook her head. All she could see was the ravine. "Can't." She thought about trying to mount the horse again. "Tired. I need to rest."

"Mariah. Look up the mountain. You might be able to see me."

Grumbling, Mariah tried to climb out of the ravine. Her hands and feet kept surprising her. She persisted. After a while she could at least feel her feet again, and her hands. They hurt. She still couldn't claw her way out of the crumbling ravine, however.

"I can't," she said finally.

"You can't see me?"

"I can't climb out of the ravine." Mariah's voice was clearer. Moving around had revived her. "It's too steep here. And I'm cold."

"Start a fire."

She looked around. There wasn't enough debris in the bottom of the ravine for a fire. "No wood."

She shivered suddenly, violently, and for the first time became afraid.

"Talk to me, Mariah."

"Do you get lonely, too?" Then, before Cash could say anything, she added, "I wish…I wish you could have loved me just a little bit. But it will be all right. I found the mine and now it's yours and now you have to believe me…don't you?" Her voice faded, then came again. "It's so cold. You were so warm. I loved curling up against you. Better each time…love."

Cash tried to speak but couldn't for the pain choking him. He gripped the phone so hard that his fingers turned white. The next words he heard were so softly spoken that he had a hard time following them. And then he wished he hadn't been able to understand the ragged phrases pouring from Mariah.

"It will be all right…everything will be fine…it will be…"

But Mariah was crying. She no longer believed her own words.

A horse's lonesome whinny drifted up faintly from below. Cash's horse answered. He reined his mount toward the crease in the land where Mariah's tracks vanished. Balancing his weight in the stirrups, he sent his horse down the mountainside at a reckless pace. Minutes later the ravine closed around Cash, shutting out all but a slice of the cloudy sky.

"Mariah!" Cash called. *"Mariah!"*

There was no answer but that of her horse whinnying its delight into the increasing gloom.

Instants after Cash saw Mariah's horse, he saw the dark splotch of her jacket against the pale swath of granite. He dismounted in a rush and scrambled to Mariah. At the sound of his approach, she pushed herself upright and held

out her hands. Quartz crystals and gold gleamed richly in
the dying light.

"See? I've p-proved it. Now will you b-believe me?"
she whispered.

"All you've proved is that you're a fool," Cash said,
picking Mariah up in a rush, ignoring the gold that fell from
her hands. "It will be dark in ten minutes—I'm damned
lucky I found you at all!"

Mariah tried to say something but couldn't force herself
to speak past the defeat that numbed her more deeply than
any cold.

Her gift of the gold mine had meant nothing to Cash. He
still didn't believe in her. She had risked it all and had
nothing to show for it but the contempt of the man she
loved.

He was right. She was a fool.

Sixteen

Broodingly Cash watched Mariah. In the silence and fire-light of the old line shack she looked comfortable despite the stillness of her body. Wearing dry clothes and his down sleeping bag, sitting propped up against the wall, coffee steaming from the cup held between her hands, Mariah was no longer cold. No shivers shook her body. Nor was she clumsy anymore. The pockets bulging with gold-shot rock had been as much to blame for her lack of coordination as the cold.

She's fine, Cash told himself. *Any fool could see that. Even this fool. So why do I feel like I should call her on the cellular phone right now?*

That's easy, fool. She's never been farther away from you than right now. Your stupidity nearly killed her. You expect her to thank you for that?

Flames burnished Mariah, turning her eyes to incandescent gold, heightening the color that warmth had returned to her skin.

"More soup?" Cash asked, his voice neutral.

"No, thank you."

Her voice, like her words, was polite. Mariah had been very polite since they had come to the line shack. She had protested only once—when he stripped her out of her damp clothes and dressed her in the extra pair of thermal underclothes he had brought in the backpack. When he had ignored her protest, she had fallen silent. She had stayed that way, except when he asked a direct question. Then she replied with excruciating politeness.

Not once had she met his eyes. It was as though she literally could not bear the sight of him. He didn't really blame her. He would break a mirror right now rather than look at himself in it.

"Warm enough?" Cash asked, his voice too rough.

It must have been the tenth time he had asked that question in as many minutes, but Mariah showed no impatience.

"Yes, thank you."

Cash hesitated, then asked bluntly, "Any cramps?"

That question was new. He heard the soft, ripping sound her breath made as it rushed out.

"No."

"Are you sure?"

"Yes. I'm fine. Everything is…" The unwitting echo of Mariah's past assurances to herself went into her like a knife. Without finishing the sentence, Mariah took a sip of coffee, swallowed and regained her voice. "Just fine, thank you."

But her eyelids flinched and the hands holding the coffee tightened suddenly, sending a ripple of hot liquid over the side. A few drops fell to the sleeping bag.

"I'm sorry," she said immediately, blotting at the drops

with the sleeve of her discarded shirt. "I hope it won't stain."

"Pour the whole cup on it. I don't give a damn about the sleeping bag."

"That's very kind of you."

"*Kind?* Good God, Mariah. This is me, Cash McQueen, the fool you wanted to marry, not some stranger who just wandered in off the mountain!"

"No," she said in a low voice, blotting at the spilled coffee.

"What?"

There was no answer.

Fear condensed into certainty inside Cash. With a harsh curse he put aside his own coffee cup and sat on his heels next to Mariah.

"Look at me."

She kept dabbing at the bag, refusing to look at him.

Cash's big hand fitted itself to her chin. Gently, inexorably, he tilted her face until she was forced to meet his eyes. Then his breath came out in a low sound, as though he had been struck. Beneath the brilliant dance of reflected flames, Mariah's eyes were old, emotionless, bleak.

He looked into Mariah's golden eyes, searching for her, feeling her slipping away, nothing but emptiness in all the places she had once filled. The cold tendrils of fear that had been growing in Cash blossomed in a silent black rush, and each heartbeat told him the same cruel truth: she no longer loved the man whose lack of trust had nearly killed her. She couldn't even stand the sight of him.

Cash had thought he could feel no greater pain than he had when Mariah told him she was pregnant. He had been wrong.

"Are you sure you feel all right?" he asked, forcing the words past the pain constricting his body. "You're not act-

ing like the same girl who went tearing up a stormy mountain looking for gold.''

"I'm not," she whispered.

"What?"

"I'm not the same. I've finally learned something my
stepfather spent fifteen years trying to teach me."

Cash waited.

Mariah said nothing more.

"What did you learn?" he asked when he could no
longer bear the silence.

"You can't make someone love you. No matter what you
do, no matter how hard you try...you can't. I thought my
stepfather would love me if I got good grades and made
no demands and did everything he wanted me to do." Mariah closed her eyes, shutting out the indigo bleakness of
Cash's glance. "It didn't work. After a while I didn't care
very much.

"But I didn't learn very much, either. I thought you
would love me if only I could prove that I loved you, but
all I proved was what a fool I was. You see, I had it all
wrong from the start. I thought if you believed me, you
would love me. Now I know that if you loved me, *then*
you would believe me. So we both had a long, cold ride
for nothing."

"Not for nothing," Cash said, stroking Mariah's cheek,
wanting to hold her but afraid she would refuse him.
"You're safe. That's something, honey. Hell, that's everything."

"Don't. I don't need pity. I'm warm, dry and healthy,
thanks to you. I did thank you, didn't I?"

"Too many times. I didn't come up here for your
thanks."

"I know, but you deserve thanks just the same. If my
stepfather had had a chance to get rid of me, he wouldn't

have walked across the street to avoid it, much less climbed a mountain in a hailstorm.''

Cash's breath hissed in with shock as he realized what Mariah was implying.

''I appreciate your decency,'' she continued, opening her eyes at last. ''You don't need to worry about losing your home with Luke and Carla because of my foolishness. Before I leave, I'll be sure they understand that none of this was your fault.''

Too quickly for Cash to prevent it, Mariah pulled free of his hand, set her coffee cup aside and unzipped the sleeping bag. His hand shot out, spread flat over her abdomen and pinned her gently in place.

''What are you saying?'' Cash asked, his voice dangerously soft.

Mariah tried to prevent the tremor of awareness that went through her at his touch. She failed. Somehow she had always failed when it came to love.

''I'm leaving the Rocking M. You don't have to marry me just to ensure your welcome with Luke and Carla,'' Mariah said, her voice careful. ''You'll always have a home with them.''

''So will you.'' Cash's eyes searched hers, looking for the emotions that he had always found in her before, praying that he hadn't raced up the mountain only to lose her after all. ''You'll have a home. Always. I'll make sure of it.''

Mariah closed her eyes again and fought against the emotions that were just beneath her frozen surface.

''That's very generous of you,'' Mariah said, her voice husky with restraint. ''But it's not necessary.'' She tried to get up, but Cash's big hand still held her captive. ''May I get up now?'' she asked politely.

''Not yet.''

Cash's big hand moved subtly, almost caressingly. He couldn't free Mariah. Not yet. If he let her go he would never see her again. He clenched his jaw against the pain of an understanding that had come too late. He tried to speak, found it impossible, and fought in silence to control his emotions. When he could speak again, his voice was a harsh rasp.

"Look at me, Mariah."

She shook her head, refusing him.

"Do you hate me so much?" he asked in a low, constrained voice.

Shocked, Mariah opened her eyes.

"You have every right," Cash continued. "I damn near killed you. But if you think I'm going to let you go, you're as big a fool as I was. You loved me once. You can learn to love me again." He shifted his weight onto his knees as he bent down to her. "Forgive me, Mariah," he whispered against her lips. "Love me again. I need you so much it terrifies me."

Mariah would have spoken then, but he had taken her breath. Trembling, she opened her lips beneath his, inviting his kiss. She sensed the tremor that ripped through him, felt the sudden iron power of his arms, tasted the heat and hunger of his mouth. The world shifted until she was lying down and he was with her, surrounding her with a vital warmth that was so glorious she wept silently with the sheer beauty of it.

Suddenly Cash's arms tightened and he went very still.

"Cash? What's wrong?"

"Didn't you feel it?" he asked, his voice strained.

"What?"

"Our baby." Cash closed his eyes but could not entirely conceal the glitter of his tears. "My God," he breathed. *"I felt our baby move."*

"Are you certain?"

His eyes opened. He smiled down at Mariah, sensing the question she hadn't asked. He kissed her gently once, twice, then again and again, whispering between each kiss.

"I'm very certain."

"Cash?" she whispered, her eyes blazing with hope.

"I love you, Mariah," he said, kissing her hand, holding it against his heart. "I love you so damned much."

Laughing, crying, holding on to Cash, Mariah absorbed his whispered words and his warmth, his trust and his love, and gave her own in return. He held her, loving her with his hands and his voice and his body, until finally they lay at peace in each other's arms, so close that they breathed the same scents, shared the same warmth…and felt the butterfly wings of new life fluttering softly in Mariah's womb.

Cash's big hand rested lightly over Mariah's womb.

"Go to sleep, little baby. Mom and Dad are right here. Everything is all right."

*　*　*　*　*

CHAIN OF LOVE

by Anne Stuart

Chapter One

It was a dream, a nightmare, that she'd relived too many times. That voice, that awful, slurred voice, yelling at her, screaming at her, tormenting her, before the heavy fists followed, crashing down on her, as she helplessly tried to flinch out of his reach. But she had never been fast enough, even though he was always slowed by liquor when the rages came upon him. He'd catch her as she scrambled for the door, and her cries would go unheeded as he'd hit her, again and again and again.

"ARE YOU ALL RIGHT?"

Cathy Whiteheart turned her attention from the crowded highway to her sister's concerned gaze, and managed to summon up the vestiges of a smile. "Of course," she said, her voice slightly rusty. "Why wouldn't I be?"

"You just groaned," Meg said sharply. "And you're white as a sheet."

"I haven't been outside my apartment all summer," she reminded her. "It's no wonder I'm pale."

"You weren't that pale a few moments ago. Were you thinking about Greg?"

Cathy pushed the sunglasses back, huddling deeper into the soft leather seat of the deep blue Mercedes. "I shouldn't have agreed to come with you,'' she said, ignoring her sister's question.

"You didn't exactly agree.'' Meg's voice was caustic. "I simply wouldn't take no for an answer. It's been months since we've seen you, Cathy. We've been worried about you.''

"I'll be all right,'' Cathy replied, but the set expression on her pale, stubborn face was far from reassuring.

"I wish I could believe that,'' Meg said, equaling her stubbornness as she once more turned her attention toward the highway between Georgetown and Annapolis.

The famed Whiteheart obstinacy was about all they had in common, Cathy thought with a wryness unusual for her nowadays as she turned back to the scenery. No one would ever have taken them for sisters. Much as Meg might envy Cathy her willowy height, the shoulder-length curtain of silver-blond hair, and the large, wide-set green eyes, it was Meg who had been inundated with suitors, surrounded by handsome, friendly, eager young men. Pert, short, dark-haired Meg, with her much lamented tendency to put on weight and her less-than-perfect nose was the acknowledged belle of the Whiteheart clan, while Cathy, with her classic, untouchable looks had led a surprisingly cloistered existence. It wasn't that she had actively disliked men, she thought musingly. Far from it. But no one had, in most of her twenty-six years, been able to arouse her interest, and the most dedicated men had fallen away in the face of her intractable calm. If only it had stayed that way.

But owning and running a day-care center hadn't put her much in the way of eligible men, so that by the time Greg Danville had appeared in her life, with his handsome face, puppy-dog air and absurdly vulnerable demeanor she had fallen hard, too hard. And then had been unable to pull herself out of the quicksand of a suddenly destructive relationship until it was too late, and she was scarred for life, emotionally if not physically. Why hadn't she stayed in her apartment, hidden behind the drapes, instead of out here in the bright, merciless October sunlight that reached behind her large, opaque sunglasses? She wasn't ready to face life again. There were times when she doubted she ever would be.

Meg had kept up an inconsequential flow of chatter, refusing to be discouraged in the face of Cathy's monosyllabic answers. They were almost at the marina when she once more broached the subject that never seemed far from her conversation. "He's not worth it, Cathy."

For a moment Cathy considered not replying. She continued facing out the window, mesmerized by the scenery she had seen many, many times. "Don't you think I know that?" she said finally in a weary, disheartened voice. "I know perfectly well that I was a fool—I never spend a day without realizing it. And I know that my pride was more damaged than my heart. Sometimes I wonder whether I'm capable of falling in love. If I'd loved Greg more maybe I would have put up with less." She sighed bitterly. "I thought he needed me."

"He did, Cathy. But in ways that were no good for either of you, don't you realize that?"

"Of course I realize that. I realize quite a bit," she added, staring out the window with listless eyes. "But then, I haven't had anything to do but sit and think."

"Sometimes I think it's a damned shame Brandon Whiteheart is our father," Meg declared with belated wrath. "It would have done you good to have had to go out and work every day. I still can't imagine why you sold out your share in the day-care center. The work was perfect for you."

"If Brandon Whiteheart wasn't our father, Meg dear," Cathy replied with a trace of her old humor, "and if we each weren't the proud possessors of embarrassingly large trust funds, not to mention all sorts of expectations from Auntie Flo, etcetera, then Greg Danville would have found me less than irresistible, and I wouldn't be in the mess I'm in now.''

"If you think he was only after your money, then you haven't looked in the mirror, sweetie."

"I know only too well he was only after my money," Cathy replied wearily. "It was made appallingly clear to me."

Meg, never blessed with a large amount of circumspection, plunged right in. "What exactly did happen? One moment the two of you were all hearts and flowers, engaged to be married, and the next thing I know you've barricaded yourself in a new apartment and Greg had moved in with some politician's daughter."

A shaft of remembered pain shot through Cathy. "Please, Meg. I don't want to think about it."

"But you obviously are. And I think it might help if you talked about it to someone," Meg persisted, her concern and curiosity inextricably entwined.

Cathy knew that nothing but shock tactics would silence her. Turning to face her sister's pert, inquisitive face, she pulled off the enveloping dark glasses that were like a second skin, and her cold, despairing green eyes bored into Meg's startled brown ones. "Do you remember the time I fell off a horse last winter?" she queried calmly enough.

"Of course I do. You were a real mess—two black eyes, a broken rib and a concussion. But what does that—"

"And the time I told you I fell down a flight of stairs?" she continued inexorably.

"Certainly. But why…" Horrified disbelief washed over her face as she swerved over into the opposite lane. She pulled back into her own just in time to avoid an irate

Volvo station wagon. "Cathy, I had no idea! How hideous for you! But why didn't you leave him sooner? Why did you let him continue to do that to you?"

"It's very hard to escape from a situation like that," Cathy said wearily, returning her glasses to their customary position on her aquiline nose. "I don't think I could explain, even if I wanted to. Do you suppose we could just drop the subject? Have a nice day sailing, with no bad memories and no broken hearts? Please?" The plea wasn't far removed from tears.

"Of course we can drop it, sweetie," Meg soothed, instantly contrite. "I didn't mean to push. And I'm certain that Charles won't bring it up either. He's always the most tactful of men, my dear husband is, and you can be sure he wouldn't mention something like that in front of a stranger. Not that Sin's a stranger, mind you. We've known him for years—he's one of Charles's very best friends. But you haven't met him yet, so we would hardly be likely to…" Meg's mindless chatter trailed off in the face of Cathy's suddenly wrathful expression.

"Margaret Whiteheart Shannon, if you have dared to fix me up with a blind date I will never, ever forgive you! At this moment I have no interest in men whatsoever, and if I ever do I will be more than capable of finding my own. I've spent the last three months feeling angry, hurt, and frightened, and I'm not in the mood to have some willowy senator's aide paraded for my inspection. Stop the damned car!"

"He's not a senator's aide, and he's not there for your inspection," Meg said mildly, her face mirroring her guilty conscience. "It's his boat, after all. I couldn't very well tell him he couldn't come along because my sister is afraid of men."

"Damn you, Meg," Cathy said bitterly, determined not

to let her see how close to the mark her words had come. "It's not without justification."

"I know it's not," Meg said in a reasonable, sympathetic tone. "I shouldn't have said that. But I'm not trying to fix you up—I can understand you need time. I wish you wouldn't be so suspicious. Charles and I were thinking of buying a boat, and Sin's seemed just the right size."

"So he's a used-boat dealer."

"No, dear. Sin doesn't need our money, and he's very happy with his boat. We're thinking of buying one like it, and he suggested we come along for a day's outing and see if it suited us. As a matter of fact, I expect he'll probably have some sweet young thing along, and you won't have to worry about him making a pass at you. You can sit on deck and glower to your heart's content. Does that make you any happier?" She pulled into a parking lot beside the marina, sliding to a halt with a sqealing of tires that years of driving and her husband's exasperation had failed to cure.

"I should never have come," Cathy mumbled.

"Maybe not. But I'm not about to turn around and drive you back to Georgetown. You're here and you're going to enjoy yourself, or so help me I'll throw you overboard as soon as we get out of the harbor." Meg's dark eyes were quite fierce in her heart-shaped face, and there was a pugnacious tilt to her pointed chin; it was a battle of wills. After a moment Cathy laughed—a weak laugh, but it gave Meg hope after she'd all but abandoned it.

"All right," Cathy said, raising her hands in a gesture of defeat. "I'll be good. I'll tap-dance around the deck, flirt with Mr. Whatsisname, keep Charles in stitches…"

"His name is Sinclair MacDonald, and he isn't your type at all."

Cathy followed her sister out of the car and down the

docks. "And what do you consider my type? Why wouldn't your wonderful Mr. MacDonald do?"

"Because Sin is fairly good-looking, intelligent, charming, well-bred, amusing, somewhat dangerous, and quite, quite kind. Since your only previous lover lacked all those qualities, I'm certain that Sin would never do for a girl with your peculiar tastes."

"A great many people have said Greg was handsome," Cathy said with ill-placed defensiveness.

"His eyes were too close together. And don't go telling me he was charming. I could see through that manufactured bonhomie the moment I saw him. And he certainly wasn't intelligent. If he was, he would never have thrown you over for a round-heels like Susie Daley."

"Could we just possibly stop talking about Greg?" Cathy begged. "I'll make an effort, I promise. I'll even be nice to Mr. Sinclair MacDonald, if you promise me it's not a setup."

"Have I ever set you up before?" Meg demanded, properly incensed.

Despite her overwhelming gloom, Cathy found she had to laugh at her righteous indignation. "Well, there was Charles's assistant at the Division, there was your next-door neighbor." She listed them on her slender, ringless fingers. "There was the young man you took your pottery course with, there was—"

"Enough! I plead guilty. But I know well enough that you're in no mood for matchmaking right now. I have *some* sensitivity, you know," she said, a vague look of guilt hovering around her dark eyes.

"There you are, ladies," Charles's east coast drawl hailed them from up ahead. "We'd just about given up on you."

"Cathy took a bit more persuading than I expected,"

Meg replied, moving toward the boat with quickening steps. "But I got her here, and that's the main thing. Come along, Cathy," she called back over her shoulder, racing up the gangplank and into her husband's welcoming arms.

Cathy trailed behind, wondering if she could come up with some last-minute excuse. The bright sun, blue sky, and the trim, shining white yacht were all conspiring to bring back the headache that had been her constant companion during the long, sweltering summer months. Desperately she wanted to race back to Georgetown, to her silent apartment with the drawn curtains and the air conditioner, shut away from the fresh sea air and the smiling faces and laughing voices all around her.

She hesitated at the top of the gangplank. "Look, why don't I just catch a bus back to town? I'm not really in the mood for this."

Meg sent her husband a long-suffering look. "You see what I mean? She seems to have developed an allergy to sunshine and fresh air. If you come up with one more complaint, Cathy..."

"All right, all right," she acquiesced, giving Charles a kiss on his proffered cheek. "This is a lovely boat, though why you'd need anything quite so large is beyond me."

"It sleeps four. We're planning on using ours to sail down to the Caribbean in the winter like Sin does. Think of the money we'll save in hotel bills!" Meg announced brightly.

"That sounds like your usual idea of wise financial planning," Cathy scoffed. She cast a searching glance about the shiny decks. "Where is our host? Did I scare him away?"

"Sin's gone to pick up some cigarettes. I thought I could do without, but..." Charles shrugged.

"And his lady friend?" Cathy inquired in silky tones.

Meg was off to one side, making frantic gestures that Charles failed entirely to notice.

"Oh, there's no one else coming. I think Sin's between ladies for the moment. Though he seldom stays that way for long. I've never known anyone with such phenomenal luck with women." Meg's grimaces and signals finally penetrated his abstraction, as did Cathy's motionless stance, her generous mouth compressed in a thin line beneath the large, enveloping sunglasses.

"Oh, you don't need to worry," he added hastily. "I don't think you're Sin's type. He likes them a little more worldly, and a little more rounded, for that matter. You've lost weight this summer," he added bluntly.

"Tactful as ever," Cathy murmured, relaxing her tensed shoulders for the first time that day. It was good to be around Charles and Meg and their tactless concern. She hadn't allowed anyone that close in months.

"No, really, you don't need to worry about Sin. He's absolutely harmless. I'm sure he'll take no more notice of you than if you were a piece of driftwood."

"That bad, am I?" Cathy laughed, the sound rusty from long disuse.

Charles's fair skin flushed. "You know what I mean, Cathy. It's just that Sin is…well, you know, he's…"

"Yes, Charles. What exactly am I?" An amused voice came from directly behind her, though well above her head. With a curious sense of fate, Cathy turned to meet Sinclair MacDonald.

Chapter Two

She had been prepared for height, but not quite the overwhelming size of the man directly behind her. She squinted up at him, way up into the face above her, the mobile mouth, laughing hazel eyes, and she took a hasty step backward, away from all that vibrant masculinity. In her rush of nervousness she tripped, her ankle turning beneath her, and before anyone could move a large, well-shaped hand reached out and caught her elbow, righting her again with just the proper amount of strength and gentleness, and then released her.

"Thank you," she said shakily, the imprint of his hand still burning on the soft, tender skin of her upper arm. Keeping better control of her feet, she backed away, well out of range of that almost overwhelming masculine intensity.

"Sinclair MacDonald, this is my sister-in-law, Cathy Whiteheart. Cath, this is Sin. You've heard me mention him," Charles added with a winning smile that had a nervous edge to it.

"Not that I remember," Cathy said with a stubborn, unencouraging glare at her demure sister. All that potent attraction was having a perverse effect—she was determined to keep this astonishingly attractive man at a distance. There was a look of a sleek, jungle beast about him, for all his affable smile. *Like a panther,* she thought fancifully, edging farther away.

Her host smiled lazily down at her. "Well, you haven't missed anything," he dismissed her rudeness lightly. "Why don't you ladies go below and see if you can rustle up some lunch while Charles and I get under way? It's past noon and I, for one, am starving."

Cathy met the charming grin with stony rage. "Why don't you *gentlemen* fix lunch? Or is that too much like women's work?"

Instead of the anger she expected and hoped for, the amused smile deepened, revealing a disconcerting dimple in one lean, weathered cheek. "A liberated woman?" he inquired smoothly. "I beg your pardon. Why don't Charles and I make lunch, then, while the two of you cast off and get us out of the harbor? You can call us when we've hit open sea." He started toward the cabin.

Cathy's sense of humor, long dormant, surfaced for a brief moment before being engulfed in irritation. "I don't know anything about sailing," she admitted, as her eyes unwillingly took in the length of him.

God, he had a beautiful back! He was wearing a teal blue Ralph Lauren polo shirt stretched across broad, well-muscled shoulders, and the faded jeans that hugged his impossibly long legs looked molded to him. He stopped, turned casually and shrugged. "Well, since I know absolutely nothing about cooking, why don't I take care of the boat and you take care of the food? You can pick your own assistant—I'm sure Charles will be happy to help you if you want to keep everything sexually integrated."

All this was said in such an innocent drawl that Cathy was hard put to control an overwhelming desire to shove his large frame overboard. She wasn't used to verbal spar-

ring, especially with one whose looks were quite distracting, and she suddenly felt the almost desperate need to get
away from the hot, bright sun, the blue sky, and the tall,
disturbingly handsome man who had already overwhelmed
her. She had had enough of being bested by handsome men
to last her a lifetime, she thought with a sudden upsurge of
self-pity that brought stinging tears to her eyes behind the
sunglasses.

Swiftly she headed toward the cabin. "C'mon, Meg,"
she ordered in a muffled voice.

There was still one problem left to negotiate. Sin Mac-
Donald had stopped in the middle of the narrow passage-
way to the cabin, his large frame filling the small aisle, and
he didn't look as if he was about to move. Cathy moved
in on him, determined not to be the first to give way, and
he held his ground, the hazel eyes surveying her with lazy
amusement as he lounged against the bulkhead. She was
forced to stop in front of him, feeling dwarfed, helpless,
and frustrated.

The look in her tear-filled eyes was pure hatred. She
allowed herself to glare at him, mistakenly thinking the
oversized glasses hid her expression. But the anger in the
set of her mouth and a stray tear slipping down from beneath the glasses told more than she suspected. "Would
you please move?" she requested icily. "Unless you prefer
to do without lunch?"

He continued to stare down at her, his expression changing only slightly before he reluctantly straightened, allowing her a narrow passage in front of him. "You mustn't
mind me, Cathy. Charles should have told you I can't resist
teasing young ladies. Forgive me?"

Kindness was the last thing she wanted from him just
then. It stripped her of her defenses, and Sinclair MacDonald already made her far too vulnerable. "How entertaining

for you, Mr. MacDonald,'' she said, avoiding the last part
of his speech. He was still much too close. Holding her
breath, she edged past him, her arm inadvertently brushing
against his lean, taut body. She pulled back as if burnt, and
practically ran the remaining distance to the cabin, dashing
down the steps and collapsing on a cushion, her heart
pounding. They would all be laughing at her up there, she
told herself, wrapping her long arms around her knees and
rocking back and forth. Nothing but silence came from the
deck for several moments, and slowly Cathy's deep, shuddering breaths slowed to normal.

"Are you all right, Cathy?" Meg's voice was soft with
concern and guilt as she followed her sister below. "I
didn't mean to make matters worse. I thought—"

Cathy took a few deep breaths, whipping off her sunglasses in the darkness of the cabin. "You didn't think,"
she said bluntly. "You call *that*"—her tone was filled with
deep loathing—"*that*, fairly good-looking? I suppose you'd
describe Robert Redford as just all right."

"Well, I guess I understated it a bit. I just thought you
should realize that a handsome man can be nice too," she
replied defensively, dropping down on a cushion beside her
sister.

"Sinclair MacDonald hasn't yet convinced me. Macho
pig," she added bitterly.

"Well, I can't argue with macho, but I really wouldn't
call him a pig."

"I would," Cathy shot back, rising from the cushion and
wandering toward the porthole. Sin MacDonald was directly in sight, and for the first time Cathy allowed herself
a long, leisurely look, trying to inure herself to his unde-
niable attractions.

He must have been at least six foot three or four, with
broad shoulders, a trim waist and hips, and those long,

beautiful legs encased in faded denim. He wore ancient topsiders and no socks, and the V neck of his polo shirt revealed a triangle of curling golden brown hair. Cathy had always detested hairy men; Greg had been smooth and hairless. But somehow the sight of those brown curls was having an inexplicable effect on Cathy—one she told herself was disgust. She found herself wondering how far down his stomach the curls went. She hoped he didn't have hairy shoulders.

And she hadn't even taken his face into account yet. The square chin, and the wide, sensual mouth beneath a broad mustache gave him a faintly piratical air. Add to that lean, weathered cheeks with that seductive single dimple when his mouth curved in a smile, a straight, decisive nose, laugh lines radiating out around those smoky, unfathomable, uncomfortably *kind* hazel eyes, and the combination was as potent a blend of masculinity as Cathy had ever been subjected to. The slightly long, curling brown hair had a splash of gray in it, and as Sin pulled his sunglasses from the top of his head and placed them on the bridge of his nose, Cathy bit her lip, turning back to her sister's knowing gaze.

"Macho pig," she repeated defiantly. "But a handsome one, for all that."

"I thought you'd see it that way," Meg said with a satisfied smirk. "Do you want to see what Sin brought for us to work with? I brought a salad and French bread—he said he'd take care of the rest."

Cathy busied herself rummaging through the picnic basket on the pocket-sized table, pulling out a surprising assortment of things. "Does he have a cook?" she inquired silkily, unwilling yet to refer to Sin by name. Given the contents of the picnic basket, Sin's disclaimer of kitchen abilities seemed a blatant lie.

"Not that I know of," Meg replied. "He prefers complete independence and self-sufficiency, or so Charles tells me. Why?"

"There's a beautiful quiche here, a crock of pâté, an icy Soave, Russian black bread...."

"Sin would be sure to know the best delicatessens," Meg responded before Cathy's accusing look. "God, what a feast! It will be all I can do not to make a perfect pig of myself. Aren't you famished?"

Cathy forced herself to turn casually away. "Not really," she replied from force of habit, surprised to find she was lying. For the first time in three months she was actually looking forward to a meal. It must be the sea air.

"Oh, dear, you aren't seasick yet, are you? We're scarcely out of the harbor." Meg eyed her with concern.

"No, I'm fine."

"You should go out on deck and get some sun. I'm sure you won't be in their way."

"I'd rather stay here."

"You can't hide in the cabin all day, Cathy!" Meg cried in exasperation.

"I can do anything I damn please," she shot back. "I feel trapped, maneuvered, *set up,* and I don't like it."

"So you're going to sulk and ruin the entire day?"

There was a long silence. Cathy turned to her angry sister, suddenly contrite. "I'm sorry I'm such a wet blanket, Meggie," she murmured. "I'll make an effort, I promise. Just give me a few minutes, okay? We don't want to eat for a while yet, anyway, do we?"

Meg's piquant face softened. "No, sweetie. We can wait as long as you want. I'll go topside and give you a few minutes to pull yourself together. Unless you'd rather talk?" She offered it tentatively, knowing from experience not to push her sister toward confidences before she was ready.

"Not now, Meg. And definitely not here. Tell Charles and Macho-Man I'll be out shortly, okay?" Wearily she pushed her silky blond hair away from her pale face.

A moment later she was blessedly alone in the tiny cabin. It was very quiet—the creak of the wood, the *snap-snap* of the sails overhead, the small, subtle sounds of wind and water against the sleek lines of the boat. And the sound of voices, soft, easy camaraderie with shared laughter floating down to her. *I should be out there,* she thought disconsolately, *not sitting alone in this tiny cabin the way I've been sitting alone in my apartment for the last three months. Surely Greg wasn't worth such prolonged mourning?*

Reluctantly she looked down at her clothing. Pale beige linen pants, a thin cotton knit shirt in a subdued gray, and running shoes made up her outfit. It would be too cold out there, she decided, wandering around the small room, peering with never ceasing fascination at the complete compactness of the living quarters. From the pocket-sized galley, miniature bathroom or head, and comfortable, blue-duck covered bunks, it was efficient and welcoming. Stepping past the head, she peered through the door into the forward cabin, then hastily backed away. The master cabin consisted of a large mattress, covered by a duvet, and nothing else. The perfect spot for a sybaritic weekend, she thought with an odd combination of nervousness and contempt, and took another step backward, her slender back coming up against something tall, solid, and unyielding. She didn't have to turn around to know with a sinking feeling that Sinclair MacDonald had caught her peering into his bedroom.

Turning, she tensed, waiting for some crack. In the darkened cabin he seemed impossibly huge, towering above her, his sea-blown brown curls almost brushing the ceiling. His sunglasses were still perched on his nose, and Cathy wished she still had similar protection from his probing eyes. She could only be grateful the dim, shadowed light hid her reddened complexion.

"Did you bring a windbreaker?" he questioned after a long moment, and Cathy's shoulders relaxed. "You'll be too cold without one—the breeze is pretty stiff."

"I forgot," she mumbled, dropping her gaze from his face. Unfortunately, in that tiny space, there was little else to look at besides his body, and she decided that concentrating on his stomach or anywhere else below would be unwise. She stared fixedly at the curling hair at the open collar of his shirt, keeping a blank expression on her face.

To her intense relief he backed away, rummaging underneath one of the bunks and coming up with an Irish knit sweater that would probably reach to her knees. He tossed it to her, showing no surprise as she adeptly caught it, and pulled another out for himself. "Put that on," he ordered casually, pulling his over his head. "It'll be too big, but it's the warmest thing I've got." Still she stood there, holding the sweater in motionless hands. He started toward the steps, turned and gave her a semi-exasperated glance. "Look," he said, running a harassed hand through his already rumpled hair. "I promise to stay at the other end of the boat if that's what's bothering you. Your sister and brother-in-law are really worried about you. It would be nice if you could make an effort to be sociable."

She hesitated for a moment longer. "I'll be out in just a minute," she said finally, shrugging into the heavy sweater. "And you don't have to stay at the other end of the boat," she mumbled into the sweater.

He moved back, a glimmer in those hazel eyes. "What did you say?"

"I said you didn't have to stay at the other end of the boat," she repeated patiently, hoping he couldn't see the deepening color on her pale cheeks. "I'm sorry if I was rude to you." She placed her sunglasses back on her nose and gave him a trace of a smile.

His smile widened, the dimple appeared, and the laugh lines around his eyes crinkled behind the dark glasses. "That's perfectly all right," he murmured. "I'm quite rude on occasions too. Truce?" He held out one hand. Cathy stared down at it for a moment. Her father said you could always judge a man by his hands and his eyes. She had already observed that his eyes were kind and humorous, much to her dismay. The hand in front of her was large and capable and well-shaped, the fingers long and tapering, the nails short and well cared for, unadorned by any rings. She put her slender hand in his, feeling it swallowed up in his strong grip. He let go far too quickly, his hand reaching out to take her elbow.

"Shall we join the others and tell them the war's over?" he inquired, a trace of laughter in his deep voice.

"Might as well. I don't want to have to spend the entire day in the cabin," she replied with a trace of her old spirit, and was rewarded with a laugh.

"Well, for that matter, I could always keep you company. I'm sure we'd have no trouble finding ways to spend the time," he said casually.

He must have felt her entire body stiffen through the light clasp on her elbow. Yanking her arm from his grasp, she started for the steps. "No, thank you for the kind offer," she snapped, shaking with an overwhelming rage and something not far removed from panic. She had barely taken two steps when his hands reached out and caught her, turning her to face him and holding her upper arms in an iron grip.

"Hey," he said softly, his forehead creased, "what's gotten into you? I was only kidding."

"Well, kid with someone else," she cried, knowing she sounded neurotic and completely out of control. "I don't need Meg finding someone to flirt with me to take my mind off my problems, and I don't need—"

He shook her, briefly but quite hard, and the words rattled to silence. "Let me make one thing clear," he said in his deep still voice that had a curiously enervating effect on her. "I flirt with almost every pretty lady I see, unless I'm with someone, and you, despite your monumental bad temper, are one of the prettiest women I've seen in a long time. I don't need Meg to encourage me, and she knows she wouldn't get anywhere if she tried. Is that understood?" When she refused to answer he shook her again, hard. "Is it?"

"Yes, sir," she muttered, with little grace.

He laughed then, loosening but not releasing his iron grip on her tender flesh. "Now are you ready to go above and be the nice, sweet girl I know you are beneath that bitchy exterior?"

He was smiling down at her, that beguiling little smile, and Cathy could smell the salt spray and tangy scent of his cologne, combined with the intoxicating smell of his sunheated flesh. She made a face. "Yes, sir," she said again, deceptively meek.

"Good," he said, leading her toward the steps. "But let me tell you one thing, my girl. You don't fool me for one moment."

"I wasn't trying to," she shot back, starting up the stairs. "And you, Sinclair MacDonald, don't fool me either." She didn't know why she said it, and she was totally unprepared for his response.

"Really? I wouldn't count on it." And he followed her out into the bright sunlight.

Chapter Three

After their disturbing little confrontation in the cabin, things were surprisingly better, Cathy realized as she leaned back against the duck-covered cushions out on deck. If she didn't know it was impossible, she would have said she was enjoying herself. The blueness of the sky, the sea all around them, the easy, non-demanding company, including Sin MacDonald, seemed calculated to relax her wary suspicions. Stifling a yawn, she shook her silver-blond hair about her shoulders, staring out at the horizon with a preoccupied air. The breeze was chilly, but Sin's sweater was more than up to task of keeping her warm. She would have liked to dispense with it—it was a toss-up as to which would be more disturbing: chattering teeth and blue lips or the insidious scent of Sin's aftershave as it clung to his oversized sweater.

"More wine?" Sin offered lazily, and for a moment Cathy hesitated. The chilled white wine was delicious, but she had no head for alcohol. To be sure, Meg would take care of her and see that she got home safely, but...

"No, thank you," she replied politely enough, not missing the amused light in his eyes at her somewhat stilted courtesy. "I'm so full I couldn't move." As if on cue, Meg rose from her seat behind her sister and wandered forward to join Charles. Cathy tensed her muscles, prepared to join them, when Sin's broad hand reached out and stayed her. She sat back down on the shiny wood deck, unwilling to come in actual contact with him again. She was far too susceptible to his very potent charm.

"I think your sister and Charles would like some time alone," he said, making no effort to cross the three feet that separated them on the small square of deck. "They're still practically on their honeymoon."

"They've been married eighteen months," she shot back.

"As I said, they're practically newlyweds. You know, Cathy," Sin observed meditatively, "I am hardly likely to throw you down on the teak deck and rape you. Particularly with an audience."

Embarrassment and irritation warred for control, with embarrassment having a slight edge. She lowered her confused eyes to the deck, thankful once more for the sunglasses. "Is it teak?" she inquired with just a trace of agitation in her voice. "I assumed it was some sort of synthetic."

"I'm not much for synthetics," he stated, not bragging, merely as a statement of fact. And Cathy found she was inclined to agree. Everything about him was alarmingly real. "Why don't you relax?" he added. "I promise you you're safe from ravishment right now."

"I always assumed I was," she said boldly. "After all, I doubt I'm the type to interest a man like you."

"A man like me?" he echoed, arrested. "And what would you think that is?"

He had a lazy half-smile on his face as he leaned back against the bench, his long legs stretched out on the deck in front of him. Cathy hesitated, wishing irrationally that he would take off those shielding sunglasses, at the same time maintaining her own for protection from his all-seeing eyes.

"Afraid to tell me?" he taunted gently. "I know enough about you already to be certain you've made some very arbitrary judgments about me. I'd be interested in seeing how astute you really are. Not that I think I'd have a snowball's chance in hell of changing your mind once you make it up."

"You're quite right." She sat up straighter, curling her legs up underneath her to put even more distance between his overwhelming masculinity and her own frailty. "You strike me as someone who's very sure of himself."

He raised an eyebrow. "Overly so?" he inquired pleasantly.

"Bordering on it," she shot back. "You're used to being found attractive by women, and can't quite comprehend that any poor female would be immune to your charms. You spend a lot of money on your pleasures, like your boat and the wine. You're probably quite vain, indolent, and you've already proven yourself to be sexist…"

He took this litany in quite good part, reaching into the cooler by his side and retrieving a beer. An imported German one, of course, Cathy noticed as further proof of his sybaritic tendencies. "I sound like quite a worthless fellow," he observed easily. "Haven't you anything good to say about me? No redeeming qualities?"

She considered this. "Since Charles and Meg like you, you can't be all bad."

"Dogs and children like me too," he offered meekly.

"You sail well," she continued sternly, ignoring his interruption. "And you have excellent taste in your expensive wines and such." She hesitated for a moment. For some reason Sin seemed to be waiting for more. Determined to be frank and bold and take the wind from his sails, she added, "And you're not bad on the eyes, either."

Whatever he had been expecting, that obviously wasn't it. A slow smile creased his tanned face. "High praise, indeed. You, however, are staying immune to my overwhelming physical attractions?"

"Completely!" she replied, edging slightly farther away from him. No matter how far she moved, he still seemed too close. She supposed he couldn't help being intimidating, he was so damned huge. "Just as you are to mine."

He pushed the sunglasses up to his forehead, surveying her through half-closed eyes, that smile still playing beneath his mustache. "What makes you think I'm immune to you, Cathy?" he asked softly, and the caressing sound of his voice sent a small shiver down her back, despite the heavy sweater.

"You assured me I was completely safe from—from ravishment, I believe was the word you used." She could feel the color come up in her face once more.

"That wasn't exactly what I said. I said you were safe, 'right now.'" He rose in one fluid, graceful movement, towering over her. "That doesn't mean I'll wait forever." And before she could reply with more than a gasp of outrage, he had made his way forward to join Charles and Meg.

Cathy stared after him for a long moment, awash with conflicting emotions. Emotions that couldn't be completely defined as outrage. There was something akin to excitement at the thought of Sin MacDonald directing all that tightly leashed masculine energy in her direction. Aghast at her own wayward thoughts, she hastily got to her feet, gathering up the debris of their luncheon and carrying it below. She couldn't tell whether it was the effect of the hot sun, or that intense look Sin MacDonald was giving her from across the boat, but she suddenly felt it imperative to have a few moments to compose herself before subjecting herself again to that piercing, hazel stare. And her sister was far too knowledgeable, besides.

She delayed as long as she could, cleaning up the remains from their picnic, straightening the tiny galley and removing every last trace of their occupation. It was half an hour before she finally ran out of things to do, and she considered returning Sin's heavy sweater to the footlocker. But they were still about an hour out of port and the wind had gotten substantially chillier as the afternoon shadows deepened. Obeying an impulse, Cathy slipped into the head, shut the door behind her, and turned to stare at her reflection in the mirror. The sunglasses covered fully half of her face, with only her pointed chin and hollowed cheeks and pale, tremulous mouth visible beneath the long curtain of silver-blond hair, now rumpled from the salt breeze. Taking off the glasses, she peered at her reflection. The green eyes were large and sad and wary in her pale, oval face, and the hours in the sun had brought forth a faint trace of freckles across her delicate nose. Ignoring the beauty that she had always failed to recognize, she decided she looked like someone recovering from a long illness.

With a sudden start she recognized the key word. Recovering. She never thought she would, or could, recover from the devastating blow Greg Danville had dealt her heart and her pride, not to mention her body. But recovering she was, slowly, unsteadily, but quite definitely, thank you. The very thought was amazing. Crossing her eyes and sticking out her tongue at her Ophelia-like reflection, she planted the protective sunglasses back on her nose and joined the others on deck, curiously cheered by her short moment of insight.

"What are you looking so bouncy about?" Meg inquired casually, turning to survey her.

"Why shouldn't I be bouncy? It's a beautiful day, I've been entertained and well-fed. There's no reason I shouldn't be feeling good," she replied evenly, keeping her eyes averted from Sin's interested expression.

"No reason at all," her sister echoed, obviously mystified. "We've been hatching up a marvelous plan while you were below."

"Really?" She leaned against the railing, folding her arms across her chest and willing herself to relax.

"Several, as a matter of fact," Meg continued blithely. "First off, Sin's been planning on taking *Tamlyn* down to the Caribbean, and we thought it would be fun to accompany him. Charles would sail down with him, and I could follow by plane. We wondered if you wanted to come along. You know you've always loved the Caribbean, and I think you need to get away."

Several things flew through Cathy's mind, as her eyes caught Sin's seemingly occupied figure. "Who's Tamlyn?" she blurted out, and then could have bitten her tongue at Sin's amused expression.

"*Tamlyn* is the most important female in my life," he replied, watching her expressive face beneath the glasses. "You've already berated me for spending too much money on her."

"I did?" she echoed, mystified. "Oh. *Tamlyn* is the boat," she realized belatedly.

"*Tamlyn* is the boat," he agreed with a smile. "Jealous?"

Her temper flared again, just as he had obviously planned. "God, you're conceited," she stormed.

"And you rise so nicely to the bait," he countered.

"Children, children!" Charles admonished, raising a restraining hand. "You two squabble like a couple of teen-agers. Would you listen to your sister's idea, Cathy?"

"Okay," she agreed meekly, shooting a darting glance at the unrepentant Sin.

"I'd love your company, Cathy," Meg continued persuasively. "Sin and Charles will be spending all their time messing around with the boat, and you could keep me company. We could shop, and go exploring, and all sorts of fun things. Please say you'll come with me, Cath. I've hardly seen you at all since Charles and I got married and you met—I mean, I've missed you. We'd have so much fun, please, Cathy."

"Oh, I don't think…" she began vaguely.

"There's no reason why you shouldn't go. You're not working anymore, and there isn't anyone to keep you in town," Meg added with her usual lack of tact.

"But I'm not—"

"We won't be going for another month," Charles chimed in. "Not till sometime in November, when the rainy season is well past. I'd consider it a personal favor if you'd come, Cathy. I wouldn't feel right about abandoning Meg if you weren't there."

"Not that he should feel right about abandoning me at all," Meg laughed, sharing a tender glance with her obviously doting husband. "But you know what men are like. I doubt we'll even see them the whole time we're down there."

Cathy could feel Sin's speculative hazel eyes on her averted face. "I still don't think—"

"I think she's afraid we'll all have to crowd on the boat," Sin's slow, deep voice broke through. "Maybe you'd feel better about it when you realize we'll be staying at Pirate's Cove on St. Alphonse. This boat is definitely too small for four people, particularly when two of them scarcely know each other."

Meg added the most telling argument. "I mentioned the idea to Father and he thought it was terrific, Cath. Please say you'll come. I'll have a miserable time if I'm left to my own devices."

Cathy hesitated, torn by indecision. She knew perfectly well that to agree would be succumbing to Meg's blatant matchmaking and tantamount to throwing herself at what now appeared to be a supremely disinterested Sinclair Mac-Donald. But for that matter, she too was supremely disinterested. So what could be the harm in it? If neither of them had any interest in the other, then there was no reason why they couldn't have a very pleasant time. And the warm trade winds and aqua water ought to do wonders toward her recovery, she thought, still savoring that word.

"She'll go," Sin announced suddenly, nearly catapulting her into disagreement once more. Shooting him a glance of irritation that had absolutely no effect, she nodded.

"I think I'd like that a lot," she agreed.

"Terrific!" Meg cried, enveloping her sister in an enthusiastic bear hug. "We're going to have a ball."

"This all depends on whether Father is feeling all right," Cathy warned, immediately having second thoughts.

"Pops is as strong as a horse, and you know it as well as I do," she shot back. "That tiny heart seizure has been the best thing in the world for him, forcing him to slow down. The pace he was keeping was killing him."

"I hope the boredom isn't finishing the job," Cathy replied. "Though I think he might actually be enjoying his curtailed activities."

"I have little doubt that he is. You know how he loves having his grandchildren around," said Meg, a faint blush rising to her cheeks. Cathy noticed the rise in color, and opened her mouth to query her sister, then shut it again. Perhaps Meg was still suffering from the memory of her miscarriage just six months after her marriage. This was certainly not the moment for Cathy to bring it up.

"Well, that's settled," Charles announced, his smooth, tanned face looking quite pleased. "Why don't we all go out to dinner to celebrate? You've been dying to go to that new Chinese restaurant down by the water, darling, and now's our chance."

"No, thank you," Cathy said hastily. "I really have to be back. I—uh—promised Rosemary I'd be there. She wanted some help on a sweater she was knitting, and—and she was going to come over."

Meg eyed her in surprise. "Since when have you learned to knit?" she asked sharply.

"Since this summer. You promised me I'd be back by late afternoon," she added, rather desperately, and then felt awash with guilt at the disappointment on both her sister's and Charles's faces.

"Well, that's simple enough, then," Sin spoke up. "I have to get back to town myself. I'll take Cathy back, and the two of you can go out for your dinner. I think an old married couple like yourselves need a romantic dinner alone every now and then, anyway." Cathy opened her mouth to protest, then shut it before his quelling look. "You don't have any objections, do you, Cathy?"

She wished desperately she could think of one good reason not to accompany him. But there was none. None that she could bring herself to mention. Being in Sin's company with the protective presence of the Shannons was one thing; spending at least an hour in the confines of an automobile was most definitely another. The cynical expression on his lean, dark face told her he knew everything that was going through her mind, but there was nothing she could do. Reluctantly, she nodded. "That would be fine," she lied, and Sin's amused smile deepened.

Chapter Four

It was all she could do to control the little start of panic that swept over her as she watched Charles and Meg drive off into the gathering dusk. What in the world was she doing alone here on a deserted dock, trapped in the company of a man she had only just met, a man she found more than unsettling? What was it Meg had called him? "Somewhat dangerous," hadn't she said? And kind. Cathy stared after the retreating taillights, wondering if she could count on that vaunted kindness.

"The car's just over there," Sin's voice came from directly behind her, and she jumped, emitting a small shriek. Immediately his strong hands caught her arms, turning her to face him in the twilight shadows. "Hey, calm down. I didn't mean to startle you." The hazel eyes were staring down at her with a worried expression.

"That's all right." She pulled away from his grip quite easily. "I'm just a bit on edge."

The right side of his mouth curved up in a smile. "I'm sure you are. Would it help if I promise I won't do anything more than shake your hand? Scout's honor?"

"I doubt you were ever a scout," she scoffed.

"Your doubts are misplaced. I was an Eagle Scout, and the pride of my pack. So you see, you're perfectly safe with me." He gestured to the right with a flourish. "I'm afraid my car isn't quite as new as your sister's, but I promise it won't break down or run out of gas." He reached for her elbow to guide her to the car, but she nimbly side-stepped him. His grin widened.

"Suit yourself, princess. Follow me." He headed for the car, and Cathy stuck her tongue out at his tall, broad back before following him. He was already in the driver's seat of the small, green BMW. "I'd have held the door for you but I didn't want to expose myself to a blistering attack," he apologized with mock regret as she slid into the passenger seat and fastened the safety belt.

"There's nothing wrong with common human courtesy," she replied crossly. "It should simply go both ways. Women have just as much of a duty to be polite and considerate as men do."

"Exactly." His voice was dry as he started up the car.

It took Cathy ten full minutes to apologize. "Sin," she said, her voice small in the darkened car.

"Yes?" The voice wasn't terribly encouraging. He had spent the last ten minutes in silent contemplation of the highway, not even glancing once in Cathy's direction.

"I'm sorry if I've been rude. I've been going through a pretty hard time, but I shouldn't take it out on you." It took all her determination to come out with that, but she knew she had to apologize. No matter what her provocation, there was no excuse for her behavior.

"I know." At the understanding note in his voice Cathy's resolve nearly broke. And then his meaning came through.

"What do you mean, you know?" she demanded, horrified. "What has Meg been telling you? Damn it, I warned her—"

"Calm down. She only said you'd had a rough time of

it recently. Your sister is worried about you," he explained patiently, as if to a child. "She talked to her husband and her husband mentioned it to his best friend. It's only to be expected."

"Only to be expected that when I make a fool of myself the whole world has to know?" she inquired bitterly.

"I hardly qualify as the whole world," he said reasonably. "And I know this will come as a great shock, but the previous love affairs of Miss Cathy Whiteheart are not of great importance to me. I have a great many other things on my mind."

"I'm sorry," she said again, and then laughed ruefully. "I always seem to be apologizing to you. Maybe it would be better if I just kept my mouth shut to begin with."

"Better, perhaps, but not half as interesting." His hazel gaze raked her averted profile. "That was very noble of you, to let your sister and Charles go out tonight. I know a ride home with me was the last thing you wanted."

Guilt flooded Cathy's pale cheeks. "That's not true."

"Oh, then you wanted to be with me?" he inquired, a satanic lift to his brows.

"No, of course not. I mean—" She broke off, floundering. "I wish you wouldn't trap me into saying what I don't mean," she said irritably.

"Then maybe we'd be better off not talking at all," he suggested in a neutral tone.

"Better, but not as interesting," she shot his words back to him, and was rewarded with a laugh.

"Check and mate." He chuckled. They fell into a silence, but a surprisingly comfortable one. It was odd, Cathy thought, that neither of them seemed to feel the need to fill the silent car with idle chatter. Leaning back against the leather seat, she shut her eyes, the tension slowly draining out of her weary body. A moment later she was sound asleep.

She dreamed she was back with Greg, lying in his arms. It was a dream that had haunted too many of her nights during the past three months, a nightmare that had no ending. Night after night she had felt the warmth and love turn swiftly into ugly, blinding hate and pain, physical pain as she flinched from the raging fury that confronted her.

But this time it was different. She felt the sweetness of his breath on her face, the smell of his skin, his aftershave strong in her nostrils, and she knew if she opened her eyes that Greg's warm, hazel ones would be smiling down at her. But Greg had cold blue eyes, she thought suddenly, struggling out of the mists of sleep, and he favored a sickly sweet cologne, not the spicy tang that assailed her. Her eyes opened to stare into the hazel gaze of her dream, but it belonged to Sin MacDonald.

"Don't you think it's a little dark for sunglasses?" he inquired gently, reaching out and taking them from her face before she had a chance to gather her wits and stop him. The car was parked outside her apartment building, and he was hunkered down on the sidewalk, inside the open passenger door, staring at her face in great concentration. The streetlight was very bright overhead, and she heard his sudden intake of breath.

"My God, they're green," he murmured, his voice low and husky. "If I'd known that I wouldn't have let you wear those damned sunglasses for so long."

"Give them back," she demanded, feeling naked and horribly vulnerable in the face of his piercing regard.

"Cathy, it's almost nine o'clock at night. You don't need sunglasses at this hour," he said in an almost tender voice. "Besides, you're home."

She looked past him at the ancient building that held her

apartment and three other luxury flats. "How did you know where I live?" she demanded suspiciously. "I don't remember telling you."

Sighing in exasperation, he rose to his full height, catching her arm and pulling her out of the car at the same time. "That's because I'm a Russian spy and it's my duty to know these things," he said wearily. "How come the paranoia?"

"Charles must have told you." Cathy satisfied her own curiosity, not noticing that Sin neither confirmed nor denied it. She held out her hand politely. "Thank you for driving me home," she said, her voice hatefully stiff and priggish. She knew she should invite him in for a drink, or even some dinner, but Sin MacDonald was a fairly overwhelming man, and at that moment she felt she had to be by herself, back in the safety of her apartment, able to hide from the confusing sensations and emotions that had assaulted her during the long, tiring day. And yet a perverse, totally irrational part of her wished he'd somehow prolong the evening. Force her to invite him upstairs, or drag her out to dinner. He hadn't taken no for an answer before.

This time, however, it appeared that he would. He stared down at her politely outstretched hand, the sun-lines around his smoky hazel eyes crinkling in amusement. "That's right. I did promise to shake your hand." Clicking his heels together, he took her hand in his and bowed over it, for all the world like a Prussian officer. "Madame," he uttered in a thick, guttural accent, "the pleasure is all mine."

And without a backward glance he strode back to the driver's seat on his impossibly long legs, got in, and drove away. Cathy stared after him, an unaccustomed pricking in her eyes. What was she crying about? she demanded of herself angrily as she strode past the doorman, giving him an automatic friendly nod. Greg Danville had given her more than enough to weep about for the next few years; she didn't need to start crying about Sin MacDonald besides!

THE APARTMENT WAS STILL and silent as she let herself in, and unbearably stuffy after being shut up for the day. Out of habit she strode to the air conditioner, then made a detour to the long, Palladian windows that overlooked a mini-balcony. Pulling back the heavy curtains that had stayed shut the past three months, she opened the French door onto the cool night air. A fresh breeze ruffled her hair, and there was a scent of fall in the air. *Maybe the summer of my discontent is over,* she thought, wrapping her arms around her slender body.

At that moment she realized she was still clad in Sin MacDonald's Irish knit sweater. Damn, she thought. Now she'd be forced to get in touch with him to return it. And for that matter, where were her sunglasses? Still in his hand, last time she'd seen them. Double damn. She'd have to call Meg tomorrow and find out how to reach the enigmatic Mr. Sinclair MacDonald. What a pain, to be forced to communicate with someone she found quite…bothersome.

Humming beneath her breath, she moved into her kitchen and began assembling a gigantic sandwich. There was scarcely any food in the house—she'd have to remedy that tomorrow. Funny, but she hadn't felt much like eating since she couldn't remember when. And now, all of a sudden, she was eating like a weight watcher let out on probation. First stuffing herself that afternoon, and now she was wolfing down a sandwich that would have put a glutton like Charles to shame. Back to the refrigerator to discover, to her unalloyed joy, a single beer, the same imported brand that Sinclair MacDonald favored. *I'll have to get some more,* she thought, opening the bottle and pouring it into a heavy pub mug, and taking another bite of her sandwich. You never know who might turn up and want a beer.

The shrill ringing of the telephone interrupted her meal and she reached for the phone, spilling half of her drink in her haste to answer it. "Hello?" she said breathlessly around the remains of her sandwich.

"Cathy? Is that you? It's Meg." Her sister's voice sounded somewhat disgruntled.

"Hi, Meg. Who else would answer my phone?" she replied, taking a drink from her depleted beer.

"You're back so soon?" She sounded disappointed, Cathy thought. But not as disappointed as I was when I answered the phone.

"Of course I am. It's only forty miles from the marina," she said reasonably.

"But I thought Sin might take you out to dinner or something." Her tone of voice was plaintive. "You didn't scare him off, did you?"

"Of course I did," Cathy shot back. "Isn't that what I always do with importunate young men?"

"I wouldn't call Sin importunate. Or that young, either. He's older than Charles—probably around thirty-five or thirty-six. That would make him ten years older than you, so I hardly think that qualifies him—"

"Enough, Meg. You know I don't like matchmaking."

"Yes, ma'am. How did you manage to scare him off?" she questioned, a very real interest in her voice.

"It was quite simple. I don't think he was the slightest bit interested in the first place."

There was a long, disbelieving pause. "Well, we shall see. Sin isn't one to give up easily, and—"

"He's *not* interested in me, Meg. If I thought he was, I wouldn't be coming with you to the Caribbean."

"But you don't dislike him, do you, sweetie?" Meg's

voice was anxious.

"No, Meggie. I just have no intention of getting involved with someone at this point. If I ever do, I will let you know, and you can rush right out and round up all your eligible friends for my inspection."

"Well, all right. Maybe I should encourage Sin to bring a girlfriend along, if you two really aren't going to hit it off. Though I don't know if I like the idea of some nubile young thing accompanying those two horny men on that very romantic boat for however long it'll take them to sail down. I've never seen Sin with anything less than a bona fide beauty."

"Do whatever you think is best. That might be a very good idea," she said, lying through her teeth. "Let me know what's happening, will you? Oh, and I forgot to give him back his sweater. Do you suppose I could drop it off with you and you could return it for me? And maybe get my sunglasses back?"

"Why don't you do it? I'll give you his number."

"No, please. I'd prefer it if you'd take care of it." All Cathy's earlier good humor was rapidly vanishing. "I don't want to see any more of Sinclair MacDonald than I absolutely have to."

"Hmm." Meg's voice was knowing. "I'll see what I can do. In the meantime, take it easy, okay?"

"Sure thing. Don't I always?"

"Not recently," her sister said wryly, hanging up.

The last tiny bit of sandwich went into the trash, the rest of the beer down the drain. Heading toward the bedroom, Cathy hesitated listlessly by the open windows, then shrugged and continued on her way. Tomorrow morning she could pull the curtains again.

SHE WOKE UP suddenly, her slender body in the light cotton nightgown shivering in the predawn light. Another dream, another nightmare. With no Sin MacDonald to save her, she thought muzzily, huddling down under the light summer blanket. Still her body trembled, both from the cold and the aftermath of her nightmare.

Five minutes later, she sat up, sighing. A heavy flannel nightgown hung on the hook inside her walk-in closet, a cardigan sweater lay across the chair beside her, her quilted robe was just inside the bathroom door. Getting up, she padded all the way across the apartment in bare feet, out to the front hall. Sin's sweater lay there, where she had left it the night before. Pulling it over her head, she made her way across the apartment and got back into bed. The scent of her perfume mingled with the traces of his aftershave and the faint smell of the sea. Pulling the blankets around her, she shut her eyes, snuggling down into the Irish wool. A moment later she was asleep.

Chapter Five

Putting Sinclair MacDonald out of her mind was far easier said than done. During the next two weeks, Cathy found herself jumping every time the phone rang, racing to answer it, all prepared for the scathing denunciation that she had reworked several times during the ensuing days. But the phone had remained silent.

In the meantime she was torn. Part of her hated the thought of leaving the apartment and possibly missing a phone call, but the overwhelming emotion that haunted her was a need to escape. After three months of immuring herself in the four walls of her luxurious Georgetown flat, she found that she would go mad if she didn't get out for at least part of the day. She went shopping, buying unsuitable clothes that she would never wear, food that turned bad in the refrigerator and had to be thrown out. And for some obscure reason, she always kept a supply of imported German beer in the sparsely filled refrigerator.

By the second weekend after her daylong sail, the inactivity broke her will, and throwing her bathing suit and a change of clothes in the back of her small red Honda, she drove the forty miles to her father's estate in Virginia. Brandon Whiteheart's health had not been good, and Cathy never thought of him without a pang of worry.

As the youngest of Brandon Whiteheart's large brood, she had always held a special place in her father's affections, affections she returned fully. Her mother's death when Cathy was two years old had sealed her close dependence on her father, and Brandon had always found time to be there for her, despite his myriad interests. A brusque businessman, it had taken the gentle vulnerability of his youngest to pierce his hard-boiled exterior. Meg had still been young enough to benefit from his softening, but the three elder siblings—snobbish and overbearing Georgia, always so aware of her position as the daughter of one of the wealthiest industrialists in America; pompous Henry; and venal Travis, Cathy's least favorite of all her siblings—had been too well set in their ways. Too many years of parental disinterest had done their damage, and the three elder Whitehearts viewed their father's absorption with Cathy and her elder sister Meg with jealous exasperation.

All this was going through Cathy's mind as her little red car sped across the countryside. There was little doubt all three of them would be in residence. Georgia and her husband Allen had moved in with Pops when Allen's business had gone bankrupt. Henry and his wife Milly were in the midst of moving, and were staying at Whiteoaks until their extravagant new house was completed. And Travis, dear, darling Travis with his little ways that bordered on sadism, came every weekend to ensure his inheritance. Despite the fact that Brandon Whiteheart had always been scrupulously even and fair in his dealings with his children, Travis could never find it in his heart to trust either his father's fairness or his siblings' greed. Since the heart spasm last winter Travis had raced down to Whiteoaks each and every weekend, eyeing his siblings with a jealous sneer and confining his conversation to snide remarks and sycophantic fawnings on his father. The absurdity of it was, Cathy thought as she pushed her silver-blond hair back from her face, that of all the wealthy Whiteheart children, Travis had done the best with his inheritance, more than tripling it in the last twelve years. Yes, she thought with a sigh, Travis would be there, and all the others, with the lamentable exceptions of Meg and Charles. They were too busy getting ready for their Caribbean trip. Maybe one afternoon with her father would be enough, she thought. Surely she could manage a few hours alone with him, long enough to assure herself that he was in good health, and then she could dash back to town before she got roped into one of those noisy, backbiting, unappetizing orgies known euphemistically as a family dinner.

As she turned into the long, winding driveway that led to Whiteoaks, a dark green BMW sped past her, too quickly for her to see the driver, but long enough for a shaft of unhappiness to mar her determinedly cheerful state of mind. Seeing a car so similar to his brought Sin back full force. Perhaps she could cancel her part of the Caribbean trip. Despite Meg's assurances that they would scarcely even *see* him, Cathy had her doubts. Circumstances would throw them into a "couple" situation, where the obviously disinterested Sin would be forced to act as her willing escort. The very thought made her blush with incipient embarrassment, and she told herself she would call Meg the moment she returned home. If she needed to get away, perhaps Hawaii would be a refreshing change. If only there weren't so damned many tourists marring the spectacular landscape! But doubtless St. Alphonse in the Caribbean would be equally tourist ridden. Maybe she would go to Europe.

"Well, Catherine, you were the last person I expected to see," her eldest sister's stentorian tones greeted her as she stepped lightly from the compact car and ran up the front steps. Georgia stood poised at the top of the wide, marble steps, her silvery blond hair perfectly coiffed as always, the blue eyeshadow heavy on her sunken lids, the thick coating of powder over the perfect Whiteheart features taking on a sickly mauve hue in the afternoon shadows. "And frankly, my dear, you don't look your best," she continued, tilting her head to one side in a deliberate attitude she had long ago perfected. "Do you think blue jeans and a khaki shirt are the proper garb in which to visit your father?"

Ignoring the rising temper always provoked by her contentious sister, Cathy clinked cheekbones dutifully, wondering if her pale, smooth cheeks had taken on some of Georgia's purple talc. "Pops is more than used to me," she replied evenly. "You're looking elegant as always, George," she added, not missing the tightening of her sister's thin lips at the hated nickname. "Is that a new suit?"

Georgia allowed herself a small preen. "Do you like it? Bendel's, of course. You really ought to do something about your clothes, darling. They're either disgraceful or terribly plain. No doubt you've brought some terribly staid off-the-rack thing for supper."

"I'm not staying for supper, Georgia," Cathy decided hastily, moving past her sister into the house. "And you know perfectly well that I don't care about clothes."

"You never have. You're not going to win a man that way, my dear. Take some advice from your sister, jeans and shirts will not do at all. I could also give you some advice on makeup. You don't take advantage of your looks, you know. You don't have to settle for being plain. With the proper makeup and clothes you could be passably pretty. I do wish you'd let me take you in hand."

"No, thank you, Georgia." Cathy accepted her sister's strictures with her usual stoic forbearance, having heard them all her life. If she had ever had any doubts about her possible attractiveness, Georgia had done her best to stamp them out, leaving Cathy feeling plain and gawky, not recognizing her own lithe charm and unusual beauty. Georgia had worked her black magic once more.

"Where is everybody?" Cathy queried, changing the subject quite firmly. "Is Pops resting?"

"You know your father, Catherine. Nothing can make him slow down. He's been conducting some very nefarious sort of business, and both Travis and Henry are livid. They've done everything they can to get him to confide in them, but your father does like to be mysterious."

A tolerant smile lit Cathy's face as she recognized her father's childish traits, a smile that turned her palely pretty face into a thing of beauty. "He's your father too, Georgia," she reminded her.

Georgia's beautifully shaped hands had curled into fists at her sister's smile. "Not so you'd notice," she said bluntly, turning her back on Cathy and leaving her without another word.

Cathy stared after her elegant, well-dressed back until her sister disappeared into the house, the all-too-familiar waves of guilt washing over her. "Damn it, Georgia," she whispered, "I won't let you do that to me anymore. It wasn't my fault."

"What wasn't your fault, darling?" Travis's slightly husky voice startled her into another polite curse. Reluctantly she turned to face him, wondering for not the first time how someone so endowed with physical charms and financial well-being could be so unpleasant. Her brother was just above medium height, with the same dark, wavy hair that Meg had, warm brown eyes, a beautiful nose and well-modeled lips. Unfortunately those lips were permanently carved in a sneer, and the brown eyes frequently glittered with malice.

"None of your business, Travis," she replied pleasantly enough.

"You should be used to your sister by now, Cathy," Travis purred. "She still hasn't recovered from the fact that Father couldn't care less whether she lived or died, and he thinks the sun rises and sets with you. Added to that the fact that you're far lovelier than she could ever hope to be, along with being seventeen years younger, and I think you can understand her irritable mood. She's usually much better when she's warned you're coming."

"I'm hardly lovelier than Georgia, Travis, and if you've been telling her so I wish you'd stop. Everyone knows that Georgia is the beauty of the family, and will be when she's eighty."

"All those people don't know my hermitlike youngest sister," Travis said smoothly. "What brings you down here?"

"I wanted to see how Pops was doing."

A frown creased his brow. "Don't you think we're capable of taking decent care of him, Cathy? Or are you expecting—"

"Travis, I just wanted to visit with him." Cathy interrupted him with a patience that was rapidly wearing thin. It was no wonder she avoided this place like the plague. "How is he?"

"Up to his ears in intrigue," Travis snapped, obviously nettled.

"By the way, who was that driving away as I arrived? In the green BMW?" she inquired casually, following him into the house toward her father's library, the only place he could still call his own in a house filled with visiting children.

"No one you know, little sister. Some business acquaintance of his, part of his hush-hush plan. Don't bother asking—even you won't get any further with him on this one.''

"I have no intention of cross-examining him about his business. I doubt it would be all that exciting once I found out, anyway," she replied, stopping outside the paneled door to the library.

"Will we be seeing you at dinner, Cathy mine?"

A bitter smile lit her pale face. "Not likely. For some reason my family destroys my appetite."

"You don't look as if you've had much appetite recently, anyway," her brother observed sweetly.

"You know what they say, darling," she shot back. "A woman can't be too thin or too rich."

"And you know, from your experience with Greg Danville, that both of those things aren't true."

Cathy recoiled as if from a physical blow. "How do you know about Greg Danville?" she demanded hoarsely.

"You should know by now, dear Cathy, that nothing stays a secret in this family." Travis was unmoved by the reaction he had caused.

"Does Pops know about it?"

"Who do you think told me?" he purred. "Have you forgotten that Father employs a veritable army of private investigators?"

Slowly Cathy withdrew her hand from the antique brass doorknob, noticing with absent fascination that her slender, ringless hand was trembling slightly. "Good-bye, Travis," she said coolly, and turning on her heel, she strode out of the house without a backward glance. Travis's light, malicious voice floated to her.

"What shall I tell your dear Pops?"

She paused for only a moment at the front door. "I'm certain you'll think of something," she replied without bothering to turn around. A moment later she was in her car, speeding down the driveway, away from the house, away from her hateful family. And away from her insensitive, prying, *controlling* father. Damn them all.

Chapter Six

The insistent ringing of her doorbell finally penetrated Cathy's heavy, drugged sleep. Without bothering to check her digital clock glowing malevolently in the darkened bedroom, she buried her head under the feather pillow with a groan. Still the buzz of the doorbell intruded. She pressed the pillow closer over her head, swearing beneath her breath.

Someone was leaning on the doorbell now, the shrill noise penetrating the pillow, Cathy's hands, and her aching head with a sadistic vengeance. With a groan she threw the pillow across the room and struggled out of bed, moving in a fogged stupor toward the front door.

It had been four in the morning before she had slept. The thought of her father's betrayal had been the cruelest blow of all, with her siblings' customary malice a mere frosting on the cake. From the moment she arrived back in her apartment, just after dark, the phone had begun to ring, and ring, and ring, until she took it off the hook in desperation. For the first time in her life she wished she hadn't been so adamant in turning down the sleeping pills and tranquilizers her family practitioner had offered her. After all, everyone else took them, why shouldn't she? If she only had some, maybe she'd be able to sleep. Or at least stay awake calmly.

Even her most faithful friend, the television set, had failed her in her moment of need. The only thing on late night TV had been a turgid romance, far too well suited to her morose mood. The only alcohol in the house had been the imported German brew. It had taken two and a half beers to make her pleasantly tipsy, tipsy enough so that when she scrambled into her now customary sleeping apparel of shorty pajamas and Sin's Irish sweater, she fell asleep with only a few maudlin tears. To dream once more of Greg Danville, his blue eyes narrowed in rage as he stalked her, until she woke up with a muffled scream of terror in the predawn light.

It had taken another hour for her to sleep again. For two weeks Greg had been absent from her dreams, only to turn up now, when she least needed him. She had hugged her sweating body tightly, willing the panic to subside. She was safe, the door was locked, there was no way he could get to her.

The buzzer was still ringing in her head as she stumbled across the darkened living room, tripping over the pillows she had thrown, knocking over the stale, half-empty beer bottle in front of the television. Reaching the door with its damnable buzzer, she pounded furiously against the thick paneling.

"Shut up, damn you!" she shrieked. "I'll open the blasted door if you just give me a moment."

The buzzing stopped, leaving a silence even more deafening in her pounding head. Peering through the peephole, all she could see was a broad chest. She knew only one man that tall. She didn't even hesitate. With fumbling fingers she undid the three locks and flung open the door into the hallway. And there, leaning against the doorjamb, lounged Sin MacDonald, looking, if that was possible, even more overpoweringly handsome than he had two weeks ago. The faded denims encased his long, long legs, though this time he wore old cowboy boots in place of the sneakers. His lean, powerful torso was shown to advantage by a chambray western shirt, and the green sweater he had worn as a sop to the chilly weather brought out his hazel eyes. On his lean, tanned face was a tolerant half-smile, in one hand he twirled her missing sunglasses.

Cathy stood there, staring, her mouth agape, unaware of how completely appealing she looked, her silver-blond hair tousled around a sleep-smudged face, the long legs bare beneath the enveloping sweater. At the sight of her his smile broadened beneath the mustache, and he stood upright and strolled past her into the apartment, for all the world as if he belonged there, she thought wrathfully.

"I'm glad you're enjoying my sweater," he said mildly enough. "Isn't it pretty scratchy to sleep in, though? Or are you wearing something underneath it?"

Color flooded her face as she realized just how little she *was* wearing. She stood there, torn as to whether to order him from the house, or dash to the bedroom to put on something a bit more enveloping. Sin must have had the uncanny ability to read her mind, for he walked back past her dumbstruck body, closed the door, and turned to her, that lazy smile playing about his mouth but not quite reaching the eyes.

"Don't you think you'd better put something else on?" he inquired gently. "Not that you don't look absolutely lovely, but the sight of all that delicious female flesh is a bit unsettling for a red-blooded American male."

"I—I—" She gave it up and fled to her bedroom, banging the door shut behind her.

She was in no hurry to put in an appearance after her embarrassing encounter. The clock by her bed read the unbelievable hour of 2:00 p.m., and she had obviously still been in bed. How did he know she was alone? She should have pretended there was someone waiting for her in the bedroom, someone who kept her in bed the better part of the day. Maybe that would wipe that amused smile off his face, she thought viciously, ripping off her clothes and turning on the shower, full blast. Maybe she could still pretend there was someone in here—after all, he was hardly likely to—

She had underestimated him. She had barely put her head under the heavy stream when his voice came horrendously close. "Do you like your coffee black?"

Cathy let out a shriek of outrage as she saw his tall, strong figure through the rising steam of the shower. "Get out!"

"Do you like your coffee black?" he repeated, obviously unmoved by her outrage.

"Leave this room!"

"Not until you tell me how you like your coffee," he said easily, leaning against the sink, his eyes hooded in the hot steam. Cathy knew perfectly well the smoky glass of the shower made an adequate protection for those knowing hazel eyes, but at that point she wouldn't have put it past him to open the shower door to get her attention.

"I like it black and in private," she ground out.

He straightened to his full height, a good twelve inches over the top of the shower enclosure. She could see him towering over her, like Godzilla over a Japanese village, she thought furiously.

"Would you like me to wash your back?" he inquired sweetly. She took the wet washcloth and flung it over the door, watching it land with a satisfyingly wet smack full in his face.

There was an ominous silence, with nothing but the sound of the shower in the small bathroom. Sin dropped the washcloth back over the shower stall, wiped his streaming face on the thick blue towel she'd left out, and let himself out of the bathroom without another word. As Cathy quickly finished her shower, she tried to rid herself of the ridiculous feeling of guilt that Sin's silent exit had instilled in her. Perhaps she should have laughed it off, invited him to join her in the shower. After all, it wasn't as if she was still an innocent....

She dressed quickly in jeans and an oversized shirt before padding into the living room on bare feet. The room was transformed. Sin had pulled the drapes, picked up her spilled beer and the pillows and articles of clothing that she'd tossed about in a rage, and was now sitting on the sofa, his boot-clad feet up on the coffee table, casually drinking his coffee. Another cup was on the table in front of him, obviously meant for her. Cathy could see faint traces of water in his thick brown hair, but the hazel eyes that looked up at her were lacking anything other than polite interest.

"I decided you'd rather have your coffee out here than have me bring it to you," he said, his slow voice warming her. "I've already had one shower today."

With what grace she could muster she entered the room, picked up the coffee, and took a seat as far away from him as possible. "I have a temper," she allowed, taking a sip of the coffee.

"Apology accepted," he replied.

"There was none offered!" she snapped.

"No? That's what it sounded like," he said, unmoved by her wrath. "Why haven't you been answering your phone?"

"You tried to call me?" she questioned, her feelings warming somewhat. Maybe it hadn't been his fault that two weeks had gone by without a word.

"All last night and this morning," he confirmed, ruining her temporary mellowing.

"I didn't feel like talking to anyone," she replied coldly, taking another sip of coffee. It was extraordinarily good coffee; thick and black and strong, and she found herself leaning back in her chair.

"I gathered as much. I was hoping I could persuade you to have dinner with me tonight."

"I don't think—"

He overrode her objections. "We're leaving for St. Alphonse in a matter of days, with you and Meg following a week later. I thought it would be a good idea if I filled you in on the details. Where we'll be staying, what we'll be doing, what sort of stuff you'll need to bring."

"I've been to the Caribbean before," she said haughtily. "Besides, Meg could tell me all that."

"Meg and Charles have gone to visit his parents in Connecticut. Come on, Cathy, don't be difficult. There's no reason why we can't be friends."

Yes, there is, she thought silently, taking in the long, lean beauty of him. "Of course we can be friends," she said abruptly. "It's just…"

"You don't have anything planned, do you?" As she shook her head he rose to his full height. "Well, then, that's settled. I'll be back here around seven. Have you ever eaten at Champetre?"

Politeness forced her to rise and follow him to the door, politeness she wished she'd ignored as he towered over her, dwarfing her slender height. He was so close she could feel the heat emanating from his body, smell the faint, male smell of him, his bittersweet aftershave that had clung to the sweater. Keeping her face averted, she opened the door for him. One strong hand reached out and caught her willful chin, forcing her rebellious green eyes upward to meet his rueful hazel ones.

"Cheer up, Cathy," he said gently. "It won't be so bad. I promise you, I can be a perfect gentleman when the occasion calls for it."

"But will the occasion call for it?" she wondered aloud. And she also wondered if gentlemanly behavior was what she really wanted from him.

His smile deepened, so that the one, unforgettable dimple appeared beside his sensuous mouth. Suddenly, as if on impulse, he bent down and brushed his lips against her unwary mouth, his bushy mustache tickling her deliciously. It was so fleeting Cathy wondered if she dreamed it. Sin straightened and moved away. "I'm afraid, knowing you, that I'll have to be on my best behavior, or you won't come with us to St. Alphonse."

"True enough," she agreed, wondering if it really was. "Does it matter that much whether I come or not?"

He nodded. "Meg really needs you." They were not the words she would have chosen to hear. "See you at seven."

The door closed behind his broad shoulders with a tiny, well-oiled click. Cathy stood there, staring at the blank, white expanse of the door, lost in thought. *Haven't I learned my lesson,* she demanded of herself dazedly. *Haven't I had enough of handsome men to last me a lifetime?* With a sigh, she went back to her coffee, wondering what on earth she would wear that would both entice and discourage Sin MacDonald.

In the end she settled on a simple black silk dress, one that clung to her high, firm breasts, swirled around her gently rounded hips and hugged her slender waist. It was a very deceiving dress, seemingly demure until Cathy's graceful body moved beneath it. She both hoped and feared that Sin would notice.

She shouldn't have had any doubts. When he arrived at five past seven the look in his hazel eyes was both guarded and more than flattering. "That's a very dangerous dress, Cathy Whiteheart," he said in a low, deep voice after a long, silent stare.

She controlled the impulse to say, "What, this old thing?" She had bought the dress for Greg, bought it the day she returned back home from shopping to find him in bed with a strange woman. She had never worn it, and suddenly she was glad she had decided to ignore her misgivings. It wasn't the fault of the dress that she associated it with Greg. Besides, Georgia's cutting words had an unpleasant edge of truth to them. The remainder of the clothes that took up only a small portion of the space in her walk-in closet were unimaginative, unflattering pastels and flowered prints. She either looked like a schoolgirl or a housewife in most of them—even Greg at his most charming had been far from pleased with her wardrobe. But she had never had much interest in clothes. At least, not until recently.

"I'm afraid I don't have anything to offer you in the way of a drink." She made her voice cool and composed, something she was far from feeling. The mere sight of his tall, strong body, clad in gray flannel slacks, a black turtleneck, and a Harris tweed jacket that showed off the set of his broad shoulders was enough to send her pulse racing. His lazy smile and the promise in his smoky hazel eyes just about proved her undoing.

"That's all right, Cathy." He draped her jacket around her shoulders, the hands lingering for a delectable moment. "We can easily have a drink at the restaurant. I wouldn't want to put you out."

For one mad, impetuous moment Cathy knew the overwhelming desire to lean her head against that broad, deep chest and close her eyes, give over her troubles and responsibilities into his large, capable hands. She looked up, her green eyes meeting his for a long, pregnant moment, and then she blinked rapidly, moving away. "We'd better leave," she said, and her voice was noticeably shaky.

Damn him and the devastating effect he had on her. Tender amusement lit his eyes as he took her unwilling arm. "Certainly, Cathy. It's just as well. When I promised you could trust me to behave like a gentleman I didn't know you were going to wear that dress."

His skin seemed to burn through her clothing. She couldn't free herself from the nerve-shattering effect of his presence. In the luxurious confines of his BMW he seemed overwhelming, magnetic, and far more man than she was capable of dealing with at that point in her life. But the invisible wall she tried to erect toppled every time he smiled at her, touched her, and it took far too long to rebuild it each time. The day would come when she could no longer do so, and she didn't know whether she dreaded or longed for it.

She had steeled herself for an ordeal during dinner, fending off all that flirtatious charm, but as they took their seats in the elegant, secluded confines of the restaurant Sin suddenly became completely businesslike, treating her with a polite, distant charm that left her both relaxed and ever so faintly disgruntled. She scarcely tasted the delicious food he ordered for her, drank far too much of the excellent Bordeaux, and watched the candlelit shadows play across his strongly handsome face with bemused fascination.

That swift smile lit his face as he finished his brandy. "Have you been listening to a word I've said?" he asked. "You look like you're in another world, although it's obviously a much pleasanter place than the one you usually inhabit. What are you thinking about?"

"You," she answered forthrightly enough. "I know absolutely nothing about you. Do you work for a living?"

The smile deepened. "Now and then."

"At what?" she persisted.

"At whatever takes my interest at the time," he replied. "Any more questions?"

"If I had them, you'd be unlikely to answer," she shot back, nettled.

"How can you say such a thing?" he mocked gently. "Anyway, I bet I can answer them without your having to ask. I'm thirty-six years old, six feet four, two hundred and ten pounds, single, unemployed, unattached, and I drink Scotch."

"Fascinating," she murmured.

"And then we come to you. You're five feet eight or nine, about a hundred and twenty pounds, twenty-six years old, independently wealthy, currently unemployed, unattached, and suffering from a mysterious and ill-advised broken heart. You drink imported beer and anything else I offer you, probably from a lack of interest rather than alcoholic tendencies. And for some reason I make you damned uncomfortable."

"Maybe it's because you outweigh me by a hundred pounds," she retorted, draining her brandy glass in a defiant gesture. "And I'll have you know I'm the family wino. It's a deep, shameful secret, but I should have known I could never hide anything from you."

"Hardly an alcoholic if it takes only two and a half beers to give you a hangover. You forget, I straightened up your living room today." He signaled for the waiter, tossing his linen napkin on the table. "And you're going to feel a lot worse after tonight. Two daiquiris, half a bottle of wine, and a brandy should make you practically comatose," he said affably. "I expect I'll have to carry you out to the car."

"Don't count on it," she snapped. "I didn't have anything to eat last night. Anyway, I think I'm getting used to drinking. What are you staring at?" she demanded as his eyes narrowed with sudden intensity as they roamed over her face.

"How did your nose get broken?" he asked abruptly.

Cathy's hand flew to her face. "I didn't think it was that noticeable," she said with a shaky laugh, determined to treat it lightly.

"It isn't. I've been staring at you for hours now and I just noticed. How did it happen?"

He wasn't going to leave it alone, she realized dismally. "Oh, I had it done. I thought it would give my face more character," she said breezily.

Sin continued to stare at her, his silence unnerving. "He did it, didn't he?" he said finally. "Greg, I think his name was?"

There was a sudden roaring in her ears as the last vestige of color drained from her face. For a long moment she was afraid she would pass out. And then the need to run overcame her. Pushing back the chair, she grabbed her purse and ran from the room, past the crowded tables, blinded by tears, not knowing where she was going, only knowing that she had to escape from those all-seeing hazel eyes. When she reached the sidewalk in front of the restaurant she continued to run, panic-stricken, down the darkened street, the roaring sound in her ears so loud she didn't hear the sound of his pursuit until strong arms reached out and caught her from behind, spinning her around to fall against his broad, strong body.

Sin's arms came around her, strong and comforting, holding her trembling body against his with a solid tender-

ness. One hand came up and caressed her tumbled hair as
she buried her face against his shoulder, wanting to hide
away from the horrifying memories and this man's uncanny
knowledge of her. But there was no hiding place, not even
in Sin's arms, and after several long, shuddering minutes
she pulled away, tilting her head back to stare up at him
bravely.

The smile that curved his mouth and lit his eyes was
curiously tender. He still retained a loose hold on her body,
and one tanned hand reached up and caught her willful chin
in a gentle grasp. "Sorry for trespassing," he said softly.
"Do you want me to drop the subject?"

"Yes, please." Her voice came out in a husky whisper,
and for a brief moment his hold on her tightened reassur-
ingly. And then she was released.

"I'm afraid your precipitate exit rather precluded dessert," Sin remarked casually.

"I'm not really hungry."

"You may not be, but I'm still starved. And I'm sure
you wouldn't say no to the best ice cream in the Washington area."

A faint glimmer of interest penetrated Cathy's abstraction. "Ice cream?" she echoed. "What kind?"

"Any kind that takes your fancy. Blueberry gem, maple
walnut, apple-banana. Of course, the true test of a great ice-
cream maker is my personal favorite—coffee." He took her
elbow in the most casual of gestures and led her back toward the car.

"Don't be absurd," she replied, making an effort to
match his light tone. "The real test of a great ice cream is
vanilla. Anyone can make a decent coffee ice cream—all
you have to do is add enough coffee. They're basically all
alike anyway."

"Oh, you think so, do you? Wait until you try Benwards'. You'll never settle for bland vanilla again.'' He smiled down at her wickedly as he opened the car door for her. "You're too much of a woman to settle for anything as unexciting."

"As vanilla ice cream?" she retorted, knowing perfectly well he was talking about something far removed. As always she was much too aware of the tall, strong body next to her, even more now since she'd felt those strong arms around her, that formidably gorgeous body hard against hers.

"You're not a coward, Cathy. I'm sure that once you decide what you want out of life you'll go for it with no holds barred," he replied mysteriously, shutting the door behind her and moving around to climb into the driver's seat.

"And I don't want vanilla ice cream?" she inquired.

His eyes met hers across the soft leather seat of the BMW. The streetlight above provided an eerie illumination, making Sin's face curiously brutal. "It would be a waste," he said, and then turned his attention to the demands of city driving, leaving Cathy to stare out into the brightly lit nighttime streets of Washington.

Chapter Seven

It was almost three o'clock in the morning when they finally arrived back at Cathy's apartment. If the sight of the augustly demure facade of her building set off small alarms in her brain, then Sin's relaxed, friendly, completely non-threatening behavior of the last few hours allayed those fears. It was almost as if, she thought with just a faintly disgruntled air, he had switched off his considerable sexuality like a light. The result had been more than enjoyable charm, but Cathy couldn't help but wonder when the panther would re-emerge.

The doorman nodded pleasantly as they walked back into the building, Sin's hand resting lightly on the small of her back. His touch was so gentle, in fact, that Cathy wondered why it seemed to burn through the thin material of her dress. "You certainly have a great deal of security around here," he observed as he followed her into the elevator. "I hadn't thought Georgetown was such a dangerous area."

"It's not. I just feel better knowing there's someone down there to keep out unwanted visitors. Speaking of which, how did you manage to get up to my apartment this afternoon?" she demanded.

"Speaking of unwanted visitors or security?" he returned, unabashed. "I have my ways, Catherine Whiteheart.

You can rest assured, it wasn't your very ample security's fault. When I set my mind to something there's very little that can stop me.''

A tiny, anxious shiver ran through her at his calmly implacable words, a strange sense of inevitability washing over her. ''It certainly is late,'' she said nervously. ''You should have told me the best ice cream in the area was in Maryland.''

Standing in the close confines of the elevator he seemed even taller than his six feet four inches. The smile he gave her was no longer as innocent as it had been. ''I didn't want to give you the chance to refuse.''

''Yes, but did you have to force me to eat so much?'' she groaned, holding her stomach in mock pain. ''I agreed with you that the coffee ice cream was the best in the world.''

''But how were we to know for certain unless we checked their other flavors?'' he argued persuasively as the elevator doors opened with a soft swoosh.

''But twenty-four flavors?'' she questioned plaintively, determined to keep up a light banter until she got safely behind her locked apartment door. ''I doubt I'll eat for days.'' They were already at the shiny, black-painted door, and it was with a feeling of déjà vu that she held out her hand, remembering all too well her forced politeness in dismissing him the last time he saw her home. ''Thanks for a lovely dinner,'' she said stiffly. ''I'd invite you in for a nightcap, but it's far too late. There's nothing I want to do but fall into bed.''

He cocked an eyebrow at her last sentence and she felt her pale face flush a fiery red. ''Still keeping me in my place, Cathy?'' he inquired gently, ignoring her outstretched hand. With an easy shrug he turned. ''Good night.'' Seemingly without another thought he strode back toward the elevator, leaving Cathy staring after him with mixed emotions, foremost among them a perverse disappointment that he had given up so easily. As he waited for the elevator to return to the floor, he turned and leaned against the wall, hands in pockets, giving Cathy an absolutely devastating smile. And then he began to whistle.

The elevator arrived; the door swished open beside him. Those searching hazel eyes looked at the elevator, and then back at Cathy's motionless figure waiting by her door. Slowly he straightened up, and the panther look was back on him in full. He headed into the elevator, did a sudden about-face and turned back toward her, stalking her like the jungle beast he so resembled.

Before she had time to react he had pulled her slender body against his, hard. Her hands were caught between them as she instinctively raised them to ward him off, trapped against his broad chest. "To hell with keeping my place," he said succinctly, and lowered his mouth to hers, gently at first, as if not to frighten her. His arms were an iron band around her slight frame, allowing her room enough to move, but not to escape, as his lips nibbled at hers, slowly, sweetly, drawing from her a response she didn't want to give. One hand slipped down her back to press her closer to him, to make her fully aware of the strength of his response to her, and the slight loosening of his embrace allowed her enough leverage to free her arms. She slid them up his chest, pushing against him for a futile, angry five seconds, and then, uttering a quiet moan somewhere in the back of her throat, she slid them around him, entwining her fingers in the long brown curls at the back of his neck.

His lips left hers for a moment, trailing a line of slow, deliberate kisses across her pale cheeks to her ear. The tip of his tongue flicked out, tracing the delicate outlines of her ear, his strong white teeth capturing her lobe with gentle nips. "Open your mouth, Cathy," he whispered as he moved back to recapture her lips. Closing her eyes, she obeyed, letting him regain possession of her mouth even more intimately than he had before. His tongue explored every inch of her warm, moist mouth, demanding and drawing from her a response that she had never given another man. Her heart was pounding, her breath coming in quick, shallow pants, and her entire body trembled from pent-up desire. She could feel the flat surface of the wall behind her while every square inch of his body seemed burned into her flesh, and still he kissed her, as if he could never get enough of her willing mouth.

And then suddenly he moved away, out of her nerveless arms. Opening her passion-drugged eyes, she found his damnable hazel eyes staring down at her with a look of intense satisfaction.

He looked infuriatingly calm and collected, but Cathy couldn't help but notice his somewhat quickened breathing, and her yearning flesh had felt the imprint of his desire just moments before. He was scarcely as unmoved as he was striving to appear.

But his control was certainly a great deal better than hers. A disturbingly pleased smile lit his mouth beneath the mustache. "See you," he said lightly, and headed back to the still waiting elevator. Whistling, damn his soul!

She waited until the elevator had reached the bottom floor before she began to fumble through her purse for her key. Her hands were shaking so much she couldn't make it work for precious moments. When the lock finally turned she stumbled into her darkened apartment, racing across the living room to the French windows, pushing aside the curtains to stare out into the street.

Sin's tall body emerged from the entrance and strode

casually, almost jauntily to his car, apparently as unmoved by the last few minutes as she was devastated.

As he opened the door to his car he hesitated for a moment, staring up at the darkened facade of the building. His eyes went unerringly to her windows, and in the bright streetlight she could see his strong white teeth flash in a grin. The same bright streetlight, she realized with belated mortification, that would doubtless illuminate her presence at the window, staring down at him like a lovestruck teenager. Quickly she let the curtain fall, moving away from the window as if she was burned.

The open door let in the only light in the darkened apartment. As she moved across to close and lock it, she reached a stray hand to brush her still trembling lips. Never in her life had she been kissed like that. Greg hadn't cared much for kisses, saving them for public occasions. Sin MacDonald had put more sexual energy, more sensuality and caring into that kiss than Greg had in the entire act of sex. If Sin's mouth was that devastating, what would the rest of him be like...?

"Stop it!" she cried out loud, trying to wipe such disturbingly erotic thoughts from her mind. But a short while later, as she lay sleepless in bed, the thoughts returned, the feel of his body against hers, the imprint of his questing mouth on her comparatively virginal lips. It was a long, long time before she slept. And when she finally did, her dreams took up where Sin had left off that evening.

Chapter Eight

The shrill, insistent ringing of the telephone broke through the mists of sleep. Cathy fought the nagging sound valiantly, and then was suddenly, completely awake. Her digital clock winked back at her—seven thirty. Immediately Cathy's thoughts flew to Sin, only to release them. Sin and Charles had left five days ago, were halfway to St. Alphonse by this time.

Struggling to sit up, she glared at the white princess phone by her bed.

"Hello!" Cathy snapped into the receiver, giving in to its demands at last.

"Cathy, thank God you decided to answer," Meg's voice came back over the line, blurred with worry. "I was afraid you might have unplugged the phone or something equally dismal."

"What's wrong?" Alarm shot through her body. "Has anything happened to the boat?" Horrifying visions of Sin MacDonald sinking beneath the angry Atlantic had her heart pounding and her palms sweating.

"The boat? Heavens, no. As far as I know, Sin and Charles are just fine. No, it's Pops. He's had another mild seizure."

Cathy didn't waste time with amenities. "Where is he?"

"At Littleton Hospital, but they're only going to keep him overnight. It's really not that bad, Cathy. They just want to watch him. Apparently whatever project he's been working on has been much too stressful. And I doubt Georgia or Travis has done anything to help matters. They tend to nag at him, and you know how Pops hates nagging."

"Have you seen him?" She hopped out of bed, the receiver tucked under her chin as she rummaged through her sparsely filled closets. "Can he have visitors? How does he look?"

"He looks fine." Meg chose to answer the last question. "A little tired, but not bad otherwise. He's resting right now, and the doctors think the fewer people here the better."

"But surely that doesn't go for me?"

"I'm afraid so." Meg's voice was uneasy with regret. "He really does need his rest, Cathy. I'm sure the doctors will let you in for a few minutes this evening. After all, you won't have another chance to see him for three weeks. Our plane leaves tomorrow evening and on this short notice I doubt we could change for a later flight."

"Don't be ridiculous, Meggie! I have no intention of going to the Caribbean when Pops is sick," Cathy shot back. "I wouldn't abe able to enjoy myself."

"You won't be able to enjoy yourself out at the house. Not with Travis breathing down your neck and Georgia set on an improving course. Pops will have a private duty nurse, and there won't be anything for you to do but sit in the middle of family squabbles. Besides, *I* need you, Cathy."

The thought of her resilient, self-sufficient sister needing her younger sibling was beyond comprehension. "Don't be silly—you're more than able to take care of yourself, and always have been. And besides, you've got Charles. Pops has no one that he can really trust.''

"How do you think he'll feel, with a tug of war going on around him? You and Travis can never be in the same room for more than five minutes without being at each other's throats. And Georgia's getting impossible—she must be going through the change of life.''

A reluctant laugh was drawn out of Cathy at the thought of her elegant sister allowing her body to betray her. "Don't be absurd—Georgia's only forty-three.''

"But with her disposition she's old before her time,'' Meg shot back. "And she's more than capable of keeping the house in running order while Father takes it easy. You have to come with me.''

"I can't.''

"But what will Charles and Sin think?'' Meg wailed. "They'll be expecting you to meet them there.''

"Then their expectations will have to be dashed,'' Cathy replied coolly. "I can't leave when Pops needs me.''

"Even though I might need you more?'' Meg's voice was distraught.

"Meg, I can't! You, of all people, should know I have to be with Pops when he needs me.''

BUT BRANDON WHITEHEART seemed to have little need of his youngest daughter after all. He greeted her from his hospital bed, looking deceptively robust despite the faint, grayish tinge around his mouth, with a gruff, "What's all this idiocy about not going to St. Alphonse with Meg?''

Unintimidated, Cathy shot back, "And what's all this nonsense about another heart seizure? I expected to see you flat on your back, looking at least slightly cowed, and instead you sit there looking hale and hearty. Faking again, Pops?'' she queried as she bent to kiss his cheek.

"You know me, daughter, always looking for attention," he replied gruffly, pleased by her concern. "My doctor tells me I've been working too hard. Too much stress, he called it. As if anyone could live without stress in this crazy world today."

"I'm sure he's right. Travis has been telling me you're up to your ears in intrigue—secret meetings, mysterious phone calls and the like. What's going on, Pops?"

"None of your business. Since when have I confided in a young thing like you about my personal affairs?"

"Don't try to look fierce with me, Pops," Cathy replied, unmoved. "Though I know from long experience that if you don't want to tell me anything I may as well not even bother asking. When are they going to let you out of here?"

"Tomorrow afternoon. And don't you bother about coming to see me—I know you'll be getting ready for your trip to the Caribbean."

"I would be if I had any intention of going," Cathy responded demurely. "As it is, I'll just move my things out to the house and await your return."

"No!" There was something curiously akin to panic in his husky voice. "I don't want you out there. I can't bear having everybody fussing over me."

Cathy's forest-green eyes met his calmly. "I can be just as stubborn as you, Pops, and if I've decided that I'm not going to St. Alphonse there's nothing you can do to make me go."

"You don't think so?" He met the challenge stonily. "We'll have to see about that. I'm not so sick that I can't still get exactly what I want. I have ways, daughter, that you wouldn't even begin to imagine."

"Really?" she shot back. "You should know by now that I'm more than a match for you."

"We'll see," he promised grimly. "We'll see."

THE NEXT DAY WAS FAR TOO busy to allow Cathy much time for second thoughts. There was no way in heaven she would spend the next few weeks at Whiteoaks unless armed with a large enough stack of novels to keep her safely occupied, away from the myriad delights of backbiting and gossip offered by her discontented siblings. Then she had to unpack her suitcases, dumping the warm-weather clothes and replacing them with jeans and sweaters to keep her warmer, although they were certain to turn Georgia pale with horror. At the last minute she packed Sin's Irish knit sweater. After all, he'd have no use for it down in the Caribbean, and he hadn't asked for it back.

For a moment she allowed herself to wonder whether he would regret that she hadn't come. Meg had maintained a stony silence since her final plea last evening, and Cathy couldn't decide whether she was relieved or disappointed. Heading down to St. Alphonse with Meg would have been playing with fire. Despite the fact that Sin MacDonald seemed scarcely interested in her, hadn't called her in the three days before he'd set sail, Cathy couldn't shake the remembrance of his devastating kiss in the hallway. If only she could decide what had provoked it. Was it a mere whim, a passing fancy, or a matter of habit? Maybe he was so unsure of his masculinity that he had to go about forcing it on any female who was less than interested.

Much as she wanted to believe that, it was too farfetched. Sin knew only too well that beneath her cool exterior she had been fascinated despite herself. And she had yet to meet anyone *less* unsure of his masculinity.

She couldn't think of Meg without a wave of guilt washing over her. It wasn't often that her sister asked anything of her, and to have to turn her down was painful beyond belief. But Cathy's family ties were strong, and her thwarted need to be needed overwhelming. As long as she felt her father truly needed her, and Meg only *wanted* her companionship, then there was no question where her duty lay.

Glancing at the clock by her bed, she allowed herself a noisy, far from satisfactory sigh. Six fifteen, and Meg's plane would be leaving in less than two hours. Knowing her sister's almost excessive punctuality, Cathy had little doubt that Meg would already be en route to Dulles Airport, without having placed a last minute call to her sister, to cajole, to threaten, or at least to let her know she was forgiven. It was unlike Meg to hold a grudge, but in this matter she had used every trick she could to change Cathy's mind. Cathy had remained adamant, but now, as she watched her clock and sighed, she wondered whether she had made the right decision.

The ringing of her doorbell interrupted her reveries, the buzz shrill and angry in the silent apartment. It was amazing, Cathy thought as she closed her suitcase and headed toward the door, how expressive a mechanical device such as a doorbell could be. There was little doubt that whoever was ringing was quite furiously angry, a supposition that was borne out as a loud pounding began.

"All right, all right, I'm coming," she shouted crossly as she fiddled with the various locks and bolts. Before undoing the final one she peered through the peephole, encountering a broad, blue-clad chest.

"If you don't open this door, Cathy," Sin MacDonald's voice came unbelievably from the other side, "I swear to God I will break it down."

Hesitating no longer, Cathy slid the final bolt on the door and opened it. Standing there in all his towering six foot four glory stood a deeply tanned, furiously angry Sin. The last few days on the deck of the *Tamlyn* had turned his golden skin mahogany color; his hair was streaked by the sun, and his eyes, blazing as they were with anger, looked more green than hazel. He was still dressed in sailing clothes—faded denims, sneakers and a collarless white knit shirt opened at his darkly tanned throat. His teak arms were crossed on his broad chest, and the expression on his face was enraged.

If this man had been handsome before, the added days in the sun had made him well-nigh irresistible, Cathy thought dazedly, backing away from his panther stalk. "I— I thought you were halfway to the Caribbean by now," she stammered, cursing herself for showing how unnerved she was.

"I was, and still would have been if it weren't for your self-centered foolishness," he shot back. "When Charles called Meg last night she couldn't stop crying. Of all the selfish, adolescent gestures...." He ran an exasperated hand through his thick brown curls. "Don't you ever think of anyone but yourself? Meg needs you right now."

"Meg has Charles," she snapped. "And I fail to see what business it is of yours, or what you're even doing here, for that matter."

"I had to fly up for an important meeting, and I promised Charles I'd get you on that plane if I had to drag you kicking and screaming through Dulles Airport. If it were up to me I wouldn't give a damn what you did, but Meg and Charles need you." His voice was grim. "Now are you going to go pack your bags or will I have to do it for you?"

"If you take one step toward my bedroom I'll scream," Cathy replied furiously. "How dare you come in here and tell me what to do? Meg knows perfectly well why I'm staying behind, why I can't leave."

"And why is that? Because you're afraid to be around me?" he taunted with uncomfortable accuracy.

"Of all the conceited—!" Words failed her. Determined

to calm herself, she took three deep, slow breaths. "I don't think we have anything more to say. I was in the midst of cooking dinner," she lied. "I'm going to continue, and when I come out I want you to be gone." Turning her tall, straight back on him with all the dignity she could muster, she strode into the kitchenette, praying, hoping, and dreading for the door to slam behind his retreating figure. Her nerves were strung taut as a wire, and when he came up behind her, his strong hands grabbing her arm and pulling her to face him with too much force, she grabbed the first thing she could to ward him off. Which happened to be a rather small, dull, and completely ineffective paring knife.

It happened so fast her mind blurred. One moment she had turned on him, brandishing the tiny knife, in the next he had spun her around and shoved her against the wall, her arm twisted behind her, the knife dropping from numb and nerveless fingers. For a moment she was dizzy from the pain, convinced her arm was about to be dislocated. And then she was released as Sin moved away, breathing rapidly in the tiny kitchen.

"That was a very stupid thing to do," he said shakily. Slowly she turned around to face him, her face paper white in the fluorescent light, her breath coming as rapidly as his.

"Yes," she agreed in a whisper. "It was." The look of the panther was back about him in full force, and for the first time Cathy was actually frightened of him. It wasn't so much the violence with which he subdued her pitiful attack. It was the speedy professionalism of it that filled her with horror and suspicions she couldn't even begin to name.

Sin's breathing slowed to a normal rate, and that dangerous look began to recede. He checked the thin gold watch on one tanned wrist, then met her wary gaze. "The plane leaves in an hour and a half. You have exactly fifteen minutes to get ready, or we'll leave without your luggage."

"I'm not going." She could have wished her voice was somewhat stronger than the reedy whisper, but she continued to glare at him defiantly.

Bending to pick up the knife and toss it back in the drawer, he took her arm in a gentle grip that belied the steel in his long fingers. "Haven't I made it perfectly clear?" he inquired silkily. "You're going to do what I say if I have to knock you unconscious and carry you aboard in a suitcase."

"You'd do just that, wouldn't you, if you thought you could get away with it?" she stormed. "You're nothing but a—a—" Various words flitted through her mind. What exactly was he? A terrorist, a gangster, a mercenary?

Apparently Sin was just as interested in her opinion. A faintly amused light entered his previously grim eyes. "I'm nothing but a what, Cathy?"

"A bully!" she said defiantly, her voice stronger.

The smile reached his mobile mouth beneath the mustache. "I can't argue with that. Are you going to pack?"

She tried once more. "Give me one reason why I should accompany you?" she demanded. "Just one."

"I can give you several. First, because I'm a hell of a lot bigger than you are and I'm not giving you any choice. Second, because despite your martyred air, you know perfectly well that your father doesn't even want you around. So all this noble self-sacrifice is a joke. If you're worried about me being around let me assure you that I'll keep as far away from you as you like." Why did he have to look so desperately handsome when he made *that* magnificent concession? "But most of all, your sister really needs you. She's desperately afraid she'll lose this baby like she lost the other one, even though her doctor says it's fine for her to travel. She needs another woman with her, one she can trust and confide her fears in, and…'' His voice trailed off before the combination of wrath and concern in her sea-green eyes.

''Someone she can confide in? It seems unlikely that I'm that person, since she didn't bother to confide the simple fact that she was pregnant again. How was I supposed to know why she needed me so desperately? Do you think I'm completely heartless? No, don't bother to answer that. Obviously you do.''

Concern wiped the last trace of anger from Sin's tanned face. ''I'm sure she meant to tell you before your father got sick. She only found out a couple of weeks ago, and she's been afraid to talk about it to anyone but Charles.''

''And you,'' Cathy added bitterly.

''And me,'' he agreed. ''Well, now that you know, what do you intend to do about it? Are you going to let her make the trip alone and worry herself sick?''

''Don't be absurd,'' she snapped. ''I'll be ready in ten minutes.''

''Make it five. I don't know about the traffic at this hour,'' he ordered lightly, taking her acquiescence quietly. If he'd gloated, Cathy thought, she would have gone for him again, no matter how efficiently he managed to repel attackers.

The ride to the airport was accomplished in silence. Sin kept his eyes straight ahead, all his concentration on rush hour traffic, while Cathy leaned back against the seat and closed her weary eyes, trying to remember what she had thrown in the one suitcase she'd had time to pack. For all she knew she'd end up in St. Alphonse with very outdated ski-wear, and she had the overbearing man next to her to thank for it. Stealing a glance at his uncompromising pro-file, she allowed herself a small sigh. No matter how she tried to hold on to it, the resentment had slipped away once she had committed herself to accompanying him. Perhaps he was right, that she had sought any excuse because she was afraid of him.

Well, she wouldn't have to be afraid of his attentions or that devastating light in his hazel eyes anymore. He had made it more than clear how little he thought of her. Self-centered, martyred, hadn't he called her? Well, perhaps he was right.

They had turned off into the airport complex when she finally found her voice and her courage. "Sin?" Her voice was slightly shaky. Sin kept his eyes straight ahead of him, his face expressionless. "I'm sorry." Her voice broke somewhat, and she cursed her vulnerability.

For a long moment it didn't appear that he heard her. And then, without taking his eyes off the road, his large strong hand reached out, covered hers, holding it in a gentle, reassuring grip that almost wiped away the last tiny bit of self-control she possessed.

For countless, breathless moments his hand held hers. In the darkness of the car her slender hand felt lost in his large, capable one, the calluses rough against her smooth skin, the strength and warmth flowing from his body to hers, calming and steadying her. It was like a tangible thing, the feeling flowing through them. And then, as they pulled up in front of the departure lounge, he gave her hand a brief, reassuring squeeze before releasing it to shift gears. And as Cathy turned her attention to the scurrying passengers, she couldn't shake the feeling that something incredibly intimate had just passed between the two of them. That knowledge was both enticing and threatening, and it was with a sense of relief that she watched as he stopped the car in front of a walkway outside the air terminal.

"Meg's got your ticket." When he spoke his voice was entirely normal, and Cathy took her cue from him.

"She knows I'm coming?" she inquired steadily.

A flash of white against the dark tan signaled his amusement. "She knows I don't take no for an answer," he replied. "I'll see you in St. Alphonse."

"Aren't you flying with us?" She was startled into asking, then cursed herself for betraying her interest.

He shook his head. "I have some business to attend to, and then I'm flying back down to meet Charles outside of Miami so we can sail the rest of the way. We should follow you by two or three days at the most."

"Don't hurry on my account," she snapped. "We'll be just fine without you."

He threw back his head and laughed out loud, a warm, lovely sound on the autumn air. "I have little doubt that you will be. Try not to pull a knife on anyone before I get there. I might have difficulty extricating you from the results of such a foolish move."

"Don't worry. I'll save my knives for you," she replied in dulcet tones as she climbed out of the car. He seemed to hesitate for a moment, then, giving her an abrupt nod, he put the BMW back into gear and drove off, leaving her standing there, staring after him a bit woefully, her small suitcase clasped in her hand. Then, squaring her shoulders, she turned her back on his retreating taillights and went in search of her sister and her enforced flight to St. Alphonse. And as she moved through the crowds she was humming to herself.

Chapter Nine

There was a silvery sliver of a moon, hanging lopsided in the clear night sky. As Cathy stepped off the plane onto the tarmac she stared up at the night, unable to shake a strange feeling of expectation. The air was velvety warm on her skin, a soft breeze blowing her hair away from her face, and she wanted to stretch out her arms and embrace the night and the sea breeze. Instead practicality reared its ugly head, and she turned back to her slightly green-tinged sister.

"That is the most horrifying landing I've ever had to sit through," Meg gasped as she reached the tarmac. "I thought for sure we were going to end up in the ocean."

"The landing strip was a little short," Cathy conceded, taking her sister's arm as she stumbled slightly. Cathy was feeling very protective now of her older sister; they had spent the whole flight talking about Meg's pregnancy and her fears. Cathy sent a silent thanks to Sin for having forced her hand; Meg *did* need her. "That's why we had to fly in on such a small airplane. But look on the bright side—at least we came in when it was dark. Can you imagine having to watch that landing in broad daylight?"

"Oh, please!" Meg moaned. "I may not leave St. Alphonse for nine months."

"Oh, taking off should be easier than landing," Cathy reassured her blithely. "And Charles will be with you to hold your hand." Unbidden the memory of Sin's hand capturing hers filled her mind and flooded her pale complexion. She averted her incriminating face. "Why don't you find a seat in the airport while I see to our luggage and a taxi? You look beat."

"I *am* tired," Meg admitted. "I don't seem to have much energy nowadays."

"That's perfectly normal for the first part of your pregnancy, isn't it?" Cathy couldn't keep the anxiety from her voice. "You've checked with the doctor and everything?"

"Perfectly normal," Meg reassured her with a smile. "Dr. Gibson says I'm strong as an ox and in perfect health."

"Well, stay that way, or you'll have me to answer to," Cathy threatened, her broad smile taking the sting out of her words. As she made her way to the baggage claim she reveled in her sense of well-being. It was a beautiful night, she would soon have a new niece or nephew, and she was away from Washington and the painful memories that she never could seem to shake. And whether Sin MacDonald disapproved of her or not, he was undoubtedly moved by her, and the thought of his incipient arrival caused a pleasant blend of apprehension and excitement somewhere in the vicinity of her stomach. And when she remembered the night he kissed her, the feelings made her dizzy.

IT HAD BEEN A TENSE FEW minutes after Sin left and Cathy searched the crowded airport terminal for her sister. She had finally caught up with her at the ticket counter. Meg had turned and met her searching gaze with a faint, guilty flush and a beseeching expression.

"You idiot," Cathy had announced succinctly, enveloping her petite elder sister in a tight hug. "Why in the world didn't you tell me?"

"I didn't want to force you to come," Meg mumbled, looking guilty.

"Oh, you didn't?" Cathy said lightly, skeptical. "Then why did you sic Sin MacDonald on me? He informed me he never takes no for an answer."

"I can believe that," Meg said soulfully. "Who in their right mind would want to tell him no? Anyway, I did try to tell you. Several times, in fact. But you were so caught up in Pops that you wouldn't listen." She gave her taller sister a tentative smile. "It's all right. I know how worried you were."

"I still should have given you a chance to explain," Cathy replied absently, her brain still distracted. "And I don't think you're right. Just because one wants to protect oneself doesn't mean one is out of one's mind."

"What?" Meg was justifiably mystified.

"You said no one in their right mind would say no to Sin MacDonald, and I said—"

"Oh, heavens, never mind that," Meg cut her off, the merest trace of mischief in her dark eyes. "You'll have more than enough chances to say no to him once we're in St. Alphonse. You can convince me of your sanity then. In the meantime, we're going to miss the plane if we don't hurry. Where's your luggage?"

"This is it." She had held up the small carry-on valise that contained heaven knew what.

"Is that all? I guess you'll have no choice but to live in your bathing suit."

"You won't like the one I brought. It's seen better days."

"Not that hideous flowering thing?" Meg cried. "The

one that looks like a two-hundred-pound matron should wear it?''

"The same. You can always pretend you don't know me.''

"Humph,'' Meg had replied unpromisingly. "I can see someone's got to take you in hand.''

"Did I ever tell you,'' Cathy retorted in dulcet tones, "how much like Georgia you are?''

"Bitch,'' Meg said genially. "Very well, I'll drop the subject. But not permanently, mind you.''

SHE WENT OVER THAT conversation in her mind as she unpacked her meager belongings. Moonlight was shining in the sliding glass door of her hotel room, silvering the sea-green carpet that was thick and soft beneath Cathy's bare feet. She was used to traveling first class, but she had to admit that Pirate's Cove Resort outclassed most of the other places she had stayed. The grounds had the absolute best landscaping, the kind that always looked natural and un-planned. The foyer of the hotel had a romantic, old-fashioned air to it. Any moment Cathy had expected to see Humphrey Bogart lounging near a potted palm, or Lauren Bacall slithering across the oriental carpet in clinging for-ties satin. And the rooms were absolute perfection.

Charles and Meg had a small, luxurious room on the second floor, with a king-size bed with brass headboard, silver-gray carpeting and a country French effect that was curiously suitable in that exotic climate. Their balcony looked out over the tiny cove from which the resort took its name, somewhat to the left of Cathy's view.

Her room was on the fourth floor, and nearly twice the size of her sister's. There were two king-size beds instead of one, with wicker headboards in place of brass and rough, natural Haitian cottons on the beds and at the sliding windows. The Gauguin above the love seat was, to Cathy's amazement, authentic, and she vowed to take a closer look at the Degas in Meg's room.

"There you are." Her sister emerged from the bathroom looking pale. "I guess that plane ride was a bit more than I could take."

"I think the taxi ride did more of a number on your stomach than the plane," Cathy observed. "Listen, Meg, I've been thinking. It's absurd that I should be in this big lovely room by myself while you and Charles share the smaller one. Why don't we trade? I can't imagine why the hotel arranged it this way. Are you sure they gave us the right rooms?"

Meg's pale face flushed with something curiously akin to guilt. "I'm sure. Charles and I had that exact room last time we were here, on our honeymoon. I had to request it several months ago to be certain of getting it. Pirate's Cove is *very* popular."

"But are you sure you wouldn't rather have this room?" Cathy persisted. "It's absolutely gigantic for one person, and..." Her voice trailed off before her sister's miserable expression. "It is for one person, isn't it, Meg?" she asked quietly.

Meg shook her dark head. "Apparently not. The hotel got the reservation mixed up and they've put you and"— here she gulped—"Sin in the same room."

"Well, they'll simply have to make other arrangements. I'm not sharing a room with a man I hardly know, and I'm sure it's the last thing Sin wants," Cathy announced with great assurance.

Meg shook her head. "I tried," she said in a voice that was little more than a whisper. "They've been booked solid for months. There's not a room or bed to spare, not here, and not on the whole island. I'm sorry."

"Sorry?" echoed Cathy. "You've got to be kidding! I can't share this room with Sin! He's going to think I planned it this way, I know he will. I can't bear it, Meg. I—"

"Calm down," Meg's voice, eminently practical, broke through the rising hysteria. "Sin has been treated to enough of your charm to know that such a setup would be the last thing on your mind. They won't be arriving for another couple of days. If there's not a last minute cancellation then you and I can share a room and Sin and Charles can have this one."

"Don't be ridiculous. This is your first vacation in ages—I'm certainly not about to break you up like we were at summer camp. I'll fly back."

"You'll do no such thing, Cathy! You promised me you'd keep me company, and I'm going to hold you to it. If worse comes to worst Sin can always sleep on the boat. He's done it before, and I'm sure he wouldn't mind."

"How can you be sure there's not another room on the island?" Cathy persisted. "I wouldn't mind staying at another resort. As a matter of fact, it might be easier. While Charles and Sin went off you could come over and—"

"You really are afraid of Sin, aren't you?" Meg mused. "He said you were, but I thought he was imagining things. Why don't you like him?"

"It's not that I don't like him," Cathy admitted, tossing herself down on the bed nearest the balcony and staring at the ceiling. "I'm just not ready to get involved with another man. The wounds still haven't healed from Greg."

An angry look closed down over Meg's usually cheerful face. "Some time," she said, "I would like to put out a contract on Greg Danville. The man should be shot."

"You know, Meg, I rarely even think of him anymore,"

Cathy admitted, surprised at her own truthfulness. "It's just the thought of anyone new that throws me into a panic."

"And what makes you think Sin is going to be that somebody new?"

Cathy rolled over to face her sister, pushing her silver-blond hair out of her shadowed face. "I don't know. It's probably just a combination of paranoia and wishful thinking," she admitted with a wry grin. "I'm too tired to sort it out tonight, anyway. I'm sure after a few days of having nothing to do but lie in the hot sun I'll be able to think of a way out of this mess. I could even stay on the boat while Sin enjoys this room and the nubile young ladies who will doubtless fall at his feet."

"What makes you think they'd fall at his feet?" Meg questioned curiously.

"Wouldn't you, if you were single?" Cathy shot back.

"You're single. I hadn't noticed you falling at his feet."

Cathy hesitated for a moment. "I hide it very well," she said quietly. "Now go to your room and get some sleep. I'm sure Junior doesn't appreciate these late hours you're keeping. It's no wonder your stomach is setting up a protest."

"But I want to continue this conversation," Meg insisted stubbornly. "Did you really just say—?"

"Forget what I said. Sometimes I talk too much. If I happened to notice that Sin MacDonald is an incredibly attractive man it's only because I'm not yet blind. That doesn't mean I'm going to jump into bed with him, it doesn't mean we have anything at all in common. It merely means—"

"Yes, I know," Meg interrupted, a twinkle in her dark eyes. "You can spare me all the rest of your denials and justifications. I'll just have to take you at your word."

"Do that." Cathy jumped from the bed, filled with sud-

den restless energy. "Do you want me to walk you back
to your room?"

"No, dear sister. You get a good night's sleep. We have
an arduous day ahead of us, lying in the sun and broiling
our delicate Whiteheart skin. I want you to be completely
rested. Sweet dreams."

There was a distinctly mischievous look on Meg's face
as she shut the door. Cathy strolled to the balcony and
stared out into the moon-shadowed stillness. The quiet
sound of the surf attempted to soothe her, but Cathy's nervous imagination was too strong for it. She knew only too
well what she'd dream of that night. The nightmares of
Greg seemed banished forever, to be replaced by the most
lasciviously sensual dreams, all involving Sinclair Mac-
Donald's six foot four body in erotic detail. Cathy wasn't
yet sure which dream was more upsetting.

Chapter Ten

Lazily Cathy squinted into the mid-afternoon sunlight, the large sunglasses cutting the glare only slightly. Something nice and tall and icily fruity would be divine at that moment. As she burrowed deeper into the soft white sand she considered raising her hand in a languid gesture she'd observed others using. Within seconds a white-coated bartender would appear at her side, eager to cater to her every whim. There was something so wickedly sybaritic about Pirate's Cove, the way it encouraged indolence and self-indulgence. A self-indulgence that was frankly sensual. No, it would do her good to get up from her comfortable position and go in search of a drink herself. Besides, she'd been lying in the hot tropical sun for almost two hours. By using all her latent caution she'd managed to acquire a light golden color all over her body. Any more than two hours and that honey gold would turn to lobster red.

Sighing, she rolled over and struggled to her feet, thrusting her arms into the terry cloth coverup. Not that the old-lady bathing suit showed much, she realized with a flash of humor. Nevertheless, she just couldn't bring herself to stride around the sand or the hotel lobby wearing so very little. The terry cloth robe reached to her ankles, although it was slit up the side, halfway up her slender thigh. She ought to get a needle and thread and sew the slit, she thought absently, heading toward the shade and a cool drink.

There were a good half dozen single men sitting around the bar. All in bathing suits, exposing indecent amounts of flesh, most of it sunburned and flabby. For a brief moment Cathy allowed herself to wonder what Sin would look like in one of those brief excuses for a swimsuit, and then she shook that disturbing thought from her brain. The luxurious atmosphere of Pirate's Cove really had addled her brain.

Six pairs of eyes watched her approach. Even the enveloping white terry cloth couldn't disguise her long, shapely limbs or natural grace, and the large sunglasses beneath the silvery blond hair added to the mystery. Cathy recognized those avid expressions, and without missing a beat she did a right turn and headed back to her hotel room.

Meg had returned to her room an hour ago in search of a mystery novel. When she hadn't returned Cathy had presumed one of the all too frequent bouts of nausea had hit her. She would check on Meg, then head back to her room and order a piña colada from room service. A nice, cool shower before dinner would add just the right fillip to an already perfect day. And it was likely to be her last one. Sin and Charles were due tomorrow. The very thought of all the garbled excuses and explanations she'd be forced to offer before Sin's amused eyes brought a chill to her sun-heated flesh.

There was no answer at Meg's door. A momentary panic filled her, before she remembered her spare key. Opening the door a crack, she peered into the deserted room. Meg's bathing suit lay in a wet pile on the floor, her sundress from the morning tossed across the bed, a towel in the chair. Ever the neatly organized person, Cathy thought with amusement as she picked up her sister's clothing and hung it away. She must have gone back out, and somewhere they'd missed each other. Well, they would doubtless meet up again before long. In the meantime her skin was beginning to feel a little clammy in the wet bathing suit, and she hurried on ahead to her room two flights up, eager to get into clean, dry clothes.

Her feminine intuition must have been at an all-time low. She had locked the door behind her and come halfway into the room before the sight of Sin MacDonald brought her up short. And what a sight.

He was standing in the middle of the bedroom, clad only in a pair of faded denims that hugged his lean hips and encased his long, long legs. The entire expanse of bronzed torso was bare, and Cathy found herself mesmerized by the broad, mahogany shoulders, and the triangle of golden curls that started at his chest and then trailed down in a line beneath the belt of his jeans. Abruptly Cathy jerked her eyes upward, to meet those warm hazel ones that had haunted her dreams. And the moment she had dreaded was upon her in full force. She could feel her face turn red with embarrassment.

"Hi, there," he greeted her composedly. "I wondered where you were. Meg and Charles went off into town— something to keep her mind off her stomach, she said. I was just coming to find you."

"Uh—er—" Completely tongue-tied, Cathy continued to stare miserably as Sin pulled a polo shirt over his head, emerging with his brown curls tousled.

"Have you been enjoying yourself?" he inquired solicitously, sitting down on a bed, *her* bed, and putting on a battered white sneaker. "You look a bit sunburned. How is the water?"

"It's not sunburn, it's embarrassment," she said frankly.

"And the water's beautiful. Look, we can't share this hotel room."

He said nothing, merely raising an eyebrow, as she stumbled onward. "It's not my fault, really," she stammered. "Somehow the hotel got the reservations mixed up, and they put us in together. And they insist that there's not another room here, or on the whole island, for that matter."

"That wouldn't surprise me," he said calmly. "Even though it's not quite peak season, St. Alphonse is very popular."

"But you have to believe me, I didn't plan this. I don't like it any better than you do, and I know it's bound to put a cramp in your style, but there's nothing we can do about it. Meg offered to share her room with me while you and Charles—"

"Out of the question," Sin interrupted, a trace of a smile beneath his mustache. "I've had to put up with Charles's snoring for the past eight days. I more than deserve a break. That is, presuming you don't snore?"

"Of course I don't!" she said, affronted. "But I can't ask you to share this room with me. It wouldn't be fair to you. I'll take a plane home as soon as I can make arrangements."

"You'll do no such thing." He was off the bed in one fluid leap and standing in front of her, towering over her, that lean, panther look about him once more. She could feel the body heat emanating from him. "I know it's not your fault that the hotel got our reservations mixed up, and that's no reason to cancel your plans. Meg still needs you; you must know that after spending the last few days with her, Charles is devoted, but men leave something to be desired in a delicate situation like this."

"I don't know why you keep assuming I'd know any

more about this than a man would," Cathy broke in irritably. "After all, I've never been pregnant."

"I hadn't thought you had," he said mildly. "Maybe I'm romantic enough to think the mystical bond between all women comes through at a time like this. Meg needs you as much as ever, and I think *you* need this vacation. Despite this latest tantrum, you look a lot more relaxed than you did in Washington. Listen, we're both adults, and this room is gigantic, with two nice, large beds. I don't see why we can't manage to share this room very comfortably."

"But what if—if you meet someone?" she stammered, flushing beneath his ironic gaze. "And you wanted to take her to your room? Wouldn't that present somewhat of a problem?"

"I didn't come down here to 'meet someone,'" he mocked her delicate phrasing. "One-night stands have never been my thing. And if I happen to get carried away by my passions I could always go to *her* hotel room. The same goes for you."

"No!" she refuted the idea instantly. "I have no intention of...of..." Her voice trailed away.

"Well, then, that's settled. We'll live a very peaceful, celibate life while we're here. I'll be an eagle scout and you can be a nun, and we should get along beautifully. Anyway, I intend to spend most of my nights at the casino. I only allow myself to gamble two weeks of the year, and this is one of my weeks." He sat back down to put on the other aging Adidas.

Cathy let out a small sigh of relief, trying to squash the last traces of uneasiness. It should all work out after all. "I didn't know eagle scouts gambled," she said pertly.

He grinned at her. "That's the girl," he approved, somewhat mysteriously. "And I didn't know nuns wore gold earrings."

"By the way, roomie," she said after a long moment. "That's my bed you're sitting on. I got first dibs."

"Would you care to toss for it?" he shot back.

"My, my, you are going to spend all your time gambling, aren't you?" she mocked. "No, I don't want to toss for it. Possession is nine tenths of the law, and that bed is mine."

"Yes'm. I'm going down for a drink. Would you care to accompany me?" He rose to his full height, stretching luxuriously. Every muscle seemed to ripple beneath his bronze skin, and Cathy felt a sinking feeling in the pit of her stomach.

"No, thank you. I've been out in the sun too long as it is. I'm going to take a shower and then a nap." She managed a convincing yawn, despite the fact that her earlier lassitude had vanished.

"See you, then." A moment later he was gone, the door closed and locked behind his tall, well-shaped back. There was one problem with this situation, Cathy thought belatedly. It was all very well and good to share a room platonically, when Sin MacDonald had as much interest in her as if she were his sister. And an older sister at that.

But it would have been a hell of a lot better if she were equally indifferent to him.

Chapter Eleven

A long, cold shower might not have worked wonders, but by the time Cathy had washed the salt out of her hair and dried it in the soft trade winds off her balcony, then dressed for dinner and downed an icy piña colada, she was feeling up to facing almost anything. If only, she thought mournfully, she had managed to pack some of her new clothes. The one dinner dress was a boring cotton A-line with a high neck, an outfit that Georgia had once stigmatized as worthy of a grandmother from Hartford. It wasn't quite that bad, Cathy thought, twirling in front of the full-length mirror and posing coquettishly. The predominant colors were a shell pink that gave her skin a special glow and a sea green that matched her eyes. If the cut did nothing for her figure, well, then, at least it didn't make her look dumpy. Just sort of boring. It was fortunate she wasn't out to entice any man, wasn't it? she demanded of her reflection. Her reflection responded with a frankly skeptical look.

The bathroom had almost broken her resolve. Sitting on the shelf beside her meager stash of makeup was a brown leather shaving bag. Hanging on the back of the door was a velour robe, still damp from his shower, and on top of the sink was his toothbrush. It was all so uncomfortably intimate, just as if they were an old married couple.

But damn it, if he could survive this situation unmoved, then she would hardly be the one to cry coward. She could be just as cool and remote as he could, she told herself. She could take things in her stride....

It was a decided shock to watch all six feet four of Sin MacDonald stride into her bedroom as if he belonged there. As indeed, he did, Cathy reminded herself from her perch by the window.

"You're already dressed," he observed as he crossed the room. "Good. It won't take me long to change. I told Meg and Charles we'd meet them down in the Windjammer Room." He already had his shirt halfway over his head. Cathy allowed herself one furtive glance at all that sun-bronzed flesh before returning her attention to the sea outside the balcony. Tossing the shirt on his bed, he stood there, his eyes alight with amusement. "I bet I'm supposed to change in the bathroom."

"You guessed right. I may as well go down." Cathy headed toward the door, only to have her bare upper arm caught in his iron grip. He held her gently, but there was steel in his fingers, and Cathy knew perfectly well she wouldn't escape until he was ready to let her go.

"You may as well wait for me," he corrected gently. "If you were rooming with another woman you'd wait, wouldn't you?"

Reluctantly she nodded. "I suppose I would."

"So, you see. You can be just as polite with me. Besides, I hate to enter a dining room alone. Makes me nervous," he announced cheerfully.

"Liar. Nothing short of a great white shark would make you nervous," Cathy joked back feebly.

Sin's grin broadened, and with his other hand he gave her a mock clip on the jaw. "That's it, kid. Don't let me browbeat you." He released her arm, grabbed a pile of clothes and disappeared into the bathroom, leaving Cathy to stare after him with a bemused smile on her face.

Dinner was a great deal more relaxed than Cathy had anticipated. For one thing, Sin seemed to go out of his way to be charming in an easy, comfortably nonthreatening manner. Not a glance, not an innuendo that wasn't entirely proper was cast in her direction. The subjects ranged from the lengthy trip down on *Tamlyn* and the various squalls the men had run into, to Meg's morning sickness to the myriad delights of the shopping on St. Alphonse.

"You mean to say you haven't been into town yet?" Sin demanded, astonished, as they were finishing their after-dinner coffee. "I don't believe it. I've never heard of a woman who passed by the chance to go shopping."

"Sexist," Cathy replied lazily. "Not every female jumps at the chance to spend a day wandering around crowded shops."

"Every one I've ever met has," he replied frankly. "You must be a very unnatural woman."

The lazy smile vanished from Cathy's face instantly as her blood seemed to freeze. *I won't make a scene,* she told herself. *I've already stormed out of a restaurant once, I won't allow myself to do it again. If I just take a few deep breaths it should be all right. One. Two. Three. There, I'm just fine.*

"Are you all right, Cathy?" Meg's worried voice broke through her abstraction. "You suddenly look quite pale."

Managing a light laugh, Cathy shook back her hair. "It's nothing. I'm just tired, I guess. Too much time in the hot sun. I don't think I'll come to the casino with you. Gambling doesn't hold that great an attraction for me anyway, and I'm quite exhausted."

"But it won't be any fun without you!" Meg pouted.

"Don't be silly. You'll have two handsome men at your

side—you'll be in seventh heaven,'' she replied weakly. ''And if you'll all excuse me, I think I'll go on up now.'' Before anyone could do more than protest she had slid from behind the table and headed for the door with as much speed as a graceful departure could manage.

The beach in front of the hotel was blessedly deserted. The moon was getting on toward full, shining down on the water and up the sand in a trail of moon fire. Slipping off her high-heeled sandals, Cathy moved down the beach by the water, the cool, wet sand beneath her bare feet soothing. It was very peaceful and quiet, with only the sound of the water lapping gently on the shore and the trade winds rustling the palm trees to keep her company. The lights of the hotel were hazy behind her, casting a soft glow over the beach. Heading for the farthest beach chair, she sat down on the wide chaise longue and pulled her knees up to her chest, wrapping her arms around them and hugging herself against the loneliness of the night.

His voice was gentle on the night breeze. ''May I sit with you?''

She had felt his presence from a long way off, though his approach across the sand had been silent. Somehow she had known Sin MacDonald wasn't going to leave her to her misery alone on the beach. She kept her eyes on the shimmering water in front of her, wondering what would happen if she refused to answer. Would he take matters into his own hands and sit beside her? And then she could fence with him and perhaps take his comfort without having to put forth anything of her own.

But Sin knew her too well. He continued to stand there, calmly, patiently, awaiting her answer.

''Yes, please,'' Cathy whispered in a very small voice. Without a word he settled down beside her, his long, tuxedo-clad legs stretched out in front of him, the moonlight shining on his white shirtfront. It had been a considerable surprise to Cathy—how well he looked in evening clothes. She had imagined with his broad shoulders and craggy good looks that he'd appear out of place in anything besides corduroys or faded denims. But he had confounded that vague hope, appearing in black tie and looking, if possible, even more devastating.

The chaise longue, built for two occupants, was suddenly far less roomy. Cathy could feel the length of his thigh pressed against her hip, and the intimacy of it sent her heart racing.

Sin, however, appeared unmoved by her proximity. He leaned back and stared up into the starry night sky. "There. That wasn't so hard, was it?" he inquired gently. He reached out and took her hand in his large, capable one, and immediately Cathy felt the same feelings of power and warmth flowing through her. It was a comfortable feeling.

"No," she agreed. "Not so hard." They sat in companionable silence, and the sound of their breathing mingled with the sea and the wind.

After a long moment he spoke. Cathy could feel his breath stirring her hair, knew his probing eyes were upon her. "What did he do to you, Cathy?" The question was gentle, and for the first time in four months Cathy knew she could answer.

"You don't really want to know." She hesitated with a trace of grimness. "It's not very pleasant."

"I hadn't imagined it would be. I wouldn't have asked if I didn't want to know," he replied. His hand reached up behind her neck and she felt herself being drawn inexorably closer, to rest against his broad shoulder. One arm was around her, holding her close to the sweet-smelling warmth of him, as the other kneaded the base of her neck with slow, sure strokes. "I don't think you're going to get over it until you tell someone. And I think your roommate is as good a person as any. I'm not likely to condemn you or pass judgment.''

Cathy could feel the tension drain out of her as she was enveloped in his calming strength. ''I condemn myself,'' she said in a soft, bitter voice. ''For being such a fool, and for going back for more. I should have known he was only interested in my money. There were enough signs of it. But I simply refused to see it.

''You see, I loved him. He was the only man I'd ever slept with, the only man I trusted enough to go to bed with. And he was so patient with my problems, and understanding, so how could I help but be grateful? He had to put up with so much from me, I felt I should...I should...'' Her voice strangled to a stop, and she shut her eyes. Sin's gentle hand kept stroking the back of her neck.

''What problems, Cathy?'' His voice was a deep, gentle rumble beneath her head. ''What did he have to put up with, that you should be so grateful?''

I don't believe I'm talking about this, Cathy thought mistily. *It's as if he has some magic power over me, enticing from me all my deepest secrets.* ''I...I don't enjoy having sex,'' she confessed finally.

''Says who?'' His arm tightened around her, and Cathy could feel a strange tremor pass over his body, followed by another. Almost like a smothered laugh. But he couldn't be laughing.

''Greg. You see, I didn't—didn't respond at first. It was a long time before I could even enjoy the thought of making love with him. And even when I could, it took me so long to warm up, to respond to him...that he'd be finished. He said he didn't mind, but I know he did. And he told me I was unnatural, once when we were having a fight.''

"No wonder you got upset at dinner. He sounds like a real charmer, your Greg. When did he break your nose?"

"I don't—don't remember," she said faintly.

"Why not?" He was inexorable. "It won't help you to block things out. The sooner you remember and face it, the sooner you'll get past it."

"It's not that—that I've forgotten the night," she confessed. "It's just that...it could have been one of several."

The soothing fingers stopped for a moment, then continued in their circular, gentling motion. "He used to hurt you a lot?" There was a grimness in his voice.

"Only when he got so frustrated with me that he couldn't help himself. He was always miserable afterward." Cathy's voice was urgent with the need to find excuses. "Or at least, that's what he said," she added lamely.

"And how long did you put up with this?"

She bit her lip, stealing a hesitant glance up at his moonlit profile. She could read no condemnation in his shadowed features, only dark concern. She took a deep breath. The worst was over anyway—there was little more he could find out to disgust him. "Until the day I came home and found him in bed with a strange woman. In my apartment. In my bed. I never went back. I found another place to live and bought all new things and I haven't seen him since. So I suppose I'm not the abjectly miserable coward I thought I was. I did finally say no."

There was a long silence. And then his hand slid around from behind her neck and caught the side of her face in a gentle hold. "Cathy," he said softly, "did it ever occur to you that Greg did more than abuse you physically? That his lies about your sexuality were just that, lies to cover up his own inadequacy." His eyes were glittering down into hers in the moonlit night, and there was sadness and a great tenderness in them.

"But then why am I still so frightened of men?" she cried. "And why do I freeze when anyone gets close? The very idea of making love makes me break out in a cold sweat, and…" Her voice trailed off before the faint smile that lit his eyes and played on his face.

"It'll pass," he said softly, and bent his head down to hers, blocking out the moonlight. His mouth caught hers, gently, sweetly, his lips teasing hers with little nibbles, refusing to let her escape, until she opened her mouth beneath his to let him deepen the kiss, his tongue searching every corner of her mouth until she was overcome by a longing she had never felt before, except for a few moments in her hallway two short weeks ago. He was seducing her with his mouth, enticing her, and all this time his hands stayed decorously in place, one cupping her face and the other her shoulders, holding her slender body close to his. When she started to slide her arms up around his neck, to pull him closer, he suddenly broke off the kiss.

"That's enough of that," he said with a slight shake in his voice. "I think I've proved my point."

"You kissed me to prove a point?" Cathy asked in a dangerously low voice, her heart still pounding.

His smile broadened. "I kissed you because you're a delectably beautiful, incredibly desirable woman with a wonderfully kissable mouth, and because we're both sitting here in the moonlight with the Caribbean all around us. *And* to prove a point." He kissed the tip of her nose lightly. "Does that mollify you?"

"I suppose so," she said, not quite certain if she was telling the truth. "Shouldn't you be heading toward the casino? Are Charles and Meg waiting for you?"

"I've been dismissed, eh?" he inquired with a trace of mockery. "Very well, Catherine Whiteheart." He rose in one fluid motion, pulling her to her feet beside him. "I'll take off, after I make sure you're headed back to the room. I don't know that it's perfectly safe for you to wander alone on the beach.''

''Especially with such a kissable mouth,'' she shot back.

''You've become a saucy wench all of a sudden,'' he laughed. ''I told Charles and Meg to go on ahead. I'll follow them as soon as I put you in the elevator.'' Taking her arm in his loose grip, he led her back along the beach to the hotel entrance. ''So tell me, Cathy.'' His voice was studiedly casual. ''Have you heard from Greg Danville since you found him with that woman?''

A sudden, unformed suspicion caught Cathy off guard. ''Why do you ask?''

''Just curious,'' he said easily. ''Did he accept his dismissal without a fight?''

She hesitated for only a moment. ''No, of course not. There was too much money at stake. He kept calling me, trying to explain. And when I refused to receive his phone calls or answer his letters, he sent me the most awful, vicious letter…telling me just how useless and pathetic I was. I burned it, of course.''

''Did you memorize it?'' His arm slid around her waist protectively.

She looked up at him, managing a wry smile. ''You know me surprisingly well for such a short time. I know parts of it by heart, quite against my will. Memory is a very stubborn thing on occasion.'' They were outside the elevator, the hallway deserted at that late hour.

''You need something new to replace those memories. New words, such as'' —his lips brushed her forehead— ''you have the eyes of a sea nymph, all blue and green mysterious depths. Or'' —and his lips brushed her cheekbone— ''your hair is like a curtain of silver rain. Or'' —

and his lips caught hers for a brief, lingering moment—
"or...but maybe I'll finish that later. Sweet dreams."

Before she realized what had happened he had placed
her in the elevator, smiling at her as the door slid shut, a
disturbingly tender, maddeningly possessive grin. And then
the elevator moved up, carrying her away from him.

Chapter Twelve

She slept very lightly that night, a part of her always alert for the sound of his footsteps, the opening of the door, the feel of his presence in the room. But time after time she'd sat up, wide awake, to find the bedroom still deserted. It was past four when she finally fell into a deep sleep, and when she first heard a quiet rustle of clothing her sleep-fogged mind insisted it was another false alarm. She turned over lazily, stretching her arms out into the darkness. And saw Sin towering above her dressed, no doubt in deference to her, in a brief pair of cotton running shorts. Her defenses momentarily abandoned, she smiled sleepily up at him.

"Are you still awake?" he demanded in mock severity. "It's five o'clock in the morning."

"Five?" she echoed hazily. "You must have had a good night."

He squatted down beside her bed, bringing his face level with hers. "I had an excellent night," he said lightly. "I won absurd amounts of money. The only way it would have been better was if you'd been there." He reached a tentative hand to brush a stray lock of hair out of her eyes, and she rubbed against him like a contented cat. He pulled his hand back as if burned. "Don't do that," he ordered sharply, not moving from his position by her bed.

Cathy burrowed deeper into the soft, comfortable bed, deciding not to question his irrational behavior. "Aren't you going to get in bed?" she questioned sleepily.

He seemed to hesitate for a moment. "Yes," he said, as Cathy felt the mattress sag beside her.

She sat bolt upright in outrage, but a moment later he had yanked her back against his body, fitting her against him, spoon-style, his long arms around her, holding her in place. "Go to sleep," he murmured in her hair.

"How dare you?" she fumed, fighting the delicious lassitude that washed over her. "You must be drunk. Get out of my bed!"

In answer he pulled her closer still into his warmth, and against her will she felt her body melt against his. He must have sensed her weakening, for he gave her a gentle, approving kiss on one bare shoulder. "That's right," he whispered, his breath hot on her skin. "All we're going to do is sleep together. For now." A moment later he was, to Cathy's mingled outrage, relief, and amazement, sound asleep.

She knew afterward that she was partly to blame for what happened. Still, he had insisted on getting in bed with her, against her vociferous protests. So was it her fault that hours later, half waking, half asleep, she had snuggled deeper against the long, warm body wrapped around her? That she had, sighing peacefully, turned in his arms and rested her sleepy head on his hair-roughened chest, had slid her arm around his lean waist and pressed her slender, unconsciously yearning body to his. One of his hands had moved down her back, to urge her slender hips against his, while the other gently cupped her chin. Opening her sleep-filled eyes, she gazed into Sin's probing hazel stare. He gave her more than enough time to turn her head, to elude his slowly descending mouth. Her arms tightened around his waist, her fingers splayed out across his leanly muscled back, as she willingly drew him closer. With a muffled groan his mouth met hers.

There was nothing tentative about this kiss, none of the reassuring gentleness of the night before. He kissed her long and deep and hard, with a kind of savage tenderness that was inexplicably arousing. Pressing her back into the soft mattress, he half covered her body with his, his long, bare legs holding the lower part of her body captive, as he plundered her willing mouth. His hand, which had been stroking her neck with long, sure strokes, moved down to caress one full, straining breast, his thumb rubbing gently until the tip hardened in fevered response beneath the silk gown. All her free will seemed drained away, leaving her a grateful captive of his knowing hands.

"Oh, God," he muttered against her soft mouth. "I want you so much." The hoarse words warmed her fluttering heart as she pressed closer.

Trailing fiery kisses down her jaw and the slender column of her neck, his mouth caught her breast, his tongue flicking over the rosy-tipped peak. Her nightgown had somehow gotten pushed down to her waist, leaving both breasts free for his sensuous attention, and as he moved his mouth to the other nipple she moaned deep in her throat. His hand trailed along one slender thigh, moving upward with inexorable determination, until he reached the innermost center of her being. She stiffened for a moment, then arched her back, reaching blindly for the waves of pleasure he was coaxing from her.

She slid her hands lower on his firm, muscled back, reaching the waistband of his shorts, and then stopped, confused. Greg hadn't liked her to be too bold—he wanted her lying there, passive, accepting his orders. She tried to blot out the memory, concentrating on Sin's wickedly clever hands and mouth, and a small moan of pleasure escaped from the back of her throat.

"That's it," he whispered against her silken skin. "Let me love you. I could make it so good for you, if you'll let me love you. Please, Cathy."

Through the sinking, swirling mass of sensations and emotions his enticing voice filtered through. "Let me love you," he'd said. Greg had another word for it. Many other words, all obscene, all necessary to him, the constant litany of filth as he hurt her....

"No!" she cried, yanking herself out of his arms and stumbling from the bed. "No, no, no, no!" she wept, shaking with panic and something else as she huddled on the floor, her arms wrapped around her shivering body. Pressing her face against the rough cotton bedspread, she sobbed in frustration and despair.

There was nothing but silence from the man in the bed for a long, breathless moment. Cathy was too miserable to look, certain he hated her, certain he was in a towering rage, so that when she felt gentle hands on her bare shoulder she flinched away in panic.

"I'm not going to hurt you, Cathy," Sin said gently, reaching down and lifting her shaking body into his arms, holding her against his broad, bare chest. Carefully skirting the bed, he moved to the upholstered love seat on the far side of the room, sitting down very carefully so as not to disturb his comforting hold on her.

Cathy knew she had no right to accept his comfort when she had led him on so shamelessly. "I'm so sorry," she wept into his warm, bare shoulder, awash with guilt, fear, and frustration. "But I can't. I just can't."

"Shhh," he soothed, stroking her back with long, sure, calming strokes. "I know you can't. Not right now. It's my fault anyway. I didn't mean to rush you—I thought I had more control. It's just that you're so damned enticing." He reached a hand under her chin, forcing her tear-drenched face up to meet his. "Come on, Cathy. It's not so bad, is it? The big bad wolf stopped in time, didn't he?" He smiled down at her, a dazzling smile that melted the last of her panic.

"I guess so," she whispered, managing a shaky smile in return. He stared at her for a long, breathless moment, and Cathy wondered if he was going to kiss her again. If he did, if he took her back to that bed, she didn't think she'd be able to stop him.

Gently but determinedly he put her to one side, standing up and stretching, moving quite definitely out of her reach. "Why don't you get a shower while I go for my run?" he suggested, grabbing a sweat shirt out of the closet. "I'll see you at breakfast." He disappeared into the bathroom and emerged with a towel.

Cathy watched him from her perch on the love seat. "How much do you usually run?" she questioned, striving to put a casual note in things.

"Usually a couple of miles. This morning, however, I think I'm going to need to run twice that much, and take a nice, long swim. I'm afraid I have a lot of excess energy to work off." He bent over her, brushing a stray lock of hair out of her troubled eyes. "See you at breakfast?" His voice and touch were incredibly gentle.

"I...I guess so."

"Good. I'll be hungry," he announced with a grin that bordered just slightly on a leer, and left. Cathy watched him go with mixed emotions, foremost among them regret. And a stubbornly optimistic sense of promise.

To CATHY'S IMMENSE RELIEF Meg and Charles joined them for breakfast. To have had to make casual conversation

facing Sin's tender, all too knowing eyes would have been
a bit more than she was up to just then. Fortunately, the
other three were all in excellent spirits, with more than
enough to chatter about. Cathy would have thought her abstraction had gone unnoticed, had it not been for the small
attentions Sin paid her. A soft touch on her arm as he offered her muffins, the reassuring momentary press of his
knee against hers, the lingering of his fingers as he handed
her the salt.

"I can't believe I feel so splendid!" Meg crowed. "It
must be having you here, darling," she purred to her husband. "This is the first morning I've had without nausea in
three weeks. I feel like doing something to celebrate. What
should we do, Cath?"

All Cathy's attention at that moment had been directed
to the strong backs of Sin's hands, the light splattering of
dark hairs, the thin, long fingers, strong knuckles and well-
shaped nails. Hands that had already discovered ways to
give her untold pleasures. Startled by Meg's question, she
looked up, to meet Sin's knowing gaze. She blushed, a
deep, fiery red. "I—I don't know. Whatever you'd like to
do," she said lamely.

"I know what you can do," Sin broke in, the light in
his eyes telling Cathy he had read her mind. "You can go
shopping. There are a few things I want to do in town, and
I would be more than happy to take you in. We can spend
the morning on our various errands and get back here in
time for lunch and an afternoon swim. How does that
sound?"

"Perfectly divine," Meg breathed. "Don't you think so,
Cathy?"

"Fine. But I don't really have anything I need to buy,"
she murmured.

"Now there I take issue with you." Sin's eyes were

laughing. "What was that pink and green flowered monstrosity on the back of the bathroom door?"

Cathy's blush deepened. Sin's tone and words sounded so terribly connubial. "That's my bathing suit," she replied with a trace of defiance.

"I was afraid of that," he sighed. "Your only one, no doubt."

"One is sufficient," she replied haughtily.

Sin ignored her, turning to an amused Meg. "I can rely on you to see that she buys something more suitable, can't I, Meg? Suitably scant, I mean."

"You can, indeed," her traitorous sister agreed enthusiastically. "I've always told her it's a damn shame to have her lovely body and then cover it with old women's clothing."

"Am I to be consulted in this?" Cathy asked with dangerous calm.

"Oh, by all means," Sin said airily. "I'm sure Meg will let you have your choice, as long as you restrain your Quakerish tendencies. After all, this entire hotel thinks you're my woman, and I have *some* standards to maintain."

"You—you—" Words of outrage failed her. She had to content herself with a murderous glare that Sin met with a bland smile. A sudden, wicked plan began to form in her mind. She would buy a new bathing suit if he insisted. The largest, most old-fashioned, enveloping old lady's swimsuit she could find. Let him put *that* in his pipe and smoke it, she thought with satisfaction.

That plan, however, was much easier to envision than to carry out. The small, elegant boutiques that were scattered about St. Alphonse's main city of Verlage had nothing that would cater to senior citizens. The most enveloping of swimsuits were demure two-piece ensembles that still showed an alarming expanse of skin.

"Foiled again, eh, sis?" Meg questioned with amusement, having been the recipient of Cathy's evil plan. "Serves you right. Of course, you can always reverse your plan."

Cathy was in the midst of perusing an unbelievably scanty sea-green bikini, wondering who in the world would have the nerve to wear it. Although the scraps of material looked better suited to a precocious ten-year-old, the tag and label insisted it was her size. "How would I do that?" she inquired absently, holding the suit up to the light.

"You could buy the skimpiest, slinkiest swimsuit available. Something so outrageous Sin would be sorry he ever opened his mouth. The one you're holding looks like a good candidate," Meg observed.

"Oh, heavens, I couldn't do that," Cathy laughed, quickly shoving the suit back on the rack with a clatter of plastic hangers.

"And why not? You haven't got an ounce of extra flesh on your body. There's no reason why you, of all people, couldn't get away with something as skimpy as that."

Cathy's eyes strayed back to the rack. "He would be flabbergasted," she admitted with a wicked chuckle.

"He'd be speechless," Meg encouraged her. "And that's something I'd like to see. Sin always seems in complete control."

Not always, Cathy thought silently, retrieving the suit. "Maybe I'll try it on," she said aloud.

"Don't do that. If you try it on you might chicken out. You're a perfect size eight; you know that as well as I do. Just ask the lady to wrap it for you. The color matches your eyes perfectly."

On the verge of backing down, Cathy hesitated, torn. "It does?"

"Absolutely. Look, let me buy it for you, as a present," Meg urged.

"Nope. I'll buy it myself," she said with sudden decisiveness. "After all, it's time I learned to live dangerously. I…" Her voice trailed off as she headed toward the smiling saleslady. Her eye had caught the dress behind her. "Oh, my heavens."

"I see what you mean." Meg's voice was awed. "Who in the world would have the nerve to wear a dress like that? Not that it isn't beautiful. But gracious, it would cling to every single line and curve…and that hot pink! I've never seen such a seductive dress in my entire life." She reached out and touched a silky fold reverently, sighing loudly. "That's the sort of dress I've always wished I could wear. But I just wouldn't have the nerve." She eyed her sister's meditative expression with a secret smile, then added to the effect. "I couldn't get away with it, though. I haven't got the frontage to fill out that décolletage, and there doesn't seem to be any back to the thing at all. Why, it would fall right off me. But God, what a dress!"

"What size is it?" Cathy asked in a curiously resigned tone.

"Size eight, mademoiselle." The saleslady had rushed over, quite willing to be of service in the matter of the most expensive dress in the shop. "Would mademoiselle care to try it on?"

"Oh, why don't you?" Meg encouraged her eagerly. "Just for fun! No one will see you—it would be such a lark. How often does one come across a dress like that in one's life? It looks as if it was designed with your body in mind."

"No, I won't try it on," Cathy said with unshakable certainty, and Meg's and the saleslady's faces fell. She turned to her sister with a mischievous smile. "After all, as you just said, I'm a perfect size eight. If you would just wrap that with the bathing suit?'' she asked the beaming shopkeeper.

By the time the two sisters met up with Sin and Charles they were absolutely laden down with packages, all containing clothes for Cathy. Silk blouses in jade green, hot pink, and deep plum, lean-fitting linen pants, evening sandals with tiny gold straps, and several pairs of quite the shortest shorts Cathy had ever seen filled their packages. Sin watched their approach with amusement, taking the bulk of their purchases in his arms.

''You didn't buy anything after all?'' Meg questioned as they headed toward the Land Rover with its striped awning. ''I thought you had urgent shopping to do.''

''Good things come in small packages, nosy,'' he replied mysteriously, and refused to say anything more.

It took her a surprisingly long time to put all her clothes away after the light, sinfully delicious lunch served at Pirate's Cove. Silky little wisps of underwear replaced her serviceable cotton briefs and plain white bras; the pink dress she hid in the back of her closet. Her old bathing suit had mysteriously disappeared, thanks, no doubt, to Sin's meddling. One look at her body in the new, sea-green bikini was enough to send her rummaging through every corner of the spacious room. It was well and truly gone.

''I can't be seen in public in this,'' she gasped aloud to the mirror, tugging uselessly at the thin fabric. Her high, round breasts seemed about to spill from the thin, banded top, and the bottom was cut high on the thigh, slashed low across the hipbones, and just managed to cover her firm, rounded buttocks. If she didn't die of embarrassment she would undoubtedly strangle on it as it came off when she tried to swim. Of all the stupid, frivolous ideas. The color may have matched her eyes, but who was going to look at her eyes when everything else under the sun was exposed? She let out a helpless little groan, shaking her long blond hair down about her shoulders in a vain effort to provide more covering. The sun-tipped strands stopped several inches short of the rounded curve of her breast.

"I wondered what was keeping you," Sin's lazy voice came from the open door. "I was afraid you might have—" His voice trailed off as his wide eyes swept over the full, scantily clad length of her. Straightening from his lounging position in the doorway, he moved into the room, shutting the door behind him with an ominous little click. His face was completely unreadable in the early afternoon sunlight streaming in from the sliding glass door. Very slowly he walked all the way around her, his eyes raking her body in a fashion that in anyone else would have been incredibly offensive. With Sin, however, the effect made her tremble slightly with confused longing.

When he had finished his circuit and his eyes finally lifted to meet hers, there was an unmistakable light in their hazel depths, and the dimple in his right cheek was in full evidence.

"Are you trying to give me high blood pressure?" he asked mildly enough.

"I've seen people wearing less on the beach," she said in self-defense, not sure whether she actually had.

"At this particular moment I'm not interested in what other people are wearing," he said huskily, moving away from her and heading toward his dresser. "I guess my shopping was successful after all. I bought you a present." His eyes flickered briefly over her body, then back to her face again. "Something to go with your new image."

He tossed her a small, velvet jeweler's box. Startled, she caught it with one hand. "Don't look so frightened." He grinned suddenly. "It's not an engagement ring."

"I hadn't thought it was," she said with chilly dignity, wondering for not the first time how he managed to read her mind. Quickly she snapped open the lid. Nestled in the black velvet was a long, thin, gold chain, with a small, clear emerald. "What—what is it?"

He moved up close to her, his lean, strong body dwarfing hers, and took the box out of nerveless fingers. "It's a chain for your waist. It's supposed to be worn with a bikini." Suiting action to words, he unclasped the tiny clasp and drew it around her waist, his arms snaking around her. She drew in her breath at the potent touch of his hands on her bare flesh, and he laughed. "You don't need to hold your breath—it's more than big enough," he said casually, reclasping it and letting it fall. It rested just above her hipbones, the emerald winking up at her.

"Sin," she breathed, mesmerized. "I can't accept it."

"Why not?" He stepped back to admire the effect.

"Well, it's too…expensive."

"I can afford it."

"But it's too…intimate."

His grin broadened, threatening to split his tanned face. "Nothing's as intimate as that damned bathing suit," he said. "And I thought you'd learned that I don't take no for an answer."

"You did this morning," she said breathlessly, then felt herself blushing.

He surveyed her for a moment, and then, before she could divine his intention, he moved toward her, put a hand behind her neck and kissed her briefly and quite, quite thoroughly. Her mouth was seared by the contact, but before she had a chance to respond he moved away. "Now go on out and get some sun on that magnificent body of yours," he ordered lightly. "I'll be along shortly."

Cathy hesitated, still bemused by his kiss. He took a

mock threatening step toward her. "Unless you'd rather spend the afternoon up here with me...?"

Grabbing her terry cloth coverup, far better suited to her new bikini than to her grandmother-suit, she ran.

Chapter Thirteen

It had been an exhilarating afternoon, Cathy decided as she surveyed her reflection in the bathroom mirror still clouded with steam from her shower. A perfect, golden glowing moment in time, when all that seemed to exist were the sea and the sun and the sand. And Sin's long, leanly muscled body lying by her side, the teak-bronzed flesh glistening in the hot sun. If she hadn't known better she would have thought he did it on purpose. That brief excuse for a swim-suit that stretched across his slim hips left little to Cathy's imagination, an imagination already overactive. The laughing light in his hazel eyes as he caught her hand and pulled her after him into the warm, salty water was far too knowing, but for some reason Cathy no longer minded. It was enough to be with him, laughing in the sunlight, her body drifting against his in the turquoise sea, collapsing exhausted side by side, arms brushing, legs touching, hands reaching, innocently, knowingly.

Sin had sat up abruptly, shaking the water out of his brown curls as he rested his arms on his drawn-up knees. He turned his head to meet her questioning, lazy glance as she lay there in the sand. Reaching out one tanned hand, he gently brushed the sand from her flat stomach, then smiled as she tautened her muscles in an involuntary reaction to his intimate touch. His eyes met her troubled green ones, and she had the uncanny feeling that he knew everything that was going through her head that afternoon. Knew it, and was amused by it. And yet the smile on his face was so tender as he leaned over her that she couldn't summon forth her usual outrage. Or even any fear, she thought with belated wonder. Sometime during the last twenty-four hours, some way, she had given her trust to him. And she knew with a sudden, blinding clarity that if he climbed into her bed that night she wouldn't stop him.

She took more than her usual care dressing that evening. Sin was sitting on the balcony, already in the elegant black dinner clothes that suited him so well, a German beer in one hand and a paperback thriller in the other. He'd barely looked up when she'd disappeared into the bathroom, content with lazily telling her to take her time. Such a domestic scene still unnerved her, filling her with all sorts of strange emotions, foremost among them a wistful longing for what was doubtless out of reach.

"Ridiculous," she told herself out loud, brushing a gold-tinted blusher across her high cheekbones. Sin MacDonald was hardly the marrying sort, and besides, she had only met him a couple of weeks ago. With an artfulness that she seldom employed she creamed her eyelids with a bronze-gold, then darkened her lashes with a practiced hand. Pursing her warm red mouth, she eyed her reflection warily. With the gold-tinted makeup she looked vaguely exotic, and her silver-blond hair tumbled down her back in artful waves that owed more to the moist sea air than to a hairdresser's art. Taking a few steps back, she stared at the pink silk dress. It clung to every soft, ripe curve of her body, a body, she told herself firmly, that Sin had already seen far too much of in the bathing suit. At least this covered her, although the front hugged her round breasts beneath the décolleté and the back was nonexistent. It certainly had to be considered a bit more demure than the bikini, although looking at it Cathy was assailed with sudden doubts. Perhaps the cotton dress…

"*Courage, ma vieille,*" she whispered stoutly. There was nothing wrong with her appearance. As a matter of fact, she looked almost beautiful that night. Her sea-green eyes glowed with anticipation, her mouth was tremulous with inner excitement. "You'll do," she whispered.

"Who are you talking to?" Sin's voice queried amiably through the door. "I thought you were alone in there."

Bracing herself, she opened the door. "I was talking to my former self," she said bravely, strolling to her closet with a casualness that took her a huge effort to maintain. Her thin, gold-strapped sandals were on the floor. They would have made her tower over Greg, but Sin would need more than a three-inch heel on his lady to feel dwarfed. *His lady,* she thought wistfully, sitting down on the bed nearest her and slipping on a sandal.

The thick silence penetrated her determined air of calm, and she looked up suddenly, still holding the second sandal. Sin was standing a few feet away, watching her with a completely unreadable expression on his face, his eyes hooded in the twilight evening.

"Is something wrong?" she inquired anxiously, and discovered that her heart was pounding. He took a slow, menacing step toward her, followed by another, and the look of the panther was about him again. He stopped when he reached the bed, and it took all Cathy's willpower not to cower back against the pillows. Determinedly she stiffened her spine, and looked way, way up into his enigmatic face.

"That dress," he said finally, "is outrageous." His voice was low and husky, setting her nerve ends to trembling.

"Outrageous?" she echoed, wondering if she should feel flattered or miffed.

"Outrageous," he confirmed. "You better hope your father never gets a look at it—he'd lock you away from all us voracious males. What do you call that color? Pink?"

She licked her suddenly dry lips. "I guess so." She still couldn't quite read his reaction.

"I've read there's a certain shade of pink that's supposed to be soothing to the savage breast. They've been experimenting with it in mental hospitals and jails, trying to calm dangerous inmates. I can tell you right now that isn't the shade of pink they're using," he growled. Suddenly he leaned over her, one long arm on either side of her, his face close enough to hers that she could feel his warm breath on her face, see the light in his eyes that removed the last trace of self-doubt.

"That color," he continued huskily, "makes me very, very dangerous. And you're sitting on my bed." Slowly, inexorably, his mouth descended, giving her more than enough time to escape from its overwhelming claim on her senses. But she had no intention of escaping. At the warm, wet taste of him her last defense crumbled, and she opened her mouth willingly to his probing tongue, her hands reaching up to clutch his shoulders in a convulsive grip. Slowly she felt herself lowered onto the bed as his body followed her down, his hands trailing up her silken body to catch her full, straining breasts. "No bra," he murmured against her mouth. "You shouldn't be allowed out." His mouth left a slow, deliberate trail of kisses down her neck as he rolled over and covered her slight body with his, one leg between hers as he continued his leisurely exploration of her soft, warm body. The peaks of her nipples had hardened beneath his practiced touch and with aching deliberation he let one strong hand trail down her midriff, across her abdomen and then below, his long fingers spread out over the pulsing warmth of her, his fingertips caressing lightly, teasingly through the clinging material, until she arched her back, pressing her hips against his hand in mute supplication.

Her hands slid from his shoulders to his chest, to meet the frustrating expanse of cloth that separated his body from hers. She wanted to feel his warm, heated flesh beneath her hands, let her fingers trail through the short curls of hair. She reached up to fumble with his tie when one hand reached up and caught her wrists, yanking them over her head and holding them there as he moved to cover her body completely with his. The clothes between them only seemed to heighten the sensations.

"Don't mess with the tie," he said lightly, his eyes smiling down into hers. "I spent almost half an hour getting the damned thing right, and I'm not about to let you undo all that hard work."

Cathy's breath was coming in short, heavy gasps as she looked up at him. Never had she felt more vulnerable, her body at his command, completely open to him as he continued to hold her arms above her head in a grip that for all its gentleness would allow no escape until he was good and ready. If it weren't for his slightly quickened breathing and the feel of his desire against her hips she would have thought this was no more than a game to him. But instinct, long dormant, told her this battle was just as important to him as it was to her.

"Sin," she began hesitantly, only to have her mouth stopped by the gentle pressure of his lips. Before she could move to deepen the kiss he had pulled away, getting to his feet with one lithe move and pulling her with him. She swayed for a moment, then caught herself.

"You'd better keep off the bed when you wear that dress," he said briefly, turning his back on her and running a cursory hand through his rumpled hair. "We're running late." He moved to stand by the door, ill-concealed impatience in his large frame.

Cathy started toward him, then realized belatedly that she still had only one sandal on. "You go ahead," she said. "I have to find my other shoe." It was nowhere in sight. Getting to her knees on the thick shag carpet, she peered under the bed, keeping her face averted. Confusion and hurt were warring with the remnants of warmth that lingered from his embrace.

"Where did you last have it?" He sounded subdued, preoccupied. Keeping her back to him, Cathy sat back on her knees, staring about her with unseeing eyes. "Don't worry about me," she said in a muffled voice. "If I can't find it I'll wear something else. Go on ahead," she repeated, her voice catching a tiny bit. She could only hope he didn't notice.

Two strong hands reached beneath her elbows and pulled her to her feet before turning her unwilling body to face his stern regard. "Cathy," he said wearily, "we're only playing this by your rules. There was nothing I wanted more than to stay in that bed with you just now. But you aren't ready, are you?" She refused to answer, staring mutely at her feet, and he gave her a little shake. "Are you?" he repeated, his fingers tightening on her soft, golden arms.

"No," she said, meeting his gaze fearlessly, wondering if she lied. The scent of him was a powerful aphrodisiac, that mixture of aftershave and sun-heated skin, brought out by the sensual exertion of the last few minutes.

His smile was just cynical enough to make her uncomfortable. "Your shoe is over by the balcony," he said coolly, releasing her arms and moving away.

She slipped it on as quickly as she could, not daring to

stop by the mirror to check her appearance. She must look
a wreck, she thought with a sigh as she preceded him into
the hallway.

They rode down in the elevator in silence, Sin's expression abstracted. "Wait here for a moment," he ordered
when they reached the lobby. He disappeared and Cathy
wondered for a miserable moment if he'd abandoned her.
It was probably no more than she deserved, after having
led him on like that. A tease, that was what she was. Just
a cheap, selfish little tease. She wouldn't blame Sin if he
never wanted to see her again. He was probably trying one
more time to find another vacancy on the tiny island of St.
Alphonse rather than have to spend another night with—

Long, cool fingers pressed against her hot skin, lifting
the silk curtain of her hair. "Hold still," Sin's voice murmured as she jumped nervously. The strong, intoxicating
scent of gardenia assailed her nostrils, and she watched
with mingled wonder and suspicion as Sin fastened the
flower above her ear with deft fingers.

"A peace offering," he said lightly as he took her arm.
"I don't usually sulk."

"Sin, I'm sorry..."

"Hush. You don't need to apologize," he murmured.
"We can talk about it later."

"Good heavens, Cathy!" Charles greeted her approach
with flattering amazement. "I always said you were beautiful, but that dress is a knockout."

"It certainly is," Meg endorsed her husband's approval.
"It looks even better on than I would have expected. And
that flower is just the perfect touch."

Cathy slid into the chair Sin was holding for her, her hair
brushing his fingertips. "Meg helped me pick it out."

"Meg Whiteheart Shannon, I should have known you'd

be to blame," Sin mocked. "Always leading innocents astray."

"But you've got the flower wrong," Charles said with a sudden frown. "Didn't Sin tell you? You're supposed to wear it behind your right ear. If you wear it behind the left ear it means you're already taken. Engaged, married, in love, whatever."

Cathy turned to meet Sin's bland expression. He had always struck her as a man who left little to chance. "You should have told me," she said accusingly. She reached up to move it, but his hand forestalled her, the hard fingers cool on her heated flesh.

"Leave it."

Her eyes met his for a long, startled moment. And then she dropped her hand.

Chapter Fourteen

The music was soft and seductive, flowing gently around them. It was all Cathy could do to keep from swaying slightly in time with the hypnotizing rhythm. Determinedly she stared into her champagne glass, swirling the dregs, and keeping her attention as far from the dance floor as she could. Never did she think she would be jealous of Meg, but there she was, looking up into Sin's interested gaze, her still slender body cradled tenderly in his strong arms. Where she had absolutely no business being, Cathy thought, slopping a bit of champagne onto the tablecloth.

"Are you sure you don't want to dance?" Charles queried with a trace of anxiety.

"Not right now," she replied a trifle shortly, allowing herself a brief, painful glance in her sister's direction. Sin chose that moment to laugh uproariously at one of Meg's witticisms, and the unrestrained amusement was like a sharp pinprick to Cathy's already exacerbated temper.

"I can't imagine why Sin hasn't asked you to dance yet," Charles observed with tactless curiosity. "It's not like him to be remiss in these things."

"I think the problem, Charles," Cathy explained with deceptive calm, "is that you're assuming Sin and I are a couple. We happen to be sharing a room, but we might as well be strangers for all that. I assure you, our relationship is strictly platonic."

"Is that why Sin had your lipstick on his mouth?" her brother-in-law queried in dulcet tones. "I know you too well, Cath."

The music ended at that moment, before Cathy could come up with a suitable retort. And then Sin was towering over her, a bronzed hand on her arm.

She turned and gave him her frostiest glance. "Yes?"

He was unabashed. "Are you ready to dance?" he inquired evenly.

"I don't really think so," she drawled. Paying absolutely no attention to her demurral, the hand tightened, she was pulled unceremoniously to her feet, and moments later she was out on the dance floor, securely captured in his arms. One hand had captured hers, the other pressed against her waist, pushing her gently against his lean male strength.

"Now who's sulking?" He pulled her a tiny bit closer, with bare inches between their bodies.

"I am not sulking," she said defiantly. "I'm merely a little—a little…"

"Irritated?" he supplied sweetly.

She glared up at him. "That's as good a word as any," she shot back. "You've danced three times with Meg, and now, finally, you deign to ask me to dance, never for a moment considering that I may have lost interest—"

"I was waiting for a nice, slow one," he broke in, pulling her the rest of the way into his arms and pressing her head against his shoulder. She knew she should struggle, try to move away, but she did seem to fit so well.

"Why the sigh?" he inquired, his voice rumbling pleasantly beneath her ear.

"You're a bit too much for me," she confessed, lulled by the intoxicating warmth of his body and the slow, sensuous strains of the music. The hand at her back was caressing her lightly as it pressed her closer to his hips, and little tremors were dancing up and down her narrow and mostly exposed spine. The hand stopped for a moment, then moved onward.

"You forgot to take off the chain," he said lightly.

Cathy found she could be grateful to the dim light and her position against his shoulder. There was no way he could see the telltale color flooding her face. "I didn't want to," she whispered, and had the dubious satisfaction of having his arms tighten around her.

"Sin, darling!" A shrill, affected voice broke through her reverie, and she jerked herself away as if burned, to come face to face with a tiny, vivacious brunette. One red-tipped hand was on Sin's black dinner jacket, and the look on her sophisticated face was, to Cathy's mind, frankly acquisitive. "I couldn't believe it was really you! When I've been searching high and low for weeks now, all over Washington and New York. I never for a moment thought I'd find you here in St. Alphonse. Isn't this rather far afield for you, darling? I mean, it isn't your vacation, is it? You're always so terribly frugal with your vacations, when I don't see why you need to be. After all, what's the good of owning your own company if you can't do as you please?" Her light laugh rang out. By this time the music had stopped, the band had departed the bandstand for a short break, and Cathy longed more than anything to escape. But Sin's hand was still firm on her arm, not about to let her go.

"Hello, Joyce," he greeted her evenly when the flow of words had come to a temporary halt. "I hadn't expected to see you here."

"Well, of course you didn't, darling. And I scarcely expected to find you here either, though I remember the time we came down together...." She let the phrase trail meaningfully, more than aware of the effect her supposedly art-less conversation was having on the female half of her au-dience. Her luminous brown eyes swept over Cathy's figure, a flash of envy for the dress clouding them momen-tarily. And then her red lips curved in a bright smile. "And who's your little friend, darling? I hadn't heard you were seeing someone new. Unless, of course, she's involved in—"

To Cathy's complete amazement Sin dropped his grip on her arm, taking Joyce's slightly overripe one instead. "Joyce VanDeiler, this is Cathy. I'll see you back at the table." With that hasty dismissal he turned and positively rushed the petite beauty toward the opposite end of the room. Cathy stared after them in mingled rage, hurt, and sheer surprise, before making her solitary way back to the table and Meg's and Charles's interested faces.

"Who was the femme fatale?" Charles inquired. "I don't think I know her."

"Her name is Joyce VanDeiler," Cathy offered in neu-tral tones as she took her seat. "Apparently she's an old flame."

"Oh, yes, I remember Sin mentioning her." Charles nod-ded, looking after the departing couple with more interest. Cathy followed his gaze long enough to see the intent con-versation, complete with soulful eye-flutterings from the black widow. Sin's back was to her, his head bent in an attitude of rapt attention. Cathy looked away.

"Well, I'm glad he's found someone," she managed to remark in a suitably languid tone. "I was afraid he'd feel bound to hang around with me, which, as you can imagine, is the last thing I wanted." Picking up her refilled cham-pagne glass, she allowed herself another look over the rim of the glass. Just in time to see Joyce VanDeiler reach way up and wrap her black-clad arms around Sin's bent neck and press those bright red lips against his mouth. At that distance Cathy couldn't tell who had initiated the embrace, but then, she really didn't care, she told herself, setting the glass down with a tiny snap.

"I think I'll go up to bed," she said brightly. "I wouldn't want to be a fifth wheel."

"Don't leave yet, Cath," Meg begged, her dark eyes troubled. "I'm sure Sin will be right back. He couldn't have known that—that creature would show up. I'm sure he's just trying to get rid of her gracefully."

"Well, if I disappear then perhaps he won't feel that he has to get rid of her." Bending down to brush her sister's cheek, she left them with one more determined smile before vanishing out of the lounge.

The night was still and quiet, with the full moon bright above her head. *I seem to be making a habit of this,* she told herself grimly as she stepped onto the sandy beach. Silhouetted against one French door was a couple, sensuously entwined. The man was too short to be Sin, but the damage was done. Cathy yanked off her sandals, abandoning them in the sand, and started running down the beach, away from the noise and the laughter and the loving couples.

She ran until her heart pounded in her ears, throbbed in her chest, and her breath came in painful rasps, and still she ran. She fell once, skinning her knees in the wet sand, and then she was up and running again, as if Satan himself were after her. When she fell again by the rocks at the end of the small inlet she stayed down, letting her breath come in long, shuddering gasps into the wet sand, as hot, angry tears flowed down her face.

Slowly, slowly her sobbing breath quieted. The tears stopped their heated trail down her face, and her heart's rapid, frightened pounding slowed to a more reasonable rate. With her face still buried in the sand, she slowly became aware of her surroundings. The quiet *hush-hush* of the sea rolling onto the sand and the rocks. The smell of salt water and sea vegetation in the air, the burning of her skinned knees and the wet, sandy grit that bit through the clinging dress that was now irrevocably ruined. So much for the damned dress. It had hardly accomplished what she hoped it would.

There was another scent on the night breeze. For a moment Cathy thought it was her gardenia perfuming the air, then realized it was Sin's spicy aftershave. Did it still cling to her flesh, she wondered, after that all too brief embrace in their room? Or was it that interrupted dance?

Slowly, without moving her head, she opened one eye. A black-clad leg was beside her. Tilting her head, she looked up at Sin's motionless figure sitting in the sand next to her prone figure. His eyes were staring out at the ocean, as though looking for some sort of answer. She couldn't tell whether he had found it or not when he turned to meet her questioning gaze.

"Why did you leave?" His voice was low and beguiling on the night air. "Meg said you'd gone up to your room but I knew better. Particularly when I found these"—he held up her gold-strapped sandals—"on the beach."

"I wanted some fresh air," she said huskily, knowing full well how ridiculous the excuse sounded as she lay in the cool wet sand, her face wet with tears.

"You like running helter-skelter down a beach and then flinging yourself into the sand in tears?" he queried in soft mockery. "Mind you, I have noticed an unfortunate tendency to go racing off at the slightest provocation, but I would have thought—"

"I didn't fling myself onto the sand." She rolled over and sat up, brushing the clinging grains from her dampened front. "I tripped and fell." She lifted her skirt, took a brief peek at the graze which was now bleeding with a cheery profusion, and dropped the material back over it with a small shudder. "And I don't have a tendency to do any such thing," she added with a glare. "You bring it out in me."

"I'm sure I do." He brushed her hands away and lifted her skirt unnecessarily half way up her thigh, considering that the scrape was on her knee. "You did a good job with that," he remarked. "Come back with me and I'll get it cleaned up."

"It's nothing but a scratch," she muttered gracelessly. "I'll take care of it myself."

"I know that perfectly well. And I have no doubt you can clean it just as well by yourself. But I wanted to make sure you were all right."

"Did you promise Meg you'd check on me?" she shot back bitterly.

"Damn you, Cathy, are you never going to trust me?" His hand shot out and yanked her body across his, so that she was half sitting, half lying in his lap. She was so astounded she just sat there, without struggling, until his mouth came down on hers with a savage, bruising passion that seemed more of a punishment than a caress. And yet, curiously enough, Cathy responded to the savagery and unleashed desire as never before, opening her mouth beneath his and twining her arms around his neck, pulling his body closer to hers until she thought they might melt together.

Her tongue met his in a furious battle for dominance, until suddenly everything changed, and they were no longer waging a war but communicating needs and wants and desires in a silent sharing that reached beyond anything Cathy had ever known. And then Sin pulled his mouth away with a groan, burying his face against the curve of her neck.

"Damn you, Cathy," he said quietly, his breath coming rapidly. "And damn this dress, and most of all, damn Greg Danville." He looked up suddenly, and his eyes blazed into hers. "Tell me, Cathy, did Greg ever make you feel like this?" His mouth took hers, briefly, savagely. "And make you quiver in his arms like you do in mine?" He shook her. "Did he?"

Numbly she shook her head, and the smile of grim satisfaction that lit his face frightened her. "You're about as passive as a volcano," he muttered thickly, his mouth tracing hurried little kisses along her exposed collarbone. "And you're going back to your room right now, or I won't answer for the consequences."

Before she could protest he was on his feet, yanking her after him. "But I don't want..." she began, but his hand covered her mouth with surprising gentleness.

"Don't say it," he whispered. "You try a man too much, Cathy Whiteheart. And I can stand just so much at one time. You go on ahead to the hotel. I need to go for a long, soothing walk."

"But, Sin..." she tried again, but his hand covered her mouth again.

"Don't talk anymore, Cathy," he whispered. "We'll talk for hours tomorrow. But unless you're willing to ask me to come back and make love to you, now, tonight, then don't say another word." He drew his hand slowly away, and his eyes burned down into hers wordlessly.

Once, twice, she opened her mouth to say the words that she wanted to say. But somehow the thought of coldbloodedly arranging her seduction at his too clever hands was more than she could manage. She wanted him to sweep her into his arms, drown her protests with his magical mouth, stifle any incipient revolt with those experienced hands and that lean, tightly muscled body. She wanted the decision taken from her, she realized, so that she wouldn't have to face the consequences of her action. And she wasn't ready for that, no matter how ready she was for the joining of their bodies.

A wry smile twisted his mouth beneath the mustache. "That's what I thought," he said with grim humor. Gently he leaned down and brushed his lips against her smooth forehead. "Go to bed, Cathy. I promise I won't be in until I can be trusted." Taking her shoulders in his strong hands, he turned her around and gave her a gentle push in the direction of the hotel.

She had no real choice but to go. Halfway back she turned to look at him. He was standing there, tall and stark on the moonlit beach, his face too distant to read his expression. It took all her self-control not to run back to him, barefoot across the wet sand. Resolutely she continued onward, and when she turned once more to look for him he was gone into the night.

Chapter Fifteen

Wearily she stretched her long, tanned legs in front of her and surveyed the slowly ascending sun. The coffee by her side had long since grown cold as the sun grew warmer, as cold as Cathy's hurt and fury. She had spent long hours waiting for him, lying in his bed wearing nothing but the gold chain about her slender waist, and still he hadn't come.

She dozed fitfully off and on, until her anger finally overcame her exhaustion, and she returned to her own bed, trying to shut out the image of Sin with his arms around that all too willing brunette. But still sleep eluded her, until she eventually moved from the bed to the tiny terrace, to sit in the comfortable chair and watch the sun rise over the deep blue ocean. She had already called the airline, and a ticket on the noon flight back to Washington awaited her. But first, she thought savagely, she would tell Sinclair Mac-Donald exactly what she thought of him and his kisses and promises and faithlessness and…

A flash of reason inserted itself into her slowly boiling rage. What reason had he to be faithful to her? She was falling into the same trap that Charles and Meg had—assuming she had any claims on him simply because they were sharing a vacation and a room. And a few kisses. His eyes and his hands and his body had said he wanted her, and she hadn't answered. Was it any wonder he had sought more willing diversion for the night? Cathy's hands gripped the arms of the chair tightly as she stared out at the deserted beach. It was no wonder at all, especially considering how fickle men were. And she could only be grateful that he hadn't come in last night. If he hadn't found his...diversion, he would have returned to the room to find her waiting for him with open arms, all her defenses gone. And how would she have ever built them back up again, once he'd abandoned her?

The sound of the key in the lock alerted her to his return. The first runners were setting out along the beach below her, a white-jacketed waiter began setting up breakfast tables on the hotel's terrace restaurant. Cathy heard the door open and close, heard the steady measured tread of his footsteps, heading toward her. She kept her sea-green gaze on the ocean in front of her, her back and shoulders rigid beneath the terry cloth robe.

"You aren't talking to me this morning?" His voice was low and caressing as he came to stand directly behind her.

"I have nothing to say," she said evenly. Unable to stand the suspense any longer, she tilted her back to stare at him over her shoulder. "Except to hope you had a pleasant night with Joyce."

He'd thrown his dinner jacket across the bed, and one hand was in the midst of unbuttoning the white shirt to expose his tanned chest dusted with curling brown hair. His face looked tired and somewhat surprised. Not the face of a man who had just spent a night of passion, but Cathy was in no mood to notice.

A slow, mocking smile spread across his weary face. "Why Catherine Whiteheart, I do believe you're jealous," he murmured. "Your eyes are like chips of green ice."

"Jealous?" she echoed with what she hoped was a suitably cynical laugh. "Jealous of you? Don't be absurd. I'm delighted you found someone more congenial to spend your nights with."

"Are you indeed?" He finished unbuttoning the shirt and sent it sailing onto the bed. "Is that why you spent at least part of the night in my bed?" he questioned silkily.

All hope of managing this with an icy dignity vanished. Leaping to her feet, she knocked over her chair and the half-full coffee cup. "Go to hell." she spat, storming past him to the bathroom.

His hand shot out and caught her wrist, whirling her around to face him. Instinctively she reached out and slapped him with all her strength. She scarcely had time to be appalled by her actions before he hit her back, hard.

Tears of pain and shock started in her huge green eyes, and she put her hand to her stinging cheek. "How dare you?" she whispered hoarsely.

There was not the slightest trace of compunction in his disturbing hazel eyes. "I thought you wanted to be treated as an equal," he shot back. "When an equal hits me I hit them back, whether they're a man or woman. I'm not about to let you go around demanding equality on your terms, and then turn into a helpless, clinging female when it suits you. You're going to have to expect to be hit when you slap someone."

"You're still a sexist," she fought back. "You pulled your punch. If you really looked on me as an equal you would have hit me harder."

His strong jaw tightened, and the exasperation that washed over his face was coupled with an awe inspiring rage. Flinging her wrist away in disgust, he turned and strode out onto the balcony, his broad back to her, as he took several deep, calming breaths. A moment later he turned back to her, a somewhat rueful expression on his face.

"You just made me lose my temper, Cathy," he said in a deceptively mild tone. "And I can be a hell of a lot more sexist than that. Come here, woman." Not waiting for her, he began to stalk her, a dangerous, determined glint in his eyes.

"No, Sin." She began to back away from him, panic and a strange anticipation causing her heart to pound furiously against her rib cage.

"No, Sin," he mocked. With his long legs he could move much faster than she could, and he caught up with her before she was halfway to the door. "How about, yes, Sin? Please, Sin? I'd like that, Sin?" His mouth was poised over hers as his arms held her pinned against his iron body. "Why do you fight me, Cathy? Why are you determined to think the worst of me? I spent the night on board the yacht because I didn't trust myself sharing a room with you. You sent me away last night. How was I to know you'd change your mind?"

"I—I didn't change my mind," she breathed, mesmerized by the mouth that was hovering just above hers.

"Then why did you sleep in my bed?" he queried again.

"Because I'm a fool," she whispered, closing her eyes as his mouth descended. Instead of the brutal assault she was somehow expecting, his mouth proved even more devastating. Light, clinging little kisses brushed across her tremulous lips, her cheeks, her nose, her eyelids. His mouth traced the still stinging imprint of his hand on her cheek, his lips nibbled on one pink earlobe, and then trailed down the slender column of her neck. Gentle, coaxing, teasing little kisses that left her trembling and completely demoralized. She slid her arms up his broad, naked back, pressing her body closer to his, her head flung back to give him better access to the sensitive hollow of her throat, the long blond hair a rippling curtain down her back. And then the world swung crazily about her as he scooped her up in his arms, holding her against his chest.

"Are you still a fool?" he whispered in her ear, his tongue tracing delicate little patterns as he moved toward the rumpled bed.

"Sin," she whispered, reaching up to entwine her hands in his soft brown curls. Her mouth met his, eagerly, hungrily as he laid her down on the soft bed, following her down, his body half covering hers, as the kiss deepened, her lips opening to meet his thrusting tongue as it explored the moist, sweet interior of her seeking mouth. "Yes," she murmured helplessly, as one hand cupped her full, straining breast, his thumb gently teasing the nipple until it stiffened against him. "Yes, yes, yes," she cried, as his hand slid down her thigh and began to lift the terry cloth robe.

The shrill ringing of the bedside telephone ripped them out of their dream of passion. With a precise expletive Sin rolled away from her, grabbing the phone before she could make a dive for it, and barking angrily, "Yes?"

As Cathy lay there, her robe up around her hips, her breath returning to normal, sanity began to edge back. Sin suddenly seemed to loom large and frightening beside her, his naked torso glistening with sweat, his broad shoulders tense with frustration and sudden anger.

"What?" he snapped into the telephone. "Are you sure?" He listened for another moment. "Well, Miss Whiteheart won't be needing the reservation after all. Thanks for your trouble, but her plans have changed. Yes, that's right." He slammed the receiver down, then turned back to Cathy's suddenly cowering figure.

Pulling herself upright, she managed to meet him glare

for glare. "You had no right to do that," she said. "I have every intention of going back to Washington today."

"Why?" It was a simple enough question, but it was enough to break Cathy's tenuous self-control.

"Because I don't dare spend any more time with you!" she cried. "Can't you see what this is doing to me? I don't want to have a casual affair with you, Sin. I can't take that sort of thing. I'm not sophisticated enough to take and discard lovers like a change of clothes."

"You think it would be like that?" His voice was slow and deep and his face was unreadable.

"I know it would. You'd get tired of coping with me, and some day, sooner or later, someone like Joyce Whatever-her-name-was will show up and you'll be off."

"You have a lot of faith in me," he said lightly, his hand gently smoothing a strand of hair away from her brow.

"Don't do that!" she cried desperately. "Leave me alone, please. If you don't..." She let the sentence trail.

"If I don't?" he prompted, his voice deep and infinitely tender.

"If you don't," she continued weakly, "you'll only break my heart. And I couldn't bear it." Burying her face in her arms, she gave in to the tears that had racked her body the previous night. As she lay there she could feel his hazel eyes watching her, feel his warm, soothing presence beside her on the bed. But he made no move to comfort her, merely waiting until her sobs slowly died away.

"As I see it," Sin's voice said slowly, consideringly, "we have two options. Taking as given that I'm not about to let you go back to Washington, that is."

His reasonable tone was enough to make her raise her damp face curiously. "Why not?" she asked in a husky, tear-drenched voice.

He had moved to the other side of the bed and was leaning against the pillows. "Because I'm not," he replied shortly. "I want you here with me. So my options are simple: I can either kidnap you and keep you on my yacht, or"—he gave her a devastating smile—"we can get married."

The world seemed to spin about her. "I don't consider that amusing," she snapped.

"I wasn't planning on amusing you," he replied easily. "It's very simple to get a marriage license on St. Alphonse. We could be married this afternoon and then take off on *Tamlyn* for a honeymoon. Away from telephones and old flames and other distractions. What do you think?"

Cathy sat bolt upright, straightening the terry robe primly. "I think you're out of your mind," she announced firmly. "Why in the world would you want to marry me? You aren't in love with me." There was still enough foolishness in her that she hoped he might deny it.

He leaned back meditatively. "I don't know," he said dreamily. His eyes met hers suddenly, and Cathy felt a tightening in her stomach at the desire that blazed there. "I do know that I want to be with you. I want to make love to you, morning, noon, and night. You were made to be loved, Cathy, and you've spent far too much of your life celibate."

"That's not enough of a reason to get married," she said quietly. "Simple sexual attraction isn't enough. We could sleep together without getting married."

"Who said there was anything simple about sexual attraction?" he countered. "And there's more to it than sex, my love. I want to protect you, take care of you."

"I can take care of myself."

"Nonsense. You're far too vulnerable. How you could have gotten this far in life and still have remained so innocent is beyond me." He shook his head in amazement.

"And though you're one of the toughest ladies I've ever met, you still need me."

"To protect me?" she repeated skeptically. "I don't think that's reason enough."

"What about this?" Before she could divine his intention, he had moved across the bed and caught her in his arms, his mouth crushing hers with a ruthless, demoralizing passion that was as soul-destroying as it was efficient. Part of her knew very well he was doing everything he could to turn her into a quivering mass of desire in the shortest amount of time. She knew it, and was helpless against it.

He moved his mouth a fraction of an inch away, keeping his arms securely around her. Not that she was about to struggle out of his embrace, she thought dizzily. "Marry me," he whispered.

"No." She shook her head, and his lips caught hers, gently teasing her into opening her mouth.

"Marry me," he said again, his tongue tracing her upper lip.

"No." The sound was definitely weaker. One hand released its hold on her waist and cupped her soft breast.

"Marry me." He had moved her robe aside, and his tongue swirled around the rosy-tipped peak. A small, quiet moan of surrender emitted from the back of Cathy's throat.

"Yes," she whispered.

Chapter Sixteen

Cathy went through the wedding in a dream. She had dressed in the cream linen suit that Meg had rushed out and bought her, squeezed her feet into the matching shoes that were half a size too small, and stood in front of a tall civil servant with her sister and Charles to one side and Sin, tall and somber and sinfully handsome, on the other. His voice had been low and deep and sure as he repeated the simple vows, Cathy's tone was a thin, reedy sound. *What am I doing,* she demanded of herself as she held out her hand and felt the thin gold band slip over her finger. *Am I out of my mind?*

Doubts had assailed her immediately. The moment she had whispered "yes" Sin had pulled away from her and rolled off the bed. "I feel like I've been waiting centuries," he'd said, shrugging into a forest-green polo shirt. "I can wait a few more hours. Besides, if we're going to get married this afternoon I have a thousand things to do." Dropping a kiss on her bewildered forehead, he had vanished from the hotel room.

And this was the first time she had seen him since he had seduced her into agreeing to his crazy proposal. Standing tall and straight in front of the justice of the peace, with no chance for Cathy to come up with the hundred and one objections that had flooded her mind since he'd left her.

Even Meg had seemed strangely preoccupied, chattering at a breakneck speed that allowed Cathy no time at all for reflection or even confidences. All the while her dark eyes were troubled. Now as she stood next to her, holding the small bouquet of gardenias Sin had bought her, the troubled expression was still there. Out of the corner of her eye Cathy watched Charles reach out and pat Meg's hand in a reassuring gesture. He looked slightly grim around the mouth too, and Cathy's doubts increased tenfold.

Too late. "I now pronounce you man and wife," the justice announced. In a daze Cathy felt Sin's lips brush hers, followed by Charles and Meg, the doubts erased from their smiling countenances.

"I'll call Pops for you," Meg promised. "Leave it to me. He'll probably raise holy hell, but then, that's his usual style." She hugged her again, tears bright in her eyes. "God, I hope you're happy, Cath."

"Now, now, we don't need tears, darling," Charles chided genially, and Cathy couldn't tell if the geniality was forced or not. "I thought you loved romance."

"I just want to make sure Cathy's happy," Meg wailed, casting a fulminating glance at Sin's bland exterior. "And you'd damn well better know what you're doing," she informed her new brother-in-law.

Sin took this veiled threat in good part. "I do," he said simply, his arm moving to encircle Cathy's waist. She looked up at him, belated surprise and the return of her doubts clouding her expression.

"Well, shall we see the happy couple off, Meg?" Charles tried to inject a note of normalcy into the proceedings. "There's a bottle of champagne chilling on *Tamlyn*.

I suggest we go toast the marriage and then let these two get off on their honeymoon.''

"Sounds good," Sin agreed easily, taking her arm in a lightly possessive grip and guiding her toward the door. She tripped, and his grip tightened. "Are you all right?" The concern in his warm hazel eyes momentarily banished every doubt that had assailed her.

"I'm fine," she managed. "I'm not used to these shoes."

"It's bad luck for a bride to trip on her wedding day," Meg broke in before Sin could respond. "That's why they're carried over thresholds."

"I guess we didn't get off to a very good start then," Cathy said with a shaky laugh. Sin's body seemed curiously tense beside her, and she wished she could shake this sense of impending doom.

"We'll make up for it," Sin promised firmly, smiling down at her, and the warmth in his eyes melted her misgivings. When he looked at her like that she would do anything for him, even something as abysmally stupid and short-sighted as rushing into marriage.

Smiling back at him, she slipped out of her tight shoes and handed them to a bewildered Meg. "We need all the luck we can get," she murmured. "I don't want to tempt fate again."

And barefoot, she went with Sin out into the blazing tropical sunlight.

She had changed out of her linen dress and put on slim-fitting designer jeans and an oversized white cotton tunic that emphasized her tan while merely hinting at the ripe young curves beneath its billowing lines, and then joined her new husband on the deck as they sailed out of the harbor. They hadn't talked much, Sin being involved in the navigation of the yacht and Cathy being stricken with sudden, tongue-tied shyness. They had reached the tiny cove on the uninhabited island south of St. Alphonse in just under five hours, and right now the delicious odor of broiling steaks wafted in the open cabin door. Sin had insisted on taking care of dinner that night, brushing aside her offers of assistance with gentle determination. So that all she could do was sit barefoot on the bed she'd soon be sharing with her new husband and wonder if she'd gone out of her mind.

"Do you want some wine?" he called out cheerfully as he worked on the salad. "Or a drink of some sort?"

"No, thank you," she replied politely enough, leaning her head out of the cabin door for a moment. The small dimensions of the main cabin seemed dwarfed next to Sin's height. His back was to her, the faded jeans tight across his hips and clinging to his long, long legs. The western-style shirt hugged his broad shoulders, emphasizing the latent power they contained. With a sigh, Cathy moved back into the cabin, leaning up against the bulkhead. *Why?* she asked herself one more time. And with a sudden, blinding clarity, she knew.

You're in love with him, she accused herself silently. *Of all the stupid, idiotic, blind fools! You've been in love with him for days—weeks—and you never even noticed. No wonder you were so eager to be talked into a loveless marriage. Because on your side there was more than enough love. Stupid, stupid, stupid!*

And when had all this madness started? Once she realized the depth of her hopeless infatuation, the rest was easy. She'd been attracted from the first. But she'd been blinded by her lingering pain over Greg and a fear of new commitments, fighting the attraction with every ounce of her strength and stubborn will. But it had done her no good to fight.

She'd fallen in love with him the night he followed her out of the French restaurant in Georgetown and held her trembling, miserable body against his comforting warmth. And it had taken her another month to realize it! Well, she had never been noted for her wisdom in love. Witness Greg Danville.

Not a flicker of pain, she noticed with grim satisfaction. She was over him completely—at least loving Sin had accomplished that. But would the cure be worse than the illness? She had a wretched feeling that it might be.

"Dinner's ready." He was standing in the doorway, filling it completely. He even had to duck his head to move inside. "Are you all right?"

"Fine," she lied, looking at him with new eyes. "But I'm not really hungry."

"You should be." Taking her hand, he pulled her from the bunk and drew her out into the main cabin. "Have you eaten anything all day?"

"I had a sandwich sometime around noon." She failed to mention she'd left more than half of it behind on the plate. The little booth was set with white damask, silver candlesticks, and Waterford crystal wineglasses. A trace of humor penetrated her abstraction. "Do you usually travel with all this fancy stuff?" she queried, slipping into her place.

"Wedding present," he replied succinctly. "Meg didn't want us to use the same tin plates we'd used all the way down here." He placed a perfectly cooked steak in front of her with a flourish. The salad to her left was a work of art, with thinly sliced avocados spiraling around the outside. She looked up at him suspiciously.

"You told me you couldn't cook," she accused him after she took a tentative bite of the steak. It was perfect.

"When did I say that?" he demanded, surprised. "I love to cook."

"You told me that first day I met you. When I said the men should fix lunch."

"Oh, that." He smiled wickedly, the corners of his eyes crinkling. "I only wanted to rescue you from an embarrassing situation. You were forced to admit you couldn't sail, and I didn't want you to feel any worse than you obviously already did."

"Rescue me?" she echoed. Despite the feeling of helplessness it connoted, the notion was very pleasant indeed. *Stop that*, she ordered herself sternly. *He's just got a Sir Galahad complex, and you're a damsel in distress. It's lucky he doesn't know how distressed you are, and all because of him.*

Surprisingly enough, she was hungry. After devouring her steak, she finished her salad, three rolls with butter, and almost half a bottle of champagne. Sin leaned back and watched her eat, with a light in his hazel eyes that was disturbingly tender. He was fast proving her undoing, Cathy realized hopelessly. And she knew without question that however miserable she'd been after Greg, it was nothing compared to the devastation Sin's eventual desertion would wreak.

"Penny for your thoughts?"

She forced herself to meet his eyes candidly. "I was wondering how long we'd be married," she said lightly, and had the dubious satisfaction of seeing the good humor vanish from his face.

"That's up to you," he said noncommittally.

"You'll let me go?"

A not entirely pleasant smile lit his tanned face. "Jumped at it, didn't you? No, I won't let you go. Not right now, at least."

"Then when?" she pursued it.

"Cathy." He leaned across the table and brushed her face with a gentle hand. "You agreed to marry me. Why all the doubts?"

She jumped like a frightened rabbit, pulling away from the caress as if burned. "Just nervous, I guess," she said shakily.

His eyes surveyed her for a long, speculative moment. "All right." He rose slowly to his full height, towering over her in the tiny confines of the cabin. Without another word he began clearing the table with an economy of movements. Cathy opened her mouth to offer to help him, then shut it again. If he did the dishes himself it would be longer before he turned his attention back to her. And she wasn't quite ready for the full force of that gaze.

Leaning her arms on the back of the bench seat, she stared out at the inky water beyond the porthole. "Do you mind if I go out on deck?" she asked suddenly.

Sin's eyebrows rose in surprise. "Of course not. As long as you don't jump overboard and try to swim for it. I wouldn't take kindly to a runaway bride."

"Where would I run to?" she asked in a low voice as she climbed the three short steps to the deck.

Once alone in the inky blackness, she took three long, deep breaths. The water was all around her, still and black, with a wide trail of moonlight cutting across it to the beach several hundred yards away. She could hear the quiet sounds of the water lapping on the hull, the soft breezes ruffling the palm trees on the shore and jiggling the hardware on the masts. Cathy sat cross-legged on the bench seat, drinking in the cool, sea-tanged night air, reveling in the deserted stillness, the calm and peace that surrounded her. For a moment she could almost forget the inexplicable mess she had landed herself in. Married to a man who didn't love her, a man whose presence sent her heart pounding and her pulses racing.

He moved so quietly she accepted his presence before she was completely aware of it. One strong, tanned hand reached out with a brandy snifter.

"I don't think—" Cathy began.

"Take it." The order was gently spoken, but an order nonetheless. "You need it. It's been a long, long day, and you didn't sleep much last night."

She took a tentative sip of the brandy, letting it burn its way down. He was so very close. She could feel the heat emanating from his body, smell the enticing male smell of him. Like a magnet she could feel her body being pulled toward his, and the idea panicked her.

"Let's go for a walk on the beach," she said suddenly. "It's such a pretty night and—"

"No." The word was quiet but inexorable.

Cathy swallowed once, twice, and took another sip of her brandy. "What about a swim, then? It looks like a lovely beach, and I love swimming at night."

"No." He leaned back against the cushions, his eyes glittering in the moonlit darkness.

"But it's early and I—"

"No." His voice was calm and implacable. "Finish your brandy, Cathy."

"I—I don't think I want it," she said nervously, getting to her feet and edging out of his way. She half expected him to catch her, but he made no move to impede her escape. "I think I'll go below and—and find something to read. I'm not at all tired, and reading always helps me sleep." The words came out breathlessly and far too fast. Sin had the indecency to laugh at her lame excuse, but he let her go without moving.

Chapter Seventeen

The main cabin was no escape, and the small room she would soon have to share with Sin was even worse. Cathy whirled about her in panic, wishing now she *had* jumped overboard. She didn't want...she couldn't...

Sin moved slowly down the steps, lithe and graceful as a jungle cat, despite his height. Placing the brandy snifters on the tiny counter, he turned to face her in the small confines of the cabin. There was a look of intractable purpose in his face as he moved slowly toward her.

"No, Sin," she gasped, backing away. But in that small room there wasn't much space to back into.

"Yes, Sin," he corrected gently. "Yes, indeed, Sin. Yes, please, Sin." He reached out and caught her by the retreating shoulders, his hands warm and firm and inflexible. "Don't run anymore, Cathy," he whispered, drawing her slowly toward him. His hands ran up her shoulders to her neck, cupping her face, and his eyes burned down into her frightened green ones. Slowly, agonizingly slowly, his mouth descended to capture hers, his lips moving against hers in a sensual appeal. The only parts of his body touching hers were his mouth on hers and the hands holding her throat, the thumbs stroking along the sides of her neck slowly, sensuously, as his tongue explored the wet, hungry interior of her mouth. Cathy's hands were at her side, her fists clenched, and she willed herself to resist the practiced seduction of that experienced mouth. But Sin had all the time and patience in the world, teasing, enticing, seducing her with his tongue, until her arms slid around his waist of their own volition, pulling him closer against her yearning body.

His mouth left hers to bury in her neck, the lips nibbling at the sensitive cord above her collar. "Say it, Cathy," he whispered against her heated flesh. "Say that you want me."

She shook her head helplessly. "No," she whispered. The hand on her neck slid back to her shoulders, and she felt herself pushed a few inches away. It seemed like miles, when all she wanted to do was bury herself against his leanly muscled strength.

"No?" he echoed, his eyes blazing, his voice soft but implacable. "Do you really mean that?"

They stared at each other for a long, tension filled moment. And Cathy knew that this was her last chance. All she had to do was tell him no, one more time, and she would never have to worry about being further enthralled by the strange power he had over her. One word and he would release her forever.

"Answer me, Cathy," he said, and his voice was fire and ice. "Do you mean that?"

"No," she whispered. "I mean, yes. I mean..." She stumbled helplessly to a halt. And still he waited, unwilling to help her. She had to cross that last bridge alone.

Reaching up, she covered his hands with hers, pressing them against her shoulders. "Yes, Sin," she said, her voice husky. "I want you."

A slow smile spread across his face. "You've got me," he said simply. A moment later one arm had slid under her knees and she was in his arms, held high against his chest with effortless ease. "Lady, you've got me for as long as you want me," he promised, and his mouth found hers again as he carried her into the front cabin, kicking the door shut behind them.

Moonlight was streaming in the open hatch over their heads, casting silver shadows on the wide berth as he gently laid her down, his body following hers with pantherlike grace.

"You aren't still afraid of me, are you, Cathy?" he whispered, staring down at her.

She gazed up at the bronzed, unreadable features poised above her, and she shook her head, the last of her misgivings vanishing. She loved him and wanted him, had loved and wanted him for what seemed an eternity. And now, for at least a time, he was hers. She smiled up at him tremulously, raising a tentative hand to the buttons of his shirt. He lay there on his side, motionless, his eyes burning into hers, as she fumbled with the final button of his shirt and slid her hand across the heated flesh of his chest. The skin was smooth and muscled beneath the light layer of curls, and Cathy sighed.

"To think I didn't use to like men with hair on their chests," she murmured dreamily, raising her other hand to slip the shirt off his broad shoulders. He moved a bit to help her, then rolled back on his side, one hand possessively on her slender hip, an amused smile lighting his eyes as she discovered the wonders of his body.

Slowly she let her hand trail across his flat stomach, until, on impulse, she leaned down and buried her mouth against his chest. She could feel his heart pounding against her lips, slow, heated beats that betrayed his need for her. Smiling against his flesh, she slid her hand up his smoothly muscled back, her sensitive fingers kneading his hungry skin with soft, sure strokes. His breath was coming more rapidly now, ruffling her silken hair as she moved her mouth across the muscled planes of his stomach and up his chest. Her hand trailed back across his stomach, drifted lower to the belt of his jeans, and then jerked back, her courage finally failing her.

"Coward," he laughed softly in her ear, catching her reticent hand and moving it lower. She let out a small gasp of surprise, her widened eyes meeting his. "Is that all the exploring you're going to indulge in, darling?" he whispered against her ear, his tongue tracing the delicate lines. "There's a great deal more of me to discover." His hand reached up to cup her chin, his thumb gently stroking her trembling lips.

Moving over, he replaced his thumb with his lips, kissing her slowly, deeply, with a languorous passion that set the fires in her loins burning more fiercely. She was barely aware of his hand undoing the buttons of her shirt, pulling back the cottony material and dispensing with the front clasp of her lacy bra with practiced ease, his hand caressing one soft, aching breast possessively, his sensitive fingertips gently stroking the tender nipple.

"Oh, God," he breathed suddenly, his voice husky with passion. "I can't stand these damned clothes any longer!" With an impatience that bordered on savagery he unzipped her jeans and stripped them from her body, tossing them on the floor with her shirt and bra. His jeans followed, and then there was nothing separating them but their own determination to wring every last, lengthy ounce of pleasure from a moment long denied.

His lips found one soft breast in the moonlight, his tongue flickering across the suddenly rigid nipple as Cathy moaned, her fingers digging into his shoulders. His hand trailed up her slender thigh, softly tantalizingly, until he reached the center of her soul-destroying need. She jerked away, startled, but his sure, gentle stroking first calmed, then overwhelmed her. She arched her hips against his hand, little whimpers of desire echoing from the back of her throat. The burning fires had turned into a conflagration, one that threatened to destroy her. Her body trembled and shook all over with the desperation of her need, a need she had never known before. Sin pulled his mouth reluctantly away from her breast and trailed small, damp kisses across her collarbone, all the while his clever, clever hands were driving her to the edge of madness and beyond.

"Sin," she gasped, her nails digging into his flesh. "Please, Sin. Oh, please…" she moaned, moving her head back and forth in the extremity of her need.

His hands left her, catching her head and holding it still as his eyes bored down into hers. "Are you ready so soon?" he whispered sweetly against her mouth. "I was expecting to have to coax and reassure you for hours yet."

"Don't…tease me," she gasped.

A slow, tender smile curved his mouth. "Never, my sweet." And, setting his hungry mouth on hers, he moved over and covered her body with his, joining them at last in that final embrace, swift and sure and deep. They moved together in perfect union, a masterful blend of mind, body, and spirit, until the blazing conflagration engulfed them both in a fiery holocaust that left them, weak but replete, to struggle upward, phoenixlike, from the ashes of their fulfillment.

Sin reached out a tender hand to brush the hair away from her flushed, sweat-dampened face. The cool wetness of tears caught his fingers, and very tenderly he leaned over and kissed them away.

"Sin, I…" His hand covered her mouth before she could tell him, before she could say that she loved him.

"Not now," he whispered, his warm breath tickling her ear. "Don't tell me now." He pulled her exhausted body against his, spoon-fashion, cradling her against his taut, sweat-drenched leanness. And before she had time to wonder why he would stop what would surely have been a very satisfying confession, sleep claimed her, leaving her wrapped in her lover's arms and at peace with the world.

CATHY WOKE, slowly at first, the thoughts and feelings and images drifting lazily through her sleep-fogged brain. All along her left side was warmth and comfort, and a heavy weight was pressing around her middle, a weight she slowly realized was Sin MacDonald's arm. One large hand was cupping her breast, and despite the even rise and fall of his breathing she knew he was more than aware of her. She lay very still, reveling in the feel of his strong, lean body against hers.

"Good morning," his voice rumbled in her ear, sounding sleepy, smug, and satisfied. As indeed, she herself was. "How long have you been awake?" He stretched beside her, rubbing his body against hers slowly and sensually.

"About half an hour," she replied honestly, snuggling back against him. "I felt too happy to sleep."

His arm tightened around her, and she felt her body being drawn slowly back down onto the bed. He leaned over her, pressing her against the soft mattress, and the look on his face was tender, and, even if he wouldn't put the word to it, loving. "Then you've only had a total of about an hour's sleep," he said with a lascivious grin. "Aren't you tired? You certainly should be after the workout you gave me last night."

"The workout I gave *you?*" she shrieked, albeit softly. "I'll have you know, Sin MacDonald, that I was sound asleep when you...when we..."

His grin broadened. "You can still blush," he marveled. "Not that I'm surprised—if anything could make you blush, that infamous 'when we...when you...' should. And I'll have you know, Cathy MacDonald, that I was sound asleep the time before, when you...when we..."

"You're incorrigible," she said crossly, trailing her hand up his tautly muscled arm. "And who says I don't want to keep my maiden name?" she added teasingly.

She had the dubious satisfaction of seeing his hazel eyes turn fiery with rage. Covering the lower half of her body with his stronger one, he held her captive as his hand cupped her mutinous face. "*I* say," he informed her huskily. "that five-minute ceremony made us one, a unit, and I want us to stay that way. In name, in spirit, and—" he let his hips bump against hers suggestively "—in body."

Her eyes widened in shocked recognition. "Good heavens, Sin. Not again," she breathed, her eyes alight as she lifted her mouth for his possession.

He kissed her long and deep, with a savagery that alarmed and excited her. "Is that a protest?" he murmured hoarsely against her throat.

"Hm-mn," she denied with a low guttural noise, a purr of pleasure as her tired body responded once more to his practiced caresses. "Merely an expression of awed wonder." And sliding her deft hands down his lean torso, she met his passion fully, exploding within moments of him as they reached the apex of their perfect desire. And once more they slept.

"You know, you don't really need to wear that," Sin said lazily as he stretched out on the bunk beside the small kitchen. He caught hold of the short, velour wrapper she'd appropriated from him as she tried to find her way about the pocket-sized galley. It fell to just below her knees, and must have been barely decent on Sin's lengthy frame, she thought wistfully.

"Don't mess with the chef," she ordered sternly, twitching the robe out of his grasping fingers. "If you want coffee you have to let me get to it." She fumbled with the automatic coffeemaker, mastering its intricacies with her usual difficulty with mechanical objects.

His hazel eyes were half-closed as he surveyed her lithe form, and Cathy knew perfectly well that his imagination was stripping away the robe with devastating accuracy. She could feel the color rising, and she forced herself to turn and survey him with the same sensual directness. Leaning against the counter, she let her hungry eyes roam over his tanned, muscular body. From the long, long legs, the trim hips and lean buttocks encased in the scantiest excuse for underwear Cathy had ever seen, the flat stomach and broad, hair-fringed chest that she had wept and moaned and laughed into last night. *And this morning,* she added silently. To the broad shoulders, strong arms, and diabolically clever hands that seemed instinctively to know what part of her needed to be touched, with just the right amount of gentleness or force. And the hazel eyes that looked so tenderly into hers, the mouth that had taught her things she had scarcely known existed. All in all it was a very potent package, she realized with a small blissful sigh.

The tiny laugh lines around his eyes crinkled in amusement. "I'd ask you what you were thinking but I'm sure I'd be shocked out of my mind." He accepted the coffee she offered, never taking his eyes off her. "And I don't see why I have to wear these." He plucked at the briefs. "I'll allow you your modesty, but when there's no one around for miles and miles..."

"You have to wear them," she said, sitting down cross-legged beside him and sipping at her rich black coffee, "because I find you far too distracting without them. It's hard enough to concentrate on cooking as it is. What do you want for dinner?"

His eyes roamed lazily over her. "You," he said, pulling her down to lie against his broad, hard chest without spilling a drop of her coffee.

"I think you're going to need something a bit more substantial if we're going to keep on at the pace we've started," she said, sighing happily. She let one hand trail intimately across his stomach, listening to his stifled groan of pleasure with a smile as she snuggled closer against his chest. She took another sip of her coffee. "Speaking of food—you know what the trouble with you is?"

His arms tightened companionably around her slender form, one hand dipping into the robe to touch her breast. "No, tell me. What is the trouble with me?" he demanded lazily, showering small, unhurried kisses in her cloud of silver-blond hair.

She moved her head to look down at him mischievously. "You're like Chinese food," she explained in dulcet tones. "Very satisfying at the time, but a half an hour later I'm hungry again."

A shout of laughter greeted her impish remark. Taking the half-empty coffee cup from her hand, he placed it on the table beside his, then stretched back, taking her with him, so that her slender, half-clad form was stretched out on top of his lean, strong body. It was a dizzying feeling, with his warm flesh and hardening desire beneath her, waiting for her. With a sigh she buried her head against his chest, nestling against the soft cushion of hair as his hands reached beneath her robe.

"All I can say," he sarcastically murmured in her ear, "is that it's a lucky thing you're frigid. God knows what I'd do with you if you actually liked to make love." His hips, magically divested of the restraining briefs, reached up to meet hers, as her whole body tensed.

"What's the matter?" His voice was soft and patient, unlike his passion-stirred body.

She tried to pull away from him, but his hands sensed her withdrawal and reached up to stop her, holding her frailness against him.

"It's just…" Her words faded for a moment, then strengthened. "You reminded me of something I'd rather forget."

"Greg Danville," he supplied in a short, angry voice. At her reluctant nod, his grip tightened. "Listen, Cathy," he said in a surprisingly stern tone, "Greg existed. You can't wipe him out of your life, forget that you ever knew him or that he ever hurt you. It happened. But it's over, long over. And it has nothing to do with you and me, and what we have together. Nothing at all. Is that understood?" Despite the sternness there was a gentleness in his eyes and the hands that held her captive against his still fully aroused body. "Is it?" he demanded again.

And strangely enough, it was true. Greg Danville was out of her life, never to be heard from again. He had nothing to do with her and Sin, nothing whatsoever. She managed a smile, tentative at first, then widening with real delight. "Yes, sir," she said sweetly. And then with dizzying force he turned her over onto the bunk, covering her body with his ardent one. And Greg Danville vanished completely in a torrent of desire.

Chapter Eighteen

Cathy sat on the deck, soaking up the hot, Caribbean sun with truly hedonistic fervor. Her body was turning a lovely golden brown, setting off the thin gold chain with its perfect emerald, and she felt warm, full, and completely satiated. She reached out to touch the emerald, which served as a sort of talisman for her. Any time she began to doubt what had happened to her during the past weeks, and particularly the past two days since she married Sinclair MacDonald, she would reach for the chain through her clothing or, more frequently, on her naked body, and touch it. For good luck, or to remind herself that it was real. She wasn't sure which—maybe a little bit of both. Her eyes trailed across the deck to Sin's lean frame. He was hunched over some piece of equipment, his face intent beneath the sunglasses, his tanned body, clad only in the briefest of denim cutoffs, glistening with the sun and a light film of sweat.

"I hated to leave that island," Cathy said dreamily. "Everything was perfect there. The water, the sun, the privacy."

He looked up and smiled at her, easily, casually, the very naturalness of it incredibly sexy. "I hated to leave it too," he replied, squinting out at the horizon. "But we need supplies, and Martin's Head is the closest place I know. We can sail right back.''

''No, I don't think so,'' she sighed. ''For some reason I'm afraid it will have vanished if we try to find it again. You don't even know what island it is, do you?''

''Hey, I'm not that bad a navigator. I can find it again,'' he protested. ''Or maybe we can find another island.''

She turned to peer up at him in the brilliant sunlight. ''that would be nice,'' she sighed. ''We may never run out of islands at this rate.''

He seemed to hesitate, on the verge of saying something and then obviously thought better of it. He returned his attention to the instrument in his hand, his fingers as dexterous on the intricate machinery as they were on her responsive body.

''What were you about to say?'' she questioned curiously, pulling herself to a sitting position and retying the straps to her bikini behind her neck.

''Was I about to say something?'' he murmured vaguely. ''Can't remember what.''

''Maybe it was something about when we have to go back,'' she prodded, a flicker of nervousness racing along her veins. ''You know,'' she added with an uneasy laugh, ''I don't really know what you do for a living.''

There was no mistaking the wariness in his body. She knew every inch of it far too well by that time to miss his reaction. ''Sure you do,'' he said easily, too easily. ''I told you before, I'm a consultant.''

''But for whom?'' she persisted. ''Oh, I remember. That Joyce-woman said you own your own company. Is that why you're able to just disappear on your honeymoon without telling anyone?''

He put the piece of machinery down, turning to stare at her with lazy charm. ''Why the cross-examination, Cathy?'' he inquired evenly. ''I'm more than happy to tell you anything you want to know.''

''Even about Joyce?'' she dared to ask.

''Even about Joyce,'' he agreed. ''Though I can't imagine why you'd want to know. I never pretended to be a monk before I met you, sweetheart. Joyce and I were...close at one time.''

''You mean you were lovers,'' she said flatly, miserably aware of how bitchy she sounded.

''Yes.'' His answer was unequivocal.

''And how many others?''

The last trace of a smile was wiped from his face. ''I lost count,'' he snapped, crossing the small section of deck to kneel down beside her. ''What the hell is wrong with you, Cathy?'' he demanded roughly, pulling her unresisting body into his arms with an anger that was oddly reassuring.

''I'm sorry,'' she said meekly against his firmly muscled chest. ''I guess I'm just on edge. I'm afraid that everything is going to end in disaster since we've left the island. Can't we go back?'' she pleaded.

Tenderly he pushed the hair from her face, a crooked smile that didn't belie his own misgivings playing about his mobile mouth. ''We'd starve to death, baby,'' he said softly. ''Don't be so gloomy. We'll stop at the store on Martin's Head, be there for a total of fifteen minutes and then be off. You can do the shopping while I get fresh water and fuel on board. And then we'll be miles away again, where no one can get to us. How does that sound?''

His hand was gently stroking the slender curve of her waist as he held her against his broad, firm chest. He smelled of suntan oil and sun-heated flesh, a potent combination that stirred her senses. She could feel the tension draining out of her as she wondered if she'd ever tire of his magnificent body.

"It sounds heavenly," she sighed. But still, in the back of her mind, the misgivings remained.

MARTIN'S HEAD WAS SMALLER than she had imagined, and the tiny store looked dark and depressing. Leaving Sin at the dock, haggling with a cheerful-looking pirate, she made her way up the winding path to the small store, determined to complete her business and be gone as quickly as possible. It was the sight of the telephone booth that diverted her intentions.

The only cloud on her blissful horizon the last few days was the lack of word from her father. Meg had promised to call him from St. Alphonse with the news of Cathy's precipitous wedding, but the absence of her father's good wishes suddenly overwhelmed her. On impulse she abandoned her shopping for the telephone, her heart pounding with sudden excitement and happiness. She couldn't wait to tell Pops about Sin. They'd like each other, she knew they would. And Pops would hardly object—he'd been wanting her to get married for years. While he was secretly very proud of her insistence on working at the day-care center, he still held to the antiquated notion that a woman couldn't be happy unless he had a husband and children on the way. Cathy put a tentative hand on her flat belly as she waited for the call to go through, surprised to find that she was beginning to agree with him. The thought that she might be carrying Sin's child was infinitely precious to her.

"Well, well, if it isn't my little sister Cathy," Travis's hateful voice drawled at the other end of the surprisingly good connection. "We hadn't expected to hear from you for ages. How's the honeymoon? Enjoying your stalwart private eye? Your father was fit to be tied, you know. Security is one thing, but this is carrying it a bit too far, don't you think?"

"What in the world are you talking about, Travis?" Cathy demanded. The connection was crystal clear, but Travis's conversation was definitely full of static. "Can I speak to Pops?"

"Oh, you most assuredly can. There's no way I can stop him—" His sentence ended in the middle, and then her father was on the phone, breathing heavily.

"It's about time you called," he said gruffly. "Where the hell are you?"

"On a small island called Martin's Head," she replied in bewilderment. "Didn't Meg call you? I'm married. To a—"

"Your idiot sister most certainly did call me. And I know Sin MacDonald a hell of a lot better than you do. I hired him."

Slowly, her body began to go numb. Starting at her toes, and working its way slowly upward through her loins and her heart, until the only part of her that still worked was her brain. "You what?" she echoed.

"I hired him. Haven't you ever heard of MacDonald and Anderson?" he snapped.

"They're your security firm," she replied vaguely. "But what...?"

"Sinclair MacDonald is the president of MacDonald and Anderson. He's worked for me for years, on special projects and the like."

There was a long silence. "The latest of which is me?" she questioned finally in a dead voice.

Her deathly reaction finally penetrated the miles of telephone cable to her father. "No, don't take it like that, honey. You were in danger. That psycho you hooked yourself up with last spring has been trying to extort money from me. Said he'd wreck your life if I didn't turn over a very large sum of money to him. I remember how much you seemed to love the guy—I thought he could do it. So I hired Sin MacDonald to get you out of the country and out of Danville's way till we could take care of him.''

''I see.'' She was amazed at how calm her voice sounded. ''And did Meg and Charles have anything to do with this?''

''Well, of course.'' Her father had the grace to sound somewhat sheepish. ''How else could we have managed it? You weren't about to fall for him on your own. But honey, listen, it's all over. We've got Danville dead to rights. We've gotten a restraining order, and if he comes anywhere near you he'll be slapped in jail so fast his head will spin. Even if we don't make the charges stick he won't ever try to pull a stunt like this one again.''

''Great.''

''So you can come home, honey. If that was a real marriage Sin arranged we can manage a speedy annulment. But I sure as hell can't figure out why he went that far.''

''I was about to fly home,'' Cathy said flatly. ''He probably thought marrying me was the only way to stop me. He's a very thorough man, Mr. Sinclair MacDonald.''

''He is indeed,'' her father agreed jovially, his voice plummy with satisfaction. ''In that case I'm sure the marriage isn't legal. No problem, then. You just catch the first plane home and we'll put all this behind us. Meg and Charles are already back. You can tell Sin for me there'll be a bonus for him. Not that he needs one, at the prices I pay him already.''

''I'll be sure to tell him. I'll be home tomorrow.''

''That long?'' Brandon Whiteheart was displeased.

''It'll take a while to get to an island with an airport. I won't take any longer than I have to—'' The phone was removed from her hand with inexorable force. Turning to look up at her husband's face, she let go, keeping her own face carefully blank.

"It's your boss," she said politely, and turning her back on him, she walked back to the boat.

Chapter Nineteen

It didn't take her long to throw her clothes into the duffel bag she'd brought along. Sin had insisted she wouldn't need many clothes on her honeymoon, an insistence time had borne out. Cathy was cold and dry-eyed, an icy film covering her heart and soul. Even the feel of Sin's heavy footsteps climbing onto the boat failed to break through her iron control, although her senses told her when he entered the cabin on silent feet.

"How long will it take to get to St. Alphonse?" She kept her back to him and her voice cool and composed.

"Eight or ten hours, probably." His voice matched hers for coolness. "We'd have to make it under power—there's not a breath of wind."

"Then we can make it there by tonight?" She spent more time and attention folding a pair of jeans than she had taken with the entire sum of her other clothing.

"By tomorrow. I'm not about to spend all night sailing, and it's already five o'clock. We wouldn't be in till three or four in the morning. It can wait."

She steeled herself to turn and meet his gaze. His face was completely expressionless in the dim confines of the cabin, and it was with an overwhelming effort that Cathy stopped herself from screaming at him. "Is there an island closer that has an airport?" she questioned politely.

"St. Alphonse is the nearest one. Are you going home?" The question was asked in a tone of polite disinterest, a tone that Cathy matched perfectly.

"As soon as I possibly can."

He stared down at her for a long, silent moment. She could see a tiny muscle working in his strong jaw, the only sign that her new-found knowledge affected him in the slightest.

"In that case," he said flatly, "I suppose we should get under way. There are still a few good hours of sunlight left." Without another word he turned and left her alone in the cabin.

She looked down at the wide bed they had shared, and an involuntary moan of pain issued from the back of her throat. She clamped her teeth shut on it, shoving the neatly folded jeans into the duffel bag and zipping it shut. The next twenty-four hours would take a century to pass, she thought wearily as she sat cross-legged on the bed. *And I won't cry. If I can just keep away from him I'll make it through. As long as I don't have to spend any more time with his lying eyes, that damnable smile that promised love and tenderness.*

But he never told you he loved you, she reminded herself, determined to be fair. *He may have lied about everything else, but he never told that final, unforgivable lie. Damn it, don't cry,* she threatened herself, pinching her leg fiercely to stop the treacherous weakening. *Because once you start crying,* she warned herself, *you won't ever stop.*

The hours passed at a snail's pace, even more slowly than Cathy had anticipated. At one point the faint aroma of chicken soup wafted through the tightly shut door, followed by a short, staccato knock.

"Do you want anything to eat?" Sin's voice was cool and composed, entirely in control of the situation, apparently.

And why did the sound of his deep voice still have the power to melt her bones, after his lies and betrayal? "Nothing," she snapped, more fiercely than she had intended. His footsteps moved away, leaving her once more to fight off the misery that threatened to overwhelm her. She stayed on the bunk, curled up in a tight, dry-eyed ball of despair behind her locked door, hidden away, her privacy the only solace she could find on that tiny, floating hell.

When she awoke it was just past midnight, according to the luminous dial of the thin gold watch Sin had left by the bed. The boat was dark and silent—sometime during the last few hours Sin must have dropped anchor. Not a sound issued from the main cabin, nothing to hint that she wasn't alone on the boat. But she knew far too well that she shared the boat, and the last thing in the world she wanted was to risk waking her—her father's hired man. No matter how lonely the bed suddenly seemed.

Nature, however, had other ideas. The only bathroom on the boat was just outside the tightly locked door, and it soon became apparent that she would have to leave the safety of her refuge. She would simply have to trust to a not very kind fate that Sin would be sound asleep and not notice her tiptoeing across the cabin.

There was no sign of him as she slipped out of the master cabin and into the confines of the head. Breathing a sigh of relief, she decided to allow herself the luxury of brushing her teeth and washing her face. The haunted green eyes that stared back at her out of the curtain of silver-blond hair had an eerie familiarity. She had spent the summer just like this. She recovered from Greg Danville; why did she have the depressing conviction that Sin MacDonald would be a great deal harder to forget? She had always known it.

Tears began to form in the green eyes, and she quickly splashed cold water in them. Sliding back the bathroom door, she started out into the main cabin, only to run smack into Sin's large, immovable body.

There was a quick, indrawn gasp, before Cathy jumped back. Or tried to. His large, strong hands caught her shoulders in an iron grip, holding her rigidly a few inches from him. From the glitter in his eyes she could tell he was in a deep, towering rage, from his rapid breath that fanned her face she could detect the faint trace of brandy. The look of the panther was back, overpowering in its threat of danger and savagery. It was all Cathy could do to stop from quailing before the intensity in his strongly marked face.

"Are you going to talk to me?" he demanded, all trace of composure gone. He shook her once, hard. "Are you? Or are you going to spend the rest of the time sulking in that damned cabin?"

"I'm going to spend the rest of the time sulking in that damned cabin," she shot back, her own coolness vanished in the face of his attack. "We have nothing to say to each other." She struggled helplessly. "And get your hands off me."

Her heart was pounding with a mixture of fear, anger, and a desire that nothing could destroy, not even the full knowledge that he had tricked her. *Maybe that's what love is,* she thought miserably, still glaring up into his angry eyes. *A wanting that nothing can destroy.* And some part of her wanted to reach up and smooth his tumbled hair out of his flushed face, to reassure him—to apologize, of all things! And what did she have to apologize for? He was the one who had lied and cheated, who trapped her with her own needs. She clenched her fists to keep that soothing hand from moving upward of its own volition.

The fingers that clenched her shoulders loosened somewhat, to slide down her bare arms. "Maybe you're right," he said slowly, his eyes hooded. "Maybe we do have nothing to say to each other. And maybe you *should* spend the rest of the time in your cabin. With me," he added crudely. "Because I sure as hell am not going to take my hands off you." With a suddenness that threw her off balance he yanked her into his arms, so that she fell against his broad, hard chest. Her arms were trapped between them as his mouth came down on hers with punishing savagery. Desperately she fought him, keeping her mouth tightly shut against his insistent, probing tongue, as his hands slid down her arched back and cupped her firm buttocks, pressing her up against his angry male desire. And then the room swung crazily around as he scooped her slight body up and carried her back into the cabin, dropping her unceremoniously on the bunk.

"Don't you dare do this!" she spat at him as he stripped her thin cotton knit shirt over her head with deadly efficiency. "Haven't you humiliated me enough?" His deft hands dispensed with her tight jeans, brushing aside her furious fists. A moment later he was naked in the bed beside her, her wrists held above her head in a grip of iron clothed in velvet. His other hand caught her chin and held it still, his eyes burning down into hers for a long, breathless moment.

"I'm not going to rape you, Cathy," he said huskily. "Because I know too well how to make you want me. You're my wife, dammit. And even if it's only for one more night, I intend to be your husband." And his mouth dropped down to take possession of hers, this time with none of the savagery that had marked his rage in the outer cabin, but with a slow, insinuating thoroughness that had her shuddering with a tightly controlled longing. His mouth trailed tiny, passionate kisses across her neck, down her collarbone, his lips capturing one nipple as it swelled in response. His callused hand traveled down the firmness of her flat belly, stroking the smooth, soft skin as his fingers moved ever closer to that aching, secret part of her that already knew him so well. And then his hand moved up, away, to stroke the outline of her hip, her waist, all the while his mouth concentrating on the upper half of her body, his lips teasing, tantalizing, until her slender frame squirmed with a longing she could no longer deny.

Once more his hand trailed down her body, to dance lightly across her stomach, down to her thighs, and then away. Wordlessly she arched her body, vainly trying to reach his dilatory hand. He moved up and kissed her again, and this time she opened her mouth eagerly to him, her tongue meeting his in a tiny duel of passion that promised no victor and no vanquished. And then as a reward his hand moved back, to the very center of her longing, stroking her with a knowledge that scorched her even as it brought her to the edge of oblivion.

Finally he released her wrists, levering his body across hers. She should push him away, she told herself dazedly, wrapping her arms tightly around him as her hips pushed mutely against his hand.

"Say it," he whispered in her ear, his breath hot on her yearning flesh. "Tell me you want me."

She shook her head, clamping her strong white teeth down on her lips that would have told him anything he wanted. Abruptly his hand left her.

"No," she whispered, tears streaming down her pale face unbidden, the final vestiges of control vanishing. "No," she repeated, refusing to give him his last victory.

He knew as well as she did how much she wanted him; she wouldn't give him the final triumph of begging him.

He stared down into her tear-drenched face for a long, unfathomable moment, and in the darkness his face was anguished. And then his mouth caught hers as he completed their union, his body taking hers with a mastery that left him as much a slave as she was.

Helplessly she fought the spasms that washed over her, the feel of his strong, powerful body above her, between her, inside her. But it was a useless struggle, one Sin knew he would win long before he carried her into the cabin. Wave after wave of ecstasy washed over her, and dimly she could hear a voice, *her* voice, sobbing in fulfillment.

It seemed a long time later that he lifted his spent body away from hers. Gentle hands reached up to smooth her face, and his head bent low to capture her lips. She turned her face abruptly away, her eyes shut tight, the tears still streaming down her flushed face. She could feel him hesitate above her, and the thumbs kept stroking her tear-drenched cheeks.

"Cathy," he said gently, his voice tender.

"Go away," she grated, her body stiff in his arms. "Haven't you done enough?" She opened her eyes to stare at him with unalloyed hatred. "I'll never forgive you for that! Never!" Her voice was low and bitter, and there was no doubt that she meant what she said.

Slowly his arms released her, the loving tenderness wiped from his face, leaving it blank and cold once more. "No," he said wearily, sitting up and reaching for his discarded jeans, "I don't suppose you ever will." And a moment later he was gone, closing the door silently behind him.

The engines throbbed to life. He was taking her back, she realized numbly. Traveling at night had suddenly lost its lack of appeal. Turning her face into the pillow, Cathy wept.

Chapter Twenty

Cathy pressed her foot down on the accelerator, speeding along the Virginia countryside as if the devil himself were after her. When, in fact, he'd abdicated, leaving her to wake, alone and bereft, on the docked ship on the busy island of St. Alphonse. There had been no sign of him as she hastily scrambled into her clothes, and she hadn't wasted time looking for him. At the last moment, pulling the thin cotton shirt over her head, she noticed the gold chain that still circled her waist. With a savage yank she ripped it off, breaking the delicate links. Throwing it on the rumpled bed, she pulled at her gold wedding band, intending that it should follow suit. But the wedding ring stuck. Desperately she pulled at it, all the while looking over her shoulder, terrified that Sin would reappear and once more exert that devastating power over her. Finally she gave up, grabbing her duffel bag and purse and running from the small yacht without a backward glance, racing along the busy docks of St. Alphonse until she reached the street and the safe haven of a taxi. She leaned back, her breath coming in sobbing rasps, as she sped her way to the airport. She could always send him the damned ring.

Two hours later she was on a flight to New York. She

had taken the first available plane, determined to put the island and her so-called husband behind her as quickly as she could. A night at the airport hotel provided little solace. She could wash the sand, suntan oil and the scent of Sinclair MacDonald from her body. But she couldn't wash away the feel of his hands on her, the way his long, lean body claimed hers with such deliberate lingering. Sleep had eluded her, and she was on her way by seven that morning, taking the air shuttle back to Washington and a taxi to her apartment in Georgetown.

But instead of the haven she expected, she stared at the walls in mutinous hatred. Without a conscious decision she emptied her duffel bag of the warm-weather clothes, filling it haphazardly with sweaters, jeans, and turtlenecks. Every warm pair of socks she owned ended in the bag, along with a stack of novels and her seldom used paints. She had only one duty to perform, and then she'd be free. She stopped for a moment at her bank, and then was off, speeding in her little red Honda Civic down the cool autumn highways to her father's estate.

For once none of her siblings was in sight. There was no Georgia sweeping down the stairs to cast disbelieving eyes over her disheveled appearance, no sneering Travis to puncture her with sly innuendos. She left the car directly in front of the wide front steps, prepared for a hasty exit, and made her way directly to her father's study. He greeted her precipitous arrival with a scowl, his heavy white brows drawn together.

"It's about time," he snapped. "I've sent Travis out looking for you. Why in hell didn't you call? When did you get in?"

"Last night," she said shortly, throwing herself down on the leather love seat.

His frown deepened. "That's it? Two words? No kiss? No, 'Hello, Pops, I've missed you'?"

She eyed him with deceptive calm. "No. Not until you explain what you thought you were doing, siccing Sin Mac-Donald on me. Why couldn't you have told me what Greg was trying to do? I certainly wouldn't have defended him."

"How was I to know that?" he countered, moving around the front of his mahogany desk. "You'd been pretty well hooked on him, not to mention putting up with his...peculiarities willingly enough." A look of distaste shadowed his aristocratic face.

Cathy's heart stopped for a moment, then thudded, her face flushing. "Who told you?" she gasped. "Oh, why should I bother asking?" she added bitterly. "Your hired stooge must have provided you with all the intimate details of my past relationships. After all, you were paying him to spy on me, among other things." For some reason she had thought she couldn't hurt anymore, but the thought of Sin spilling her confidences in her father's disdainful ear was still a further twist of the knife that skewered her heart.

"As a matter of fact, it was Danville who bragged about it," her father said heavily. "Just to convince me how much power he had over you." He moved closer, sitting down beside her and taking her limp, unresisting hand in his blue-veined one. "Listen, honey, I was just trying to protect you. Sin MacDonald is the best in the business—I thought I could count on him to distract you and keep you out of Danville's way. I had no idea he'd go overboard like that. I would have thought arranging to share your hotel room would have been enough."

Another blow to Cathy's solar plexus. "You mean that was part of the whole entrapment?" she demanded.

"Sin's a real professional. Of course he arranged it. And if he felt he had to marry you to do his job, then he'd do it. Trust Sin to be thorough."

"I thought it wasn't a real marriage," Cathy said in a small voice.

"Apparently it is, according to Sin. I can't imagine why, unless he thought you'd see through a phony one. Not to worry, though. My lawyers can dissolve it in forty-eight hours or less. I'll have Harris come over this evening with the papers...."

"I won't be here." She rose abruptly.

"What do you mean, you won't be here?" her father echoed uneasily. "Of course you will. Meg and Charles are coming for supper. She's afraid you might be mad at her. I told her no such thing, but I don't think she'll believe it till you tell her yourself."

"Is she really pregnant?" Cathy snapped, striding to the window and looking out at the winding drive, the neatly landscaped lawns. "Or was that all part of your master plan?"

"Of course she's pregnant! What kind of Machiavelli do you think I am?" he demanded, affronted.

"I really don't know. All I do know is that I'm not staying." She turned back to face him, and her face was bleak beneath the honey gold of her newly acquired tan. "I'm going away for a while. Where no one can find me, or bother me. I would suggest you don't try to find me, Pops. I wouldn't take kindly to another Sin MacDonald showing up at my doorstep."

"But—but what about your annulment?" he protested.

"You'll need to sign the papers if we're going to get moving on it."

"Let Sin file for the annulment," she said bitterly. "After all, with the nice little bonus you're going to give him he can well afford it."

"Cathy, Cathy, I don't know what's gotten into you, girl," her father sighed. "I was only looking out for your interests."

"I'm sure you were, Pops," she said steadily. "But right now it's time for me to take care of myself. I'll call you." Without another word she turned her back on him and left the house, ignoring his angry calls. She passed Travis's Peugeot on the winding drive, ignoring his look of surprise, her face determinedly forward. And she refused to look back until she reached Vermont.

THE NEXT SIX WEEKS were long, pain-filled ones. As she burrowed into the tiny log cabin halfway up a mountain, she reveled at first in her isolation. None of her family would ever stop to think of Alice, her old college roommate, much less remember that she owned a house and twenty acres in Vermont. She was safe to enjoy herself in her solitude. She read every book in the tiny house, then began making periodic forays to the two-room library in town to stock up on mysteries, romances, biographies, and thrillers. Deliberately she kept all thought of Sin MacDonald from her mind, even when her eyes happened to glance down at the thin gold band that still adorned her finger. It came off easily enough now. Cathy had lost weight, her figure taking on a more willowy look, but for some reason she kept the gold band firmly in place. It was when she found that she wasn't pregnant that she began to realize why.

Of course she hadn't wanted to be pregnant, she told herself sternly. Not under those circumstances. She had thought it through very calmly when she realized there was a possibility. She would have an abortion. After all, everyone did nowadays. And what kind of life would the poor baby have, born to a father who manipulated women and a mother who was hopelessly in love...?

That was the key to the matter, Cathy realized, curled up on the couch, her slender fingers wrapped around a cup of coffee. A mother hopelessly in love. Although not a mother this time. And probably never would be. At least, not to Sin MacDonald's children. And instead of relief she felt an aching emptiness.

She should write him, she thought for the twentieth time. Send him his damned ring, and inquire politely if he'd gotten the annulment. After all, she should find out whether she was still a married woman or not. Not that it mattered. In the tiny village of Appleton the only single man was eighty-four and stone deaf. She was hardly besieged by eligible admirers.

But days and weeks passed, and the ring stayed firmly on her finger, and the letter remained unwritten. Until finally, on impulse, as the steep hills were covered with a fresh dusting of snow, she drove into town and placed a long-distance call to Meg.

"Hello?" Meg's somewhat breathless voice came over the line, and Cathy realized with a shock that she hadn't seen her sister since her wedding day.

"Hi, Meggie," she said softly.

There was a long silence on the other end of the line.

"Cathy?" she shrieked joyfully. "Oh, my God, is it really you?"

"It is, indeed," she answered with a laugh, the tension draining from her. "How are you doing? How's Junior coming along?"

"Oh, he's fine. Hanging in there like a trouper. I'm fat as a pig already, but at least the morning sickness has passed. But where in heaven's name are you, Cathy? We've been worried sick. Pops calls me almost every day, asking if I've heard from you."

"Do me a favor? Tell him I'm fine, but don't tell him anything else. I—I'd rather keep away from him and the family for a while longer."

There was a long pause on the other end of the line. "It still hurts, does it?" she asked quietly.

"Only when I laugh," replied Cathy grimly. "So tell me, what's the news? How's Pops doing?"

"Pops is just fine, but madder than a wet hen at you for running out. Charles is in seventh heaven, preparing for fatherhood, and Georgia is being as meddling as ever." She paused deliberately. "Oh, and you'll want to hear the latest on your exlover."

Cathy's heart lurched to a stop. "Not really. I couldn't care less about Sin MacDonald."

"I wasn't talking about Sin. I mean Greg Danville. He's in jail, you know."

"In jail?" She was only vaguely interested. "Why?"

"He was brought up on assault charges. Apparently he beat up a young lady who just happened to be a senator's daughter. I gather he doesn't even want to be bailed out. But then, who can blame him after what happened?" There was another suggestive pause.

"All right, Meg, I'll bite. What happened?" Cathy asked wearily.

"Well, just before Greg was picked up he got into a barroom brawl. Apparently he was just sitting in a bar in Georgetown, minding his own business, when this real tall guy came in and picked a fight with him. Broke his nose in three places. The guy sounded a lot like Sin."

Cathy's hand flew to her own nose, touching it gingerly as she remembered her flight from the French restaurant and Sin. "How interesting," she managed in her chilliest voice.

Another pause. "Cathy," Meg said finally, her husky voice earnest, "Sin's in terrible shape."

"Why? Did Greg hit him back? I wouldn't have thought he'd do much damage to anyone Sin's size," she said coldly.

"Don't be deliberately obtuse. Sin's in love with you. He's been going crazy trying to find you this last month, and all his leads have turned up blank."

"Well, he'll just have to try harder. I'm sure Pops is paying him enough to make it worth his while." Cathy's voice was bitter.

"Pops isn't paying him anything. He quit. Over the phone from that island, as a matter of fact. Didn't he tell you?"

"No. Neither did Pops. Not that it makes any difference," she said staunchly. But it did.

"Don't you care about him at all, Cathy? You never used to be so hard-headed. The man loves you."

"What makes you think that? He never told me a word about it," she shot back, amazed to find her hands were trembling. She hadn't known it was that cold.

"Of course he didn't. How could he tell you he loved you when he had to keep lying to you? He was trying to protect you, Cathy. He deserves something better from you than a complete disappearance. You owe him a hearing at least."

"I owe him nothing." She rubbed her hands together to get rid of the chill. "And where did you come up with all this?"

"Sin and Charles really are old friends. They were at Harvard together. Sin's confided in Charles, and Charles has told me—"

"With strict orders to pass it on. Well, no thanks," Cathy finished for her. "He can find some other poor fool and marry her. There are people with more money than us."

"One of whom is Sin!" Meg snapped, her sympathy coming to an abrupt end. "He's George Farwell's nephew, Cath. He doesn't need our money."

"Oh." Another part of Cathy's rage bit the dust. "Well, this is costing us a small fortune. I'll call some time later. Maybe on the weekend."

"How far away are you? When are you coming back?" Meg demanded. "Can I tell Sin you called?"

"No, to the last. I don't know when I'm coming back, and I am not about to tell you where I am. Next thing I know Sin or someone equally unwelcome will show up to drag me back to dear old daddy. I'll be in touch." She hesitated, then finally asked the question that had plagued her mind. "Oh, Meg, you wouldn't happen to know whether Sin has filed for an annulment yet, would you?"

There was a disgusted snort from the other end. "Of course I know. He's done no such thing. You're still legally married. I told you, the man loves you!"

"Oh," she said blankly. And then hung up without another word. She stayed there in the cold Vermont wind, staring at the silent telephone for a full five minutes, lost in thought. Could she risk it again? Did she dare to take one last chance, on the remote possibility that Meg was right, and Sinclair MacDonald *had* fallen in love with her? Or would she spend the rest of her life running and hiding, always tied to a man she hadn't had the courage to face?

It didn't take her long to decide—the ten minutes it took to drive back up the hill to her cabin were sufficient. If Mohammed wasn't a good enough private investigator to find the mountain, then the mountain would have to travel back to Georgetown.

It took her longer than she would have expected to close up the cabin. First she had to arrange to have the water drained and the electricity turned off. The food had to be eaten up or tossed out, the house scrubbed from top to bottom to keep the winter creatures from making an unwelcome home there, to chew through mattresses and get stuck in the fieldstone chimney. Library books had to be returned, the car checked for its twelve-hour trip back to Washington. She checked off each item on the list, staring at it with a look of exhausted satisfaction. She was finally ready. In her purse was Sin's duplicate set of keys, the set that he'd tossed her on their wedding day with great casualness. The keys to the yacht, their hotel room, his BMW. And the keys to his apartment in Alexandria.

In the past few weeks she had staunchly ignored the ramifications of that casual gift, deciding several times that she would toss them out. After all, she would never have a use for them. But something had stopped her—perhaps an unconscious echo of medieval times, when the mistress of the castle was ceremoniously presented with the keys as a symbol of her rank. If Sin had expected their relationship to be a temporary delaying tactic in the Caribbean, why had he given her his Washington keys?

As she started on the first leg of her long journey, she glanced at her reflection in the car mirror. There was a light in her green eyes, a sense of purpose to her soft mouth. Some things were worth taking a chance on, worth fighting for, she thought, putting the car in gear and starting down the winding dirt road. And Sin MacDonald was, despite her earlier misgivings, one of those things.

Chapter Twenty-one

There was no sign of his forest-green BMW in the parking lot adjacent to his building, or on any of the streets around. Hedging her bets, Cathy parked several blocks away, walk- ing the distance through the autumn-cool streets of Alex- andria in jeans, high-laced boots and a thick pullover. Com- pared to Vermont's early winter the weather was positively tepid, and her hips swung with a casual sway as she strolled down the sidewalks. It was nearly evening; almost seven o'clock, and Cathy had been driving for thirteen hours. Thirteen hours that had seen her grow progressively more light-hearted as she neared the Washington area, despite the uncertainty of her reception. When she reached the outskirts of Alexandria she had hesitated, longing for a hot shower and a nap more than anything. But a belated uncertainty crept in, and she knew if she put it off she might never have the courage to beard the panther in his den. He would simply have to take her, travel-stained and exhausted, as she was. She only hoped he'd take her.

There was no answer to her ringing of the red-painted, paneled door of his apartment. By the looks of things Meg had been right—Sin didn't need her money. The under- stated charm of the building and the foyer proclaimed discreetly that here resided people of wealth and taste. Fumbling with the keys, she tried one after the other, going through the entire set twice before managing to turn the bolt. And then she slipped into the darkened flat, closing the door behind her.

It had a musty, closed-up smell about it, she realized as she moved around switching on lights. She opened a window to air it out, then turned to survey Sin's living quarters.

They suited him, she decided after a long perusal. Leather couches, brass lamps, ancient oriental carpets on the polished hardwood floors. The striking modern painting above the fireplace boasted a signature well-known to Cathy, and the impressionist print in the hallway turned out to be quite real. The burgundy red of the curtains complemented the deep hues of the carpet, and the wood shone with loving care. The place looked like Sin—casual, elegant, and comfortable. And very handsome, she added gloomily, wandering through the beautifully organized country-style kitchen with its gleaming copper and butcher block counters. But she was unprepared for the sybaritic luxury of the bedroom and bath. The king-size bed dominated the large room, the striking charcoal nudes that hung on the walls adding a touch of sensuality. Those would have to go, Cathy decided impishly. They were far more full-figured than she was—positively Rubenesque, when it came right down to it. She didn't want Sin to have the chance to make odious comparisons.

Sudden doubt assailed her. What if he wasn't glad to see her? What if Meg had read only what she wanted to read into Sin's actions? What if he was glad to be rid of her, and finding her in his apartment was the last thing he wanted?

At that moment her eyes dropped to the bedside table. There was a picture there, a snapshot of a beautiful woman in a bikini. A jealous misery washed over her, and then she stared more closely at the photo. It was a very happy Cathy. Sometime during those four days on St. Alphonse Meg had taken her picture, and Sin had wheedled it out of her. It was in a heavy silver frame, her green eyes laughing up from behind the curtain of blond hair. There was a question in her eyes, a look of doubt that told Cathy that Sin had taken it after all. The day they left their tiny island and headed for disillusionment on Martin's Head. If she looked closely she fancied she could see the hurt lingering, waiting to attack. Carefully she placed the frame back on the table. And then she noticed, lying unobtrusively beside it, the gold chain.

Tears of relief flooded her eyes as the last of her doubts vanished. He wanted her. For the first time in six weeks she found she was hungry. There was scarcely anything in Sin's refrigerator. Finally making do with a cheese sandwich and one of Sin's imported beers, she strolled over to his desk. Pieces of paper littered the top, covered with Sin's bold scrawl. Her name, over and over again. A list of her best friends, complete with addresses and phone numbers, all crossed out. A listing of her car model and license plate. And various other notes concerning her habits, her friends, her favorite pastimes and restaurants. Cathy stared down at them with a wistful smile. For all his legendary proficiency he hadn't been able to find her. She'd covered her tracks a bit too well. A yawn overtook her, and then another, and she rubbed her gritty eyes wearily.

Where was he? If he didn't show up soon she'd be sound asleep, and she had grave doubts about her ability to reenact

Goldilocks and the Three Bears. Maybe a shower would wake her up. If Sin came home in the middle of it, well... Things would simply have to resolve themselves naturally.

But the hot shower had the opposite effect. Once she stepped from the steaming stall she was barely able to keep her eyes open. Toweling her hair dry, she stepped nude into his bedroom, her toes reveling in the thick brown carpet. He'd had the chain repaired, she noticed. It hung a little more loosely around her slender waist than it had six weeks before, but at least it didn't slide off once she did the clasp.

It had been a fitting gift, she mused. For despite her hurt and betrayal, she was chained to him as surely as if she were manacled. But it was her own overwhelming love that chained her, and therein lay her power and her salvation.

There was a floor-length hooded velour wrapper behind the bathroom door. She pulled it on, and then, on impulse, moved through the apartment, turning off the lights, closing the window, effectively wiping out any trace of her early arrival. And then, switching off the bedroom light, she climbed into his huge bed, chuckling to herself, "And who's been sleeping in my bed?" And then, moments after her still damp head hit the soft feather pillow, she was sound asleep.

The voices woke her from a deep, dreamless sleep. For a moment she panicked, forgetting in the darkened interior of the bedroom exactly where she was. And then, as she returned to full cognizance, the panic deepened. That was a woman's voice out there, a light, sultry female that provided a perfect counterpoint to Sin's deep tones. *Oh, my God,* Cathy thought, the full horror of the situation washing over her. *He's brought a woman home with him.*

Silently she crawled out of the bed, pulling the velour

wrapper about her as she tiptoed to the half-opened door and pressed her ear against it, straining to hear their conversation.

"Get some sleep, Sin darling," the woman said companionably, and Cathy gnashed her teeth. "You look like hell. You've been working too hard, you know."

"I haven't been sleeping well, Barb," he confessed. Cathy could imagine him running a hand through his rumpled brown curls as he made that admission, and her stomach knotted with sudden longing. How was she going to escape before he brought that—that creature into the bedroom?

"Is she worth it, Sin?" the woman's voice came again, and Cathy pressed closer, wondering if she heard correctly.

"Yes." The answer was unequivocal. To Cathy's mingled relief and consternation he put a hand behind the lady's slender back and guided her to the front door. "Tell Frank I appreciate him letting me borrow his best girl for the evening. I don't think I could have managed to remember all that without your taking notes."

"What else is a secretary for? Besides, if Frank can't trust his brother who can he trust? I'm sure you'd do the same for him." She let out a small trill of laughter. "Not that I'm as understanding. I wouldn't care for Frank to spend an evening alone with your Cathy. She's far too pretty, if that picture is any proof." She reached up and gave Sin a sisterly kiss on the cheek. "Find her, Sin. Find her, or get over her."

"I'm trying, Barb," he said morosely. "I've got to." The light in the hall illuminated his face for a moment as he let Barb out, and Cathy drew an involuntary breath of surprise. He looked drawn and haggard, and she could easily believe he hadn't been sleeping well. Was she the cause of that? She could only hope so. Dropping the robe on the thick carpet, she scrambled back into the bed, pulling the covers up to her chin, and prepared to wait.

She didn't have long. First the chink of ice and the sound of a drink being poured filtered in from the living room. Then the sound of his boots dropping on the floor, the mutes notes of a bluesy ballad from the stereo. The lights flickered off, the bedroom door opened, and Sin stood there, framed in the doorway, his shirt unbuttoned and pulled from his pants. There was enough light from the streetlamps outside to illuminate the room, casting the bed's lone occupant in the shadows. Without bothering to turn on the light, he kicked the door shut behind him, shrugged out of his shirt, and took a long pull from his drink. And then he stepped on the hastily discarded bathrobe.

"What the hell?" he muttered, scooping it up from the floor. Faint traces of her scent still clung to it, flowering the air. He was suddenly very still.

It was now or never, Cathy thought, her heart pounding against the thin cotton sheet. What could she say? Something cute, light, and clever? Something witty and sophisticated, to set the tone, keep it casual? Slowly she sat up, searching for the right words. And it came out, one perfect word, in a tone of such longing that time seemed to stand still.

"Sin?" Her voice trembled and broke on the word. And then his arms were around her, his lips covering hers, and all that existed in the world were their bodies and their need and love.

No more words were needed. Slowly, achingly, they brought each other to the point of ecstasy and beyond, instinctively knowing what the other needed, answering that need and glorying in their ability to do so. Their union was made all the sweeter by the six week abstinence and the uncertainties, uncertainties that at that moment no longer needed explaining. And as the final moments of passion approached and peaked, Cathy knew that nothing short of force could remove her from her lover's side. As his cry echoed in the night, she knew he felt the same, and together they traveled over the edge of the mountain to dash into a thousand stars against the rocks below.

It was a long, long time before he spoke. Their bodies were drenched with sweat, still warm with the glow of their perfect love. He cradled her body against his, one hand cupping her cheek, his thumb gently caressing her swollen lips as if he couldn't quite believe she was really there. "Don't you ever," he said, and his breathing was still ragged, "leave me again. I don't think I could stand it."

She snuggled closer against his commanding length, a mischievous grin playing about her mouth. "I guess I'd better not. I waited long enough for you to find me, then had to give up and come to you. How you ever got to be so successful as a private investigator is beyond me. Can't find a simple thing like a wife when you set your mind to it," she mocked lightly, giving herself up to the sweet punishment of his kiss at her lack of respect.

"I would think," he said after a long, breathless moment, "that you're more than a match for me. Professionally, and otherwise." There was a longer pause. "I never meant to fall in love with you."

Cathy gloried in the words, even though his body had told her as much over and over again. "I should have warned you," she said sleepily, rubbing her smooth cheek against his chest. "There are times when I never take no for an answer, either."

"Is this one of them?" He cradled her head against his shoulder.

"Anything to do with you is," she replied pertly. His hands reached down and stroked her waist, resting lightly on the gold chain.

"I know why you came back," he drawled. "You just wanted your chain."

"Sin, darling." She raised herself up to look him squarely in the eye. "I didn't need this scrap of gold to feel chained to you." Her face was shining with love. "You still haven't let me say it, you know."

His eyes were very serious as they looked down into hers. "I couldn't, Cathy. I couldn't tell you I loved you when I was busy tricking you, and I couldn't let you tell me. I figured that was the only dignity I could save you."

A small smile curved her mouth. "And do I still need a shred of dignity?" she questioned airily.

His smile met hers. "No, my love. You have a natural dignity that nothing can take away."

"Then," she said, levering herself above him and resting her hands on his hard chest, "I love you, I love you, I love you, I love you..." She continued it like a litany as her greedy mouth showered kisses on his mouth, his neck, his chest. "I love you, I love you, I love you..." Until his hungry mouth captured hers once more, and there was no longer any need for words.

Chapter Twenty-two

The *Tamlyn* rocked gently beneath her unsteady feet, and Cathy squinted up through the bright tropical sunlight to her husband's amused face.

"Thank heavens you found a more tranquil place to anchor," she said with heartfelt gratitude, the green tinge beginning to leave her face. "I'm not sure if this was the best possible way to spend our first anniversary."

"You've never been seasick before," Sin said lazily, leaning back against the cushions on the deck.

"I've never been four months pregnant before," she replied, the pleased grin that touched her face whenever she thought of it taking the sting out of her words. "And now that we're relatively motionless I'll do just fine. Where exactly are we?" She peered out at the small, secluded cove with dawning, delighted recognition.

"Five hours south of St. Alphonse." He caught her exuberant body with expert ease, laughing tenderly at her. "I told you I could find it again."

"I should have trusted you," she said ruefully, her green eyes shining up at him as she settled herself into the curve of his arm.

"Yes, you should have," he returned lightly, his lips brushing hers. "But I forgive you."

A small chuckle escaped her. "Magnanimous of you. Do you suppose Alexander is going to enjoy having a new cousin?"

"I expect Meg will have them playing together in the cradle. Are you going to dote on ours as much as Meg moons over Alexander?"

"Probably worse." She cast a belatedly worried glance up at his suntanned profile. "Will you be jealous?"

"You forget, I know you pretty well by this time. I have no doubt you have enough for the both of us, and more besides."

With a sigh of complete happiness she pressed closer against his lean, sun-warmed body. "You're absolutely right. And absolutely wonderful."

"Of course I am. And to prove my devotion I'll tell you now that I'd rather sail down to the Caribbean with you vomiting all the way, than with your brother-in-law anytime."

"Charles's snoring being worse than nausea?" she queried impishly. "You're so romantic I don't know how I stand it."

In light punishment his face covered hers, blocking out the bright sunlight as his mouth caught hers in a long, slow, deep kiss. When he finally released her, her heart was pounding, her pulses racing, and the light that shone in her large green eyes was both dazzling and dazzled.

"Not romantic, am I?" Sin grumbled. "I've got a mind not to give you your anniversary present."

"But you already did!" Cathy protested. "This trip—"

"Is ephemeral. In a while it will only be a memory. I

wanted something more lasting.'' He drew a small velvet box from the pocket of his khaki shorts.

''Oh, Sin, I didn't get you anything....'' She took the box reluctantly, but he silenced her with one large, warm hand spread tenderly over her rounded belly that swelled gently over the skimpy bikini.

''Hush, love,'' he murmured. ''You've already given me the two most important things in my life.''

With trembling fingers she opened the box. There, nestled against the soft velvet, was a long gold chain, with a heart-shaped emerald pendant attached. ''Oh, Sin,'' she whispered.

''You've almost outgrown the other one,'' he said lightly, his fingers playing with the gold chain that now fit quite snugly around her thickening waist. ''So I thought I'd better get you one for your neck. I wanted to make sure you'd always have something to remind you.''

She smiled up at him tremulously, her emerald-green eyes bright with unshed tears. ''Remind me of how much I love you, how much I'm chained to you? I don't need to be reminded, Sin.''

He shook his head. ''No, darling. It's to remind you how much *I* love *you*. And that I'm chained to you just as you are to me, by chains of love as fine and strong as the gold around your waist. Never doubt it, Cathy. Never doubt me.''

It was a plea, not a command, and her answer was in her eyes, in her heart, in her mouth as she kissed him, her softly rounded body pressed against his lean strength. Passion, never far away, flared between them. As Sin scooped her up in his strong arms and started toward the cabin Cathy let out a soft laugh of pure pleasure.

"I think I'm going to enjoy this honeymoon even better than the first one," she murmured as with great dexterity he maneuvered them down into the main cabin and back toward the bedroom.

"And why is that?" he queried, one eyebrow raised.

"Because this time I won't make you wear those ridiculous jockey shorts," she laughed. And reaching around his shoulder, she pushed the bedroom door shut behind them.

MEN at WORK

All work and no play?
Not these men!

July 1998
MACKENZIE'S LADY by Dallas Schulze

Undercover agent Mackenzie Donahue's
lazy smile and deep blue eyes were his best
weapons. But after rescuing—and kissing!—
damsel in distress Holly Reynolds, how could
he betray her by spying on her brother?

August 1998
MISS LIZ'S PASSION by Sherryl Woods

Todd Lewis could put up a building with ease,
but quailed at the sight of a classroom! Still,
Liz Gentry, his son's teacher, was no battle-ax,
and soon Todd started planning some
extracurricular activities of his own....

September 1998
A CLASSIC ENCOUNTER
by Emilie Richards

Doctor Chris Matthews was intelligent, sexy
and *very* good with his hands—which made
him all the more dangerous to single mom
Lizette St. Hilaire. So how long could she
resist Chris's special brand of TLC?

Available at your favorite retail outlet!

MEN AT WORK™

 HARLEQUIN®  Silhouette®

Look us up on-line at: http://www.romance.net

PMAW2

Take 2 bestselling love stories FREE
Plus get a FREE surprise gift!

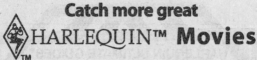

The World's Most Eligible Bachelors are about to be named! And Silhouette Books brings them to you in an all-new, original series....

World's Most Eligible Bachelors

Twelve of the sexiest, most sought-after men share every intimate detail of their lives in twelve never-before-published novels by the genre's top authors.

Don't miss these unforgettable stories by:

Dixie Browning

Marie Ferrarella

Jackie Merritt

Tracy Sinclair

BJ James

Rachel Lee   **Suzanne Carey**

Gina Wilkins

VICTORIA PADE

Maggie Shayne   *Anne McAllister*

Susan Mallery

Look for one new book each month in the
World's Most Eligible Bachelors series beginning
September 1998 from Silhouette Books.

Silhouette®

Available at your favorite retail outlet.

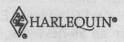

Not The Same Old Story!

   Exciting, glamorous romance stories that take readers around the world.

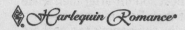   Sparkling, fresh and tender love stories that bring you pure romance.

   Bold and adventurous— Temptation is strong women, bad boys, great sex!

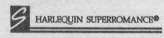 HARLEQUIN SUPERROMANCE®   Provocative and realistic stories that celebrate life and love.

   Contemporary fairy tales—where anything is possible and where dreams come true.

   Heart-stopping, suspenseful adventures that combine the best of romance and mystery.

LOVE & LAUGHTER™   Humorous and romantic stories that capture the lighter side of love.

DEBBIE MACOMBER

invites you to the

Join Debbie Macomber as she brings you the lives
and loves of the folks in the ranching community
of Promise, Texas.

If you loved Midnight Sons—don't miss
Heart of Texas! A brand-new six-book series
from Debbie Macomber.

Available in February 1998
at your favorite retail store.

Heart of Texas by Debbie Macomber

Lonesome Cowboy	February '98
Texas Two-Step	March '98
Caroline's Child	April '98
Dr. Texas	May '98
Nell's Cowboy	June '98
Lone Star Baby	July '98

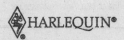